2HVØRHVNØT

TO HAVE OR HAVE NOT

JARED K CHAPMAN

APOTHEOSIS PRESS

APOTHEOSIS PRESS

ISBN: 978-1-953366-00-9

Edited by Michaelia Leigh Mendoza

Designed by Derek Smith

WEBNET.MIGHTYBASE

To thank you for reading my book, I want to grant you FREE access to the **webnet.mightybase.**

Dive deeper into the TO HAVE OR HAVE NOT Universe. Search the MIGHTYpedia. Peruse MIGHTYbase Profiles. Navigate maps of Fellowship City. Generate your own Identity Tag. Read first chapters of upcoming books and short stories. Check out concept art and much more!

To gain access, simply sign up for my email list on my author website **jaredkchapman.com** to register your MIGHTYmail account. As I continue to develop the TO HAVE OR HAVE NOT Universe, more content will be added. I hope you stay tuned and enjoy!

It has been a long-time dream to make a living as a storyteller. I love creating worlds, imagining the people who inhabit those worlds, and telling their diverse stories. If you enjoy what I have written, please consider leaving an honest review so that others may find similar enjoyment.

I truly appreciate hearing from you! Enjoy!
~ Jared K Chapman

To
My Mother for believing in me.
My Wife for inspiring me every day.
My Children for listening to my stories.
My Family and Friends for waiting this long.

In Loving Memory of
My Grandfather, Charles M. Parsons

Much of human history has consisted of unequal conflicts between the haves and the have-nots.
— Jared Diamond, *Guns, Germs, and Steel*

I teach you the Superman. Man is something that is to be overcome. What have you done to overcome man?
— Friedrich Nietzche, *Thus Spoke Zarathustra*

And when everyone's SUPER [maniacal laughter], no one will be.
— Syndrome, *The Incredibles*

EPISODE I

GOOD MORNING, FELLOWSHIP CITY

*"Broadcasting Live from Channel FC1 it's
Good Morning, Fellowship City!"*

1

THE LINE

His eyes roll under his eyelids, fluttering in harmony with the firing neurons of his dream-laden brain. Colors within this dreamscape merge into shapes and figures, but nothing so recognizable that he can focus for even a second on any single one. He searches the ever-changing flux of his surroundings, reaching out with nonexistent hands to grapple something he cannot comprehend. Beyond his reach, a billowing ominous cloud blooms from unfocused blurred colors and shapes without form. They blend as one until the one is nothing but white light swirling in a luminescent vortex.

Within the spiraling light, a pinprick of darkness emerges. It grows and grows into a massive dark figure looming just out of sight. Unable to lure the figure into view, he focuses instead on two flesh-colored forms now rising before him. They thrust their arms into the air as if to pray or surrender. Each of their left arms bears a mark. The dark blemishes cause fixation and prompt a closer examination. But as he draws nearer and nearer, the figures blur more and more, dissipating into the surrounding light.

Though he cannot bring their faces into focus, dark shapes etched into the pink surface of their skin become clear. *Are they numbers and letters of some ancient or alien alphabet tattooed upon their flesh?* He clenches one of the arms with an invisible hand, perceiving the softness of the skin, sinewiness of the strong pulsating muscle within, and the hardness of the bone beneath. As he withdraws his arm through force of will alone, the alphanumerics become clear.

ANNK ANNK ANNK ANNK ANNK

An alarm clock blares, as the sleep-laden young man springs upright in his bed. He wrenches his face, trying to preserve the visions from his dream. Finding nothing but frustration, he takes comfort in the familiar surroundings of his room. The reprieve is only momentary. His head begins to swell with the blaring alarm pounding in his brain. The LED display blinks 5:46 a.m., as he slams his fist down on the off button.

"Shit, I'm late!"

With the speed and clarity that can only result from frantic desperation, the young man leaps from his bed and salvages some clothes from a huddled black and white heap on the floor. He yanks several empty hangers loose from the rod in his closet, breaking several along the way, as he scrambles out of his room toward the bathroom down the small hall. Shimmying by the closed door of his little sister's room, a twinkle of hope glimmers in his still tired eyes.

He juggles his clothes and hangers in one hand, as he reaches for the bathroom handle and turns the knob. Nothing. The door does not budge. He tenses as his hope flickers away. He balls his hand into a fist and pounds on the door.

RAT TAT TAT

"Zelda! I'm late. I need to get—"

His blonde, 17-year-old, younger sister opens the door, eyeing him with intensity.

"Please, Zelda. I am so late."

She smirks and curtsies out of his way, as he sidesteps into the bathroom, thanking her for her help.

He strips off his clothes, trying to straighten them as much as possible before hanging them from the shower curtain. He spins the shower knob all the way to H and turns to the mirror for a brief examination of his reflection. He raises his jaw and checks for stubble, gliding his fingertips across his prickly chin. He plucks a plastic throwaway razor from a cup on the sink and shaves the patchy area before the mirror fogs up. Satisfied with his cleanish shave, he spins the knob back a bit toward C, jumps into the steamy shower, lathers, turns once, and rinses off.

Once out of the shower, he turns around and spins the knob back toward H. Steam billows out from behind the curtain, as he hoists up his white boxers with a jump, followed by his undershirt and black socks. He wipes his hand across the mirror to clear the fog and brushes his teeth. The fluoride mixed with last night's alcohol still upon his breath makes him gag, but he holds back the disgust, spitting out a giant pale blue glob into the sink before rinsing his mouth.

He fetches the slightly-dampened-now-less-wrinkled white dress shirt from the hanger and inches it on, making sure each button is fastened to the correct hole. Next, he slides on his black slacks one leg at a time, tucks in the shirt, and buckles the belt still hanging from the loops. He slips his pre-tied thin black tie over his head, keeping the knot loose under his collar. His black suit jacket still perspires with shower mist, as he stretches it over him and flips the lapels into place.

Now dressed, he shuts off the shower and faces the mirror, wiping his hand to clear his foggy image. He slicks his hair back and grins at his reflection, fogging up again from the lingering steam.

I'm on a mission from God.

He winks at himself, calling to mind a story his father once told him a long time ago about two brothers who fought evildoers through the power of music.

He opens the door to find Zelda standing in front, impatient as ever.

"You done now?" she asks with her arms crossed while stamping her foot in the most clichéd way possible.

"All yours, princess."

She nudges him out of the way and slams the door.

"Love you!" she yells from inside.

"Love you too!" he yells back.

5:56 a.m. blinks the LED display.

"Shit!" he exclaims, dashing for the door and heading outside.

The placard affixed to the outside of his door reads 3014, which means he lives in unit 14 of Camphouse 30 of the Fellowship City Work Placement Camp, also called WPC. In all, 50 such camphouses littered the island south of Fellowship City, separated by Olum River and connected by an old bridge. Aside from the different colored exteriors of the buildings, all the camphouses are identical, each housing 50 units apiece.

The young man exits Camphouse 30 on the corner of Ira Street and Citizen Way, the main street of the WPC. As he jogs past Ira Street east toward the bus stop near the entrance of WPC, he spies several people exiting camp-houses far off the central thoroughfare. *Days like today make me thankful we live on Citizen Way*, he thinks, counting the many more blocks they'll be walking. *I only wish we didn't live four blocks away from the bus stop.*

Any other day, he would've considered 3014 to be in an ideal location, but running late as he is today, the distance appears infinite. *This is going to be the longest run to the bus stop I've ever made in my life*, he thinks, sprinting by Invidia Street.

But I'm fast for a man in a black suit, he chortles at the thought. *All these other workers, leaving their camphouses now and taking their sweet ass time as they stroll toward the bus stop, are probably looking at me and thinking, glad I'm not that guy.*

Ahead of him, he glimpses an older woman with salt and pepper brown hair tied up in a bun with white lace, walking at a steady pace. As he closes in on her, he recognizes the stereotypical black and white uniform of a French maid she's wearing.

She must work for some richy-rich Mighties up in Emerald Hills, he thinks, a little jealous. *They love dressing up their workers in crazy shit like that. I'm surprised she's living in the WPC and not in the Normal slums with all the other preferred workers. I bet it's a new gig, and she'll be moving on up real soon.*

He often ponders what life might be like if he lived outside of the WPC, wondering if a place in the Normal slums (or what the Mighty call southside ghetto) would truly afford more freedom at all.

Having to wear a ridiculous outfit just to land a cushy job up there might not be worth it though, he thinks, loosening his collar and adjusting his necktie, as his short-lived jealousy fades away.

He hurtles by, startling her.

She jerks out her earbuds and yells, "Watch out!"

He waves his hand in the air without looking back or slowing his gait. At the next block, he jumps up and high-fives the Luxuria Street sign.

TWWWIIIIIINNNNGGG

"Stupid kid," barks the lady.

He laughs, picking up his pace, trying to cut ahead of the many people leaving their homes for their 7 a.m. shifts.

Come on. Come on, he thinks, racing forward, trying to ignore the soft rumbling of a crowd.

The noise builds, rising into a voluminous cacophony of chatter, as he crosses Tristia Street. He can no longer ignore the sound of the gathered mass of people waiting in the bus line, not moving an inch.

"Son of a bitch!" he exclaims, zipping by people of all shapes and sizes, costumed and uncostumed.

In the distance, he spots a lone bus exiting Olum Bridge toward Citizen Way. He bolts toward the front of the line, passing a myriad of glowering faces. The weight of their judgment does nothing to slow him down.

"No cutting!" a woman's voice shouts, but he disregards her and runs faster. The crowd's murmurs merge into some foreign-sounding condemnation where the words are unintelligible, but the tone is clear.

"I'm sorry," he apologizes, galloping past the gawking onlookers. "I need to get to work. I can't be late!"

No one is fooled by his lip-service apology, but they do understand his dilemma. Not that his boss will. He's not the most forgiving about tardiness, and the recent promotion from the kitchen to the dining room floor would likely be the first thing on the chopping block.

I don't want to be back in the kitchen all the time, he thinks. *Or worse. It could be a lot worse.*

His eyes lock onto the bus, as it creeps toward the bus stop. He rounds the front of the line, maneuvering through the crowds of other workers to inch closer to the door of the bus before it burps to a halt. He grins ear to ear.

Mere steps away from the doorway, his smile rips from his face in a sudden jolt of panic, as a massive reptilian tail drops in front of him like a boom barrier at a railroad crossing.

"Where do you think you're going?" the guard inhumanly snarls.

The young man lifts his head to meet the reptilian eyes of the guard who stands a good foot taller than his own five-foot nine-inch frame. The raised ridges of his scaly, greenish-brown skin above and around his eyes crease with tension, as he stares down the young man until he averts his eyes. They fall to the guard's chest where a laminate listing his name and badge number hangs by a lanyard around his gigantic neck. "Officer Lester Lynch, badge number AHØ7341," he reads silently, smirking.

A-Hole for one.

The guard is clad in the usual uniform of a WPC guard: blue button-up long-sleeve shirt with the sleeves rolled up above his elbows (because his forearms are just as giant as his neck), and modified black trousers with splits down each side and a not-so-black colored fabric sewn in to flare them out over his massive legs. Of course, the trousers are cut short above his monstrous green-scaled tridactyl feet that no shoes would ever fit. In the rear, his tail protrudes from an opening below the thick leather belt of his pants where a side-holster hangs.

"I asked you a question," he growls, fingering the latch of his side-holster.

"I'm late for work," answers the young man, raising his eyes back to the guard's leering lizard face. "That's the bus I need to be on."

He points to the bus behind the guard, whose only movement is to draw the handheld scanner from his side-holster, while an inhuman grunting resonates from somewhere within him. The young man shutters at the haunting sound, appraising the miniaturized, updated version of the datapads he uses to navigate the Webnet Mightybase in the WPC common hubs.

Shit, he thinks, tracking the guards fat-fingers punching the screen. *This is going to take too long.*

The guard seizes the young man by his left arm, wrapping his thick reptilian fingers around his wrist and with one pointed thumbnail, raises the sleeve of the young man's shirt and jacket cuffs away to reveal an identity tag tattooed on his left forearm. He scans the ident-tag and begins to read the results displayed on the screen.

"M. K. Rickson..."

"It's Mario," interrupts the young man, wresting his arm back and lowering his sleeve to cover it once more. "Seriously, I'm extremely late and that's my bus. I need to be at work by 6."

The guard ignores him, seizing Mario by the forearm again and forcing the sleeve. As he examines the alphanumeric code, his inner eyelids blink and vertical pupils dilate.

"Do we really need to do this right now?" Mario says, trying to reclaim his arm. "I'm going to be late."

"Ident 24VØR4VNØ, your identity tag is defaced," states the guard. "That is a violation."

"*Yes*, I know," Mario says, grimacing at the workers

boarding the bus. "Since you're new here, I'll give you a break, but I did this a long time ago and served my reprimand. It's all good now. Can I get on this bus please?"

"You cannot deface your identity tag."

"Right," Mario says, trying to slide past the guard. "I was a stupid kid going through a lot. You know puberty, the loss of my parents, being the parent of my little sister. I'm good now. Won't ever do anything like that again."

Sensing the motion, the guard clamps down on Mario's arm tighter, snarling, "Don't move!"

"Listen," Mario says, snatching his arm away from the guard and standing as tall as he can. "I've already been punished for this when I was a kid. There should be a note there on the registry about it. Maybe an asterisk by my number or a link for more info."

The guard touches the screen with a giant green, clawed finger, opening a notes page, as Mario moseys toward the bus.

"I'm sorry, Officer Lizardlips," he says over his shoulder, as he steps toward the bus. "But I really need to go."

The guard grasps his shoulder and spins him around. "What did you call me?"

"Officer Lester Lynch?" he answers, as the guard's eyes narrow with suspicion. Mario raises his hand in innocent protestation. "C'mon, I need to be on this bus, so I'm not too late for work."

PSHOOO KALLUNK

The bus closes the door and departs without any regard for Mario.

"I guess, you're going to be late," growls Office Lizardlips with a broad, serrated tooth smile. He points to the long line of people waiting for the buses. "Get in line, like all the other Citizens."

Mario ambles back toward the end of the line, peering around for other possible avenues to reach a bus faster, but at each vantage came a disadvantage in the guise of a Mighty guard. Of course, all the WPC guards are Mighty, but just like in the city, some Mighty are more Mighty than others.

The Mighty, thinks Mario. *What a dumb name. How pretentious can they get? They think they're the gods of ancient Greece or something, and Fellowship City is their Mount Olympus.*

As he hikes back to the end of the line, he glares over his shoulder, scowling at the guard.

Officer Lizardlips doesn't even realize he's nothing but the shit these god's scrape off their shoes. The other Mighty would stare him down if he even set any one of his three clawed toenails into a fine downtown restaurant. They might nod acknowledgment and thank him for his service, but they'd whisper to one another, calling him a HYBRID behind his back, if he's lucky. A HUMAN-IMAL, if he's unlucky. I've seen it happen.

??

webnet.mightybase search results...

Hybrids : MIGHTYpedia Entry

??

Of the many varieties of the Mighty, the HYBRIDS are those who possess animal-like qualities. Although they are most often found in task-based work and rarely serve in leadership positions, they are essential to the functioning of the Mighty system. For some, their appearance is animalistic, giving them gifts that allow them to serve as laborers and muscle (see Insectoids, Amphibians, Reptilians, Birds, Fuzzies, Prehensiles). For others, their abilities derive from more base animal qualities. Hybrids with less animal-like appearances are often able to find more prominent positions within the Mighty system (see SCREAMERS).

???

For more information access webnet.MIGHTYbase Profiles, a social networking platform where the Mighty can showcase their talents and cultivate relationships.

???

In a city where almost everyone is a Mighty, being a Mighty doesn't mean much, thinks Mario, reaching the end of the line. *But not being a Mighty means even less.*

Get in line, like all the other Citizens, the guard's inhuman growl reverberates in his mind, as a memory washes over him like a wave on a shoreline. He starts to view the world through the eyes of his past self, standing in the line for the bus and tugging on his father's hand. He gazes up at the ghost of his father and beams with the excited glee of a child.

Suddenly, a ruckus broke out at the bus stop in front of them. As Mario craned his neck around, trying to view the scuffle, his father tucked him close and hurried forward in the line. Several guards rushed out from different posts and started yelling, "Citizens disperse! Return to your domicile! Bus stops are now closed!"

Mario's father didn't stop. He held Mario tight under his left arm and clutched the permits in his right hand, flashing them to the guards. "We have permits!" he yelled, "It's my son's birthday. I'm taking him to Fellowship City Park to play."

One of the guards charged forward, clasping Mario's father by the right shoulder and hauling him away. The quick jolt knocked Mario off-kilter. He would have fallen, if not for his father's grip on him.

"Please, the permit is only good for today," he pleaded. "It took months to get one. Please let us through."

The guard lifted Mario's father to his face and snarled, "Citizen, you need to return to your domicile before something bad happens to you and your son."

Mario flinched, catching a whiff of the guard's foul breath from the safety of his father's protection. "Please," his father begged. "It's his birthday. I just want him to swing and slide on a real playground."

The guard shoved them backward, growling, "Leave now, or I'm taking you both to SIC!"

They turned away and shuffled back to their home 1441 Luxuria Street between Dalit Way and Potter Road.

"What does Citizen mean, papa?"

"Citizen used to be such an important word, Mario,"answered his melancholic father. "It meant you were a legitimate member of the society you lived in." His face darkened and tenor slowed. "Unfortunately, it no longer has that positive connotation. It now refers to those lesser than the Mighty. It's like how in those movies where the cops or military call people civilians. We're just not like them, Mario, and they're not shy about letting us know."

His recollection of the moment is not perfect but close, like revisiting an old film tarnished with the imperfections that come with age.

He then remembers, with slight embarrassment, how he believed his impressive memory was a power like those of a Mighty. His mouth curls up to one side. He imagines it is the exact same sideways smile he saw upon his father's face when he told him that he was a Mighty and could free his family from the WPC. The curl withers away as he recalls his father defining the word *eidetic*. Without this inherent skill, he would likely not be a waiter at one of the finest dining establishments in Fellowship City, QTs House of Jacks.

???
webnet.mightybase search results...
QTs House of Jacks (also see the Realizer) : MIGHTYpedia Entry
???

Owned by Mighty Restaurateur, the Realizer, QTs House of Jacks is the latest hot spot in a long line of culinary experiences curated by the Realizer. Unlike his earlier and now-defunct adventure dining experiences, like Gothmopolis and Glory Battles Arena, QTs House of Jacks is a simple bar and grill. The restaurant resembles a 1950s-style drive-in restaurant with a dance floor in the center and old cars used for booths. Carhops roller-skate their way around the room, while a roster of characters found in a slew of films by one of the Realizer's favorite pre-WWIII directors serve as waitstaff for the Mighty patrons.

???

With nothing but time on his hands, Mario marvels at the Fellowship City skyline north of the Island where he lives. Squinting to make out the faint colorful vapor trails of FLYERS zooming around the skyscrapers, he's reminded of something else his father once told him.

My grandfather, your great-grandfather, taught me about comic books. He said he loved to read about these people with superpowers, and he wished he could be one of them. It would be amazing to be the one person with powers among so many with-out. What good he could have done for them. Now, we live in a world where so many have those kinds of powers. I bet life for them is so boring.

The Mighty are the majority, thinks Mario, shaking his head before turning contemplatively back. *They have all the wealth, fame, power, and superpowers. But they ARE bored. Every day, they come into the restaurant with some air of author-ity, making pointless demands of the waitstaff just because they can. Something to make themselves feel important. Their lives are so mundane. They are stuck in a world where they are unable to use their powers to any potential, neither good nor evil because of the monks.*

??
webnet.mightybase search results...
Monks (see Monastery of Sol and Luna) : MIGHTYpedia Entry
???

Only the highest level of Mighty are permitted to enter the Monastery of Sol and Luna. The monks are SEER-PATHS, having the ability of sight (seeing what is happening around them or nearsight, into the past or hindsight, or into the future or foresight) and telepathy (hearing and communicating through others, animals, or machines, and physically or mentally controlling others, animals, or machines). All monks have some level of sight and telepathy. For example, some monks may only have nearsight, seeing the world around them, and may only be able to communicate with animals as ZOOPATHS or machines like TECHNOPATHS. A rare few have the highest skill in all levels of sight and telepathy (including zoopathy and technopathy). These monks are called

SEER-OMNIPATHS, like Sol and Luna, the first of their kind.

See related... *The Enclave*

The five members of the Enclave of the Monastery of Sol and Luna are all seer-omnipaths who keep constant vigil over Fellowship City, as they strive for Omnivolence or the All-Choice, seeing all choices made by everyone all at once. Because they are aware of all that is happening around them in the present and future, they can stop any misdeed from occurring by directing the lower level monks to police the Mighty. Today, there is little need for policing among the Mighty, but every once in a while, an aberrant Citizen might be punished and taken to the Solitary Internment Camp or SIC, which lies seventy-five miles west of Fellowship City beyond the Summerland Desert.

???

"Hey Mario, you gonna move up or what?" Landy, a smallish hunchback of a man with a kind heart and a shrill voice, asks from behind.

"Oh yeah, sorry," Mario says, snapping back to reality and scooting up in the line. He glances at the clock on the watchtower, 6:17. He shakes his head.

"No worries, kid. Only making sure you're not standing dead on us."

Standing dead? Mario thinks. *I've heard that before.*

2

STANDING DEAD

T*he standing dead was a real possibility right after the second Evolutionary war, but it has been many years since then*, thinks Mario, remembering his history lessons. *Things have certainly changed in that time.*

??
webnet.mightybase search results...
History (see Origin of the Mighty) : MIGHTYpedia Entry
??

The people of Earth fought wars with one another over conflicting beliefs and *necessary* resources. As the war machines grew larger and resources dwindled, the Earth soon became unable to support its vast human population. When the ice caps melted away and rising sea levels changed shorelines all over the world, desperation for resources and land heightened uncontrollably. Countries launched their weapons against one another. Biological and electronic warfare killed millions without destroying structures or machines, leaving behind only trace amounts of poisons and radiation. Nuclear weapons, however, did not leave structures intact and decimated great swaths of the Earth with long-lasting radiation. The radiation soaked into the atmosphere and rained down upon the few survivors, changing their DNA, making them the Mighty.

???

Some idiot thought it would be a good idea to intimidate another idiot by launching nukes at one another, thinks Mario, recalling images from ancient movies tucked away in his memories. *So, they both pushed their big red buttons and began World War III. After that, the Earth was like Mad Max for a while, a wasteland of only pockets of habitable areas around the globe. It took time, but the survivors rebuilt society and technology, forming a new worldwide government called the Unified Citizens of Earth.*

???
webnet.mightybase search results...
Unified Citizens of Earth : MIGHTYpedia null entry, try again
???

"The winners write the history books, son."
Mario's eyes light up, as his father's voice plays in his head.
"You won't learn about the UCE from the Mighty. That's a shared history they keep private. As far as we're to know, they have always been the ones in charge, but I've got a secret. It wasn't always like that."
Mario sat on his father's lap, beaming at his mother sitting across from them, cradling Zelda in her arms. Mario scrunched

his shoulders inward, pulling his head downward, so he appeared neckless. His eyes bulged saucer-wide with excitement, as he patiently waited to learn the secret.

"Well, I'd rather be with you playing at the park, but since it's your birthday, I guess we can begin your history lessons," his father said with a sly grin before glancing at his wife for consent.

She nodded to her husband, but her eyes questioned if their son was truly ready.

Mario flashed his puppy dog eyes at both of them.

"Pleeeeaaase."

After a few seconds, his father whispered, "This is the truth based on historical facts. We cannot write it down, but we have passed it down orally generation after generation. Not everyone in the camp knows the truth, but there are a select few who do. We pass the truth down to our children, and then they pass it to their children and so on and on, so the truth remains the truth."

Mario leaned in eager-eyed.

"What I tell you, you must remember exactly, okay?" Mario's father tapped his excited, young son's forehead. "If it's not exact, then we will not know what is their story and what is our truth. Do you understand, Mario?"

Mario nodded.

"After much of the Earth was laid to waste, only small pockets of habitable areas across the globe remained. While the majority of the human population died, amazingly a substantial number survived and struggled to regrow humanity in these livable regions, rebuild society and technology, and establish a worldwide government called the Unified Citizens of Earth."

"What's the Unified Citizens of Earth?"

His mother nodded and began speaking as if on cue, though it did not sound rehearsed. "But like any newly formed group or society, defining who belongs and who does not is necessary." She spoke softly, while deftly removing her breast from her blouse and placing Zelda's lips upon her nipple. "Although many believed all humans should belong, a small group of humans susceptible to DNA mutations caused by the nuclear fallout and various other biotechnological residues still lingering after the third and final World War made that belief challenging for the majority."

"DNA? Mutations?" Mario gaped in confusion. "New... clear?"

"It's okay, Mario," his father assured. "You won't understand a lot of this information just yet. You're young, and this is only your first time hearing it. This will become a ritual, son. We will be doing a lot of practice until you get it right. We can explain its meanings later, but for now, we just need to concentrate on getting the repetition correct. We don't want anything to change, just because you received additional information. Do you understand?"

"Yes, papa."

His father smiled lovingly upon him, mussing his hair before nodding to his wife to continue.

"An extensive range of variations resulted from the mutations. Some had practical uses, like increased strength and speed. Others were considered abominations—poor souls who remotely resembled anything human. Those humans immune to the mutations deemed themselves to be NORMAL, and over time, it became harder and harder for them to accept the differences of the others they considered to be ABNORMAL."

"Abnormal? Those are the Mighty?"

"Spoilers," his mother giggled. "Hold your little horses."

Mario's father picked up where she left off. "Now understand, the only crime these people ever committed at this time was not being immune to genetic mutations. Even so, the Normal population cast them away, considering them less than human, akin to the flesheaters or fleshies."

"Flesheaters—they ate people!?"

"Not in general, but..." His father closed his eyes and sighed.

"Mario, we cannot pause to answer questions right now. We must get through this, and you must try to remember it as accurately as possible. But know this, even the Mighty will tell you about the flesheaters, as they fear them as well."

???
webnet.mightybase search results...
Flesheaters (Fleshies) : MIGHTYpedia Entry
???

The Mighty are not the only Earth creatures to have their DNA changed from the radiation and poisons left by the humans of Old Earth. All creatures of every earthly kingdom are susceptible to such changes, but those of the animal and plant variety are the most obvious and monstrous killing machines. Collectively, these horrific, nightmarish creatures are called flesheaters or fleshies. They continue today to be a menacing danger for those who choose to reside outside of the protection of Fellowship City under the Monastery of Sol and Luna.

???

"To suppress all these threats to the fledgling society, the UCE created the Citizen Army," continued Mario's father, placing a finger on his fidgeting young son's lips. *"While the primary purpose of the army was to stamp out the fleshies threat, it was also used to pacify and control the Abnormal population, which was few in number and easily contained in internment camps. The UCE tagged the Abnormals placed into these camps with tracking implants that could be scanned with handheld registry scanners."*

"That's like us," Mario said, pushing his father's finger away. "They were like us."

Mario's father nodded, swallowing so hard that Mario felt it from his seat upon his father's lap. "This next part is going to be rough. I need you to be very quiet, very still, and listen very carefully, okay?"

Mario nodded in confused anticipation.

"Over time, the Normals allowed some Abnormals to live among them, but their names, tags, and abilities were compiled and listed publicly online in the Abnormal Registry Database. Any Normal could log onto the webnet and search for Abnormals in the area. It was supposed to provide some semblance of safety and security, but it didn't. Due to fear of the unknown or stupidly in the guise of entertainment, mobs of Normals carried out vigilante justice upon the Abnormals."

Mario's father paused momentarily, gauging his son's reaction before continuing. Mario nodded for his father to continue.

"Many fledgling Abnormals could not control their abilities, so as often as mobs of Normals lynched them, they killed Normals in self-defense. Under UCE law, Abnormals had no right to self-defense, being often sentenced to worse fates than death."

Mario dropped his head, comprehending the words. His father's grip upon him tightened around him in a hug. His mother stood up and placed Zelda over her shoulder, lightly patting her back as she took over the next section.

"With each passing year, the number of Abnormals increased exponentially, as all Abnormal parents had Abnormal children, but many Normal parents also had Abnormal children."

BUUUURRRRRPPPP

They all giggled, as his mother cradled Zelda into her arms, *trying to lull her back to sleep as she rocked back and forth in front of them.*

"Usually, the latter would be hidden away for their own protection, killed by their parents out of fear, or sent to the internment camps. Eventually, the number of Abnormals increased to a point that they were able to organize and fight back. So, began the first Evolutionary War."

Suddenly, his mother left the room, carrying Zelda into her bedroom. At the same time, Mario's father pulled Mario around to face him. Mario gazed into his father's eyes with such innocence that shame washed over his father's face. His father's eyes dropped with his head. Mario raised a hand and touched his father's face warmly. "Keep going," he quietly urged.

His father raised his head, met his son's eyes, and continued, "Not much is really known about what happened during that war, except that many people died in violent combat, especially the Abnormals. Although they fought fiercely, their lack of military skill and leadership led to their ultimate defeat against the far superior forces of the Normal soldiers of the Citizen Army. By the end of the conflict, the Citizen Army had wiped out the Abnormal population back to what they thought to be a tolerable and controllable level. They forced the surviving Abnormals into their previous positions of internment and required them to pledge fealty to the Normal rule of the government for the Unified Citizens of Earth, creating a vision of 'peace' in the world."

With empty arms, Mario's mother returned, taking over.

"Over the next few years following the Evol War—that's Evol with an O, not Evil with an I," explained his mother. "The Normals believed they found an equilibrium—harmony. They enslaved the Abnormals who could be domesticated, utilizing and controlling their abilities to serve their daily lives. Most Normal households, even the poorer ones, had at least one Abnormal to control. The Abnormals that could not be domesticated lived out

their days in the internment camps, often finding violent ends, while those with much stronger and powerful abilities had a grimmer fate. They would battle one another in gladiatorial arenas for the amusement and gambling pleasure of the Normals, becoming nothing more than their entertainment. But even as they served and entertained them, the Normals still feared them."

"They made movies, reflecting those sentiments of distrust, anger, and fear of the other and the unknown," Mario's father began. "Gone were the days of the glorification of superheroes with almighty powers. In the post-Evol War I era, the most popular films were B-Movie horrors about Normals surviving the terror of Abnormal monsters, like mutant cannibal hillbillies."

"Hillbillies," Mario laughs. "What's a hillbilly?"

"Shhh," his father reminds with his finger to his lips. "As the 'peace' endured, the concern over the Abnormals waned. A minority of Normals even sought equal rights and emancipation from slavery for the Abnormals, whose only crime they argued was by virtue of their birth. The small progress made on their behalf allowed them to enjoy more freedoms and almost shut down the internment camps. They remained necessary, however, as only domesticated Abnormals benefited from such progress. It was during this small window of opportunity that our sins caught up with us, forcing us to pay for our crimes against those who committed none."

"We do not know much about them," Mario's mother said, "but we do know that two of the most powerful Mighty to ever exist were born sometime after the first Evol war. Twins named Sol and Luna. They led the Abnormal uprising that began the second Evol War. Abnormals chanted, 'We are the Mighty! It is our time to rise!' and 'All hail, Sol and Luna!' right before they would attack Normals. Although the Citizen Army of the UCE was massive and more technologically advanced, they could not protect themselves from the new attacks directed by Sol and Luna. The Second Evolutionary War lasted less than one week."

"Wherever Sol and Luna went, Normals died," Mario's father cut in. "Not a regular death, mind you. They would lose their life in a blink of an eye and just stand there, like in a daze. Those who watched from a distance to report on the battles would later say, 'The Citizen Army surrendered their lives in subservience to Sol and Luna, standing dead without movement.' When the Abnormals left the battlefield, the Citizen Army continued to stand motionless, frozen in time. Countless hollow husks standing dead in the field like rows of scarecrows collapsed when the power of the twins faded away."

"There's no fighting back against that kind of power. Doing so almost drove us into extinction. The Normal population fell by over 90 percent across the world. They did to us what we did to them, but more so. They gathered what few of us remained and placed us into the same camp where we held many of them at the Division Base of the Citizens Army."

"They built their new city on top of the military capital of the UCE and renamed it Fellowship City," Mario's mother continued. "In the northeast of the city, the first followers of Sol and Luna began work on their monastery. After its completion, Abnormals would flock to Fellowship City from everywhere else on the earth, finding a new home there in the safety of its protection. We do not know how or why, but the dangerous threat of the fleshies does not exist within the area that surrounds Fellowship City."

"Fellowship City became the de facto capital city of the Mighty, as the Abnormals now called themselves," his father said in a voice dripping with disdain. "They rounded up the surviving Normals and forced them to labor daily, building the first camp-houses of the Work Placement Camp. Those of us deemed too aggressive, unable to adapt to the control of the new masters, were moved far away from Fellowship City beyond the Summer-

land Desert in the west where the protection of Sol and Luna ends. And so, the Abnormals became the Mighty, and the Normals became Citizens."

"Citizens," thinks Mario, as he glares at the long line of people ahead of him, also waiting for busses to take them to work. "A word stripped of all its meaning. We are nothing more than servants if we're lucky, slaves if we're not... either way, we're here for THEIR entertainment."

3

ORPHAN HOUSE

Entertainment, reflects Mario, shaking his head. He scans the crowd, counting the number of costumed Citizens waiting in line in front of him. *The Mighty don't even know what entertaining is. My father knew how to entertain. He could always make us laugh.*

"Whatchya thinkin' bout, kiddo?" Landy asks, craning his head around Mario's side.

"Oh, nothing, just my parents," answers Mario half-aware, struggling to hold onto one happy remembrance or another.

"Good people, they were," says Landy, patting Mario on the back. "Your dad and I were friends, ya know. Back in the day, all of us Camp-Rats."

"I know, I know. Born and raised in the WPC."

"Yeah, we're all Camp-Rats," Landy insists. "My parents before me. Just like your parents before you... Hell, grand-parents and maybe great-grandparents too, I bet. Who knows anymore?"

I've got an idea.

"You still got those retro-games your dad had?" Landy

reminisces. "We used to play those video games hours upon hours. Wear out the controllers and have to fix 'em. Your dad was always scrounging for parts."

"Yeah, I've got them."

"You know that's how you got your names, right? You and Zelda." Landy chortles and coughs to a wet finish. "How your mother went along with that... she must'a been real taken."

Mario ponders Landy's words as another memory resurfaces.

"Your mom never liked just sitting there, wasting her day in front of video screens," Mario's father regaled his children, who sat anxiously at his feet. "Right, dear? You always wanted to be on the move."

Mario's mother peered in from the kitchen, giving her children a quick wink before returning to her escape within. The sound of cards shuffling fluttered out of the room before their father began the story with a near whisper.

"The Mighty viewed us Camp-Rats as necessary annoyances. They permitted us certain luxuries, like video-screens, movie players, game systems, and board games—really anything that kept us busy and out of their hair. But your mom wasn't into all that noise. Whenever she'd come by, I'd have to drop my controller and chase after her."

"You would HAVE TO?" their mother questioned from the other room.

"Yes, I would," he whispered before continuing at his normal volume. "She was this little precocious girl with golden hair. A lot like you, Zelda. You couldn't help but drop everything and do what she wanted to do."

They giggled, especially Zelda. Mario peeked into the kitchen, eyeing his mother as she ignored them and played Solitaire. Unable to contain her excitement, Zelda rolled into a summersault, vaulted upwards, and ran down the hallway and back again into another summersault.

"C'mon, Mawio," she singsonged. "Let's play lost and found. I saw a flower in the garden shaped like the sun. It can be the home, and we can find something to go with it. You've got those new books. Maybe there's something in there."

Zelda tugged at Mario, trying to pull him up from his cross-legged comfort. He eyed his father skeptically, "Like Zelda? You're kidding right?"

Mario's father snatched up Zelda and placed her on his lap.

"I don't think your brother wants to play right now, baby. I think he wants to hear about how spunky and energetic your mom was when she was younger."

"I'm no longer spunky and energetic?"

"Now you did it. I'm in trouble," he tried to say with a straight face but broke into an amused smile when he glimpsed his daughter's concerned eyes. "Go run around and play. I'll keep your brother busy for a bit."

"Okay, daddy," she exclaimed, skipping down the hallway while singing some silly children's song.

"Your mother loved to run, but I was always faster than her," whispered Mario's father. "I never beat her in a race or even caught up too close, because I never wanted to hurt her feelings."

Mario darted his eyes to his mother, assessing whether she overheard the clandestine information. When she beamed at him with surprised eyes followed by a wink, he felt confident his father's secret was not revealed. He waved at her and turned back to his father. "What did she like to play?"

"Colonel Crusader."

"Who's Colonel Crusader?"

"*He was a comic book vigilante superhero without any powers,*" his father emphasized the latter part. "*I would run after her saying, 'I get to be Colonel Crusader this time, Lizbeth!' But guess what?*"

"*What?*"

"*I never got to be Colonel Crusader,*" he chortled. "*She'd yell, 'Only if you can catch me, Tommy Trickster!' And, of course, I never caught her.*"

He may not have ever caught her at that game, but he did catch her...eventually, thinks Mario, fast-forwarding to another special moment shared with his parents.

"*When we turned 18, they put us to work,*" his father's story began in a singsong lulling way, as he bounced Zelda on his lap. "*Your mother worked for the same rich Mighty family her mother worked for, and I washed dishes at one of the Realizer's restaurants in mid-town.*"

"*Your father was so stingy with his earnings, he would never take me out that year,*" interjected Lizbeth, sticking her tongue out in jest.

"*Where were we going to go? The Haberdashery?*"

"*Would it hurt to take me dancing, Tommy? You know how I love to—*"

"*You're right. We could have danced and danced, and spun around all night long,*" he said, sliding Zelda into a perch on his hip and taking Lizbeth's hand to give her a quick spin.

"*Weeeeee,*" cheered Zelda.

Then, Tommy stopped Lizbeth and held her hand up revealing the wedding ring on her finger. "*We could've had fun, but I wanted to save everything I had to get you the most perfect ring I could find and ask you to marry me, baby!*"

"*Yay!*" Zelda squealed. "*Pretty ring!*"

"*Yes, it is,*" Lizbeth purred. "*And you probably scoured every pawn shop in the Normal slums to find it, didn't you?*"

"I'll never tell," he sang, winking at Mario who sat in awe, marveling at the entire spectacle.

"Well, you were so nervous, you almost didn't give it to me," Lizbeth said, easing Zelda away from Tommy's side and sliding her onto her hip. "We're going to take a bath now."

"No, mommy," Zelda cried. "I want to listen to the rest of the story."

"You will, sweetie. Someday."

Zelda squirmed in her mother's arms all the way down the hall, trying to break free. She grunted and squealed up until the moment the faucet turned on.

"So, where'd you get the ring?" Mario asked in a hushed whisper.

"A pawn shop in the Normal slums," Tommy revealed in a normal volume, catching Mario off-guard. "It's cool, kid. I can trust you, right?"

Mario's eyes lit up and a huge smile took over his face.

"Noooo!" Zelda screamed, escaping down the hallway completely naked.

Tommy wrapped her into his arms, as Lizbeth ran toward them carrying a towel.

"I guess you really want me to finish the story, eh?" Tommy said, toweling his daughter off in his lap. "Where was I?"

"The ring!" exclaimed Zelda with a befuddled laugh, slipping free of the towel.

"Oh yes, that's right," he said, trading the towel for clothes. "Well, here's the thing. I always thought your mother was way too good for me. She's so beautiful and so smart. And back then, her long blonde hair would wave where it should and curled up at the ends without her even trying."

"Those were the good ol' days," Lizbeth quipped, wringing the towel in her hands.

Her children laughed, not fully understanding why.

"Don't listen to her," Tommy said, pulling Zelda's shirt over her head. "She still wakes up beautiful inside and out. That is something I've always loved about her."

"Well, you aren't too bad yourself. I still kinda like you all right."

The children laughed again.

"You see," their father said, as he set Zelda down next to Mario. "It's her perpetually positive attitude that keeps me going. I wanted more than anything to capture her heart."

"You always had my heart," Lizbeth said, caressing his shoulder before flicking it with her finger. "I think you might have been after something else."

Tommy let loose an awkward chuckle.

"Regardless, I psyched myself up that morning," he said, pushing his finger and thumb together in front of him, imagining the beautiful gold band with a decorative engraved lace pattern and diamond chip mounted in the center. "I stared at that second-hand ring and told myself, this is it! This is the day! She will say yes! So, I got dressed for work and ran out the door."

"Why'd you have to run, dear?"

"Because I was late," Tommy smirked before changing his voice to convey a teaching moment. "You should never be late for work. I always got to the buses way ahead of schedule, because you can never be sure that you'll catch one in time. There are so many people with the same shift as you." He returned his voice to storyteller mode, regaling, "Your mother had the same shift as me, and we always stood in the bus line together. So, she was quite worried when I didn't show up that morning."

"Quite," she mimicked.

"I ran up to where she stood in line, stepped up behind her, and put my hands on her waist." The children's eyes widened in synchrony. "She didn't even acknowledge me, because she knew my touch by heart."

Lizbeth guffawed.

"I didn't look at you, because I was angry that you were late. And I didn't respond to your touch, because I knew no one else would dare touch me so intimately in a line of workers."

"At any rate, when you did speak to me. What did you say?"

"You're late."

"And what did I say?"

"You whispered into my ear and said, I had to get something," Lizbeth said, balling the towel as she stepped toward her children. "Then, you turned me around, trying to meet my eyes, but I wasn't having any of it. I closed them tight to show you how upset I was about your tardiness."

"And when you let them open," Tommy said, standing up.

As Zelda and Mario rushed to take over his seat, he strode toward Lizbeth with his hands folded in front of him.

"Ahem. I'm kinda doing a thing here," Tommy says to his bickering kids.

The children stopped nudging one another and shrugged apologies. He gestured to his hands, and their eyes followed. His palms opened outward, displaying an imaginary box with their mother's ring inside.

She stepped forward, placing her hands in his. He caressed the tops of her fingers and went pale.

"Where's the ring?"

"In the bathroom, silly. I took it off to wash Zelda," she said, letting go of his hands. She hurried down the hallway and into the bathroom to retrieve the ring, hustled back, and flashed it at her husband and the kids before clasping his hands again. "Better?"

"Yes," Tommy said with a toothy grin. "So, your mom sees the ring and stares at me with those beautiful eyes of hers eyes, welling with tears. She stands motionless and in shock for what seemed like several minutes before I asked her, 'Is that a yes?' And she said—"

"Yes! Yes!" interrupted Lizbeth, throwing her arms around Tommy, and together jumping up and down while Zelda and Mario clapped and laughed at the spectacle.

"So, I understand there'll be a Citizen's section at the parade."

Landy's voice interrupts Mario's reminiscing.

"Oh? You thinking about going?"

"I mean... I'm thinkin' about it."

DING DING DING

A bell rings to signal a shift change of Mighty guards. Mario glares at the clock on the watchtower, as it strikes 6:30. He bites a nail, cutting a quarter moon away. He flicks it around in his mouth, as he counts the number of people standing in front of him, and then he spits it out and bites another nail. *There are still enough for two busloads*, he thinks, shaking his head. *I'm so late. The Realizer is going to kill me.*

PFFFFFFFT

Zelda sticks her tongue out at Mario, as she jogs by him. "You're so late," she says with a laugh.

Mario nods and shrugs, showing his defeat. "Some of us don't have the luxury of being able to hang out here all day and play."

"Don't be jealous," Zelda singsongs, as she spins around in a little dance.

She only has a few more months of this, and then she'll be on the work grind, just like me.

"Have fun at work, Mario!" she says, scampering away toward a group of teens her age.

Mario's reminded of the precocious five-year-old high-tailing it away from him, glancing over her shoulder and exclaiming, "*I'm the princess, and you're the prince! You have to save me!*" In his mind, his eight-year-old self responds as any big brother would. "*As you wish, your highness.*"

As he tracks her path to the large brick building on the northeast side of WPC, she scoops up her friends waiting with open arms and leads them on their way.

She still thinks she's a princess. It's probably my fault.

Seven years ago.

Rain pelted down, stinging the metal roof with every drop like a tap-tap-tap on a snare drum. Mario rubbed his reddened eyes. He couldn't believe what he had just been through, or what he had to do now. He placed an arm around the shoulders of his ten-year-old sister, who was even worse for wear.

"It'll be okay. I'm here."

Zelda frowned at him with beet-red eyes swallowed by sadness, torturing his soul. She gave him a slight nod before returning to her sulking position.

Raindrops streaked down the windows of the Orphan House like a memorial to the tears that ran across his face only moments before. He tried to wipe them away, attempting to appear less broken than he truly was and trying to be the hero his sister needed him to be.

They sat in the white upon white room of the administrator's office. Mario had been there before but only with his mother, and only when she was volunteering. The administrator clicked her pen staccato-like, almost in rhythmic timing with the tinny notes pinging from the roof. She sat behind a white desk with well-organized white papers in white folders with various identity tags scrawled upon the top tabs.

"We could put the boy in with the early-teens. I think there's some space," the sultry voice of the administrator seemed incongruous with the enormity of the situation. She was tan and tall with sleek, sharp features and a black bun pulled tight to the back of her head. Even her skin appeared to be pulled back and tied with that bun. "The girl though. There isn't room in her age group right now."

"She needs to stay with me," Mario protested, clutching his sister.

"I understand how you feel," the administrator's voice revealed empathy and even compassion, as she stood up and lumbered toward the children. "This would be a hard time for anyone. You are not alone, and unfortunately, you are not the only ones dealing with hardships like these. Thankfully, the Mighty recognize the necessity to nurture orphaned children. Years ago, you two would've been put to work. Do you realize that?"

'Yes, I actually do,' thought Mario.

He remembered his history lessons with his parents, and then he realized his last session would be the very last one he would ever have with them. His eyes lamented the loss.

"See, that's not something you'd want," said the administrator, awkwardly patting Mario's shoulder, as if to be comforting. "Our facility is designed to take care of the orphaned Citizens. While we would love to keep you two together, our facility separates the boys from the girls at your ages. So, I'm sorry. Until you turn 18, you will be housed in your respective areas."

The administrator returned to her chair behind her white desk, waving for a volunteer to come over. The volunteer looked familiar. She did not live in their camphouse block, but maybe she lived on the same street. She carried a blanket and pillow.

"I'm Maddie," she said, handing the blanket and pillow to Mario. "Follow me. I'll show you around."

"What about Zelda?" Mario questioned, standing up with the bulky package of fleece and down under his arm.

"She'll be just fine," assured the administrator. "We'll find a place for her, and you can eat your meals together tomorrow, okay?"

Mario conceded as Zelda grasped his free arm, "I love you!"

"I love you too, Z."

He struggled to free his arm from her grip, kissing her forehead and saying, "Don't worry. I'm here."

Their eyes did not part as they ushered him backward toward the door. Her sadness sank deeper with every step.

"Everything will be okay," he assured her as her hand let go.

She said nothing, as she turned around in her chair, pulled her knees into her chest, and buried her face between them. Mario's heart broke.

The very next day, Mario found Zelda at the eight-year-olds table for breakfast.

"Good morning, sir knight," Zelda greeted her brother upon his arrival. "You may take a seat."

"As you wish, your highness," he responded appropriately, sitting down with his tray of breakfast mush.

The role of Zelda's guardian was thrust upon Mario's shoulders from that day on. He tried to raise her as best he could, which included allowing her to continue playing her perpetual princess games. He thought doing so might give her a sense of familiarity and help her work out the trauma.

I had to be mature too soon, thinks Mario. I let her be a kid because I couldn't be one anymore. She's 17 now and not half as mature as I was at 13. I'm not sure that was the right thing to do.

"Ahem," Landy clears his throat from behind Mario.

Mario blinks back to the present and shuffles forward. He appraises the line and notices Officer Lizardlips' replacement moving with sloth-like speed as he oversees the current bus-loading.

Has everything gone in slow motion? Mario thinks, tilting his head and studying the guard with the big bushy eyebrows and stub nose. *He's sorta like a sloth in more ways than one.*

Landy taps Mario on the shoulder.

"You know the city a bit, right?" he asks.

"I guess," Mario responds, turning to face Landy. "Why?"

"I'm gonna get a permit to..." Landy stops, biting his lip. His plump cheeks grow rosy, as he says, "take a nice lady on a date."

"You're going on a date?"

Landy shushes Mario, placing his right hand on Mario's left shoulder to pull him into confidence range. "Well, I kinda ain't asked her yet. And, I don't want anything gettin' back to her before I do. Okay?"

"Got it," Mario says, curling his mouth to the side. "I didn't mean to let the cat out of the bag."

"So here's how you can help," Landy says, narrowing his eyes and pulling Mario closer. "Where can I take her in the city? Somewhere Citizens can go?"

4

NEITHER SERVING NOR PROTECTING

W*here can Citizens go?*
Most establishments in the city proper, aka downtown Fellowship City, do not serve Citizens. Mario calls to mind a panoply of signs of various sizes, shapes, and colors, but all saying the same two phrases: MIGHTY ONLY or NO CITIZENS ALLOWED. That is, all except for one.

We're good enough to serve them, but not good enough to serve, Mario wants to tell Landy, but he instead apologizes, "Sorry, Landy. I can't think of anything off the top of my head. If I think of something, I'll let you know."

"Thanks, Mario," Landy says, puffing his big red cheeks out and showing his jagged teeth. "And remember, mums the word." Landy pinches his lips and twists his thumb and forefinger in a motion that solidifies his secret.

Mario mimics the action and turns back around, thinking about that exception.

Unlike the many establishments further north in downtown Fellowship City, DerMööve's Arcade & Grill has no MIGHTY ONLY or NO CITIZENS ALLOWED signs posted.

??
webnet.mightybase search results...
DerMööve's Arcade & Grill : MIGHTYpedia entry
??

DerMööve's Arcade & Grill is located on 20th and B Streets right across the street from Fellowship City Park on the opposite side of the southside ghetto. It is owned and operated by the Mighty restaurateur, DerMööve.

Due to its close proximity to the living area of the select free-roaming Citizens, it is one of the few restaurants in downtown Fellowship City that will serve Citizens, even those visiting from WPC. As such, Mighty should favor caution when choosing to patron the restaurant. For many, the pre-WWIII arcade games and cuisine outweigh any other costs.

??

A common pastime of Mario's is to access the Webnet Mightybase. There are two common hubs in the WPC whereby Citizens can peruse the informational and social web space. The first and most frequented hub is in the WPC's community center, which serves as space for Citizens to congregate while locked within the walls of the WPC. Mario spends little time at that hub. The second, smaller hub is hidden in the back of the Orphan House.

Although the smaller hub has no more than three working datapads at any given time, Mario prefers the quiet of the well-lit smallish white room, which reeks of sanitizer and ozone. Inside, half a dozen semi-circular tables and colorful plastic chairs form a full circle around a central power pillar.

During Mario's stay at the Orphan House, he spent many an hour on those datapads. To use them now, however, he has to volunteer at the Orphan House on his days off.

On his most recent day off, he had to wait patiently for the children utilizing the datapads to finish.

He clutched the plastic "Data Monitor" card on his lanyard, absentmindedly pulling it back and forth, creating a friction burn on the back of his neck.

He let go of the lanyard as a hand jutted upward, catching his attention. "Mr. Data Monitor," a child's soft voice called out from behind a datapad screen.

"Yeah. Gimme a sec," Mario answered casually, moseying over to the child.

She had bright red hair tousled around the top of her head and held together by a makeshift bow. With her piercing blue doe eyes fixed on him, she handed him the datapad, saying, "This datapad isn't working. Can you—?"

"I'll take a gander," Mario interrupted, flipping the pad around in his hands. He knew how to fix it, but he didn't want to, at least not yet. "I think it has a bad motivator. It's going to take me a while. You might as well go outside and play some. I might have it ready for you later."

Her eyes welled with tears. Mario roiled with guilt but did nothing to alleviate her unhappiness. She dropped her head and sulked out of the room, glancing back at him before bolting toward the door that would take her outside to play.

'She'll be alright,' Mario tried to assure himself, triggering a reboot on the datapad. He peered out the doorway of the common hub and through the outside window, glimpsing her redhead bob

up to Zelda, who was volunteering in the outdoor play area. *'Shit... I forgot she was out there.'*

Mario flipped the datapad over after rebooting it. He toggled a few digital switches in the settings before landing on the search page for the Webnet Mightybase. He began his ritual, typing: *DerMööve.*

He always surveilled *DerMööve's* profile first, assessing any changes from the previous surveillance. Unlike other Mighty who used the Webnet Mightybase to show off their superpowers in videos or pander for dates, *DerMööve's* profile read like an advertisement for his restaurant:

Come enjoy our retro videogames, including pinball, skeeball, cabinet games, virtual and augmented reality games, and much more. Enjoy our authentic pre-WWIII BBQ! Play for the games! Stay for the food!

There was no real indication that he was even a Mighty with powers, if not for the TELEKIN floating under his name like a title.

???
webnet.mightybase search results...
Telekin : MIGHTYpedia entry
???

TELEKINS have the ability to move and control certain inanimate objects with their minds. It is a broader category that includes other kin-type Mighty, including PYROKINS who control fire, AQUAKINS who control water, TERRAKINS who control the earth and plants, AEROKINS who control the air and weather, MAGNOKINS who control metal, ELECTROKINS who control electricity, and OMNIKINS who are theoretically capable of performing all those abilities. There are no known omnikins.

Kins can be found in every part of Mighty society, from aquakin firefighters to terrakin and telekin construction workers. Although most of their abilities are limited to moving and shaping, some kins can convert their bodies into what they control, and others can even use that control to fly like the FLYERS and BIRDS.

???

'Nothing new,' thought Mario, as he scrolled his finger along the edge, sliding the information on the screen to the left, as information off-screen to the right became the forefront.

BAHAHAHA

Mario chortled so abruptly that he couldn't stop himself. The children gathered around the other datapads eyed him with displeasure. One wiry haired little girl with horn-rimmed glasses placed her forefinger to her lips and loudly shushed him.

Mario's eyes apologized before returning to the screen. At the top of the comment bar now hovering in the center of the screen, a Mighty named 4SKōR posted, "THIS IS NOT 4 ADVERTISING, LÖÖSER!"

Mario chuckled again, quieter this time, so no one heard him. Then, he touched the thumbnail image of 4SKōR in a circle frame next to her post. The image grew larger on the screen, revealing a possibly attractive young woman with short-cropped black hair and a bright red streak from the top left of her hairline back. The image shimmied, distorting her to make it appear as if she was screaming out at someone. Black mascara matching her hair color ran down her cheeks, and red lipstick as bright as the stripe in her hair rubbed away from her lips. He recognized her from QTs.

Below her comment, DerMööve replied, "You don't have to yell." His thumbnail image resembled the headshot of some famous pre-WWIII actor. He wore a tuxedo, tilting his head with a single raised eyebrow. His hair was slicked back and shiny black.

'He ages well,' Mario thought with utter disappointment.

Below DerMööve's reply, a Mighty named Tayrn Meyrgæch responded, "Loving the hair, Foursy! Keeping it feng shui down yonder?" His thumbnail image was a close-up of an eye with a rust-colored iris.

To which, DerMööve replied, "Any more comments such like this, I will reMööve you!"

Mario rolled his eyes and swiped his forefinger to the right, sending DerMööve's profile into temporary oblivion.

The ritual continued with Mario surveilling first 4SKōR's profile followed by a few others he bumped into at QTs in the past week. Finding nothing of interest on their profiles, he finished his ritual with his customary search for which he expected to find no information: EVOL and Abnormal. Nothing came up for EVOL, but when he typed Abnormal, he fat-fingered the start button before finishing the word. This time, he retrieved results he had never come across before.

???
webnet.mightybase search results...
Abnorm : over 1 million entries retrieved...
Use filter to refine search...
???

Mario scrolled through the first page. Every entry read abnorm-m_reg.db. He scrolled back to the top and clicked on the first one.

It redirected him to some random Mighty's profile page. He returned to the results and clicked another, and another, finding them all to land on a Mighty profile page, both living and dead.

The realization of what he discovered hit him hard, providing for the first time, outside evidence of what his parents had taught him in his history lessons. 'This is what became of the Abnormal Registry Database,' he thought, squinting at the hundreds of profile entries with the abnorm_reg.db tag next to them. 'When the Mighty took control, they recycled it into the Webnet Mightybase.'

"Give it up, Mario," Zelda commanded, taking the datapad from Mario's hands. "It looks like it's fixed," she said, handing the datapad to the little redheaded girl, who took it and scampered back to her spot.

Mario almost didn't keep himself from protesting, but he was thankful Zelda took her time, allowing him to find the new discovery. "I found something, Zelda. Something big."

"Yeah?"

"It confirms what Mom and Dad taught us. The history."

"Oh," said Zelda, returning to her volunteer duty.

"Wait, Zel," Mario pleaded, clasping her shoulder to turn her to face him. "It means they were right. Mom and Dad were right."

"And what's that get us, Mario? It doesn't bring them back, does it?" She turned again and hurried to her post.

Mario shuffles a bit as the line slowly inches forward. "But to me, it means something," he whispers unconsciously.

"What's that?" Landy asks. "Did you think of something?"

"What? No. I was only thinking out loud. I'm still thinking about it, Landy. I'll let you know."

"Okay, kid. Okay."

At the moment, however, Mario's thoughts are not on finding a place for Landy and his gal-pal. His mind is once again occupied with ghosts of his parents.

Seven years ago.

"Okay, kids. Are you ready?" Tommy asked, hoisting four leave permits in the air.

It was a Saturday, and they were all dressed in their finest clothes. Lizbeth and Zelda wore short dresses, while Tommy and Mario wore collared shirts and slacks. They bounded out of their cumphouse like adventurers seeking some lost treasure, full of excitement and wonder.

When they reached the bus, Tommy made a show of handing the permits to the Mighty guard on duty. The guard scanned the permits, appraised the smartly dressed family, and let them board.

Mario and Zelda sat together midway on the driver's side while Tommy and Lizbeth sat behind them. A few other Citizens sat scattered about the bus.

"Late-shifters," Tommy whispered over the back of the seat to his children, answering the question they had yet to ask.

The bus drove them across Olum Bridge Way toward downtown Fellowship City. Mario let Zelda sit next to the window, and they huddled together to admire the tall buildings.

"There's U^3," she shrieked.

"That's not it," Mario retorts. "You can't see U^3 from this far away or this low to the ground."

PFFFFFFFT

Zelda's reply warranted no further discussion on the topic. Besides, the bus turned west onto Dalton Street, heading into the

Normal slums to make a stop. Zelda and Mario marveled at the sights around them. "Citizens live here?" Zelda asked.

"Yeah," Mario answered. "Some get to live outside the WPC."

"Lucky!"

"Maybe not so lucky," their mother's voice cut in. She pointed to a derelict-looking home, where some dirty spaced-out Normals burned a bonfire in the front yard. "Out here can be dangerous."

"It's not true freedom," added their father. "Whether they're here, the WPC, or the SIC, we are all just Citizens to the Mighty. There are advantages and disadvantages, but as long as they're above us, we're going to fall to the wayside. We need to be as best prepared as possible for when that happens. Understand?"

"Yes, papa," they singsonged in unison.

Zelda pressed her face against the window, while Mario tried to find room for his. The bus turned north onto 20th street and once again headed toward downtown Fellowship City. It made two more stops before crossing the bridge over Fellowship City Park.

On the other side of the bridge, the bus driver pulled to the curb and cranked the door open. Tommy jumped up, exclaiming, "Alright, here's where we get off."

As he ushered his family out the door, the driver asked, "You sure this is where you wanna be dropped off?"

"This is the spot," Tommy said with his eyes fixated on the building across the street. It was a four-story building on the northwest corner of 20th and B, and on the bottom floor was a restaurant with a neon sign blinking "DerMööve's Arcade & Grill."

"Alright, kids! You're gonna love this!"

Tommy seized his children's hands and skipped with them across the street. Lizbeth followed in stride.

"Is it usually this quiet?" Mario asked, puzzled by the dearth of vehicles and people around.

A few streets ahead, vehicles zipped around and parked on the side of the streets, but the only thing moving in their vicinity was the bus heading eastbound.

"Most Mighty tend to stay north of B," his father answered as they stepped onto the curb in front of the restaurant. "Citizens don't usually come downtown unless they're working."

Mario nodded at his father, catching a stench in the air.

"What is that?" he said. "It smells like sweat and moldy cheese."

"It's probably the sewer," his mother said, pointing to a grating off to their side.

"Gross!" Zelda squealed.

Mario laughed, yanking her to his side and taking her hand.

"I need to protect you, my princess," he said winking at her. "There's a troll or some other giant grossness about these parts."

Zelda slipped her hand out of his.

"I can protect myself, sir knight," she protested as they approached the massive archways of intimidating size and absurdity, signaling the entrance to DerMööve's Arcade & Grill. Stepping through them, she spun around to admire their intricacy. The dizzying effect created a surreal moment, hitting her with slight vertigo and a wave of nausea. Off-balance, she reached for Mario, saying, "I don't really need you, but since you're here. I won't deprive you of protecting your princess, sir knight."

Mario scoffed, but he held her hand and much of her weight as they meandered through the front doors. She stayed a step or two behind him. He surveilled the lobby, uncertain what he would find inside.

His father, on the other hand, sped through without hesitation, heading toward a green-haired young woman standing behind a podium with a stack of menus in her hands. Mario followed, leading Zelda behind him. His mother entered last, clacking her heels on the concrete floor as she trailed them all.

In the rooms beyond the host, Mario spied several other Citizens eating in the restaurant area and playing games in the arcade, as if they had always had the privilege to do so. From his perspective, no one appeared out of place whatsoever, except the host.

Her skin twinkled with glittering green and purple sparkles. As Mario wondered whether they were the product of some sort of make-up applied to her skin or her actual skin, transparent inner eyelids blinked at him and her scaly nose crinkled. At that moment, he determined she must be a Mighty, and he was surprised by how kind she was toward his family.

Not only did she greet them with a warm, welcoming smile and escort them to an extravagant booth near the arcade floor, but she also courteously asked, "Is there anything more I can do to be of service to you and your beautiful family, Mr. Rickson?"

"Nope. I think we're all good for now," his father answered with an odd bobbling of his head.

She bowed and pranced away. Mario couldn't believe it. They were being treated like honest-to-goodness, real people for the first time in his life.

"Look," his father said with eyes shining like a toddler seeing birthday candles for the first time. Mario followed his gaze toward the array of retro-games on the arcade floor, startling as his father grabbed hold of one of his hands and one of Zelda's, exclaiming, "They have TRON and KRULL!"

"You kids go play," his mother said, as they raced toward the games. "I'll hold down the fort."

True to her word, Lizbeth held down the fort, ordering drinks and appetizers for her family, while sitting guard at their booth. She laughed and cheered for all three of her children, taking in their whimsy as her own. Every so often, Mario or Zelda would scurry back up to her, take a drink and a bite, blast her with commentary about whatever game they were playing, and skedaddle once more.

Spellbound by the magic of it all, Tommy played and played without returning to his wife. Not that she cared. She was filled with glee to witness such happiness.

"'Tschuldigung," an unfamiliar voice spoke from behind Lizbeth. She turned to face a dapper Mighty with slick-backed black hair, wearing an expensive designer suit. "Are you hier allein?"

Dumbfounded, Lizbeth answered after a few seconds to replay the moment in her head. "I'm with my family," she finally said, pointing at her family playing in the arcade. They all stood around an enormous four-player cabinet game with the word GAUNTLET scrawled upon the top.

"Mein... app... apol-o gies," the man said, excusing himself.

"No harm done," Lizbeth replied, trying her best to come off as confident and unaffected.

The man moseyed away, murmuring something under his breath, as his heavy footsteps thudded on the floor. Lizbeth dared not turn. Her fingernails bit into her palms, and she inhaled a deep breath, letting out slow bursts, one at a time.

When his footstep finally faded away, she let loose a sigh of relief and slouched forward.

"MOMMY! MOMMY!" Mario yelled, waving at her from the GAUNTLET game. "Come join us! We need a wizard!"

As Lizbeth waved back, Mario caught sight of a man sitting in a private booth not far from his mother. The man's eyes were glued to her. The way he was dressed and kempt, resembled a secret agent from one of the movies his father loved. Mario did not appreciate the way the man leered at his mother.

"Elf," a mechanical voice spoke from the Gauntlet game. "Your life force is running out!"

Mario turned back to the machine and maneuvered his Elf toward some food.

"Someone shot the food," announced the mechanical narrator.

"Zelda!" cried Mario. "I needed that."

"Sorry, I didn't mean to."

"Elf needs food badly!" spoke the game, as the death chime began.

DUH DUH, DUH DUH, DUH DUH

"I'm going to die!" Mario cried, as his character ran out of life and let loose an electronic death rattle followed by somber chip-tune music.

Frustrated, Mario turned to his mother, wondering if she witnessed the calamity befallen him. She flashed him a knowing smile and tilted her head. His frustration melted away with her smile. Suddenly, something shimmered in the corner of his eye, catching his attention. Mario focused, eyeing salt and pepper shakers floating freely about on the man's table.

As the man burned holes into his mother, his hands folded almost motionless in front of him. Almost. Several of his fingers flittered in unnoticeable staccato movements.

Without warning, the man faced Mario.

Some reflexive impulse forced Mario to turn away, but after a second or two, he turned back.

Dancing at least six inches above the man's left palm were the salt and pepper shakers. Mario was mesmerized. He was used to the Mighty WPC guards who were more monstrous than super-powered, but this was different. He had never beheld this kind of power before. It was too astonishing for any Citizen to ignore.

Not long after dying at Gauntlet, Mario and his family sat at their booth, scarfing down a meal of barbecued cheeseburgers, French fries, and malt chocolate shakes. As Mario ate, his skin prickled with goose flesh, and he shuttered. Something or someone had their eyes on him and his family.

He scoured the room, being as inconspicuous as possible as he searched the entire restaurant and arcade floor for the missing creeper. Not finding the man in his private booth or anywhere, Mario swelled with the eerie sensation. He continued darting his eyes around the room, relentless in his quest, until a massive cabinet game against the back wall of the arcade caught his attention. Although no one at all was near the game, it shifted, budging forward and to the right.

Mario believed the creepy man was a telekin, so doing such things would be second nature to him. But Mario also understood telekins needed to be in view of whatever it was they manipulated, and he did not find any sign of the man. Perplexed, his eyes lingered on the cabinet, agape with anticipation.

A flutter of leather fingertips alarmed Mario, as two gloved hands grasped the side of the cabinet from behind. With eyes peeled, Mario scooted to the edge of his seat, certain he was privy to something he should not be. He did not expect an older man with a mostly bald head, gray beard, and dark, ashy skin to peek his head around the corner. The veil of mystery disappeared, as the man exited, revealing the DerMööve logos on his dull gray coveralls and toolbox at his side. Mario slumped back into his seat.

"What's wrong, buddy?" Tommy asked. "You wanna play some more games?"

"Skeeball!" shouted Zelda.

Lizbeth patted Mario's shoulder and said, "Now that's something I would play."

Mario nodded and turned from his mother to slide out of the booth, finding his way blocked by an unforeseen obstacle.

"'Tschuldigung," said the man, casting a devilish grin at Mario.

Mario shook the shock from his face, regaining some composure as he let slip a lip service apology.

"I'm sorry. I didn't see you, mister," were the words his mouth delivered, but he continued in thought, 'and I was looking all over for you.'

"No harm," assured the man with a wink. Then, his eyes fell upon Lizbeth. "I am the proprietor of dis restaurant. You may call me DerMööve." He thrust a fist forward, dropping a handful of gold-colored tokens onto the table. "Enjoy some games on me, bitte."

"Thank you," Lizbeth said, gathering up the tokens while trying to keep her eyes away from the man.

"Don't mention it," replied DerMööve as he sauntered to his private booth.

Moments later, Mario and his family were at the skeeball machine, plunking tokens into the slot for their lane. The balls kicked loose with a thud and thunder as they rolled into place. With eyes alit with excitement, they all picked up their first balls and lobbed them underhanded up the ramp. That is, everyone except for Zelda.

KLANK KLANKETY KLANK

"It's not working for me," Zelda cried, recovering the skeeball that just bounced off the ramp.

"Come on, princess. You can do it," Tommy encouraged.

"Dad, she's throwing overhand."

Zelda stuck her tongue out at Mario.

PFFFFFT

Lizbeth plucked a ball from the dispenser and showed Zelda how to throw it down the ramp. "Now watch me do it, sweetie.

All you have to do is toss it underhand."

"Duh," Mario wisecracked.

"Mom!" cried Zelda.

"MARIO!" shrieked a frustrated Lizbeth.

"Sorry, mom," Mario said with a slight quiver as hairs on the back of his neck began to bristle.

He sought out the man in the private booth, finding DerMööve's eyes locked onto his family once more. Mario wished he had power like the Mighty, so the creep wouldn't think they were merely Citizens. He wanted to rip the man's eyes right out of his head. Alas, he was only a powerless Citizen, and he could tell DerMööve knew by the intense pleasure written all over his face as he ogled his family. Mario did not like it at all.

At his private booth, DerMööve levitated the salt and pepper shakers above his palm, but he allocated the bulk of his concentration to Mario's family.

He laughed when Zelda kicked her feet into the ground and crossed her arms with contempt whenever Mario jumped up, shouting, "I win! I win!" He licked his lips when Tommy's fingers traced the length of Lizbeth's spine then drifted to her waistline as he kissed her. He stiffened when Mario and Zelda threw their arms around their parents to make a big family hug. He frowned when Lizbeth kissed Tommy.

With each kiss, his face grew more and more contemptuous, and his eyes flared with primal fury. No longer able to bridle his wrath, he tossed the salt and pepper shakers into the wall and flicked his finger in her direction.

As if by an invisible hand, Lizbeth's short dress lifted from behind, revealing her white lace panties beneath.

Mario and Tommy were too busy playing, but not Zelda.

"Mommy," she wailed.

Lizbeth immediately turned to chastise Mario, "Quit messing with her..." but she stopped, seeing her children's shocked faces as they both pointed to her dress.

Within seconds, Tommy was on top of her, trying in vain to wrench the dress free from the unseen force. Even Mario and Zelda tried to help, stretching their arms and legs out to make a human shield. Lizbeth hunkered down, blushing a deep red as she hid within the protection of her family.

"Bwahaha," bellowed hysterical laughter from the private booth of DerMööve, catching Tommy's attention and anger. DerMööve raised his hands in innocence, as Lizbeth's dress fell back down into place. He then turned away as if he had done nothing wrong.

Tommy took a step in DerMööve's direction, but Lizbeth clasped his shoulder, wrapping an arm around him below his chest. She whispered, "Wait for the monks. They'll do something about..."

"They never stop the Mighty from messing with Citizens," interrupted Tommy, breaking free from her. "They're not coming to help us."

As he took another step toward DerMööve, she clung to him, pleading, "Calm down, Tommy Trickster. Please. You can't..."

"Bash his fucking brains in!" he interrupted again. The profanity and anger surprised Mario and Zelda, who had never seen their father in such a state before in their lives.

"You can't even think it, Tom!" she pled again. "They'll know."

Tommy turned around to face his wife.

"It's not right," he said, pushing her away and dashing toward DerMööve. He crossed the room and slowed down as he approached the private booth. "What the hell, buddy?"

DerMööve turned to face Tommy, shrugging with a smirk, he asked, "Who me?"

"Yeah, you!" shouted Tommy, as he stepped toward

DerMööve. "Who do you think you are? You may own this place, but that does not give you the right to treat my wife that way!"

DerMööve showed Tommy his palms and a face full of innocence, saying nothing in his defense.

"What the hell do you think you're doing?" Tommy shouted, slamming his fist on DerMööve's table.

"Nichts," DerMööve answered, leaning toward Tommy while making a gesticulating motion with his right hand. "You like... Citizen?"

Lizbeth squealed behind him, as her dress burst open, sending buttons flying across the room and revealing her breasts. In frantic desperation, she wrapped her arms around herself, trying to hide her modesty.

Tommy raced back to his wife's aid, removing his shirt as he approached.

"Take Zelda and hide!" he ordered Mario, as he covered his wife.

Mario obeyed, grappling Zelda's hand and dragging her to the stairwell. She whimpered, gawking in horror until Mario took her into his arms and hid her face in his chest.

"Your knight is here, my princess," he whispered, leading her up the stairwell. "We can find a safe place to hide..."

"I want to see," she interrupted, scrambling toward a balcony overlooking the restaurant.

Mario followed, giving little protest.

On the floor, Tommy protected Lizbeth, his face reddening with rage.

"I'm going to take care of this."

Lizbeth gripped for Tommy from behind his shirt, begging, "Please Tommy, no."

"Go keep him busy," Tommy whispered the command. "I'll be right back."

Dumbfounded, Lizbeth stared as her husband fled toward the exit.

DerMööve stood up from his booth and yelled with a victorious guffaw, "Run away, kleiner Mann! Run away!"

Lizbeth regained her composure, straightened her posture, and stood surefooted before striding toward DerMööve with the grace and poise of someone who had not just been embarrassed in front of a group of complete strangers. She pressed Tommy's shirt to her chest with her left hand and pointed a condemning finger at DerMööve with her right.

"Leave my family alone!"

DerMööve guffawed once more, stopping mid-laugh to eyeball Lizbeth with lustful intensity.

Her face screamed an alarm, and he liked it.

Without pause, he lunged forward, almost gliding above the ground in a hover. He flicked his wrist, forcing the shirt to fly from her hands and reveal her nude form once more. This time, she made no attempt to cover herself, but instead glared icily at the man, tightening her lips with contempt.

"You are a disgusting pig!" she growled as he slithered closer to her.

"And you have perfekte Brüste," he purred, raising his right hand toward her chest. He regarded her hate-filled eyes and smirked. Then, he groped her naked breast, giving it a slight squeeze before drawing his fingers to her nipple. His thumb and forefinger clamped tightly upon her nipple and tugged outward, as he asked, "You like it rough?"

Until that moment, their eyes never parted. Lizbeth could take no more. She broke away, scanning the room for help, but no one met her eyes. She understood their cowardice all too well. They were powerless and in no position to take on the wrath of a Mighty. She searched for Tommy but only found the demoralized gapes of her children. Locking eyes with Mario, she shook her head.

Mario turned Zelda away, hiding her in his embrace.

DING DING DINK

An iron rod broke free from a window near the exit. Tommy hustled back toward the arcade with his weapon ready. As he drew closer, he heard DerMööve shout, "I vill taste your Mutter's milk, junge Frau!"

"Leave me alone!" cried Lizbeth.

She tried to fight off DerMööve, but the swiftness of his flickering fingers stripped away the rest of her clothing.

"You vill like it," he crooned, turning his hand in the air, forcing her to turn with it. Then, he pushed at the air and she flew face-first into the table. Her arms stretched to each side while her legs fought against the invisible hands pulling them apart.

"Please stop," she pleaded, tears streaming down her face into tiny puddles on the table.

DerMööve stepped between her legs and unbuckled his belt, saying, "Alle Frauen lieben DerMööve."

With the iron rod in the air ready to strike, Tommy sprinted toward DerMööve, but he never stood a chance. Before he could get close enough to strike, a monk wearing the traditional hoodless brown robe of an adjudicator burst through the doors of the arcade.

Mario turned toward the commotion. His eyes lit up at the appearance of the 32-year-old monk, who resembled an old toy figure his father had passed down to him a few years earlier—Max Windu, Jedi warrior or something like that.

"Mein Gott!" shouted DerMööve, stepping back and re-buckling his belt.

The monk took stock of the situation and then drew his

nonlethal shock-cannon from his side holster between the folds of his robe. Tommy ignored him, focused solely on saving his wife.

"Nooo!" she screamed, flailing her naked body away from DerMööve.

ZZOOOZZ

The shock-cannon roared, blasting its non-lethal force into Tommy's back before he could strike DerMööve. He fell to the floor convulsing in chaotic seizures, as electricity rippled across his body. Mario and Zelda crouched, watching in horror as their father twitched upon the ground.

Jakandy firmly planted his foot onto Tommy's forearm, forcing him to open his hand and drop the iron rod he still clutched. Then, he charged Tommy, "Citizen, by order of the Justice Assembly and the Enclave of the Monastery of Sol and Luna, you are hereby reprimanded to the Fellowship City Solitary Internment Camp for hard labor for the rest of your days. So says Adjudicator Jakandy, monk step 7."

"No, please!" Lizbeth cried, rushing to Tommy's side, unconcerned with her nudity. She protested, "He was only..."

"Violating the Citizen Peace Statute," interrupted Jakandy, as he clicked the bindings around Tommy's wrists. Tommy's body still quivered as he muttered in pain.

"No, no. He was protecting me..." she tried again, but Jakandy stepped toward her, raising his hand.

"For aiding and abetting in such a crime," Jakandy began, clapping a binder onto her wrist, spinning her around, and binding her other wrist. "You will be given under the guardianship of the Mighty known as DerMööve."

Upon hearing the sentence of her mother, Zelda's eyes somehow widened even wider than they were before. She tried to stand up to scream, but Mario kept her down, covering her mouth with his hand.

"Shhhh," he whispered, his eyes beckoning her to calm down.

"Nooo! Please have mercy!" Lizbeth begged, dropping to her knees.

For a brief second, she believed her appeal to the monk's sense of decency and justice worked. His eyes gleamed with kindness, as he picked up the shirt from the ground and placed it over her. He helped her to her feet, and then he turned her toward DerMööve and shoved her toward him.

"Do with her as you please!"

Mario remembers that moment with vivid clarity. *My father was sent to SIC by that godforsaken monk*, thinks Mario. *He's still there. At least, I hope he's still alive. There's been no word about my father, or my mother, since that day. There's no justice in this world for Citizens. That fucking monk placed my mother in the captivity of the Mighty who was causing all the problems in the first place. We rate so low to them that we are unseen.*

As Mario stares blankly at the Orphan House still absorbed by his memory, a tap upon his shoulder jolts him into the present. He shakes his head and glances around him, catching view of the clock on the watchtower. It strikes 6:43. He surveys the crowd ahead, tallying the number of people in front of him in line. *I may make it on the next bus*, he thinks.

Then, he feels the tap again.

"I don't have an idea yet, Landy," Mario answers without looking back. "When I figure it out—"

"No, kid. What's that?" Landy asks, pointing at the sky.

Mario follows Landy's finger to two tiny, dark blemishes within the voluminous blue expanse above.

"Birds, I bet," clucks the lady in the French maid uniform from a few places in front of Mario.

"Can't be birds," Landy shoots back. "They don't have wings."

"They're too far away to see if they don't have any wings," the French maid retorts.

"They're getting closer," Landy says, pointing. "See any wings?"

The French maid gasps, hiding her face in her hands.

Mario eyes the dark dots getting closer and closer.

"They're definitely not birds," he says. "Or Big B birds. They've got to be flyers. There are two of them, and one of them is carrying something."

"Flyers!" screams a scared somebody from somewhere in the line.

Landy places a hand on Mario's back, "What are they carrying?"

"I can't make it out," Mario answers, trying to focus his eyes on the incoming flyers.

"Not what... who?" growls Officer Lizardlips from the side of the line as he passes them. Without saying anything further, he continues marching his way toward the front of the line of Citizens to relieve Officer Slothface.

"It's a monk," Landy squeals, recognizing the garment of the passenger.

All the Citizens waiting for the bus straighten into an orderly single-file line and keep completely silent. Their heads remain straight, but their eyes follow the two hulking flyers and their precious cargo as they descend to the front of the line. A dark-haired flyer with a goatee lands first with an ominous thud, kicking a swirling spiral of dust around him. He kneels, resting his right arm on his bent right knee with head held high.

Awestruck, Mario thinks, *He's like one of those superheroes from my great-grandfather's old comic books my dad told me about.*

AAAAACHOOOOOO

The flyer sneezes, flailing his arms about to drive away the dust, as he wipes snot streaming from his nose onto his left sleeve.

Maybe not so much.

Mario chuckles, spying Officer Lizardlips puff his chest up and release slow bursts of breath like he was restraining a huff of laughter. Oblivious, the flyer falls into a protective stance, stretching both arms outward. His raised right palm faces Officer Lizardlips, while his raised left palm faces the Citizens. Mario observes a slight glitteriness on the flyer's sleeve.

"Stand back!" The goateed flyer commands, circling around to make an empty space between the guard and the Citizens in line.

Everyone steps backward in automated unison, even Officer Lizardlips. Mario chuckles, thinking, *Pecking order.*

When the grounded flyer is satisfied with the compliance level around him, he signals for the flyer in the sky to descend. They both wear matching black skintight outfits with a checkered pattern down each side. The second flyer lacks any hair, facial or otherwise on his unnaturally pale bulbous head protruding from the black turtleneck. His equally pale hands lower the monk into the space created by the goateed flyer.

"At least one of them is a *strong*," Mario whispers to Landy, as he cranes his head to the side to get a better view.

The hoodless brown robe flows around the monk.

An adjudicator, Mario thinks, recalling the robe as one he had seen once before. *It can't be the same...*

His thought cuts away as he glimpses the long fiery-red, curly hair of the monk braided back across her face. Her rounded forehead's dark skin glimmers in the early morning sun, reflecting light from wetness on the surface.

Tears? thinks Mario. *Sweat maybe? Do monks sweat?*

As she shakes her head and brushes herself off, Mario appraises her from afar.

Just a few years older than me, I bet, he thinks, as everything slows to a crawl. *Wow. She's beautiful...*

Landy nudges Mario's ribs, interrupting his thoughts and sending his slow-motion daydream back to real speed. "Why's a monk here?" he asks Mario.

"I dunno, but I bet we're about to find out," Mario answers, unable to take his eyes from her. "She's questioning Lizardlips about something."

Her soft features tense as she speaks to the guard. She points a finger into his chest and says something with passion. Then, she turns to the crowd and examines the surprised faces of the many Citizens standing in line. From somewhere within the folds of her robe she retrieves a handheld registry scanner.

No matter how attractive they are, it's never a good thing when a monk arrives at the camp, Mario thinks.

She shows the screen to the reptilian guard. He nods and points in Mario's general direction. With that gesture, people around Mario begin to fidget.

He shakes his head, thinking, *They always cause panic and fear among us.*

The monk tucks the scanner under her arm and marches down the line of waiting Citizens. As she passes them, waves of relief wash over their panic-stricken faces, and they turn around to track whom her sights are set upon. Behind her, the two flyers follow like puppy dogs hoping for scraps from the table.

Mario giggles.

The French maid whips around, flashing her judgy eyes. He shrugs.

You never want to be the person they're looking for, he thinks, as the monk and flyers head toward him.

He turns to Landy.

"Sorry, kid," Landy says with a shrug. "I think your clock is punched."

Oh, shit! thinks Mario, turning to face the monk. His eyes become moons, as he gazes into her eyes.

"I like your eyes," he blurts out. "They're hazel. That's pretty."

She shakes her head and grits her teeth. The bald flyer steps forward and grunts at Mario, who recoils, uncertain if it was due to fear or bad breath. The flyer chortles. Mario grimaces as the monk retrieves the scanner, asking, "Are you Ident 24VØR4VNØ?"

"Doesn't that thing tell you that?" he quips, clenching his fingers and cracking his knuckles.

The bald flyer's eyes flash with anger as he reaches Mario. He takes a step toward Mario, but the monk signals him away.

"Are you Ident 24VØR4VNØ?"

"Who's asking?"

"I am Adjudicator Tanalia, monk step 5 of the Monastery of Sol and Luna. By directive of the Justice Assembly and the Enclave—"

"Yeah, I've heard that before," interrupts Mario.

Confused by his apparent disinterest, Tanalia narrows her eyes, giving him a once over. Before he can say anything else, she grabs his arm and yanks him toward her. The flyers grasp his shoulders, keeping him still.

"If you asked nicely—" he says but gets cut off as she tugs up his sleeve to reveal his defaced ident-tag.

She scans his tag without taking her eyes from his. He gestures his innocence, shrugging with opened palms.

"So, where do you guys work out?" he asks, peeking over his shoulder.

The bodyguards do not even pretend to notice his question. Unfazed, he asks, "I bet it's one of those places with a track on a skyscraper, right? I mean you could just fly up there. You're obviously not scared of heights. I'm not really either, but then again, I've never been up that high."

Tanalia touches the registry screen, selecting his ident-tag number. His picture pops up on the screen with his height, weight, and current location listed below. The ident-tag numbers for three relatives are listed below his with an F/39, M/39, and S/17 next to each.

"Oh man, that's an old one," Mario says, peeping at his digital image. "I look much better now, don't ya think?"

Tanalia squints at him, shaking her head in frustration. "Don't talk, except to answer my questions, okay Citizen?"

Mario signals his lips are sealed. Tanalia prods with her eyes for an answer.

"Oh, do you want me to answer that? I thought it was rhetorical."

She vocalizes her frustration in a huff. "You worked at QTs House of Jacks until 11:17 pm last night, correct?"

"Yeah."

Tanalia holds up the scanner displaying the log screen, "You were scanned in at the WPC at 2:14 am?"

"Yeah," Mario answers, thinking for a second before he

continues. "After work, a few of us went to a Normals club south of B. I got the last bus at 1:45 down the street."

"You need to come with us," demands Tanalia, turning and motioning to her bodyguards.

Instantly, the rest of the awkward humor Mario held in reserve for the situation washed way.

"I'm being taken into custody?"

"Yes," a flyer says, seizing his arms and lifting him off the ground.

"What the hell is going on?" Mario yells, as Landy and the remaining people waiting in the line shrink into ants below his dangling feet.

"I've never been in the air like this before—" he starts to say to the flyer before the vomit wins over his words.

5

THE SWIFTGLIDES

"God, I'm sorry," apologizes a green-faced Mario, trying to wipe the vomit from his mouth. The act proves difficult when dangling 10,000 feet in the air from the arm of a flyer. He tries to stop himself from looking down but fixating on the sky is just as nauseating.

He closes his eyes and takes a deep breath, counts to ten, and releases his death-grip on the flyer, trying to find a better balance. Feeling more secure, he opens his eyes as they glide above Olum River. In his peripheral vision, he glimpses the island. Ahead of him is the familiar dilapidated landscape of the southside ghetto.

They fly over the slums, bearing north along 20th street below. As they cross Dalton Street, Mario spots a familiar landmark jutting into the air.

"Club Haberdashery!" he yells, but the flyer pays him no mind. With eyes filled with awe, he admires the tall art deco spire holding the remains of a sign that once named the theater below. "My parents used to go there a long time ago. I've never been, but someone once told me that it's now a haven for the delirious and deplorable dregs of society. What do you think? Ever been?"

Mario speaks without expecting a response, trying and ultimately failing to distract himself from another bout of sickness; his fixation on the object below makes his head swim and his face turns green again.

The flyer groans in dismay, brushing some of the putrescence from his arm. Mario senses the flyer's eyes rolling.

"I really am sorry about that," he apologizes again.

Up ahead, Tanalia and her flyer dip into view.

Her flyer is the bald one. That means the guy carrying me has dark hair, right? Maybe a goatee?

Although Mario's long-term memories are virtually perfect, they are not so accurate in the short-term. Everything happened far too quickly this morning for anything to process correctly in his mind.

Mario twists his head around, trying to confirm his mental image with reality, but the flyer only tightens his grip on him.

"Ouch, man. That hurts."

He envies Tanalia, riding on the back of her black-checkered flyer.

That's gotta be more comfortable, he thinks. *She's out here taking a sky taxi, and I'm getting carried like trash.*

"Hey, sky taxi," Mario shouts, trying to break the sound barrier. "Where are you taking me?"

"Quiet," commands the sky taxi.

"I get it! You're the strong silent type!" he shouts, but the flyer clamps down tighter, causing the end of the sentence to die off in the wind.

As they swoop toward Fellowship City Park between A and B Streets north of the Normal slums, his apprehension begins to build. Mario clenches his eyes tight as visions of his parents flood his mind. The sounds of swing set chains clanging and children squealing down slides echo in his head so clearly, he cannot be certain if they are real or imagined.

As they approach the northwest corner of 20th and B streets, the children's laughter morphs into screams of terror, as his own nightmare becomes a distinct reality before him. A putrid scent of regurgitation wafts into his nostrils, and he gags, again uncertain of its origin in reality. He glowers at the restaurant below, mustering as much crud-filled saliva as possible to spit upon the unlit neon sign of DerMööve's Arcade & Grill.

HAAPHOOOOOT

He tracks the cruddy wad's plunge toward the sign, hoping it lands on its mark, but just before it hits, the flyer veers away. Not witnessing the conclusion of his bombardment leaves him unsatisfied.

Ever since the loss of his parents, he avoided any route that would take him near that restaurant ever again. He took the Central Park bus to work, even though QTs House of Jacks was only a few blocks from the arcade. Sure, the ride was a little longer and required him to walk south three and a half blocks to get to work, but it freed him from daily panic, which was well worth the extra walk. Over time, it became habit, and he had forgotten why he took that route in the first place... until now.

As they fly east, the two tallest buildings in the city fight for supremacy over the landscape.

??
webnet.mightybase search results...
Tallest building in Fellowship City : MIGHTYpedia Entry
??

Two giant skyscrapers towering above the rest mark the
Fellowship City skyline: Upton Tower number three and
the Chronicle Building. The Chronicle Building on G
Street and Cornerstone Way houses the Fellowship City
Chronicle Newspaper. It was the tallest building in
Fellowship City until Upton Tower number three was built
a couple blocks west on G Street and Fellowship Way. The
actual structure of Upton Tower number three is 18 feet
shorter than the Chronicle Building, but the towering
neon sign with the giant U and superscript 3 on top of the
building adds 33 feet, making it the tallest building in
Fellowship City.

Over the last thirty years, members of the Upton
family have built seven structures within Fellowship City
collectively known as Upton Towers. Each of the buildings
has giant signs with the enormous U and superscript
building number emblazoned in neon, indicating their
involvement with the brand. While Upton Tower number
three is the largest, Upton Towers number one and two are
large in their own right, but nowhere near the heights of
the Chronicle Building and Upton Tower number three.
Although all seven Upton Tower buildings lease offices
and condominiums, the most popular and expensive are
in number three. The Mayor and other city government
officials have offices in Upton Tower number three.

??

Even in a world of super-powers and handheld video screens, people still want their daily news in written form to collect, discard, or possibly recycle. Mario contemplates, as he compares the heights of the Chronicle Building and Upton Tower number three. *That sign definitely gives Upton the edge.*

From this height, he glances myriad lit and unlit neon signs throughout the city. *Hell, everything in this city has a damn neon sign.*

As they career toward 17th and D Streets, Mario tenses, grasping the flyer tighter.

"Hey man, you got me?" he shrieks, as the familiar red and yellow neon sign for QTs House of Jacks blinks dully in the early morning light. *That shouldn't be on yet.*

Mario cranes his head around to peek at the time on the flyer's watch. Only the last digit is visible from his uncomfortable position, a solitary 4.

7:04? Maybe 6:54? Mario surmises, trying to fathom the speed it would take to get them this far given each time.

If one flyer leaves the WPC traveling at 50 mph and another leaves... he interrupts his thought, as he eyes a small crowd of people gathering in front of the restaurant. *Great. People think we're already open.*

The bald sky taxi carrying Tanalia lands close to the front door. As soon as the ground touches her feet, Tanalia pivots toward the crowd, yelling something at them while raising her hand.

With compliant synchronicity, the crowd shifted backward, creating a semi-circle perimeter around her. Mario's sky taxi heads straight toward that space in a speedy descent. Bracing for impact, Mario latches his hands tightly around the arm of his sky taxi and closes his eyes. Suddenly, the flyer stops in midair above the space between Tanalia and the crowd, hovering momentarily before dumping Mario to the ground like trash to a curb.

Mario hits the ground with a painful thud upon his knees, slamming his right palm onto the pavement.

"Ouch!" he yells, over-embellishing the pain. "Maybe a heads-up next time!"

His sky taxi huffs in a way that could be considered laughter, as he hovers to the side of the other flyer by the front door.

Mario tries to collect himself, but his head spins and legs wobble. He starts to say, "You can just forget about a tip!" but before he can finish, his checks puff out, and he covers his mouth to stifle the spewing vomit.

I won't be late again. I promise, he thinks, as the vomit sprays through his fingers.

"What the hell?" screeches a shrill voice from the crowd.

Mario waves his hand, apologetically, as bits of barf drip off his fingers.

"I'm sorry. I'm not used to flying," he says, flinging most of the stinking sick from his hands before shoving them into the pockets of his suit jacket to indiscreetly clean them off. The overwhelming urge to vomit returns, but he gulps the sour, metallic taste back down his throat.

He peers up at the dark-haired flyer with the goatee standing next to the bald one. *I was right*, he thinks, letting loose a quiet laugh.

Not so quiet, he realizes, as the sky taxis fold their arms and snarl at him, while Tanalia glares with her hands pressed to her hips.

He attempts to feign innocence, but it is cut short as he turns away and doubles-over in a dry-heave. The crowd jolts back, rumbling in disapproval as their faces flush with a mix of revulsion and irritation.

"What the fuck you lookin' at?" squawks a short, podgy man carrying an umbrella.

An overpowering odor of rotten fish looms from his breath. Mario turns away, green once more. Out of patience, Tanalia gestures to her flyers. They hover to Mario, grab an arm on either side, and lift him from the ground.

As they carry him to the monk, Mario asks the bald one, "So, you're a strong-flyer, eh?"

"Gravity manipulator," came the response in a monotonous baritone.

"A what?"

The flyer sighed and then replied, "I can manipulate gravity fields around me, allowing me to lift heavy objects and propel myself from the ground."

"So, you're strong and can fly?" queried Mario.

"Yeah."

"Like I said, so you're a strong-flyer, eh?"

The bald sky taxi rolls his eyes, but Mario is in no position to see him. After they lower him next to Tanalia, Mario folds his hands together and bows.

"Much appreciated. Thanks for not dropping me this time!"

They ignore him, returning to their positions guarding the entrance of the front door.

Tanalia turns to Mario and asks, "Do you recognize anyone here?"

He surveys the crowd, but his attention is captured by the fish-smelling man, waddling away and muttering something under his breath.

"Ahem," Tanalia coughs, bringing Mario back to the task.

"I don't recognize that guy," Mario answers. "But he seems creepy and odd. I'd keep an eye on him if I was you."

Tanalia's eye twitches.

"Just tell me who looks familiar."

Mario scans the crowd, spotting a hooded figure hovering motionless a foot from the ground. He lingers on him, trying to place the man.

"That guy looks like he belongs in one of the Hoarder of Rings stories my dad told me and Zelda when we were kids," says Mario, pointing to the man.

"The what?"

"Nothing."

The man is dressed in armor with a burnished red cape or cloak. Two hefty handles protrude from his back, making him resemble some kind of kiddie ride.

He seems so out of place, thinks Mario. *Like, he's straight out of a superhero comic book.*

"Is he familiar?" Tanalia probes.

"I guess so."

As if threatened by Mario's response, the armored man rises another foot in the air, grasps one of the handles, and retrieves an ornately carved battle-axe. Brandishing the weapon, he hovers toward Mario, determined to strike.

"Stand down!" bellows the bald flyer, as he and his companion maneuver into defense positions between the imposing danger and their charge.

Infuriated, the hooded man hovers higher, but he no longer presses forward. "Oh, thou wretches," he says with an unfamiliar accent. "Dost mine visage escape thee?"

"What?"

"Do you not know who I am?"

"Don't know! Don't care!" the dark-haired flyer shouts. "Stand down now or face consequences."

"I am the Arcane Sawyer," the hovering man says, tapping the axe in his palm. "I never stand down. You will inform your mistress posthaste that the Swiftglides are present to observe and serve as necessary."

The bald flyer turns away, muttering under his breath, "Fucking club kids."

"Yeah, that's right," Mario recalls, "The Swiftglides. That's the Realizer's club. I haven't seen the Arcane Sawyer before, but I know his name, and I've heard about his... eccentric nature."

The bald flyer approaches Tanalia.

"He says they're—"

Tanalia interrupts, "the Swiftglides. I know."

The bald flyer nods and returns to his position.

"Did you know that because I told you?" Mario queries. "Or did you already know that because you're a seer-path?"

"What do you think?"

"Shouldn't you already know what I'm thinking?" Mario snarks. "I mean, you knew I was going to say that, right? There's not really anything I could do that would surprise you, is there?"

"No, not really. Just tell me what you know about them."

"The Arcane Sawyer is one of the higher-ups," Mario starts. "The Realizer said something about that recently. As far as I understand, he's not a people person. He lives in a cabin out in Beacon Woods near Mount MacGuffrey. I think he owns a store that sells wooden trinkets and stuffed fleshies. I mean, the head of some kind of monster is mounted in the Realizer's office courtesy of this fine fellow."

Tanalia nods and motions for him to move on to the next figure in line, a perfectly manicured brunette with voluminous blown-out hair that cascades around her face and falls onto her shoulders. She wears a tight yellow jump-suit with a white stripe down one side and a big red SWIFT-GLIDES emblazoned vertically on it.

Mario's eyes bulged out of his skull, seeing her cleavage all but pop out of the formfitting outfit that accentuates her shapely figure.

"WEATHERGIRL!"

"That's right. She's Velacruz Belch, the meteorologist on FC1."

"Yeah that too," he says with a laugh, as he is transported back into a memory.

"You've got eyes for that one, eh?" The Realizer said, placing his hand warmly on Mario's shoulder and giving it a slight squeeze.

Mario startled, averting his eyes from his female coworker finishing a plate at the prep table.

"Don't worry, kiddo," the Realizer chortled. "I won't rat you out."

"I'm just making a salad, sir," Mario said, trying to appear busy prepping a salad.

"Sure, you are," said the Realizer with a Cheshire cat grin. "So, have you taken her out yet?"

"Nah."

"You better be careful with that one. She reminds me of someone I am very familiar with. Someone a bit fiery," the Realizer said, nudging an elbow into Mario's ribs. "Maybe a bit too much for you to handle, if you catch my drift."

"Yeah?"

"You don't understand, do you?" the Realizer asked, mussing Mario's hair. "Okay, I'll explain. In my—little circle, we have a member we call Weathergirl. Now, she's not called that because she's an aerokin or an actual TV weatherperson. I mean, she's both those things—she's feisty. She's hot, always wearing tight little outfits that accentuate her shapely curves. But, if you take her out, there's no telling whether you're going to get some or whether she's going to bolt like lightning and never see you again.

Usually, it's the latter and she leaves you with a little shock just for fun."

"Oh, I see," Tanalia says, having experienced the flash-back with Mario. "So, have you seen her before?"

"No, not in person," Mario answers. "I've seen her on TV, I guess, but also on the Webnet Mightybase. She posts a lot of videos and gets a lot of comments. I didn't realize she was the Weathergirl though until right now, but it makes sense. She's got tons of videos showing her control the weather and such. There's also this one where she goes to a beach in a bikini and—"

"It's fine," Tanalia interrupts.

"You sure, because it's a pretty awesome one."

"I get the gist. Thanks."

Mario advances to the next person and nods in recognition.

"That's Ifton Upton III. His dad or grandfather built the Upton Towers, and he's heir to that fortune. He's always in QTs entertaining investors. People call him a wunderkind in the trade market."

"Probably because he's a technopath," Tanalia quips.

"Really?" Mario lingers for a moment, giving him a once over. "How can you tell?"

Tanalia sighs.

"This one's new to the group," Mario says, gesturing to the younger female wearing a tight red jumpsuit with a white stripe down the side and a blue SWIFTGLIDES on it. Her dark hair is short-cropped, and she is not voluptuous like Velacruz. "Why do the women have to wear those tight outfits and the guys all look normal?" asks Mario. "Well, not the Arcane Sawyer, but they're... I mean Ifton could be a stockbroker in that designer suit."

"Stay on task," snaps Tanalia.

"Right. Well, her name is 4SKōR. She's been in a few times, meeting with the Realizer. I think they might have been an item, but I can't be sure."

"How do you mean?"

"Well, I don't think he was the dating type," Mario explains. "He had several women he entertained here and there, but no one he kept around very long, as far as I could tell. She seemed to meet with him much more than the other women. At least, the ones I had seen come through here. And, the Realizer told me she was useless as a Mighty. He said that she was just a pretty hybrid with one gift that only had a use in one way, as far as he saw it. She's a screamer."

Tanalia rolls her eyes and motions to the next body, "And him?"

Who? Mario thinks confused, checking if he missed someone. Sure enough, behind the others with his back to them all stands a slender man in a designer suit. *Well, that's not the Realizer.*

He catches Tanalia's swift questioning glance in his direction but shrugs it off, intent on focusing on the man. He narrows his eyes and tries to turn him around through the force of his will alone.

If it's not the Realizer, thinks Mario, *and if all the other Swiftglides are here, then that is...DerMööve.*

Mario clenches his fists and bites hard, shifting his posture enough to indicate a potential attack. Before he shows any signs of movement, Tanalia places her hand on his shoulder and squeezes. Mario gazes at her with innocent eyes showing anger within.

They know what we think before we do.

Tanalia nods slightly as if she agrees with his thought. Then, she squints at him, showing only the whites of her eyes and little red veins between her narrow lids. Mario shutters at the unexpected sight. Within seconds, she turns away from him, saying, "You do not want to join your father."

Mario drops his head, untenses his body, and opens his fists.

"What do you want from me?"

"Only the truth."

"But you're a frigging seer-path."

"Yes. I am."

Tanalia stares deep into Mario's eyes, her hand still on his shoulder.

"This isn't about me being late, is it?" he asks.

"No. It isn't."

Mario scans the crowd again. Each of the Swiftglides glare at him with contempt, especially 4SKōR. Suddenly, Tanalia braces Mario.

"What's... what..."

KKKKKKKRRRRRRAAAAAAAAAHHHHHHHHHHHH

6

ABOUT LAST NIGHT

When Mario opens his eyes again, everything is blurred and his head buzzes with a high-pitched ringing. A muffled sound wafts in the distance, sounding much farther away than it should.

What happened? he thinks, rubbing his eyes into clarity.

Bewildered, Mario takes stock of his current predicament. He sits in a booth next to a gigantic window inside QTs House of Jacks. Tanalia paces near him, possibly speaking. Her lips appear to be moving, but he cannot make out her voice. He rubs his palms to his forehead, drops them back to his ears, and then startles from unexpected wetness.

A reddish-brown colored liquid covers his right palm. He tries to rub it away with his left hand. *Blood*, he appraises, tracing a shaky finger up the side of his cheek to find the origin.

As he feared, blood pooled in the concha of his right ear. He snatched a napkin from the table and pressed it to his ear, applying pressure. *That's what you're supposed to do when you're bleeding, right?*

As his hearing also becomes clearer, the clock on the

wall chimes, capturing his attention. *8 a.m.? Already?* he thinks and starts to speak, but nothing comes out. His throat radiates with pain. He envisions himself taking a shot of nails and chasing it down with glass shards.

Across the room, he spots Tanalia and begins to lift his hand. Without looking, she waves hers.

"There's a glass of water in front of you."

Mario finds the sizable glass, raises it to his lips, and downs it with wet, sloppy gulps. When finished, he sets the empty glass down with a loud clank that resounds throughout the empty restaurant. He catches Tanalia's judging eyes on him and realizes they are the only ones inside. He darts his eyes to the window, finding most of the Swiftglides standing out front glaring at him with eyes filled with venom.

Craning his neck sideways, he spies the two sky taxis standing guard at the front door. To his left, Velacruz paces back and forth between DerMööve and Ifton. Her face beams bright red as she yells, possibly arguing with one or both of them. Mario cannot be sure. He scans around for the other two Swiftglides, finding 4SKōR sitting cross-legged on the sidewalk at the base of the stairs leading to the front door. Her hands are bound behind her back, and her head is bowed. Behind them all, the Arcane Sawyer hovers about eight feet from the ground.

He looks like a buoy bobbing up and down in the Olum River, thinks Mario, mesmerized in the moment.

Velacruz belts out something that draws Mario's attention. "...think he did it?" is what he thinks matches the words from her lips.

The muffled voice of DerMööve says something long-winded in response, or at least he thinks it is DerMööve's voice. Only the back of his head is visible. Through a process of elimination, he rules out everyone else, as they all face him with unmoving mouths. When he finally turns enough for Mario to glimpse his lips, DerMööve mouths the words, "who else," before turning back around.

Seconds later, 4SKōR erupts into hysterical laughter. Mario turns to face her, finding her eyes already locked onto his. Her eyes narrow in apparent contempt as she mouths, "he's only a Citizen."

Ifton steps toward 4SKōR, turning his back to Mario and saying something with grand gesticulation. Suddenly, the giant viewscreen mounted on the wall next to Mario's booth snaps on.

Mario startles, as the screen bursts to life. He glances at Tanalia, who is completely unfazed by it, and then he returns his eyes to the screen to find an early morning news show.

Boring, he thinks, returning his focus to Ifton.

"Great question," Ifton mouths, as the voice on the news show speaks the same words before snapping off with a pop and a click.

That was fucking weird.

Tanalia turns abruptly and questions, "Do you think this situation is funny?"

"No," Mario responds before processing Tanalia's words, invoking a sense of uncertainty as to whether he answered her appropriately. "I... I..."

"Have no clue what is happening?" she finishes for him.

"Exactly," he says with great exasperation. "I don't understand what is happening right now. I was late for work and..." Mario surveys the restaurant. "Where is everyone? The others on my shift should be here."

"They were called off," snaps Tanalia.

"Why?"

"Drink more water," she says, stepping toward him.

"What?"

She fetches a second cup from the table and shoves it into his face. "Here, take it."

"I'm so confused," Mario says, taking the cup and drinking the water. "Can you just tell me what's going on?"

"Not until I know the truth... You're going to need to sit very still."

"What are you doing?" Mario asks, stiffening his back and bracing himself in the booth.

"You need to do this willingly, or it will hurt. A lot."

Mario gapes at Tanalia's hand inching closer to his forehead. Her frigid palm touches his warm skin, sending a shiver down his spine as a light beams into his head, right between his eyes. He closes them tight, but still, the light shines somehow within his head, shooting from the front to the back of his skull.

He screams, but there is no sound. There is nothing but the silence of the light, ever-expanding and all-encompassing. As soon as the white light covers all, it turns black in the center with reddish hues casting outward. No matter where he directs his attention, the redness continues to engulf everything—until the sound of flowing water from a faucet consumes his headspace.

From within the enveloping darkness, a small pinprick of white light pulses, growing larger in harmonious synchrony with the sound of the flowing water. The light belches and throbs as sounds of metal upon metal and clinking glass drown away the red rim until only the white light exists ever so briefly. The fleeting light dims into an image, becoming clearer and clearer, like an old television set turning on for the first time.

Mario wonders where he had seen an old television set

turn on before, but he lets the thought go, as the image rushes at him with violent force. The pain surges through him as he falls forward into the light of the image. Light rays elongate while little lightning bolts flash around the image now encompassing everything. He screams in agony, but the only sound is splashing water.

As the pain subsides, Mario opens his eyes to find his hands covered by black gloves and submerged in hot soapy water. He tries to control them, but they do not yield to his commands. They go about their task all on their own, washing dishes in the sink. He attempts to look elsewhere, but the eyes do not budge no matter how hard he wills them to. Each movement his body makes is not his own. He is not in control. He is merely a spectator, and the more he tries to influence what he cannot, the more the pain courses through him.

He resolves to surrender to the passivity of viewership, allowing the agonizing pain to subside. Now no more than a dull ache, he observes his right hand rise out of the water with a scrub brush. His left hand follows, carrying a plate from the wash sink to the rinse sink. The chime of a clock strikes. His eyes dart to it. 11:00.

This is last night, Mario realizes. *I'm watching my memory.*

"Hey kid, the Realizer wants you in at 6," says a tall brown-haired man in his early 30s, wearing a black suit and tie. "He apologizes for the short notice, so there's that."

"Shit," says his voice from last night. "I'm going out tonight, Vic."

"Not my problem. You wanna be a waiter or a dishwasher?" Vic asks, not expecting an answer as he heads to the exit. "Dead or alive, you better be here, 'cause you know the big boss'll be."

"Dammit," he says, sloshing a dish back into the sink.

This is too surreal, Mario thinks in utter amazement.

"That sucks you got the AM shift, bro," says one of his co-workers, moseying past the dishwashing station. "Gonna miss you at the club tonight."

Mario recognizes the twitch in his right eye at that moment. *I really hate that sleazeball*, he thinks, eyeing the greasy line cook as he clocks out and saunters over to the prep table. His own eyes linger on Christiana and his eyelids narrow as he approaches her.

Even this second time around, their conversation is too quiet for Mario to pick up over the sound of the splashing water of dishes being washed. The tension tightens every fiber of Mario's body, as he becomes aware of emotions he had not realized or processed previously. This forced reliving experience is not like revisiting his own memories in his head. There is so much more he can pay attention to. He almost likes it.

"You're not going tonight?" says Christiana.

He raises his gaze from the dishes to fall upon her beautifully sad frown. Without pause or consideration, Mario from the night before blurts out, "I'll be there."

When her frown morphs into a big toothy smile, he returns to his dishes.

"This is tedious," says Tanalia's voice echoing from within his head.

Without warning, lightning bolts flash across his vision, as he warps into a not-so-distant future moment. The kitchen is empty, except for him. He finishes sanitizing the last dish and places it on the drying rack. He shuffles toward the exit and punches his timecard to clock out.

'11:17 pm and back at 6 am? *I'm going to pay for this in the morning,*' his thought from last night plays in his head as he closes the self-locking door behind him.

As he exits the alleyway next to QTs House of Jacks, he catches sight of the restaurant's neon sign. Still blinking red and yellow, it casts an eerie intermittent glow upon the empty street below.

'*The boss usually turns it off by now*,' he hears himself think.

He cranes his neck to spy the Realizer's apartment window above the restaurant and just beyond the neon sign. A light within fades in and out with a sporadic glow shining through the window.

'*Still up watching something*,' thinks his inner voice. '*Or just working late? Either way, he'll take care of it.*'

But he didn't, did he?

Mario turns back to the empty streets ahead of him and races down 18th Avenue toward Fellowship City Park. As he reexperiences these moments, he realizes why he avoided the more well-lit and safer route along 20th Avenue.

Anything to avoid it.

"*Avoid what?*" Tanalia's voice rings in his head.

"The arcade," Mario responds in thought with a dismissiveness that does not invite further explanation or conversation.

When he reaches B Street, he slows down, assesses the traffic in both directions, and drops into a four-point starting position. "Dun-dun-dun-dun-dun duh, dun-dun-dun-dun-dun," he hums the first bars of the 8bit theme from the 1983 Track & Field arcade game by Konami, which borrowed the theme from the 1981 film Chariots of Fire, originally performed by Vangelis.

Not that Mario knew any of that. For him, it was a sweet memento of his father. Whenever they raced each other, his father would hum that little tune in a kind of countdown before saying, "GO!" As he had done with his wife when they were kids, he always let Mario win.

"GO!" Mario says before springing across the street toward the brick and iron fence of the park. As he approaches the fence, he jumps at it, grapples it near the top, and climbs over, utilizing the momentum built from the sprint. He lands on a patch of soft grass, wipes himself off, and dashes toward the pedestrian bridge.

Once again, lightning bolts flash before him, fast-forwarding him across the bridge, through the park, and toward the small crowd of people in the distance. Mario winces in pain, smelling the sweet stench of burnt metal as he refocuses.

As everything slows down, his head wobbles with vertigo.

I feel sick.

"It'll pass," assures Tanalia's resounding voice.

As he approaches the crowd, a cacophony of laughter blooms.

"Hey, guys!" his voice calls to them.

They all turn, but Christiana stops, waving for the others to keep going. The sleazeball lingers momentarily by her side, but she dismisses him, and he sulks away dissatisfied.

"Thanks for waiting."

"Thanks for coming," she says with a smile that accentu-ates her sleek jawline and high cheekbones.

He stands for an awkward second, grinning at her, unsure of how to respond. Then, she grips his hand and tugs him toward her. He tries his best not to resist as she tucks her arm under his, saying, "You will be my escort."

As they stroll together, Mario pays attention to the things he missed the night before. He admires her beauty, how her olive skin shimmers in the moonlight, and the way several strands of her black hair dance around the sides of her forehead with each bouncing step she takes. He realizes how tall she is standing next to him, acknowledging that even in flats she is slightly taller than him. Her hand touches his arm with a slow flutter of her fingers. Mario senses his heart beating faster as his vision flushes red with excitement.

As if on cue, the lightning bolts flash, spinning his head in nauseous bemusement.

Can you please stop doing that? It hurts, and I feel like I'm going to hurl.

"I'll stop when I find what I need."

She speeds through their jaunt to the club and several drinks before stopping at a moment where Christiana grabs Mario's hand.

"Let's dance," she says, dragging him to the dance floor.

Then, it speeds up again. His head swirls, as he passively views this vivid reality for a second time. He wonders if she is as happy with him as he is with her in that moment.

Could she be the one? Mario thinks, imagining a possible future as images from the night before fly by. *Christiana, the line cook.*

Just as Mario acclimates to the fast motion, it screeches back to the normal pace.

"What time is it?" he says to Christiana in mid-dance.

"Why, you gotta be somewhere else?"

"I gotta be on the last bus to the WPC," he explains. "I'm not lucky enough to have a place in the Normal slums like you and Reggie."

Mario side-smiles, noticing the sleazeball line cook spying on them.

"It's not all it's cracked up to be. But the commute is better."

"I'm sure."

She yanks over the hand of a man dancing near them and reads the LED on his watch. Then, she lets it go as if nothing happened, returning her attention to Mario.

"It's 1:35."

"Shit. I gotta get going. It'll be here in 10, and if I'm not on it, I'll be stuck out here."

"There are worse things," Christiana says. "You could always—"

"I'll see you tomorrow," he interrupts, pulling away from her. "I've got the early shift."

WAIT! What was that? Mario shouts in his head. *She was going to say something. Was she inviting me to stay with her?*

He watches himself run away from her, bursting through the door of the club and barreling toward the bus stop.

Where the hell are you going? he yells at himself. *You should get back there. She wants you to stay. Why am I so dumb sometimes? She totally wanted me to stay, didn't she? You heard it. You're in my mind here with me, right? She was going to say I could stay the night at her place. I mean even if there wasn't any kind of fooling around going down that night, it still would have been cool to talk all night with her. Dammit!*

The bus arrives as Mario reaches the stop. He jumps on board and the frantic speed resumes, zipping Mario to the WPC. He exits the bus, dashes to his unit, and unlocks the front door. He locks the door behind him, tiptoes to Zelda's room, and peers inside. Seeing her motionless under the cover of her blankets, he tiptoes to his room, strips off his clothes, and falls into bed.

"*NOTHING?!?*" Tanalia's voice echoes in Mario's head. The memory sinks into a spiral, like a toilet flushing water down the drain. His head fills with pain as he is wrenched from the past into the present. Tanalia stands before him, her face red and angry.

"It can't be nothing! You were the last one!"

"I'm sorry," Mario says still confused. "Listen, I'm not really sure what this is all about, but if you can get the Realizer down here, I'm sure he can clear up whatever this is."

"He's dead," Tanalia lets the words die on her lips, her frustration getting the better of her. She wipes her forehead and paces away.

"He's dead? What do you mean he's dead? How is he dead?"

"I don't know."

Mario jumps up exasperated.

"How the hell does a seer-path monk not know? You're supposed to know everything?"

"I know," Tanalia says, shrugging him off and storming toward a booth at the other side of the large restaurant. "I need support on this. I'm bringing in my mentor."

Mario drops back to his seat, elbows on the table, and head in his hands. *This is bad*, he thinks, glancing out the window at the Swiftglides still eyeballing him with contempt-filled faces. *Oh shit. They think it was me.*

On the other side of the restaurant, Tanalia sits cross-legged with her hands palm up and outward in front of her. Her forehead creases, showing the strain on her face as she attempts to telepathically communicate with her mentor.

"*I need your help*," the thought strikes the hooded brown-robed monk, as he meditates in a small empty room of the Arborium. "*I need your help.*" It repeats in the familiar voice.

7

A FAMILIAR FACE

I can't believe he's dead.

Mario appraises the empty restaurant, triggering little reminders. *I only got this job because of my dad. Now, what am I going to do? These Mighty think I killed him.*

"Yes, it's dishwashing," Mario recalled his father saying to him when he was very young. "Yes, it's something I do at home too, but it's more than that, Mario. It's not the work I enjoy. It's working for the Realizer. He treats me like I'm a regular guy... maybe not an equal, but certainly not a servant."

"A servant?"

"Yeah," Tommy said, picking up his son and setting him on his lap. "When they think of you as lesser, as not really human, they don't feel as bad for mistreating you. That's why they call us Citizens. It helps them to see us as dregs on society."

"Dregs?"

"It means worthless. But guess what?"

"What?" Mario probed with eager eyes.

"We're not worthless," Tommy said, poking Mario's nose and

winking at him. "We make this city run. Not them. Without us, they'd have no idea what to do."

"So, we're important?"

"Yes, Mario," Tommy answered, mussing up his son's hair. "We're very important."

"The Realizer thinks we're important?"

"Well," Tommy responds, taking a second to figure out how to word his response. "I don't know that I'd go so far as to say that, but he hasn't mistreated me at all. I've had some bosses in the past who have been downright awful. Although, I've seen and heard a lot worse from other Normals about their employers."

"I don't want a bad boss," Mario said with a shiver.

"One day, I hope you get to work for a boss like the Realizer," Tommy assured his son. "He truly is a good man, and he takes an interest in those who work for him."

Little Mario tilted his head and asked, "What do you mean?"

"The other day while I was doing dishes. He walks over to me, puts his hand on my shoulder, and pats it," Tommy regaled his son, illustrating the story with grand gesticulations. "He tells me what great work I'm doing. No other boss I've had before ever did something like that. I thanked him, of course, but I was nervous about it."

"Why?"

"Well, because he's the boss," continued Tommy, grinning on his right side. "It's not every day the boss stops by and pats you on the back while you're doing dishes. I didn't want to make a bad impression. He seems to like me all right, and I don't want that to change. So, I smiled at him and continued to do the dishes just as hard as ever. He puts his hand on my arm to stop me, turns me toward him and says, 'tell me about yourself.' Now I got even more nervous, because I'm over here trying to do his dirty dishes, and he's stopping me to ask some get-to-know-ya questions. So, I tell him, 'I'm married and have two kids.' Guess what he says?"

"What?"

"That's wonderful."

The first memory fades as another takes over.

An 18-year-old Mario wrung his hands, standing in front of a door marked OFFICE. He lifted a shaky hand to knock and then dropped it at his side.

'You can do this,' he thought. 'It'll be fine. He'll remember him. It'll be just fine.'

He raised his hand again and knocked this time with three booming raps.

"Who's there?" shouted a deep, burly voice from behind the door, sounding a bit irritated by the interruption.

"Uhm, Mario Rickson, sir," answered Mario. "Tommy Rickson is my father."

"Come in," the voice shouted in a much more pleasant tone.

Mario opened the door and peered in, finding himself welcomed by the hum of a giant viewscreen buzzing in his ears and blinking its artificial light. He blocked the annoying glow with his right hand, trying to focus on the figure across the room.

On a dirty, old plaid couch sat a flabby man, sloppy and overweight. He wore oversized pajamas that were still too small, allowing his belly to protrude from them, rising and falling with each labored breath. Food crumbs rode that Ferris wheel up and down, even though he wasn't currently eating anything.

"Come in, boy," the voice bellowed once more. "I'm not going to bite."

Mario took two steps inside, keeping his head bowed as he tried not to show on his face the surprise he felt inside.

"So, you're Tommy's kid," the man said, scooting himself up a bit and motioning for Mario to come closer to him. "Come'ere. Let me get a good look at you."

As Mario stepped toward the man, he noticed a stack of books propped up next to the couch and a long white box full of comic books behind him. On the other side of the couch, he saw more boxes brimming with newspapers and magazines. Behind those were board games stacked alphabetically beside various boxes marked videos and video games.

Mario swivels his head around in amazement, settling his eyes on a dozen different controllers displayed on an oversized ottoman. He turned toward the giant viewscreen, which was in fact four decent-sized viewscreens stacked together with each connected to a different system.

Mounted above the wall of viewscreens was the most hideous head of a monstrous creature Mario had ever laid eyes upon. He gasped.

"That's the head of one of those fleshies," the man chuckled, unknowingly spitting chewed food from his mouth. "It can be jarring at first sight. A companion of mine hunts them for fun. He thought I'd like this one."

"Do you?" Mario asked, trying to hide the disgust on his face.

"I've grown accustomed to it," answered the man. "So, what brought you here today, Mario?"

"Well, Mr... the..."

"Just Realizer is fine," he said, smiling from ear to ear.

Mario nodded, trying to shake away his nervousness before beginning again.

"Well, Mr... err, Realizer," he corrected himself. "I'm turning 18 next week, and I need a job. My father spoke very highly of you, so I wanted to talk to you first and see if you had anything for me."

The Realizer squinted at Mario, giving him a once over. Then, he picked up one of the controllers, tapped a button, and nodded toward the viewscreens.

"Have you seen this show?" he asked.

When Mario turned, the four viewscreens merged to form one image behind a black cross. The cross pattern resembled a window from which the Realizer could spy on people. Paused on the screen was a scene from the 1955 film, The Seven Year Itch, showing Marilyn Monroe in her iconic white dress standing with Tom Ewell in front of a store with a Costume Jewelry sign.

Mario shook his head.

The Realizer clicked a button on the controller, unpausing the scene. "Oh, do you feel the breeze from the subway?" she asked, as she maneuvered into a position above the subway grating. "Isn't it delicious?" she added, as her dress blew upward. She lowered her hands down, keeping her dress from blowing off of her. The Realizer paused it again when Marilyn's face returned to the screen.

The scene triggered a grim reminder of his mother, but he tried to suppress it.

"That seems familiar," Mario remarked.

"Did your dad tell you what my power is?" the Realizer asked, changing the subject.

"No, sir, he didn't," Mario answered with a sheepish shrug. "I searched for you on the Webnet Mightybase, of course. I found your Mightypedia entry, but it didn't say much about you other than being a restaurateur."

"And you couldn't find my personal profile page, eh?"

"No," responded Mario. "Why is that? I thought all the Mighty are on there."

"Privacy, kid," he said. "I'm there, but I've got my personal profile limited to a select few."

"Oh. I see," Mario said but didn't fully understand.

"I'm considered a rarity, a special. There's no one else with a power like me," said the Realizer matter-of-factly. "Would you like to know what it is?"

"Yes."

"Good," he said with a Cheshire cat grin. "You have the job."

"Okay," Mario said without reservation. Then, he asked, "What's the job?"

The Realizer pointed his finger at the viewscreens. A light emanated outward from the screens in a conoidal shape toward the Realizer's finger. He beckoned it toward him. From the light, a shape took form, becoming a person. And then, a very puzzled Marilyn Monroe in her white dress with her hands still pushing down the front was standing in front of the stacked viewscreens.

"Take her downstairs and give her to Vic," the Realizer said. "He'll make her into a waitress. Ask him to point you to the dishes."

"Thank you, sir," Mario said, escorting the bewildered Marilyn Monroe out the door of the Realizer's office.

"Oh, and Mario," the Realizer said before Mario closed the door behind him. "Mum's the word on my powers. Got it?"

Mario nodded and closed the door.

???
webnet.mightybase search results...
The Realizer : MIGHTYpedia Entry
???

Entrepreneur, restaurateur, and innovator, the Realizer is known for creating and curating experiential entertainment for the Mighty. From humble beginnings, he rose to fame with his early sports spectacular, the Midtown Players. Citizen athletes would compete in all manner of physical games and feats of athleticism in the Midtown Stadium erected in Central Park for that purpose. Unfortunately, the Midtown Players as such only lasted one season, but it gave birth to a more grandiose idea. After renaming the Midtown Stadium to Fellowship City Coliseum, the Realizer made a small fortune by capturing a larger audience interested in Citizens fighting to the death in gladiatorial-like competitions.

"My mother was one of the biggest influences on me. I didn't have a father, and she raised me working as a telekin tailor for the wealthy Mighty in Emerald Hills. We didn't have much, but she did the best she could. I only wish I could have made my fortune before she died, so I could give her the finer things in life, like a better home, better food." Taken from an Interview in the Fellowship City Chronicle.

With a hit on his hands, a mansion in Emerald Hills, and the world at his feet, the Realizer decided to take a new leap by becoming a restaurateur. His first foray was supposed to be a combination of fine food and gladiatorial entertainment. "It will be the most elaborately entertaining spectacle Fellowship City has ever seen!" Taken from an interview in the Fellowship City Chronicle. The Realizer's new restaurant, Gothmopolis, was a three-story building with a central arena for gladiatorial-like battles. All of the booths in the restaurant faced the arena. It was dubbed a comic book hero themed culinary experience. However, the idea of pitting super-powered heroes and villains against one another in bloodless skirmishes that could be rehearsed, choreographed, and orchestrated was not appealing to the bloodthirsty Mighty audiences or the monastery. Nearly two weeks after its grand opening, the monastery forced the Realizer to shutter Gothmopolis forever.

He lost a fortune, his home, and his fame, but he never lost hope. He knew adventure dining would work if done right and within the law. So, he pulled his resources together and created the Glory Battle Arena, which was popular for several years, gaining him much of the income back that he lost from the Gothmopolis debacle. In recent years, he's become a recluse, hiding from the public, and even removing his personal profile from the Webnet Mightybase. His newest restaurant, QTs House of Jacks, which is nothing at all like any of his previous projects, is currently a Fellowship City hot spot (see QTs House of Jacks).

???

There was no other information about the Realizer on the Webnet Mightybase unless you were one of the lucky ones privy to his personal profile.

"So, are you gonna stick around, green bean, or are you gonna bolt?" *Vic said with a drawl, as he took Marilyn off Mario's hands.*

"I got the job," *Mario said with a brimming smile.* "I'll be back."

"Listen, kid, it's not all fun and games here, all right?"

"I get that," *Mario says with a nod.* "I'm just happy to follow in my dad's footsteps."

"Well, if you're absolutely gawdamn sure, head into the Manager's office," *Vic pointed toward a small room in the kitchen marked* MANAGER. "You've got some paperwork to fill out before you can come back."

With a shaky fist, Mario knocked on the door once and it creaked open.

"Hello?" *Mario called, peeking his head inside. The room was empty, except for some filing cabinets and a desk with a folder marked* NEW EMPLOYEE.

Mario stepped inside and sat at the desk. He opened the folder. There were several pages, and at the top of the first page was written *New Employee Agreement*.

As you are now aware, the Realizer's power is unlike any other Mighty. He can realize any being he chooses into existence, be it from old movies, television shows, posters, comic books, and even novels.

"When I was young, I thought my power was restricted to mere images, but over time, I learned how to synthesize those images from words and realize written characters into reality."

He is one of the most powerful Mighty in existence. As an employee of the Realizer, you must maintain a sacred bond of silence concerning his abilities and how he utilizes them. If you accept this demand, you will be paid handsomely and treated better than you would be by any other Mighty employer. If you agree to these terms, turn to the next page and continue reading.

Upon reading the agreement, Mario questioned whether this was the right time and place for him, as any potential employee would do. He took a few seconds to gather his thoughts.

As he peered through the window of the Manager's office and checked out what working in the kitchen was like, a dark-haired girl moseyed by, carrying a tray of some sort. Held hostage by her beauty, he couldn't take his eyes off her. He stood up and pressed his face to the window to follow her walk away. She was tall and slender, but she had curves—not the curves of a woman yet. She was still a girl, close to his age, and captivating.

Suddenly, he visualized himself working in the kitchen and washing dishes. He flipped the page.

There are two kinds of staff at QTs House of Jacks. 1) Citizens, like you. You probably live at the WPC or in the southside ghetto.

Regardless, it will be necessary for you to always be at work on time. "If you're fifteen minutes early, you're almost on time." The Realizer does not abide by tardiness or truancy. 2) Realizations, like whomever you brought down with you to give to Vic. Although Realizations are real people, they are not Citizens but the property of the Realizer. Do not fraternize with Realizations.

Mario wondered if his future wife was a Citizen or a Realization. He shook his head, determining that she must be all Citizen. Then, he continued reading.

Because they are the property of the Realizer, he can do whatever he pleases with them. He can bring them into this world one day and take them out the next.

"I brought you into this world, I can damn well take you out," whispers Mario, recalling the Realizer's voice and words. Another memory begins to take hold as a pinkish glow develops a few feet from him. It grows larger and larger until it surrounds him within his memoryscape.

He sat next to the Realizer in a booth on the restaurant floor while the Realizer asked him various questions.

"How much do you enjoy your job?"

"More than I can say, sir."

"What do you like best about working at QTs?"

He thought about Christiana.

"I know it's a hard one to answer," the Realizer interrupted his thought, dropping his pen onto the ledger with a quiet thump. He fingered through the pages of his ledger, flipping to somewhere in the middle. "I take you as a clever young chap, Mario. Would I be wrong?"

"I don't think so, sir."

"Good, I don't like being wrong," he said, giving Mario a wink and picking up his pen. "So, here's what I want to do. Let's play a game."

"What kind of game, sir?"

"What's your favorite book or movie?"

Mario took a few moments to think about his answer. He wasn't sure if this interview had to do with a promotion or something, and he didn't want to lose any possible advancement. "Uhm, I guess it depends on the genre. I've got so many favorites."

"Yeah?" The Realizer asked, genuinely intrigued. "Can you name a few?"

"Sure," Mario started to answer but was interrupted by Marilyn bursting through the kitchen door and bee-lining it to the Realizer's booth. She said something, but it was drowned out by a skinny, dark-haired man with a Van Dyke goatee and wearing a slim black suit, who came crashing through the kitchen door behind her.

"Don't listen to that bitch!"

Marilyn reached the Realizer and whispered something in his ear, something Mario couldn't overhear.

"Mr. Pink," said the Realizer, turning to face the man. "What do you have to say for yourself?"

"I didn't steal any tips." Mr. Pink pleaded.

"Hmm." The Realizer handed Marilyn a slip of paper and a pen, and then he whispered something. "Empty your pockets, Mr. Pink. I want everything on the table."

"I don't believe this," Mr. Pink said, emptying the contents of his pockets onto the table. "C'mon. I didn't steal any tips."

"The girl says you did," the Realizer said, studying Mr. Pink. He peeks at the paper Marilyn handed him and counts the money on the table. "She gave me an amount, and wouldn't you know. That's the exact amount you have on you."

"Don't give me that," Mr. Pink responded. "She didn't make that money. She's a bitch!"

With an unexpected swiftness for a big man, the Realizer jolted forward from his seat and towered over Mr. Pink. He tilted his head sideways and narrowed his eyes, as he scrutinized the skinny man in the suit and tie. Then, he tapped his finger on Mr. Pink's shoulder.

Mr. Pink jumped back jerking his tie away from his neck. His face flushed with panic as he gaped sorrowfully at the Realizer, gasping for breaths. He turned to Mario, pleading with his eyes as he reached out for help, but Mario recoiled, trying to hide the horror in his eyes. Mr. Pink fell onto the table in front of Mario and their eyes met. Unexpectedly, his blue eyes popped from their sockets and he started to glow. In an instant, he vanished, leaving nothing behind of Mr. Pink but a dissipating pink glow.

As Mario finishes his silent requiem for the Realizer, he lifts his head from his palms and assesses the empty restaurant. Tanalia still sits in a meditative pose on the other side of the room. Outside, the Swiftglides no longer cast him threatening glares but instead all stare out in the same direction.

Mario twists his head around, trying to catch a glimpse of what captures their attention. He smashes his face against the window glass, as another sky taxi carrying a monk lands in front of QTs House of Jacks. The moment his feet touch the ground, the hooded monk dashes toward the front doors. Mario pivots around in time for the doors to swing open.

"I'm here," the hooded monk says, sounding inconvenienced in some way. He rushes toward Tanalia without looking around, already knowing exactly where she is in the restaurant. "What was so pressing, Tanalia, that required you to interrupt my patience?"

Without shifting her meditative posture, she speaks to him through her voice-thought, "*The Realizer is dead.*"

Those words haunt him, twisting his face in bug-eyed confusion and horror. The expression is one that never before appeared on the monk's face and he hopes to never wear such an expression again in his life.

Mario scrutinizes the hooded man. Though no words are exchanged between the two monks, he can tell they are communicating telepathically, given his immediate change of emotion.

He looks familiar.

The hooded monk darts a stand-down-and-shut-up side-glance at Mario and then turns back to Tanalia.

"Show me!" he commands in a voice that startles Mario.

Tanalia jumps to her feet in a single swift movement, turns on her heels to face the hooded monk, and raises her hands. He steps forward, his hands meeting her hands and interlocking with her fingers.

AAAAAGGGGGHHHHH

She winces in pain, as her headspace fills with a bright white blankness, emptying itself of all else. Every little thought forces itself away and into her mentor's mind, burning in aching discomfort and leaving only a dullness.

With confused apprehension, Mario eyes the two monks, wondering, *How could these seer-paths, who always know what is happening, will happen, and has happened in the past, not know what happened to the Realizer? This doesn't make any sense.*

A swirling white light blinks out of existence, as Tanalia's mentor readies himself to relive her experience in his own mind. His hindsight is hyper-focused, like tunnel vision, as he witnesses the world through her eyes.

She sits at the Pieromancer's Coffee Shop and Bakery, eating a cheese Danish and sipping a—it smells like it could be—hot chai tea latte. She quietly laughs, as the pyrokin barista reheats a mug for a needy, elderly customer using a flame from his fingertips. Her soft chuckle reverberates in his mind, as she surveys the room. The clock on the wall blinks 6 o 8.

They're both late this time, she thinks. *Ifton is chronically late, but the Realizer is always on time, if not early.*

Something red outside the window catches her eye. She double-takes, confirming the familiar red van edging up to the curb. Slightly relieved, she takes another bite of her Danish followed by a sip of tea, continuing her decompression. She taps on her datapad screen, sliding her finger to the right until she finds the file marked SOL & LUNA DAY. She opens the file and takes another sip of her tea. A cursor blinks after the words PARADE POSITIONING.

She glances back toward the window. Ifton crosses over from the driver's side, but the passenger side door does not open. Ifton saunters inside and waves at the monk before approaching the counter.

"Ifton!" she barks.

"Hold a sec," he says, raising one finger without looking in her direction. "I need some pick-me-up juice. I'm sure you two have everything under control anyway."

Tanalia bolts up, pushing her chair back with a haunting screech, causing patrons around the coffee shop to collectively cringe. She marches toward Ifton.

"The Realizer is not here!"

"What? He's..." Ifton scans the shop but cannot find him.

"He's really not here?"

"Affirmative."

"That's weird," Ifton says, stepping out of line and over to Tanalia. "Have you tried using your—gifts?"

"Of course, I did," she confesses. "But I could not find him. I figured he was blocking again."

"Yeah, that sounds like him," Ifton agrees, heading to the enormous viewscreen mounted on the wall broadcasting *Good Morning, Fellowship City!* He touches it, saying, "I'll try to get an eye on him."

Ifton's face contorts. His eyes close hard, rapidly moving under the lids. He clamps onto the screen so tightly that it cracks under the pressure. After a few seconds, his eyes pop open in panic.

"I'm not getting anything. QTs is a complete void."

"You wait here in case he shows up," commands Tanalia.

Ifton shrugs with concern, but Tanalia is already tapping on a black and white checkered icon on her datapad. As she exits, Ifton still stands by the screen, clutching a piece of the viewscreen in his hand. Patrons and baristas throw dagger eyes at him.

"I'll replace it," he says, whipping out his wallet.

Outside, Tanalia takes a few steps before spying a bald flyer wearing a black skintight uniform with a checkered pattern down each side descend toward her.

"17th and D!" she directs, as she climbs onto his back. He levitates, rising high above the coffee shop on the corner of 15th and N Streets.

She gazes over Fellowship City, admiring the view. A wave of happiness washes over her, drowning out her anxiety about the whereabouts of the Realizer. Her mentor senses this emotional shift, her love of flying, and he squeezes her fingers tenderly in their interlocked grip.

As they approach QTs House of Jacks, the soft glow of the neon sign still flickers in the morning light. Like some ominous light at the end of a tunnel beckoning her forward, it calls her closer. But whether it leads to danger, despair, or reward, she is uncertain. She tries again to focus her near-sight, but all is blank. This strange unknown causes her anxiety to return once more in a flood.

"There," she commands, pointing down to the restaurant.

The flyer stands by the curb like a silent guard, as she races up the stairs and pulls hard upon the doors. They do not budge. She traces her hands down the doors near the latch between them, sensing an electronic mechanism. Her eyes light up as she places her right hand flatly against the latch. She closes her eyes, twisting and tightening in painful asynchronicity.

KALICKK KAHKIK

Her mild technopathy sometimes comes in handy when needing to open doors with electronic locks. She beams with pride as she opens the doors and creeps inside.

Dark and empty, an eeriness fills the restaurant, especially as she continues to sense nothing. Tanalia hastens into the kitchen and surveys the area, noticing the old-style employee punch card placard on the wall.

How quaint? she thinks, examining the antique. *Still in use?*

She fingers the punch cards, removing them one by one and inspecting the last date and times punched. She discovers the last clock out belongs to the punch card with ident-tag 24VØR4VNØ.

She scans the ident-tag with a handheld datapad. It

pings, filling the screen with all identifying information for the Citizen. *Mario Rickson. Male, age 20. Occupant WPC 3014 with sibling Zelda. Female, age 17. Father, Tommy Rickson, age 39. Occupant SIC 7734. A troublemaker. Maybe it runs in the family,* thinks Tanalia before swiping left on the scanner. *Mother, Lizbeth Rickson, age 39. Whereabouts unknown.*

Tanalia returns the datapad to a fold in her robes, questioning, *how can it be unknown? We know everything.*

She searches the main floor of the restaurant, finding nothing of consequence. She heads upstairs to the Realizer's apartment, finding the door swung wide open.

"Realizer!" she calls, receiving no response. She reaches her thoughts outward, trying to sense something in this void, but again finds nothing. She shutters, as she creeps to the open door.

Suddenly, bursts of static and lightning flash in the mind's eye of her mentor. Before she reaches the door, everything fades, blurring out of focus and filling his mind with the sound and imagery of painful static. The intensity of the sight and sound increases, trying to eject him from her memory.

"Ugggh," the hooded monk grunts in pain, gripping the fingers of the other monk even tighter. Her face grimaces as well, but not with the same intensity as the older monk.

He wrestles against the static, clinging to the memory and trying to gain access again. As he reaches out from the oblivion of his mind's eye, all seems lost until the static clears with Tanalia fleeing down the stairwell and out the front door.

Tears stream down her face as she crashes into the unsuspecting flyer. He grapples her by the shoulders and attempts to calm her. She senses that much but shoves his hands away and climbs onto his back.

"Take me to the WPC!" she commands. "Signal another transport immediately! Make sure it's a strong-flyer. We will likely need the support"

With an exhausted sigh, Tanalia falls to her knees, fingers still interlocked with her mentor's. "Jakandy," she exhales with labored breath.

8

WHEN A MIGHTY HAS FALLEN

Jakandy?!? cries Mario's inner voice. *I remember this monk*, he thinks, fumbling with a napkin roll of silverware. *He's the bastard Mighty who took my parents from me.*

He jerks the napkin free, allowing the silverware to clank upon the table. He finds the steak knife and grips the wooden handle tight. The whole action is instinctual, subliminal. As soon as it reaches his awareness, he drops the knife and glances at the monks to make sure they do not view him as a threat.

"Stand up, Tanalia," Jakandy says, reaching out his hand.

As he helps her to her feet, a momentary relief flushes over Mario.

"I need to see it," Jakandy urges, clasping her shoulders and meeting her eyes. "Your memory was damaged."

"Damaged?"

"Void," he clarifies, starting toward the stairwell.

"You don't want to see it," Tanalia pleads. "It's—"

"A necessity, Tanalia," he specifies. "Not a want."

Tanalia follows Jakandy up the stairs.

"So, should I come with you?" Mario calls, jumping from his seat and following them.

"No, Citizen," Jakandy's voice bellows from the stairwell. "Stay back. This is monastery business."

Mario slumps back into the booth. In his periphery, the ever-agitated Swiftglides continue pacing, pointing, and yelling at him through the window. He shakes his head and stares downward at nothing.

Upstairs, Tanalia directs Jakandy toward the Realizer's apartment doorway.

"It's a gruesome sight, Jakandy," she warns, stopping midway down the hall, raising an arm over her nostrils. "I've never seen anything like this."

The sweet, rancid scent of death lingers in the hallway, becoming more and more putrid the closer Jakandy gets to the open door. As he reaches the door, he peers in and promptly flinches.

By Sol and Luna, he thinks, casting desperate eyes at Tanalia.

He throws back his hood and wipes sweat from his brow, sensing the warming sickness radiate within. He swallows hard, tasting the metallic tang of vomit ready to spew from his insides. He covers his mouth and nose with one of his arms.

"*You don't need to do this*," Tanalia urges through thought.

"I do," he says with a long exhale before turning back to the doorway.

Red bathes the room from top to bottom, casting an eerie glow from the lights burning blood. *There's so much blood,* Jakandy thinks, scanning the room. Crimson gore still drips from the walls, windows, and ceiling. It pools into a massive maroon puddle in the center of the room. The Realizer's headless body sits on the couch, sprawled as he ever was. The stuffed head of the flesheater, ripped from its mount, rests awkwardly behind the Realizer. He resembles a god from ancient Egyptian hieroglyphs. Entrails spew forth from his splayed open stomach, scattering like reaching red tendrils around the room.

"Where's his head?"

Tanalia fills him with the urge to step into the room. He perceives her and tiptoes forward, trying to keep off the bloody patches of carpet near him. Then, the sensation drives him to turn toward the four connected viewscreens on the opposite wall from the Realizer. All four are broken and bent inward. However, the bottom right is splattered with blood and brain matter. Blood drips down into a box where the Realizer's head rests. His mouth is agape, and his eyes are moons, staring directly at Jakandy. He shutters violently and turns away.

"By Sol and Luna," he mutters in a dying voice.

As he turns back toward the Realizer's body, something shimmering in the puddle on the floor catches his eye. He steps forward onto a spot of rug that appears clean. As his foot presses downward, blood gushes up from the carpet around his sandal, making a squishing sound and leaving a bloody footprint behind. He shivers as some of the sticky, cold blood touches his bare toes.

When he reaches the object, he rips a length of cloth from his robe and wraps it around his hand. Then, he bends down and picks it up. It drips thick, congealing blood, as he tries to wipe it clean.

Glasses, he thinks, inspecting the wadded clump of metal and broken glass in his hand. *Someone had to be very strong to do this.*

Moments later, Jakandy exits the room, finding the hallway empty. He takes off his sandals and wipes the bottoms clean on the carpet outside of the Realizer's apartment door. As he does so, he rubs the tips of his toes into the carpet, hoping the tacky blood comes off. Without confirming the cleanliness of his feet, he slips the sandals back on and proceeds down the hall.

He finds Tanalia around the corner with her face in her hands.

"The smell is atrocious," she complains. "I've never smelled death like that. Death is usually clean. This is chaos."

"How did this happen? How did we not see it? Everything about the Realizer is clouded."

"I know. That's why I needed your help." Tanalia spies the clump of metal and glass in Jakandy's hand. "Glasses?"

"Yeah," answers Jakandy. "Did the Realizer wear glasses?"

"Not at any of the meetings I had with him," Tanalia answers.

"But he was a vain man," comments Jakandy. "He might not have made them prominent if they were his."

Tanalia nods in agreement and then draws closer to Jakandy, explaining, "I've been trying to invoke hindsight since I've arrived, but I can't see anything. That is partially why I retrieved the Citizen. You're stronger than me. Can you get anything?"

"No, nothing. It's like it's a void," he answers. "I'm having difficulty with nearsight and foresight as well. There seems to be some kind of psychic dead zone emanating from this location."

"What do we do now?"

"I have no idea," Jakandy confesses. "I am ill-equipped for this kind of situation."

Downstairs, their muffled voices echo through the

empty restaurant, but they sound like the chatter of small animals. Mario listens for words he can decipher, as he slides his jacket off and hangs it over the side of the booth. He stretches his arms, rolls his sleeves below his elbow, and loosens his tie before unbuttoning his collar.

The tie has to go, he thinks, stripping it off and tucking it into his jacket's pocket.

As the two monks descend the stairwell, their voices become clearer, and Mario perks up.

"He was always shifty, but he had money," says Jakandy.

"The Realizer?" Tanalia questions.

As they reach the bottom of the stairwell, they ignore Mario and continue toward the kitchen.

"Don't tell me you didn't notice. His creations," Jakandy accentuates the final word. "We've always had trouble with them, but he paid everyone off."

The monks' muffled voices echo from behind the kitchen wall. Mario tries to decipher their unintelligible words, as they pace from one end to the other.

Looking for something? he thinks. *I can probably help with that. I do work here.*

After a few minutes, the kitchen door opens.

"...and you have a suspect?" asks Jakandy.

"Yes, there he is," Tanalia answers, motioning to Mario as they glide in his direction. "He works here as a—"

"He didn't do it."

Mario sinks into the booth sighing in relief. Over his shoulder, he glimpses the Swiftglides ogling him from outside.

"Can you tell them that?" he asks the monks. "I don't think they got the memo."

"They'll find out soon enough," says Tanalia before

turning to face Jakandy. "What are we going to do? There's been no word from the Enclave."

"I'm not sure if we will hear anything but silence from them." Jakandy clarifies, "They are just as equipped to handle this situation as we are. As far as I'm aware, there has never been a crime like this since the birth of Sol and Luna. And, our Order is not trained to solve crimes... only eliminate them before they can even happen. So, none of us know what to do."

"Maybe you need a detective," Mario chimes in. "Like in the old movies."

Jakandy and Tanalia share a quizzical glance before facing Mario.

"What do you suggest?" asks Jakandy.

Mario bolts from the booth, roaring to go.

"The Realizer pulled workers from movies all the time. He must have REALIZED a detective at some point." Mario explains, rushing toward the kitchen. "We just need to find him!"

Jakandy and Tanalia shrug at one another before following Mario with far less enthusiasm than he displayed. When they enter the kitchen, Mario is rummaging through drawers in the manager's office.

"You know the Realizer's power?" Tanalia questioned.

"Yeah," Mario answered matter-of-factly without looking up, still searching for something. "All his employees know... knew... it was a hiring requirement."

"And how do you suggest we find a detective?" she asks.

Mario retrieves a ledger, raises it triumphantly, and says, "With this!"

"What is that?" Jakandy questions.

Tanalia smirks.

He turns to her, probing a thought, *"Do you have a clue?"*

She shrugs and shakes her head.

"It belongs to the Realizer," Mario says, stepping toward the stainless-steel prep table as he thumbs through the ledger. "He used to write in this thing all the time. A year ago, he was asking all of us for ideas. He wrote them all in here. It's gotta have what we need."

Jakandy and Tanalia eye one another skeptically.

"Ah hah!" Mario exclaims, landing on a page with GLORY BATTLES scrawled upon the ledger heading. "Here we go! Glory Battles!"

"I remember those," claims Tanalia. "They stopped when I was a kid. Why are you interested in them?"

"So, this was just after the Gothmopolis debacle," Mario explains. "The Realizer was trying to recoup some losses by promoting violent fights between his REALIZED not-so-Normal powerless heroes and their archenemies. They were like the old gladiatorial arena battles the Roman Caesars put on to placate the masses. Battles to the death," Mario says with a shudder, as he flips through the ledger. He lands on another page and reads it in a voice meant to mimic a major event announcer, "Who will win? Hero or villain. I think the Realizer thought of himself as Caesar of Fellowship City."

"Well, he wasn't," Jakandy says, yanking the ledger from Mario's hands. "The means by which you wish to seek an answer is exhaustingly slow."

Jakandy balances the ledger in his left hand and places his first two fingers of his right hand upon his temple.

"There are two," he says almost as soon as his fingers touch his head. "One dresses like a bat and the other dresses like a woman."

"A woman?" asks Tanalia.

"No. HE dresses like a woman," Jakandy explains.

Mario's eyes light up. "This is GREAT! Let's get moving!"

Jakandy and Tanalia ignore him, as they turn away and stride out of the kitchen. Mario follows, watching them react to one another like they are having a conversation without speaking aloud.

That is so creepy, he thinks.

Tanalia turns around, narrowing her eyes at him. Mario slows his pace behind them, gulping. Without missing a beat, she turns back to Jakandy, who nods, agreeing with her about something Mario cannot hear.

As they approach the front doors of QTs House of Jacks, the doors swing open.

Shit! Mario thinks, *They're telekins, too?*

Jakandy chortles and waves his hand, sensing Mario's astonishment. Then, the telltale checkered pattern of the sky taxis come into view, as they secure the doors for the fast-approaching monks.

"Son of a bitch," groans Mario.

The two monks hurtle down the front stairs toward the Swiftglides with Mario following a few paces behind. All three sky taxis break into flanking positions around the monks and Mario.

4SKōR jumps up from her cross-legged position and lunges forward in a clumsy, awkward run. Her bound hands bounce behind her.

"I'm all better now. Please, let me go free. I'm very sorry. I won't do anything crazy. I promise."

Jakandy squints at her and then turns to DerMööve, giving him a slight nod. DerMööve flicks his finger, telekinetically severing her bonds. They fall to the ground, as 4SKōR waves her arms free.

She glares at DerMööve, grumbling, "You could have done that the whole time?"

He shrugs, stepping past her, toward Jakandy.

"Was ist das?" he says, pointing at the ledger. He flicks his finger again and the pages open in Jakandy's hand. Jakandy slaps the ledger shut. "Das belongs to mein president, Der Realizer."

"He has no more belongings," Jakandy says, waving his arm toward QTs House of Jacks and directing the sky taxis. "Everything is evidence. Put it on monastery impound."

The bald flyer nods, lifts off the ground, and hovers to the door. He turns around and stands in front of the door with his crossed arms, becoming a caricature of intimidation.

I guess he's the impound, Mario thinks.

Jakandy whips around to face Mario. Mario's eyes flutter back and forth, as he reflects on everything he just thought, trying to find something that may have offended the monk.

"Here," Jakandy says, handing the ledger to Mario. "See if you can discover anything else with your slow method."

"I don't understand," Mario confesses with a confused expression, as he takes the book from Jakandy's hand.

"What is there to understand?"

As Jakandy speaks, his black-checkered transport steps behind him. This one is a woman, a very muscular woman.

The dark-haired flyer steps in front of Tanalia. He gestures for her to take hold of him, waits for her to get secure, and carries her away.

"I'm not coming with you?" Mario asks, appraising the threatening faces of the angry Swiftglides.

"No! Stay here and inform us if you find anything of use."

"How?"

"Think it!" Jakandy says from the back of his sky taxi.

Humiliated, Mario lowers his gaze from the flying

monks back to the Swiftglides encircling him. *They're like a circling pack of flesheaters*, he thinks.

"So, you killt mein president?" DerMööve asks, stepping toward Mario.

"Nope. I certainly did not," Mario mumbles, as he steps back and attempts to summon the bald flyer for help. He gets no response at all. *Great,* he thinks, shuffling slowly up the first step, waving an arm in surrender, while tucking the ledger under the other. "Listen, I'm not really sure what's happening here."

"Der Realizer ist nicht mehr," DerMööve says with his palm facing Mario.

Mario halts his slow climb backward. His eyes contort, revealing their discomfort. He is unable to move. "Did... you... kill... him?"

"No."

"If he had," 4SKōR interjects. "They wouldn't have let him go."

Ifton steps forward, placing his hand on DerMööve's shoulder. DerMööve scowls at the hand until he withdraws it.

"Foursy's right," Ifton says, as he turns away.

4SKōR beams with pride. "Thanks, Threeway!"

Velacruz, always the voice of reason, paces between DerMööve and the others, "If it wasn't this... Citizen... who did it?"

"That's what we're trying to figure out," says Mario as he thumbs through the pages of the book.

"WE?!?" exclaims the Arcane Sawyer, dropping from his constant hover and stepping toward Mario. "You're merely a Citizen! What can you do?"

Mario presents the ledger to the Arcane Sawyer, saying, "I can read."

He turns the ledger around to an open page with a comic book cover stapled to it. The title of the comic is *The Arcane Sawyer*. The rest of the page is filled with art of a battle behind a big white blank space in the shape of what should have been the Arcane Sawyer.

"You're realized." Mario's contempt toward him read like an accusation. He points at the Arcane Sawyer. "He pulled you into this world!"

The Arcane Sawyer startles, shifting his gaze away from the other Swiftglides. 4SKōR snatches the ledger from Mario, squealing, "Give me that!"

"It means nothing," demands The Arcane Sawyer as he rips the ledger from her hands.

She laughs at his apparent discomfort.

"Mr. Veep, you're a realization?"

Fed up, the Arcane Sawyer juts his axe forward and steps toward Mario.

"Wait!" Mario shouts at him with arms up in surrender. "It's important that you were realized."

The Arcane Sawyer halts, lowering his axe and narrowing his eyes at Mario.

"Why?"

The other Swiftglides dart excited and confused glances at one another.

"Because you were at Gothmopolis!" Mario exclaims. "You know about the man dressed like a bat, don't you?"

"Yes!" booms the Arcane Sawyer. "Yes, I do!"

"Excellent! We need his help! Do you know how to find him?"

The Arcane Sawyer frowns, dropping his axehead to the ground with a clang. Before rising to a hover, he drags it a few feet, making a screeching sound that haunts their ears and sends shivers down their spines.

"After Gothmopolis closed," he says, hovering and swinging his battle-axe back up into his arms. "Some of the heroes were stuck in the Realizer's employ because they did not have powers. Unfortunately, he was one of those."

"Yeah, we know that part."

"Well, the Realizer owed a lot of money to people after that," the Arcane Sawyer hovers back and forth, pacing in the air as he tries to recount all the details. "To make a lot of money quick, he launched the Glory Battles."

"Can you fast-forward a bit?" Mario asks. "We know all this. We just need to know where he is."

"Where he is?" questions the Arcane Sawyer.

"Oh my god, yes. How can we find him? Can you help us do that or not?"

"Yes," the Arcane Sawyer nods, lifting his head high. "He was killed in a Glory Battle by some clown, years ago."

"Wait," Mario says stunned. "What? Are you sure?"

"Very sure," the Arcane Sawyer says, turning away and rising into the air.

"Shit!" Mario exclaims, retrieving the ledger from 4SKōR and heading toward the bald flyer standing at the door.

The bat is dead, he thinks with as much outward force as he can muster.

"Hey, what makes you think you can take that from me, Citizen?" 4SKōR screeches.

"Are we doing this right now?" Mario asks, turning to 4SKōR and standing his ground. "I have way more important things to do, like find the Realizer's killer. You want to continue this, or should I get to work on something actually important?"

Dumbfounded, 4SKōR stands silent and motionless.

"Good. I'll get back to it then."

High above Fellowship City, an echo of a thought catches up to Jakandy.

"The bat is dead."

He sends an impulse to Tanalia, flying no more than 20 feet from him.

"The bat is dead. We seek the drag queen now."

"Where would that be?" Tanalia telepathically asks.

"There's only one place I can think of to find a non-Mighty drag queen."

"Don't tell me it's in the southside ghetto," her thought reverberates.

"Club Haberdashery," Jakandy yells to his flyer. She nods and veers southwest.

Mario sits at a booth inside QTs, flipping through the ledger. *Why am I helping them find the killer? If something killed an Abnormal Mighty, I should be congratulating it, right? They've made us their slaves. They can do anything they want to us, and we can't do anything about it. We have no voice. No rights.* Mario glares out the window, eyeing DerMööve. *I should be finding a way to help this killer go after someone like him! They think they're so damn powerful like their shit don't stink. He stinks like shit! A Mighty nasty shit! That bastard stole my parents from me!*

"Where's my mom, you son of a bitch!" Mario yells at the window before trailing his eyes back to the ledger. He flips a couple of pages forward and stops on a page that appears different. He examines it.

The writing's different.

Mario flips back through the ledger. On all the previous

pages, the writing is consistently the same and recognizable as the Realizer's handwriting. He flips back to where the writing changes.

This writing changed about a year ago, thinks Mario. *Someone else wrote this.*

Mario reads aloud the first words written by the new hand, "What a NEW world! I spent my first day catching up on as much HISTORY and MYSTERY that I could." He quickly scans the rest of the page, reading words like silly game, alternate universe, superpowers, un-extraordinary, and trivial.

None of this sounds remotely like the Realizer, Mario ponders. *It sounds like someone brand new to this world... someone who had been Realized.*

Mario flips to the last written pages. *All of this last year was written by someone other than the Realizer. Who wrote this?*

9:00 A.M

Another hour chimes from the wall clock as Mario combs through the ledger. He is either so focused on the task at hand that he does not even register the interrupting bells, or he is exceptionally skilled at ignoring such interruptions. Regardless, there is not a hint of disturbance upon his face as he reads from the Realizer's ledger:

> *Innovation requires risk. Risk triggers the Enclave. So, unless you can prove that the award outweighs the risk, or you have enough green to line their pockets, you're pretty much shit out of luck.*

He flips a page and reads:

> *Everyone who had a novel idea or thought is long dead. That's why we live here in these remnants of yesteryear. We're barely getting by, doing the best we can with what we got and what the world has handed to us.*

I applaud the effort of those few Mighty brave enough to go out
beyond the protective shield of the Enclave to face the terrors of
the flesheaters and return with machines, structures, and pieces
that help keep this city afloat. That's something for Hyrkeol to
do. Something that makes him happy. It certainly isn't my cup
of tea.

Suddenly, a ruckus ensues outside the front door, distracting Mario. He peers through the window to find the Swiftglides rushing up the stairs toward the bald flyer guarding the door

"Ooh. This is going to be good," he says, folding his hands in anticipation.

But there is no payoff. Mario's jaw goes slack, as the bald flyer step aside and let the Swiftglides slip past him.

"I guess impound doesn't mean people can't come in and contaminate a crime scene!" Mario yells as the sky taxi shrugs him off. "That's all you are anyway. Transport!"

The Swiftglides race through the front lobby and converge on Mario. He braces himself by concentrating on the ledger, trying not to give them the pleasure of a reaction.

"You find anything yet, squirt?" says 4SKōR leading the charge.

"Nothing conclusive," Mario says without looking up from the book.

"We're gonna have ourselves a little peek," 4SKōR says, motioning to the other Swiftglides.

Ifton and the Arcane Sawyer stand behind her. DerMööve stands by the door, glaring at Mario and blocking the flyer from entering. Velacruz stands off to the side, leaning against a wall next to the kitchen door.

"You're not PEEKING around!" Mario yells, tucking the ledger to his side as he slides out of his booth seat.

He sprints past them toward the stairwell.

"That's cute," 4SKōR says with a chuckle, approaching the stairwell with Ifton and the Arcane Sawyer close behind. "He thinks he can stop us."

"You can't go up there. It's a—"

"Who died and left you in charge?" interrupts 4SKōR.

"I'm not in charge," Mario confesses, stepping backward up the stairwell and hoisting the ledger in front of him in a blocking position. "It's a crime scene. No one should go in there. The detectives will need to investigate it, and you don't want to contaminate it."

As they reach Mario, who tries his best to guard the stairwell, 4SKōR gestures to the Arcane Sawyer. He picks up Mario and places him at the bottom of the stairs.

"You coming?" 4SKōR asks over her shoulder to Velacruz.

"I don't want to see his body," Velacruz chimes in from her perch by the kitchen door. "I've got a weak stomach."

"I don't blame you," Mario says, sulking back toward his booth. "What about you? Weak stomach?"

"Guard Duty," huffs DerMööve from his posting at the front door.

They don't trust me, Mario thinks. *And I seriously don't trust them.*

AAAAAHHHHH

Mario startles and turns toward the stairs. Stupefied, DerMööve and Velacruz stand motionless.

They don't want to see... Dammit. It's up to me.

Mario races up the stairs to find 4SKōR standing in shock outside the open door of the Realizer's room. Ifton doubles over on the floor puking his guts out, while the

Arcane Sawyer stands aloft with axe and saw at the ready.

"You guys, okay?" asks Mario, creeping toward them.

"I've never seen anything like this before," says Ifton, wiping his mouth with his sleeve.

"Duh!" exclaims 4SKōR. "There's no fucking CRIME anymore!"

The Arcane Sawyer picks up 4SKōR and plants her behind him. He surveys the room. "This violence...it feels personal," He says, taking a step forward.

"Don't go in there," begs Mario. "You're going to make it more difficult for the detective—"

"Detective?" interrupts the Arcane Sawyer without looking at Mario, continuing to advance. "They cannot do what I can do."

"But you'll contaminate—"

"There," he dismisses Mario, as he hovers a few inches from the ground. "Now I will not."

Mario shakes his head in disapproval but says nothing more. He leans against the wall, flips open the ledger to the pages affixed with the Arcane Sawyer's comic book, and starts to read.

As I research possible pairings for Gothmopolis, I find that many comic book heroes have more than one arch-nemesis. However, one of those ne'er-do-wells is inevitably the biggest baddie of them all—the one villain who will pull the other villains together to make a super-villain group in some stories. Pitting the hero against that villain would likely produce the most optimal storylines for Gothmopolis.

For Superman, it's Lex Luthor. For Spiderman, it's Green Goblin. For Max Justice, it's Mikhail al-Amir Aleazim. For the Arcane Sawyer, it's Myrkuriel.

A brief history of the Arcane Sawyer: A pre-WWIII comic book created by Arthur Winthrop Wright, a professor of classics, ancient history, and archaeology at the University of Birmingham, and Daniel Boyd, artiste extraordinaire who worked on a dozen different best-selling titles prior to the Arcane Sawyer. These creators endowed their hero with amazing abilities to help the citizenry. The Arcane Sawyer originally had super-strength, super-speed, and he could fly.

Due to overwhelming popularity and Professor Wright's demanding schedule, the Arcane Sawyer property was sold to Haut Saus Comics und Mangas in Berlin. After that, the Arcane Sawyer developed other powers along the way, as necessary to complete whatever tasks the new writers set before him. He soon became unfortunately known as the 'deus ex machina-machine,' losing a host of fans over time, as he was entirely too over-powered as a super-powered hero.

As such, it may be best to Realize the Arcane Sawyer from one of the Wright/Boyd comics.

The Arcane Sawyer versus Myrkuriel primer: In his world, the Arcane Sawyer started out as a demi-godlike hero in the vein of Hercules named Hyrkeol, who protected the citizenry of an ancient island of Pæleosgosia from all manner of enemies and natural disasters.

His best friend was a golden-eyed, magic-user named Myrkuriel. That is, until the day Embroglius, the majestic volcano in the center of Pæleosgosia erupted.

In a tragic misfortune of circumstance, Myrkuriel whisked his family away to 'safety' in the remote northern region of the island. Believing his family had escaped harm's way, he helped his friend to save the many villages of the island from certain destruction.

Unbeknownst to Myrkuriel, Hyrkeol diverted the path of destruction of the lava flow as far away from the people as possible to the remote northern region of the island. Hyrkeol believed the new path of destruction would have no casualties, as everyone was supposed to be evacuated to the southern villages.

By the time Myrkuriel discovered Hyrkeol's plan, it was too late. The path of the lava flow's destruction led right to his family. Although Hyrkeol apologized, confessing he would have sacrificed himself to save his friend's family, Myrkuriel turned on his former friend. He became an evil warlock bent on the destruction of Hyrkeol.

Myrkuriel could never actually end the life of Hyrkeol, because of a blood pact they had made years before, which would take his own life in the process. Myrkuriel wanted to live more than he wanted Hyrkeol to die, so he hatched a plan that would grant him immortality and put an end to Hyrkeol without his life truly ending.

Through trickery and strategic planning, Myrkuriel cast a spell to freeze his former friend in a time-lock, which could only be broken by someone of Myrkuriel's blood. For many thousands of years, Myrkuriel lived without progeny, selfishly living life to advance his own desires. Then, he met Calliope. They married and had several children. Then, those children had children. His granddaughter, Hermione, was his favorite.

In this future where his family now lived, magic was replaced by science. Hermione was a gifted scientist, earning doctorates from Cambridge and MIT in molecular biology and quantum mechanics. As a quantum biologist, she made many discoveries, but none so magnificent as the re-discovery of Hyrkeol. Although it was accidental, she somehow broke the magical time-lock her grandfather had caged him within for those many years thanks to her various experiments with the Cambridge Electron Accelerator.

This new discovery changed her attitudes about life and

love, although it would not be long-lived. She taught Hyrkeol about the new world, while she in turn learned about his previous life. She helped him re-discover his talents in this new world and fashioned him into a super-hero. He continued to use his traditional armor with the burnished red cloak on his back, but he put aside his axe and saw as Hermione wished. They became a team.

Then, her grandfather stumbled upon a news report of his former friend helping people once again. He sought to destroy him once more, fixating on that one single idea. Because he had not practiced magic for many hundreds of years, he was forced into a solitude of constant meditation and exercise. He neglected his family to once again become Myrkuriel, the evil warlock. This time, he was done with immortality and was ready to die, hating Hyrkeol more than he wanted to live.

Again, in a tragic misfortune of circumstance, Myrkuriel, bent on destroying his old friend, became so narrowly focused that he did not see anyone other than Hyrkeol. He cast a spell that would eliminate all life in its path. He did not see his lovely Hermione. He did not see his beautiful Calliope and his children and their children. He did not see that the family was gathered to celebrate something. He did not see that they were in a restaurant full of friends surrounding them. He only saw Hyrkeol, and when the spell was done, only he and Hyrkeol stood.

Hyrkeol's powers now were vast, and he was greater than he had ever been before. Myrkuriel was mentally, physically, and emotionally spent. There was no destroying one or the other, so Hyrkeol sealed Myrkuriel in the Cambridge Electron Accelerator. The last thing Myrkuriel said to him before his matter was displaced into all its molecular pieces, "You're an arcane sawyer, Hyrkeol. You'll never fit into this world. You'll never find any happiness. I condemn you!"

There was no destruction of matter, merely a change in state. Myrkuriel would forever be trying to put himself back together, only ever being able to use possession to enact his revenge and never being able to utilize his complete power again.

Hyrkeol would go on to pick up his axe and saw once again, becoming the Arcane Sawyer. In this new future, he would fight all the dregs humanity had to offer while trying to keep Myrkuriel's constant threat at bay. He had no qualms about putting to death those he judged fit to die. His brand of justice was swift and merciless. Even so, he protected the people with all his power, believing his ethics and his morality to be the only right ones. No government, military, or police force could tell him what to do. No one owned him. No one controlled him. He did exactly what he thought to be morally just and right. And, he waited patiently for that final day when Myrkuriel would regain his true form and power, and they would fight to the ultimate death.

Right now, however, the Arcane Sawyer is hovering over a crime scene, lifting heavy objects to peek under them.

"I do not see how that child could have done this," the Arcane Sawyer's voice boomed from the room. "We are looking for something much bigger, much stronger. The murderer here was something that can stop a SUPER."

"Ahem," Ifton clears his throat while leaning against the door well to steady himself. He tries to keep his eyes off everything but the Arcane Sawyer. "It's MIGHTY. We're called the Mighty!"

No longer concerned with the machinations of the Swiftglides, Mario turns his full attention back to the ledger. He flips to the last written page, which ends abruptly in mid-sentence. Upon the next page, he finds nothing, nor does he find anything on any pages thereafter.

Confused, he flips the last page back and forth over and over. Then, he stops with his thumb pressing the page against his forefinger. He rubs his fingers together through the page, and then he flips to a previous page and does the same thing. *It's too thin*, he thinks, flipping back to the last page. *This is thicker. They're stuck together.*

With care, he teases the ends apart.

Come on. Don't rip. He separates the pages, examines them, and realizes, *the handwriting is different.*

He flips the pages to compare. The final writing is the same as the writing from the earlier entries. *This is the first thing he has written in a year... And, the last thing he will ever write in this ledger.*

This new text appears to be somewhat scribbled with smudged spots in places where his hand rubbed the ink. Some portions of the writing are too blurry to read, especially near the end.

> *There is nothing new...in this world. It is tiresome, and I am bored. I am out of ideas for the first time in my life. I want some excitement...adventure.*
>
> *I want to give the people some entertainment. I want to give the people something...different, something exciting, something more than...something more than what those bastards on the hill can provide us, something more than safety.*
>
> *What are these powers good for if not to give us some reason to live?...Where can I find new ideas?*
>
> *Even if I find new ideas, they are restricted...the Enclave. Blocking is easy enough for one person to keep these ideas from The Enclave, but as soon as you add a few more into the fold,*

which is necessary to actually...somebody screws up, and the
Enclave sooner or later discovers what is happening...

"Where's DerMööve?" calls the Arcane Sawyer, as he grips the couch.

"Why?" 4SKōR calls back, glancing into the room. "What the hell are you doing?"

Intrigued, Ifton and Mario lurch forward, immediately regretting the impulse. Ifton tries to focus on the Arcane Sawyer and block all else, while Mario drops his eyes to the ground in front of him, clutching to the ledger under his arm.

The hovering hero rises, trying not to disturb the decapitated body of the Realizer. But the couch legs stick to the coagulated blood on the carpet. He tugs, making a sick, wet, slapping sound as they break free. The three spectators shutter.

"I have made a discovery," the Arcane Sawyer says. "I need him to retrieve it with his powers of telekinesis, so we do not disturb the crime scene."

"You're picking up the fucking couch he's on," 4SKōR retorts. "I'm pretty sure that counts as a fucking disturbance." She nods to Mario. "Hey, Citizen. Picking up the couch that the victim is on would constitute a contamination of the crime scene, right?"

"I mean, if he's careful, he might be..."

"See," she interrupts him, not even listening to Mario. "You're making a mess of everything. So, what does it matter?"

"Then you come here and pick it up," the Arcane Sawyer demands.

4SKōR laughs him off and then nudges Ifton. "You can go get it."

Ifton shakes his head, covering his mouth.

"Son of a bitch," 4SKōR says, turning to Mario. "Can you tell DerMööve that the acting president of the Swiftglides requests his presence?"

Mario agrees and dashes down the hall toward the stairwell.

"Hey, fuckface!" he yells at DerMööve. He laughs when DerMööve acknowledges him. "Your new president wants you."

DerMööve's face contorts in confusion.

"Vat are you speaking?"

"The Arcane Sawyer is now the acting president of the Swiftglides," says Mario. "He needs your help upstairs."

"Oh," says DerMööve, as he ascends the stairs "Make more sense next time."

He telekinetically shoves Mario to the side as he passes. Mario glowers, but DerMööve continues up the stairs, paying him no mind.

You're lucky I don't have any powers, thinks Mario. *I would have ended you long ago*. Mario follows him up the stairs and to the room but keeps himself a few lengths behind.

"Vat ist happening?" asks DerMööve upon reaching the hallway.

"Prez needs you to flick a finger to retrieve something he found," 4SKōR explains. "He doesn't want to do any MORE contamination to the crime scene THAN HE ALREADY HAS!"

"Dis is all?" DerMööve asks, moseying up to the door. He puts his hand on Ifton's head. "Und du? You sick, mein freund?"

Ifton nods. DerMööve shrugs, points a finger at the object under the couch, and flicks. The object rises into the air and flies into DerMööve's hand. Simultaneously, the Arcane Sawyer lowers the couch into its blood-puddled place before hovering out of the room.

It's a comic book, thinks Mario, peeking at the object in DerMööve's hand. *Trivial?*

He flips through the ledger and finds the page from a year ago when the handwriting abruptly changed.

What a NEW world! I spent my first day catching up on as much HISTORY and MYSTERY that I could. The last thing I remember is playing that SILLY game, but now I'm in an alternate universe, perverse in its definition of reality. SUPERPOWERS are mundane here, an ordinary part of the quotidian... un-EXTRAordinary at all, but not for TRIVIAL.

I, of little superpower, can find my way here with my extensive BRAIN POWER and UBER-GENIUS IQ!

Mario cranes his neck to glimpse the cover again. At the top is TRIVIAL #8, and at the bottom is TRIVIAL GETS QUIZZED... FOR CASH?!? A face on the cover shows a skinny man from the shoulders up, wearing a pin-striped suit drawn to be in his early to mid-30s. In one of his eyes, the pupil is a dollar sign, and in the other, the pupil is a question mark.

"It's just a comic book," says 4SKōR, snatching it from DerMööve's hand.

Plucking the comic from 4SKōR, the Arcane Sawyer says, "I was just a comic book."

With haste, the Arcane Sawyer hovers down the stairwell, carrying the Trivial comic. The others follow behind. 4SKōR presses closest to him, trying to reach the comic.

"I had it first, Paul Bunyan!" she squeals, almost grasping it.

"Correction," DerMööve interjected. "You took it from me."

"Well, if I didn't tell you to get it for him, then it would have been me, so."

Ifton wipes vomit from his suit, saying, "You kids are giving me a headache."

Velacruz scurries toward her descending teammates and asks, "So? Did you find anything useful?"

"I found a clue!" says the Arcane Sawyer, raising the comic book into the air with both hands like a trophy. 4SKōR jumps to grab it from him, but he senses her and lifts higher from the ground. She flies forward into Velacruz, who catches her in her arms.

"Thanks," 4SKōR says, worming out of her arms.

"No need to rush it, sweetie," Velacruz says with a wink.

4SKōR pushes herself away, wondering, *What was that?*

"Don't overthink it," Velacruz says, slapping her on the right butt cheek. "Let's go."

Ifton and DerMööve giggle to one another in delighted befuddlement. The Arcane Sawyer beams with pride, unaware of anything else happening around him. Mario follows them all.

"So, let me see this clue," says Velacruz, approaching the Arcane Sawyer. He hands her the comic.

"Come on!" shrieks 4SKōR. "You hand it over like it's nothing? I've been trying to get it back for ages."

"You didn't say please," he says with an over-wide smile.

"Neither did she," 4SKōR points out.

"I don't have to," Velacruz clarifies. "I have seniority. I'm the Swiftglides Secretary." She strolls to a booth to sit down and inspect the comic book. "And you're the newb!"

The other Swiftglides chuckle, nodding and shrugging. 4SKōR stomps her feet and stands off to the side, sulking with her arms folded in defiance.

Velacruz carelessly opens the book, flipping through the pages. Then, she holds it up like it's a dinner menu that she's finished perusing and wants the waitstaff to take it away. "What's so special about this comic book?"

"There was a man in my universe not unlike this Trivial," the Arcane Sawyer says, hovering forward. "He was a genius. He knew everything."

"So?" says DerMööve.

"So, if he was realized..." The Arcane Sawyer lets his words drop away, begging a response.

Ifton steps forward, still trying to clean the vomit from his suit. "That's a big if, big guy!"

"Yes," agrees the Arcane Sawyer. "But it is more than nothing."

"In your world, did you ever solve crimes?" Mario asks from behind. They turn toward him like they forgot he was there. Mario is not surprised. "You were a hero, right? Did you solve crimes?"

"No," the Arcane Sawyer answered, pounding his fist on his chest. "I stopped crimes from happening!"

"So, you really have no experience at any of this? You have no idea what you're doing, do you? You're simply making this up as you go along."

"Shut up, Citizen!" The Arcane Sawyer exclaims, but with much less boldness than he had before.

Mario marches to the booth, stretching out his hand. "May I?"

Velacruz assesses each of the Swiftglides within her view. None seem to object, as they all gaze at Mario in utter bewilderment. She hands him the comic book.

Mario flips through the pages as The Swiftglides watch, impatiently shifting around.

"Come on," Velacruz mutters under her breath but loud enough so they all can hear.

Mario ignores her. He ignores all of them. He reads, trying to gain an understanding of what kind of person Trivial is.

After several minutes, Mario finally says, "He doesn't LOOK familiar."

The Arcane Sawyer rips the comic book from Mario's hands. "Hey, I was reading that," Mario shouts to no avail. "I'm trying to identify—"

"What do you know, Citizen?" shouts the Arcane Sawyer, as he hovers toward the door. "I know he is out there somewhere, and I will not find him standing in a restaurant!"

The bald flyer steps to the side as the Arcane Sawyer flies out the front door. The other Swiftglides barrel out the door after him quick on his heels.

Mario stands unmoving at the door, trying to make sense of the situation. The bald flyer tilts his head, appraising Mario.

The Swiftglides race toward a red van with a white stripe down the side and SWIFTGLIDES written across it. Ifton makes wild gesticulations with his right hand, and the door swings open as the engine turns over with a roar. He hops into the driver's seat, while Velacruz slides in the passenger side, and DerMööve jumps into the back with 4SKōR following closely behind.

"Turn on the Navigator and locate the homing beacon," says Ifton to the van. As he says it, the van responds in kind.

"Follow that lumberjack," 4SKōR says as she jumps into the back behind DerMööve.

"Fucking idiots!" Mario says from the front door of QTs House of Jacks Bar & Grill.

The bald flyer grunts disapproval.

"What? They're fucking clown shoes. All of them."

10

SENSATIONAL SHERYL

"The southside ghetto reeks so foul!" Tanalia exclaims while covering her nose from the unfamiliar stench. She grasps onto her flyer with a one-armed death-grip, as they descend toward Club Haberdashery.

"You'll get used to it," chuckles Jakandy. His eyes glimmer with slight admiration for the old dump, as he glimpses what it once was in the hindsight of his mind's eye. "This is actually one of the better places. At least, it's historical."

An old-style film reel begins to play within Jakandy's thought space, popping and clicking the way they used to. PICTURE START flashes, followed by a giant 8 in the center of four squares encircled by two round ovals, counting down the seconds—7—6—5—4—3—and then a flash of white.

"Welcome to Club Haberdashery," a dapper man in a top hat and tuxedo spoke through the screen. The camera tilted upward to reveal him standing in front of a picturesque old theatre. "Located in the heart of the southside ghetto," the man

continued, strolling up to the theatre's box office. "This dilapidated theatre has become a hot spot for the debauched and delirious Citizens of Fellowship City."

The camera cut to a shot of the current marquee reading: LADIES, GENTLEMEN, AND BOTH | WELCOME TO CLUB HABERDASHERY | NO SHIRT, NO PANTS, NO FUN.

"While this marquee reads like a burlesque show of yesteryear," the dapper man said, standing in front of the box office and waving his hands with grand gesticulations. "Once upon a time, this theatre marquee displayed the names of the greatest touring shows Broadway had to offer."

The screen flickered to black and white, as the theatre rewound itself from its current dilapidated state to its pre-World War III pinnacle of perfection. The marquee's sign flashed with some of the greatest titles from Broadway, including The Music Man, Fiddler on the Roof, Cats, A Chorus Line, Rent, Wicked, The Book of Mormon, Hamilton, Rumspringa, and finishing with Wonderful: An American Musical. The camera returned to the dapper man at the box office.

"Shall we go in?" he asked, tipping his hat and gesturing for the camera to continue through the grand front entrance.

"Before the nuclear summer caused by the third World War that gave rise to the Mighty, people who enjoyed culture went to the theatre to see plays and musicals on stage."

The man's voice continued off-camera, as the screen filled with the overwhelming archway entrance to the theatre where four doors were opened by female door attendants. They wore double-breasted jackets adorned in faux-military regalia over pressed, buttoned shorts with flat-top hats that resembled those belonging to a clapping toy monkey. The women raised a welcoming arm open for the camera to enter.

"*Certainly, there was a proportion of the population who disregarded such experiences, considering them dull and a waste of time. However, according to renowned theatre critic of his day, E. Thomas Daly, 'Those kinds of people lack personality and creativity.'*"

"*Everything good that Broadway had to offer came through this once great theatre. There were costumes of vivid colors, set pieces of grand design, and glamorous people on stage and off.*"

Inside the theatre, the man's voice-over continued, as the camera provided imagery for everything the man presented.

"*The theatre itself was glorious in its impressive stature and Art Deco design throughout. At every turn, a patron of the arts could find themselves face to face with vibrant shapes, zigzagging here and there, bursting like stars, or just displaying simple forms. The geometric shapes and patterns colored gold, silver, and bronze filled the lobby and grand stairwells. Statues of ancient-looking figures of some exotic origin perched upon pedestals and fastened to walls, peered down upon the theatregoers with apparent pleasure. Massive stylistic chandeliers hung at each stairwell, casting vibrant colors of ambient blue tones, while an even larger one hung in the main auditorium above the best seats in the house.*"

Images of tremendous crowds of people attending past performances plastered the screen. People dressed to the nines were drinking champagne and laughing as they engaged in cultured conversations.

"*People would come from all around to admire the majesty of this theatre,*" *the voice-over continued, and the images of the screen changed to follow the man's presentation.* "*There were tours on its architecture and artistry between shows, always well attended. People would host black-tie and white-tie events, enjoying the scenery and basking in the nostalgia of the Art Deco era.*"

The screen flashed to white once more, going blurry, as the image of the solitary man in the tuxedo and top hat slowly came into focus. His head lowered and his shoulders slumped.

"No one comes to admire the theatre any longer," *his melancholy voice spoke in a near whisper.* "No one takes tours. No one wears formal suits and gowns, except for the performer upon this stage for some rare occasion."

The stage flashed onto the screen in a still image, showing a man in an old, torn tuxedo and a top hat performing while a horde of ornery onlookers crowded around the stage. As his voice-over continued, still images of the current state of the theatre flashed onto the screen.

"The building is no longer beautiful, instead being decrepit and nearly condemned. The chandeliers and statues are long gone, as well as the gold, bronze, and silver colors. The geometric patterns muddy themselves into one another with the blackened pockmarks of ruin. There are no vibrant lights or colors at all. No defining barrier exists between the lobby and the orchestra any longer, as the walls and doors have been torn away. Many of the chairs have long been removed, forcing audience members to stand for performances on the main stage, which itself has been built further into the orchestra seats where the rich people once sat. The stairwells leading to the Mezzanine are crumbled, dilapidated heaps of carpet and beams. Club Haberdashery is a dark, dank place where a one-time glory is reminiscent but nonexistent."

The man returned as the primary focus of the screen with a headshot. It clipped the top hat at the top and the bow tie at the bottom.

"The sole surviving feature from that 'once upon a time' era are the posters from the very last Broadway show performed on its stage, still hanging in the lobby as a constant reminder of what once was."

As the man spoke, the camera pulled out slowly, revealing him standing in the lobby next to a poster hanging on the wall. The camera panned over and zoomed into the poster, making it fit the screen. It is large and black with red and white writing. 'Wonderful' is the largest word, written in red with a white glow, resembling a bright neon sign. Underneath that is a smaller phrase written in white, 'An American Musical.' Followed by a smaller white phrase, 'featuring the Music of.' Then, large red letters below that spell, 'Everclear.'

At the bottom of the poster are five stars quoted in a vibrant white with a red quote in a smaller font than the stars below it: 'Full of 90's Nostalgia! Heartfelt fun!' The final quote at the bottom, written in white and the same size as the previous quote, reads, 'More than a jukebox musical; the compelling story inspired by the lyrics of Art Alexakis is a must-see for any generation!'

"Jakandy, my old friend," a dapper man in a top hat and tuxedo greets the monks and flyers at the front of the theatre. He stands behind a lectern, guarding the entrance with discolored puce ropes hanging from several cobbled together stanchions.

"You should have told me you were coming. I would have made sure we were prepared for such honorable guests."

"*Old friend?*" thinks Tanalia.

Jakandy shrugs.

"How are you, Taj?" he asks, reaching an arm forward to grip the man's forearm.

"I'm good. I'm good," Taj responds in kind before paying attention to the others. He tips his hat, saying, "Welcome guests. Any friend of Jakandy is a friend of mine. Come inside."

He unclasps the rope from the stanchion and beckons them enter. Tanalia bows her head to offer thanks and catches sight of something odd swaying behind Taj. She double-takes to discover a tail wagging behind him, flicking his tuxedo tails.

"*He's a hybrid?*" she says through telepathy.

Jakandy gives her a slight nod.

"*I didn't realize there were Mighty down here,*" she thinks, scanning the area for other possible Mighty among the Citizens.

"*Not many,*" Jakandy responds in thought. "*Sometimes certain Mighty are accepted among the Citizens; especially those hybrids who are a little more than animal but a little less than man, like Taj. They're not as threatening as the truly animalistic ones or those who could pass as, well, monks. Citizens do not trust US at all.*"

"Move aside, Citizen," commands the female flyer, as she shoves a sizeable man into a cracked glass case, still displaying a vandalized *Wonderful* poster inside the front entrance of the club.

"*I wonder why,*" Tanalia retorts, spying the frightened Citizens scurrying inside.

Jakandy smirks at her voice-thought, keeping an eye on the man freeing himself from the poster case. With the Citizen out of the way, the defaced poster becomes visible. *Welcome to Wonderland* is spray-painted in red over the *Wonderful* and *Club Haberdashery* over the quotes below. He shakes his head as if witnessing some priceless work of art similarly damaged.

A Citizen steps outside to check out the commotion. Before he can even say a word, the Female flyer sweeps him aside and presses him into the wall. Motionless and slack-jawed, his eyes follow the monks crossing his path.

As the dark-haired flyer steps inside, the Citizen starts to say, "Well, excuse me—" but stops when the flyer halts and raises a warning fist. His index finger pops up, wagging back and forth before he continues inside.

Scattered light rays from the morning sun penetrate ancient holes throughout the building, creating an eerie juxtaposition of light and dark within the club. Hard-to-see Citizens linger in the shadows, desperately hiding from the light like vampires at dawn. The combined odor of sweat, urine, and vomit stings Tanalia's nostrils, causing her to choke back phlegm and let loose a hoarse cough.

"*There are so many,*" Tanalia thinks. "*I wouldn't expect so many this early in the morning.*"

"*Club Haberdashery never closes,*" Jakandy responds. "*This is where the unemployable, nonthreatening Citizens end up. The diseased, drunken, delirious, and wasted all gathered into one place and held captive by their own entertainment. It's easier to let them wither and die in this cesspool than to deal with them out there.*"

"Move it!" the Female flyer's voice rings out, breaking the monks' connection. She stretches her arms out, corralling a group of Citizens as the rearguard flyer flanks them on the other side.

"Behind me," he gestures to the monks, maintaining a wide berth for his charges.

They shuffle into place, gaining an unobstructed view of the main stage area. Above the stage hangs a giant banner fashioned like a vaudevillian artifact from the late Victorian era with SENSATIONAL SHERYL scrawled upon it in overembellished calligraphy. Citizens surround the stage in various states of repose. Some lean, others sit, but most are simply lounging around, and all of them are drinking, eating, or ingesting something or another.

At the center of the stage, a very tall woman wearing a tight ball gown points to an audience member standing on a table. With a raspy, almost masculine voice, she exclaims in accented English, "She may be your wife, but she's still your sister!"

The crowd laughs at the punchline, as Jakandy and Tanalia share bewildered glances.

"*What is that accent?*" Tanalia asks telepathically. "*It sounds familiar.*"

"*I think it's what used to be called British.*"

"Hey baby, why don't you come over here and let me make you laugh?!?" shouts an obnoxious drunken man leaning against a pillar in the center of the room.

Tanalia eyes him with disgust, thinking, "*Is this how they behave?*"

Jakandy smirks at her discomfort. "*You haven't spent much time with Citizens. It shows.*"

"*No one is paying attention to us,*" Tanalia notes. "*They are all drunk... or delirious.*"

"*Very likely,*" Jakandy responds, stepping closer to the main stage.

"How can this much fun be legal?" asks the performer to the audience, encouraging their cheers. She lifts the front of her gown, flashing her very long legs.

Catcalls ensue.

"*They're shaved,*" Jakandy thinks, tilting his head to examine her legs. "*But they look very masculine.*" His eyes trace her form, reaching her bosom. "*Ample?*"

"*Adequate.*"

"*Hidden,*" he thinks, noticing the high neck of the gown, covering her cleavage. A pink cameo pendant dangles from a lace choker just above her neckline.

"Well, sir. You look like you could be a Mighty," she says, pointing to a man in the audience.

The man steps forward, puffing out his chest and walking toward the stage with a swagger. "Hey, honey, I'll be—"

"Oh, you didn't let me finish, sweetums," she says, raising a finger to her cheek before pointing it to her bottom cheek. "You look like you could be a Mighty pain in my arse!"

As she guffaws over her own joke, the pink cameo bobs up and down on her neck.

"*She's a man.*"

"*Is that our detective?*" Tanalia asks Jakandy in thought.

"*Yes. I think it is.*"

As the monks maneuver closer to the main stage, their guards continue to push Citizens out of the way, drawing disdain and unwanted attention. The unfiltered thoughts of the now aware audience bombard their minds all at once.

Fuckin' monks! What the fuck are THEY doing here? Normals only! Get out, you Zealots!

"*It's not only distrust, Jakandy. They have so much hate for us,*" Tanalia thinks, as she takes a now-vacated seat near the stage. "*I sense their hatred. It feels dank and viscous upon my being, and it smells of rancid fruit.*"

"*Ignore it,*" Jakandy's voice-thought penetrates the psychic humidity of their hatred. "*Feelings are not actions. Focus on real threats.*"

"*I know you can hear this, you Abnormal freaks!*" thinks another of the random Citizens near them. "*Die fuckers!*"

"Excuse me?!?" Sheryl interrupts the audience, which is no longer paying her the attention she believes she deserves. "The show's up here," she says in a singsong voice, as she glides to the front of the stage.

The audience returns their collective gaze to Sheryl and laughs. Jakandy narrows his eyes. From their new perspective, the caked-on make-up, hiding her manhood and age is obvious. Cracks in the foundation reveal wrinkles around her eyes and mouth. "*She... he...*" thinks Jakandy. "*Is around 40 years old, I would bet.*"

"*Do you notice that?*" Tanalia thinks back, relieved by the sudden cessation of the assault upon her psyche. "*She's perceptive.*"

At the very moment Tanalia sends her voice-thought to Jakandy, Sheryl shimmies in the direction of the two monks. "The FATES tell me something," she announces. "YOU are here for ME! There's been a CRIME that YOU did not foresee!"

Jakandy and Tanalia's eyes widen.

"Meet me in my dressing room," she motions with a thumb over her shoulder, indicating a doorway covered by a drape and guarded by a rather bulky Citizen wearing a suit and tie. "I'll be there momentarily. My time is almost at its end."

"Aaaaahhhh," a collective groan reverberates among the captivated audience.

The monks stand. The flyers start to lead the way.

"Just you two," Sheryl says. "They can stay here and enjoy the show."

With warranted concern, the flyers seek approval for their temporary dismissal from the monks.

"Stand by," Tanalia says, bowing her head. "We will call on you if you are needed."

Upon the stage, Sheryl continues her performance. The flyers take the monks' seats and attempt to enjoy the show. Jakandy and Tanalia exit through the backdoor.

"Take them to the queen's dressing room," the guard says

to a stagehand in a monotone growl, leaving uncertainty as to whether his use of queen was derogatory or honorific.

The stagehand ushers the monks through a maze of clutter and old costumes through the backstage area to a door with a big silver star taped to it. Sheryl is scrawled upon it in black ink with the same style of embellished calligraphy they saw upon the banner.

Jakandy opens the door for Tanalia to enter. She surveils the room, while Jakandy finds the most comfortable place to sit.

"Take a seat," he says, gesturing to a Victorian-styled chaise lounge with ornate woodwork and an intricate floral pattern.

Tanalia takes a seat, patting the fabric.

"This is fine," she appraises.

"Our detective likes the finer things, it seems," replies Jakandy, observing the other interesting antiques collected in Sheryl's stage room.

A vintage mantel pendulum clock tick-tocks atop an ionic column pedestal. "9:09," notes Jakandy, as his eyes linger on a violin case standing to the side of an apothecary cabinet. He strides to it and opens it. "I think that is a Stradivarius. Or at least an excellent counterfeit." He places his hand upon the violin and a wave of its lifetime washes over him. "It is a Stradivarius."

"Who is this detective?" asks Tanalia.

Unexpectedly, the door opens and Sheryl storms in like a hurricane, spinning around the two monks and finding her way to her vanity.

"Okay, okay," she says. "Let me fix my face and then we'll begin." She scrutinizes her face in the mirror, fixes her make-up as needed, and then speaks once more to the monks. "So, you're the veteran and she's the rookie, right?" Sheryl asks the reflections of Jakandy and Tanalia. Then, she nods to Jakandy's reflection, "Called you in for MORAL support?"

"I guess you could say that," starts Tanalia. "But, I'm no rook—"

"It doesn't matter," Sheryl interrupts. "What happened is something even a veteran can't deal with."

"How do you know this?" Jakandy queries.

Sheryl spins her chair around to face the two monks. "Because you're here talking to me, aren't you?" She spins back and finishes the last touches on her make-up.

"*I'm having difficulty assessing her*," thinks Tanalia.

"*Likewise*," Jakandy thinks back.

Sheryl opens the right top drawer of her vanity, reaches in, and retrieves an old-fashioned long-stemmed briar pipe called a Churchwarden years ago. She leans back into her chair and lights the pipe. "There's no good tobacco in this shoddy future."

As the monks share a nervous glance, Jakandy bows his head. Tanalia acknowledges, stands from the chaise, and asks, "Do you think you can help us?"

"Of course, I can," Sheryl says, spinning the chair back around to face them. "But that's not the question."

"Then what is the question?" asks Jakandy.

"Do I want to help you?"

"It's not a question of want!" Jakandy demands. "You must help us!"

Sheryl shrugs with a huff and begins to spin back, but Jakandy leaps toward her and grasps her shoulder. He turns her back around and draws her face close to his.

"If you don't help us, we'll end you!"

"End me?" Sheryl protests, playfully slapping his shoulder. "You need me, Mr. Temper-Temper. I am doing perfectly well without you."

"Are you?" Jakandy snaps, waving his arm across the room. "Maybe we should let those grubby mongrels in the audience in on your little secret."

"And what's that? That I'm a man. They already know that, and if they don't, they're too delirious to care."

"No, not that," says Jakandy, stepping toward the apothecary cabinet and picking up the violin case. He opens it and caresses the beautiful instrument. "This is real. It's worth a lot."

"So..."

"So, is everything in here. You my dear, like the luxury. Maybe we should send you to the SIC, where there'll be no luxury—"

"Oh my," interrupts Sheryl. "Mr. Patience's patience is gone isn't it." Sheryl stands up and surveys her room. Then, she steps toward Jakandy, squinting at him. "What's in it for me?"

"You get to keep your life."

"I don't care about that," Sheryl says, turning on her heels and sitting back in her chair. She crosses her arms and legs like a defiant child. "You'll have to do better, Jack."

Jakandy turns to Tanalia, thinking, "*I don't know what to do.*"

"She wants Delirium," Tanalia says, stepping toward them. "Can't you feel it?"

"I can't read her," he says, clasping his hands to his face. "I'm not getting anything."

"It's there, Jakandy," she says, placing her hands on his shoulders and staring into his eyes. "Focus. She's a blocker."

"A blocker? Well, that's good to know." Sheryl beams,

uncrosses her arms and legs, and leans forward, saying, "Now, about that Delirium."

Tanalia shrugs and rolls her eyes at Jakandy.

"I'll be right back," she says, heading out the door.

Jakandy turns to Sheryl, "While we wait, will you—"

"Ahh, Ahh, Ahh," Sheryl singsongs, raising her right index finger before crossing her arms again.

She spins around, facing her reflection once more in the vanity mirror. From the corner of her eye, she regards the grim reflection of the monk's face, boiling over with frustration. She considers each movement or non-movement he makes, as she inspects his robes, paying close attention to any blemishes or inconsistencies in his attire or on his person.

Ideas and possibilities formulate in her brain. She wants so badly to ask him about his cat.

Suddenly, Tanalia bursts through the door.

"Here," she says out of breath, tossing Sheryl a brown bag.

Sheryl snatches it up, opening it up like a present for a child on their birthday.

"And what do we have here," she singsongs. "Oh, looky looky. Now that's the cookie."

"*That was so demeaning,*" Tanalia's voice-thought shoots into Jakandy's mind. "*I never ever want to deal with another Citizen again after this.*"

Sheryl shows the little yellow cookie with a black smiley face to her reflection, cooing, "Hi, Mr. Smiley." She places it on her vanity and grabs a big hairbrush. "Buh-bye, Mr. Smiley."

KARRACK KARRACK

The monks startle, as she smashes the cookie it into little yellow pieces.

"Didn't see that coming?" asks Sheryl with a laugh, tapping her forehead. "Blocker!"

She scoops up some of the little yellow crumbs and places them into a small glass tube with a charred black bottom and a clothespin attached to it. Then, she lights a candle on her vanity and sits the tube into the flame, holding it by the clothespin with her pinky up. The crumbs bubble into a yellow liquid.

"I've never seen this before," Tanalia thinks, as Sheryl rolls up her sleeve and ties a length of cloth around her bicep.

"It's different for everyone," Jakandy replies in thought. *"But the premise is the same. I've seen people smoke it, snort it, and shoot it before. The worst is when they slice."*

"Slice?"

"They cut themselves, making a pouch in their skin, and filling it with the junk."

As Jakandy thinks to Tanalia, she gawks in horror and disgust.

"The process is painful, and the skin never recovers, leaving blotchy spots all over the body. Eventually, those spots will get infected and the person will die. Everyone who takes Delirium dies in the end. Sometimes it's just sooner than later."

Sheryl plucks a syringe from her drawer and plunges its needle into the yellow liquid. She pulls back on the pushrod, sucking the liquid into the barrel with a bubbly slurp. Then, she jams the needle into a vein popping out of her arm and forces the liquid inside.

"That's the ticket," she exclaims, as she yanks the length of cloth free from her arm. She shutters all over as if in throes of an orgasm, rubbing her hands on her face and down her body. She giggles between moans of ecstasy.

"How is a delirious drag queen going to help us?" Tanalia thinks.

"I don't know," Jakandy replies. *"But if she doesn't, I'm going to take every one of her—"*

"I'm on the case!" exclaims Sheryl, snapping up into her seat.

Jakandy and Tanalia glimpse one another in confusion.

"You are?"

"Oh yes. It's elementary, my dear monks!"

Without pause, she erupts into action, zipping by the two monks and charging through her stage room door. They scramble to follow behind her, as she navigates the labyrinthine backstage to the exit.

"Right here is fine," Tanalia says, as they exit the doors of Club Haberdashery into the back alleyway.

She and Jakandy stand still, as Sheryl continues down the alleyway.

"What's happening?" Sheryl asks, halting her frantic pace to study the nonmoving monks

"We're waiting for our rides," Tanalia answers.

The two flyers land with a sonic boom, surprising Sheryl.

"What is this?" she asks, suspicious of the two Mighty taxis.

"Our rides."

"Not on your life!" Sheryl responds, turning away from them and punching a button on a mechanism around her left wrist. Within seconds, a small 2-seater sports car careens around the corner. The car stops on a dime in front of them. "Meet Watson!"

"NICE TO MEET YOU," Watson speaks in an amplified synthetic voice, opening the door for the monks to get in.

Sheryl makes for the driver's side, calling back, "Let's go, cenobites!"

Jakandy peeks in.

"There are only two seats," he points out, trying to find a way into the nonexistent backseat.

"Thank you, Mr. Obvious," Sheryl quips. "I guess you two will have to get a bit comfy. Now get in or I'm leaving without you!"

Jakandy slides into his seat and reaches for Tanalia's hand. She accepts his hand, allowing him to guide her into the car and onto his lap. They cram together as comfortably as possible in the tiny vehicle. As the door clicks closed behind Tanalia, Sheryl rips away from the curb, driving Watson fast down the empty street.

"Brief me," she demands.

Tanalia begins, "A restaurateur called the Realizer has been—"

"The Realizer?" Sheryl interrupts. "He's dead?"

"Yes," answers Jakandy.

She spins a hard left on the wheel, whipping Watson around the corner and forcing Jakandy and Tanalia closer to one another.

"So, what's the bad news?" asks Sheryl, glimpsing the flyers following behind in the left-side mirror.

"His murderer is at large," Tanalia says. "And we have no—"

"Clue what you're doing at all," Sheryl interrupts. "Do you?"

Watson's dashboard is aglow with bright gauges and a map of Fellowship City on the screen. Sheryl jabs a blinking button.

"How did you find me?"

"I sensed your existence from the Realizer's ledger," Jakandy answers.

"Wait!" Sheryl slams on the brakes.

Jakandy and Tanalia fly forward, but Sheryl is fine thanks to her seatbelt.

"He knew I was still alive?"

11

KAAAAAATOOOOOOUUUUM

He doesn't take advantage of my brainpower... I feel like I'm dwindling in a dark age of thoughtlessness. I'm his RESEARCH ASSISTANT?!? Don't get me wrong... I love movies and comics just as much as the next Nerd on the Block, but I need information... I crave it. Something real... not these fantasy worlds. I've already lived that!

Mario sits at the booth continuing to read the ledger.

"I feel you, buddy," he says to no one. "The Mighty don't see us. They don't see that we have worth, value. I wish I could be out there figuring this out, but I'm only a research assistant too, I guess."

I wonder if the monks found the detective yet, he thinks as he stares out the window. *And where the hell did those Swiftglides go?*

At that very moment, a young Citizen points up to the sky at a blotch hovering closer into view.

"Look, Mama. It's a Mighty," she says, tugging on her mother's arm.

"That's nice," her mother says, examining some fruit in a bin.

As a shadow falls onto the fruit, she turns to find an armored flyer with a red cloak flapping behind him hovering overhead.

The Arcane Sawyer assesses the clamor of the many Citizens amassing in the makeshift market built around an old factory. He knows that factory. Rumor has it that a toy called 'My Buddy' was made there once upon a time, but that ship went south when one of them became violent and killed people. At least, that's the rumor.

He drops from the sky into the center of the market, cratering the ground around him and surprising several dozen shoppers. Without pause, he grabs the nearest Citizen and hoists the comic up in front of him.

"Have you seen this man?"

The Citizen shakes his head and scrambles away. The Arcane Sawyer sets sight on the next Citizen, as the Swift-glides van squeals around the corner in the distance.

"His name is Trivial," says the Arcane Sawyer, shoving the comic book cover into the Citizen's face. "Have you seen him?"

"I don't know him," confesses the Citizen. "I'm sorry."

"Useless Citizen," says the Arcane Sawyer, tossing her to the side.

The Swiftglides van screeches to a halt in front of the marketplace. The team exits in a flash, bolting toward the Arcane Sawyer, who is reaching for another Citizen to question.

"Have you seen this man?"

The Citizen shakes his head, frantically searching for an escape.

"Tell me! Where is he?"

He tosses that Citizen away and stalks another.

"Have you—"

AAAAAAAAHHHHHHHHHHHHHH

At the other end of the marketplace, Citizens begin to scream and scatter.

"What the fuck?!?" shrieks 4SKōR, as the mob of screaming Citizens stampede toward them. She and the others stand confused, bracing themselves to stop the oncoming traffic.

"Stop!" "Slow down!" "Wait!" they collectively yell.

The Arcane Sawyer flies up to get a better perspective, while those on the ground stand at the ready.

"Stop, Citizen!" belts Velacruz, grasping onto a scared young man. "What's wrong?"

"Something is coming!" he wails, trying to break free of her grip. "It's coming right this way."

"What? What is it?"

"I don't know!" he answers, finally freeing himself and scurrying away with the other Citizens.

From behind the enclosing mob, a bright light emanates. The Swiftglides on the ground are dumbfounded, as the Arcane Sawyer drops from the sky, ordering, "Holdfast, Swiftglides! The time is nigh!"

As the bright light blooms into a massive cloud of light pulsating toward them, the Arcane Sawyer soars back up in the air, trying to pierce the dense opaque mass.

"What's it look like from up there?" shouts Velacruz.

"I cannot see a thing. It is nothing but a growing mass of dense light. I will attack it!"

Without further warning, the Arcane Sawyer flies head-long into the light cloud with his axe and saw splayed. He screams a war cry as he descends upon the mass of light.

Prompted by his courage, the others rush into the fray. DerMööve lifts objects from the ground and throws them forward. 4SKōR yells her sonic boom into the cloud. Velacruz conjures a tornado in her palm and sends it forward to grow bigger and bigger as it gains momentum. Ifton sends electric impulses into all the electronic and mechanical things around them, including the Swiftglides van parked at the other end of the market.

"ΛAAAAAHHHHHH!!!" they scream, barreling toward the unseen enemy, as Citizens scatter away, seeking safe havens far away from the marketplace.

Sheryl whips Watson around a corner almost crashing into a crowd of Citizens running in her direction. She slams on the brakes, but this time Jakandy and Tanalia are buckled and do not fly forward.

"What are they run—" Sheryl's voice trails off as she eyes the mushroom cloud of light explode in the distance.

KAAAAAATOOOOOOOUUUUM

"What the—" Sheryl and the monks blurt in unison, as her thought fills their minds beyond anything else at the moment.

The shaky reverberations of the explosion bounce Watson around, as the Citizens grope the ground.

"I HAVE DETECTED AN EXPLOSION," Watson's robotic voice spoke.

A big white circle blinked into existence on the digital display map of Fellowship City where the explosion occurred.

The mushroom cloud of light blooms high in the distance, light dissipating as it grows upward into the sky. Mario shakes his head, recovering from being startled by the earth-quaking boom that knocked him sideways in the booth. He peers out the window. The color drains out of him, as he turns away in a daze.

"Oh my God!"

With ledger in hand, Mario bursts out the door of QTs House of Jacks.

"Hey, can you—" he says to no one. "Shit!"

He gapes at the dissipating cloud. Shaking his head back to reality, he estimates where the epicenter of the explosion could be and races down D Street toward 20th Avenue.

Watson tears down the street toward the nearly depleted mushroom cloud with Sheryl's foot pounding the accelerator to the floor.

"Keep an eye on it," she commands.

As Mario rounds 20th, heading toward the Normal slums, he discovers a motorcycle on its side, still idling across the street. He glances around for a driver but does not find a soul. He picks up the bike, searching for someone, anyone to tell him not to.

The streets are extremely empty today. Where is everyone?
He shrugs off the thought and jumps on the bike.
Good, it's an automatic, he thinks, pulling back on the accelerator grip.

BRRRRRROMMMM

The quick start catches him off guard, but he regains composure, going full throttle as he speeds toward the billowing light.

EPISODE II

SOMETHING SINISTER STRIKES

*"Something Sinister Strikes Fellowship City
will be tomorrow's headline in the Chronicle.
You can bet on that."*

12

PRINCESS ZELDA, THE BRAVE

"You peek outside the door," Zelda says from behind the three-panel gaming screen standing up on the table in front of her.

The screen is a graffiti-covered brick wall with S.O.F.A. (with a circle around the A) spray-painted on the center panel. She peers over the wall at each of her four friends sitting around the table. Their character sheets are displayed in front of them with an array of multi-colored, multi-sided dice. They lean forward to the edge of their seats, as she describes the next element of their story-game.

"In the distance are three demonic cheerleaders hovering around a giant rugby monster-jock."

Dorian gasps, asking, "Does he have the blue-flame around him?"

Zelda squints and says, "Give me an awareness check."

Dorian rolls a sparkly purple 20-sided die.

"17! With my caffeine bonus that makes it 21!"

"Excellent! You hide in the shadows, as he searches the room. Then, he turns in your direction, revealing a blue flame emanating from his ghostly white eyes."

"Okay, guys," Dorian says to the others, standing up and slamming her hands on the table. She wears a handcrafted cheerleading outfit made from scrap cloth that does not quite make a matching color scheme. Ribbons of the same colors are braided in her dark brown hair. She measures her companions with her big brown eyes as her bulging bottom lip quivers. "This is the monster we're looking for. I will use my cheer routine to distract the demonic cheerleaders away from him."

"They might still attack you," says Frankie, wearing a pair of glasses with a piece of white tape in the middle. Other than that, he does not wear anything indicative of a costume. "I have plenty of healing balm and bandages in my *Hawkeye Scout* gear. Plus, I can protect you from them with the *Red Flame broadsword* that I picked up after we beat the *zombie Phys. Ed. Coach.*"

"Good idea," she responds with a proud grin before pointing to Rod and Keely.

Rod wears a jacket with an H affixed to it, and Keely wears a black biker jacket, black gloves with the fingers cut out at the knuckles, and a black bandana tying back her auburn hair.

"You two are the muscle," says Dorian. "You're going to attack the rugby-monster once he's alone. What's in your arsenal to take him out?"

"I can blast him with my supersized electrostatic-water gun," says Rod. "That should shock the living shit out of him!"

"I'll follow that up with my melee spinning kick and switchblade blitz," Keely says. "That lets me roll a 10-sided dice twice to determine how many stabs he takes. Plus, my switchblades are still dipped in that ionic poisonous stuff, right? That'll be extra damage."

"Right," confirms Zelda. As the Story-Keeper, it is her job to keep track of these kinds of things. "The effect is in play for three more turns."

"Great, let's begin—" Dorian starts to say, but is cut off when her 13-year-old brother bursts through the door of her room. "What the hell are you doing up?"

"It's morning!" he shouts. "Mom says, you need to send your friends home now. Curfew is over."

Dorian casts a skeptical scowl at her annoyance and turns to open the blinds. The morning sun creeps through the slits. "Dammit. Fine, get out!"

"By the way," her brother says before scurrying away. "You all look ridiculous."

Rod stands up and stretches.

"Well, I guess we'll have to finish this later," he says in a yawn.

"Can we play tonight?" Frankie asks. "I wanna see if we can close the demongate in the gymnasium, so we can move onto the nightmare monster in the boiler room."

"I'm sure I'm free, if everyone else can," Zelda says, packing up her screen, books, and notebooks that prepare her for the task of Story-Keeper.

"Sure, I'm free around 6," Dorian says. "But this time, we need to finish before curfew. I don't think my mom will let you guys stay over again. She's... temperamental."

"No problem," Zelda says, leaving the room. "I'll try to pay better attention to the time."

Rod hurries to catch up to Zelda in the hallway. "So, that was a good Storyline you gave us. I can't wait to find out where it ends."

"Don't try to butter me up, Rod," Zelda says with a smirk. "I'm not giving you any spoilers."

They exit Dorian's camphouse on the southwest corner

of Avaritia Street and Precariat Way. They stand together in awkward silence for a moment, as Rod cranes to the right, and Zelda glances to the left. Finally, he turns to Zelda, saying, "You know, I wasn't going to ask for spoilers. I just wanted to—"

"I've really gotta go," she interrupts. "Mario will be waking up soon, and I don't want him to think I was out all night with some guy."

"Oh," Rod sighs, dropping his head and shuffling his feet.

"Yeah, so let's talk about this later," she says, punching his shoulder. "Okay?"

Before he can answer, she darts up Avaritia toward Precariat.

"Sure," he says to himself, watching her speed away.

It's going to be close, Zelda thinks, glimpsing the rising sun. She wills herself to go faster, as she cuts through the passageway between Camphouses 36 and 30. She barrels through the backdoor of her building and up the stairs, jumping every other row. Nearing number 3014, she retrieves her key from a shoestring around her neck. She opens the door and sets her game stuff down on a table in the front room.

ANNK ANNK ANNK ANNK ANNK

Shit! thinks Zelda startled as Mario's alarm begins to echo through the hallway.

She lurches for the bathroom, trying to hide her noise within the alarm. She locks the door behind her and waits for the return to silence and echoing click. Her sweaty reflection taunts her in the mirror, so she unrolls a handful of toilet paper. She presses it against her forehead, chest, and under her armpits.

A whiff of her odor disgusts her mirror image. She retrieves a small vial of perfume, a birthday gift from her father years ago, and sprays a mist into the air. She steps into it, thinking, *only for important occasions, he said. Making sure Mario doesn't catch me out all night constitutes such an occasion, eh dad?*

She examines the eyes of her reflection.

No dark circles. Good, she thinks, reaching for her bathrobe.

RAT TAT TAT

The hammering on the door surprises her, even though she expected it at any second. She finishes tying her bathrobe and takes a deep breath.

"Zelda! I'm late. I need to get—"

She opens the door, pretending to be rudely interrupted from some important endeavor in the bathroom.

"Please, Zelda. I am so late," her brother says in an almost whine.

She restrains her laughter, pleased about her success of pulling one over on the big guy. As she flashes him a devious smile and curtsies out of his way, a slight tinge of regret eats at her conscience. Though she hates lying to her brother, she hates the idea of him thinking she was out with some boy doing God only knows what all night long even more.

"Thank you, Zelda," he says to her, sidestepping into the bathroom. "I truly appreciate this. I'll pay you back I promise."

With her brother distracted, she zips to her room, rips

off her comforter, and returns the pillows shaped like a sleeping body back to their usual places. Then, she tosses her bathrobe on the bed, strips out of the clothes she had spent all night in, and dresses in a pair of flannel pajamas.

Tying her bathrobe back on, she appraises her room to make sure everything is in its proper place. The empty holes in her bookshelf catch her attention. She races back to the front room, retrieves her game supplies, and places them back onto the shelf in their usual spots. Satisfied that her room is back to normal, she saunters back to the bathroom to wait at the door.

The shower shuts off as she approaches. She practices crossing her arms and stamping her foot impatiently. A small commotion followed by an incomprehensible muttering signal to her that he is almost through. She strikes her pose.

The door opens, and her brother jolts back, alarmed by her unexpected presence.

"You done now?" she says in her practiced posture, trying not to crack a smile.

"It's all yours, princess," he says, waving his hand into the room in an apparent invitation. She nudges him out of the way, slamming the door behind her.

The mirror is still fogged up, except for where her brother wiped.

It almost looks like a heart.

"Love you!" she yells, thankful for keeping her brother in the dark, even though there is genuinely nothing to keep him in the dark about.

"Love you too!" he yells back, as the front door slams shut.

She breathes a sigh of relief and turns the shower on. She soaks for 15 minutes because she can. Then, she takes her sweet time drying off and getting ready. She eats her usual quick breakfast of toast and vegetable preserve while admiring her empty bed.

I should take a nap, she thinks, but her mind becomes consumed by images of Jordy and Brynn. They are the four-year-old twins she volunteers to help with at the Orphan House. She shakes away her impending sleepiness, thinking, *No. Those kids depend on me.*

She glides down the street, light as a feather and without a care in the world. As she passes people on their way to the buses for their 7 and 7:30 am shifts, she greets them with her usual courtesies, and they wave back as they always do.

I'm glad that's not me, she thinks. *I couldn't imagine the responsibility of having to wake up early to be somewhere at a given time.*

She stops in mid-thought, realizing that she is doing exactly what they are, only she is not getting paid for her work.

At least I enjoy what I do.

For Zelda, volunteering at the Orphan House is its own reward. Plus, she can pay things forward, because once upon a time someone volunteered to help her when she was a scared little girl. Of course, she always had Mario, but they were separated at night when she cried herself to sleep or woke up with nightmares. Being someone these children can count on is something Zelda loves to be. In fact, there's nowhere else she would rather work if she could get away with it.

Unfortunately, the only way she can continue to volunteer after she turns 18 is on her days off from another job OR if she becomes a parent. She shutters at the thought. *I could always adopt though*, she thinks. *There are plenty of kids who need homes, and each home can house two children. In a few months, ours won't have any. Maybe I can convince Mario to—*

Up ahead, she spots Mario standing in line. *He's going to be so pissed off*, she thinks, reading his impatience.

He stands in the most clichéd way possible with his arms crossed and stamping one foot.

I've gotta screw with him, she thinks, laughing as she jogs toward him.

The watchtower clock strikes 6:30.

PFFFFFFT

She sticks her tongue out at him, as she prances by, laughing.

"You're so late."

"Some of us don't have the luxury of being able to hang out here all day and play," he says, but she pays him no real mind, spinning around in a little dance.

"Don't be jealous," she sings as she scampers away. "Have fun at work, Mario!"

Keely, Dorian, and Frankie stumble toward the Orphan House, resembling zombies more than anything else. Zelda catches up to them with ease.

"Hey, where's Rod?" she asks when she is within earshot.

"I think he might come later," Frankie answers. "He said he needed a nap."

"We all need a nap after that all-nighter," says Zelda, giving Keely a once-over. "But look at us, we're all here, even if some of us aren't bright and cheery."

"Hey," Keely says after a slight delay.

"Wait," Frankie blurts, his face showing grave concern and provoking everyone to stop and listen. "Do you think if we don't get any sleep today, we won't be able to play tonight? I really wanna play. I need to—"

They shake their heads in almost annoyance and press onward. Always the perceptive one, Zelda senses Frankie's spirits are somewhat shattered. She elbows Dorian in the side and nods toward Frankie. Dorian shrugs a response and cozies over beside him.

"Come on, gloomy Gus," she says, grabbing Frankie by the arm. "We may play, we may not play. It's not the end of the world. But if we do play, I'm glad you're on my team."

Frankie brightens up, grinning from ear to ear like a love-struck fool.

Zelda tickles Keely from behind.

"You too! Let's get moving. We've got some kids to shine for."

When they reach the Orphan House, they are all much more alert than they had been. Zelda is always good like that, lifting their spirits when down, reinvigorating them. If anyone asked who the leader of their little group was, they would probably all point to the lanky blonde. If not in real life, she certainly was their spiritual leader in the game, as the Story-Keeper.

From the School's Out for Armageddon (S.O.F.A.)
Story-Keeper Multi-Binder:

Saturday School, 1985

Five students, a nerd, a jock, a punk, a criminal, and a popular kid, are serving detention due to their Freshman Friday antics of the day before. Unbeknownst to them, the safest place they could be on that fateful Saturday is their High School Library. As the storms of Armageddon rage in the outside world around them, they alone survive. Each possesses the experience, knowledge, and skills necessary to work as a team for their continued survival when School's Out for Armageddon!

Whereas most role-playing games draw from fantasy and science-fiction for inspiration, School's Out for Armageddon (S.O.F.A.) draws upon the popular high school films made in the USA during the 1980s. Of course, solely deriving a game on the intricacies of high school culture and navigating such hierarchies and strata within that particular realm might be fun initially, it may not provide long term entertainment.

That is why the S.O.F.A. developers created endless possibilities of stories and enemies by invoking Armageddon, the end of the world. With this element, Story-Keepers (SKs) can incorporate an array of monsters already established in other games, as well as new ones that may never have been thought of before. In any given game, you may find dragons, demons, zombies, and possessed people, as well as vampiric hockey players, angelic meter maids, and monstrous toilets. SKs are given carte-blanche freedom to combine and create any kind of thing in this world. Even story settings can be all over the place, as demons might warp reality to place characters into fantasy or sci-fi realms.

With S.O.F.A. the possibilities are endless!

Zelda and her friends love to play SOFA, as they call it. They prefer it to any of the other RPGs that survived through history. Those other games always feature hero characters who are descended from angels, controllers of the elements, flat out magical, or able to tap into some universal force for power. SOFA heroes are devoid of such powers. They are average, ordinary high school kids forced to survive a crazy situation.

Each player's *abilities* derive from their particular *category*, but none of them delve into the extraordinary. Unless of course, the Story-Keeper, AKA Zelda, deems it appropriate to do so. Like the time Dorian drank the fizzy yellow potion they found in the chemistry lab and increased her strength 100-fold for ten turns. Still, the special powers are limited, and that's what they like about the world of SOFA. The people are powerless, but they band together to defeat an enemy with all sorts of powers.

"I'm the motherfucking SOFA king!" Rod yelled once after he defeated a squad of possessed Hall Monitors all by himself because the other three were knocked out by a surprise attack.

Zelda laughs, reminiscing on that moment, as she sits cross-legged on a mat next to the twins inside a hexagonal gated play area. Jordy scrutinizes her, his face squishing in confusion. Zelda curls her lip and shrugs. He throws his hands up in the air, and then he goes back to ramming the toy car into a block. Next to him, Brynn is too engrossed in building the biggest stacking block tower she can to pay any attention to either him or Zelda.

The sound of laughter, cries, tantrums, and yelling fills the giant room jam-packed with small hexagonal gated play areas where volunteers sit with one or two children playing with a handful of toys. Zelda cranes her neck over the two-and-a-half-foot gate, trying to glimpse one of her friends doing the same thing at that exact moment. She catches sight of Frankie, who nods when their eyes meet.

Frankie sits with a five-year-old named Eli. Eli lies on his back, staring upward most of the time. Sometimes he takes a block and bangs himself in the head with it. Frankie usually lets him do it until the shift supervisor comes close, and then he takes the block away. Eli never cries or yells or laughs. He never does anything, and that is perfectly fine with Frankie, except the lack of anything exciting happening bores him to tears. So, he often spends his time scanning the room, trying to find something interesting to focus on.

Zelda notices Dorian standing up and playing with the two children in her hexagonal cage. Zelda shakes her head, scouring the room for a shift supervisor. The supervisors do not like the volunteers to play too much with the children.

You are only there to provide guidance and support, she recalls them saying at the orientation. *You are not to excite them. You must model the best behavior possible.*

Although Zelda dislikes having to sit and observe only, she is a rule follower, unlike Dorian, it seems. Even so, her eyes light up each time Dorian's head pops up and down. Zelda imagines what she might play with Jordy and Brynn if she would only break the rules. Lucky for Dorian, the shift supervisor stands with his back to her on the other side of the room, ogling a boyishly handsome volunteer named Luddy.

He's still so damn handsome, Zelda thinks, trying not to remind herself of how she fell in love with him, at first sight, all those years ago in the Orphan House.

The memory slips through, flooding her mind with painful thoughts escaping from the deep recesses of repression. Her eyes tighten. Her nose wrinkles. She envisions herself as a 10-year-old girl, recently robbed of her parents and forced to live in a new place with so many other people. Luckily, her brother was there. Before her parents were taken, he was kind of a pain, but now he was her guardian angel, watching over her and protecting her. She loved Mario. He became her hero, especially after she met Luddy.

She no longer speaks to Luddy. Not since the incident. Not since being humiliated for professing her love for him. Luddy didn't like her like that, but he was interested in Mario.

The torment of his feigned flattery that lasted mere seconds before he asked about her brother still haunted her. After that, she never wanted to talk to another boy again. But over time, the scars healed, becoming walls to protect herself from such pain again. When boys express interest, which they often do, she acts oblivious or simply ignores them outright. She will never let her heart be trampled on again.

There is not enough room in my heart for any other boys, she thinks, her mind slipping into a protective thought of her guardian angel.

WEEEEEEEEEEEEEE

The sound of children sliding down slides and swinging on swings fills the fresh air outside. Zelda always finds much more enjoyment in the outside play area than inside. Outside, she can push the kids on the swings or catch them coming down the slides. She can teach them to do somersaults and cartwheels, and she can show them how to run up the wall and flip. She loves to be active, and besides, the shift supervisors do not consider these types of interactions play. Rather, the volunteers are providing support—and possibly guidance.

"Again, again," says Brynn, as Zelda catches her at the bottom of the slide.

"Okay," Zelda says, letting her climb back up the ladder.

"Push me, please," calls Jordy from the swing, prompting

Zelda to dash over to the swing and push him before racing back to the slide to catch Brynn.

"Again, please."

How could I even think of saying no to these beautiful little faces, she thinks.

Laughing aloud, she races back to push Jordy before he asks, and then she readies herself to catch Brynn once again.

KAAAAAATOOOOOOUUUUM

The ground shakes as the thunderous clap rips through the air, forcing everyone to cover their ears with their hands. Most of the children in the play area start crying, the rest of them start screaming, and most of the volunteers try frantically to keep them calm. Zelda barely catches Brynn, as she comes tumbling down the slide.

"It'll be okay," she tells her, as she rocks back and forth to keep her calm.

"What was that?" a volunteer shouted, still plugging his ears.

"Push! Push!" yells Jordy, holding his ears.

He might be the only child still playing. Zelda hikes Brynn to her side, and staggers over to push Jordy, but stops, letting Brynn drop to the ground.

"Uppy," Brynn says, but Zelda ignores her, staring dumbfounded into the distance. Brynn follows Zelda's gaze, seeing a voluminous cloud blooming in the sky.

"Watch them," Zelda orders a volunteer, as she hurtles toward the exit of the outdoor play area.

"Where do you think you're going?" the shift supervisor asks, trying to puff his chest and show authority, but Zelda easily lunges past him. He falls back against the gate of the hexagonal play area occupied by Luddy. Luddy smiles at him. He blushes.

Zelda darts through the giant playroom, catching Dorian and Frankie's attention. They each ask another volunteer near them to take their children before chasing after her. Outside the playroom, Keely sits at a table with some older kids, trying to encourage them to return to their schoolwork after the commotion. Zelda zips right past her.

"Hey! Where are you going?"

Seconds later, Dorian and Frankie erupt through the door.

"Which way?" asks Dorian.

Keely points to the direction Zelda fled.

"Thanks," they say in unison and continue after her.

"Stay here," Keely says to a little ginger-haired girl with her hair tied in a bow. "You're the oldest. You're in charge until I return, okay."

As Keely follows her friends out the door, the little girl's redhead bobs up and down and her bright blue eyes gape open with excitement at the thought of being in charge.

Outside of the Orphan House, Zelda finds a better view of the city. The huge plumage of a cloud billows upward between the WPC and the skyline of downtown Fellowship City. Dorian, Frankie, and Keely all catch up to her.

"What is it?" Dorian asks, catching her breath.

Zelda does not answer.

As her friends approach, the ominous sight of the giant mushroom crowd growing larger in the sky stops them in their tracks.

REEEEROOOOO REEEEROOOOO

Alarms ring out, causing Zelda and her friends to shake

out of their shocked blankness. Zelda turns on her heels and sprints toward the bus stop. Dorian, Frankie, and Keely follow right behind.

Zelda screeches to a halt, as several guards rush in front of her. Her friends stop right behind her. The guards charge toward a small riot of Citizens breaking out around Luxuria Street and Citizen Way.

"Mario's in the city," she says, wrenching in pain.

"I'm sure he's okay," Dorian says, "He's—"

"He's all I have," she says, glaring at the mushroom cloud again. "I need to find him!"

"What are you going to do?" asks Frankie, "You can't go over there and demand that they take you into the city."

"I don't know," she says. "I guess I'll figure something out."

"Wait," Keely says, reaching into a pocket inside her jacket. She hands Zelda a slip of paper. "Here. I was saving it for my birthday, but I think you need it more than I need a drink at some stupid club. It's a leave pass."

Zelda wraps her arms around her.

"I'll never forget this, Keely," she says, bolting toward the front gate. "Thank you!"

"Buses are for work only," the sole guard on duty growls, dropping his massive reptilian tail to block her way.

"I have a leave pass!" she yells, displaying the pass as she slows down on approach.

As the guard inspects the pass, Zelda tries to catch her breath. Her heart pounds in her chest. She gulps loudly. He measures her with his slitted eyes.

"All right," he grunts. "Be careful, out there. Something's disrupted the peace."

"That's the point!" Zelda says, scrambling past him and jumping onto the bus. She hustles to a window and sticks her head out, waving goodbye to her friends. "Thanks again, Keely!"

"Suck up," Dorian says, elbowing Keely's side.

"She's probably going to give you a good drop after we take out that Rugby Monster," Frankie says. "Lucky, you had the pass."

"I didn't do it for the game, Frankie."

"Yeah, well...shit," Frankie says, turning to the bus. "She won't be back in time to play tonight, will she?"

"Oh, Frankie," Dorian says, placing her arm around Frankie's shoulder and pulling him toward her bosom.

His eyes light up, as they all shuffle back toward the Orphan House.

Meanwhile, Zelda sits on the left side of the bus, peering out the window at the disappearing mushroom cloud. *You better be okay, Mario.*

"So, where to kid?" asks the driver through the rearview mirror. "You're the only one on the bus. I can take you wherever you want."

"QTs House of Jacks?"

13

AFTERMATH: PART I

"QTs House of Jacks?" the bus driver repeats, studying his passenger in the rearview mirror. "Anywhere but there, sweetie. That area's been on detour for some reason, and now with that explosion, I'm not sure I can get you close enough to that side of town."

Zelda stands up, grabs hold of the rail to steady herself, and maneuvers closer to the front. She plops herself into the seat directly behind the front door.

"Why is it on detour? What happened?"

"Dunno," answers the driver, glancing over his shoulder at her. "The monks shut it down this morning."

"How close can you get me?" she asks, peering out the window.

"That explosion looks like it came from northeast of the ghetto," the bus driver says, pointing to the dissipating mushroom cloud. "I bet I can get you as far west as 21st, but that's as far as I'm willing—"

"Perfect," says Zelda. "Thank you."

The destruction in the northeast region of the Normal slums is devastating with people scattering in every direction. Watson slows upon its approach southwest of ground zero, as a group of Citizens thunders toward the car. Sheryl punches the auto-window button and leans out of the open window.

"What is it?" she asks the passersby. "What happened?"

As Mario approaches the northeast side of the market, a huge mob stampedes in his direction. He screeches the bike to a halt.

Oh shit, he thinks, jaw dropping to the floor.

He raises his arms to protect his face, as the Citizens fly by without touching him.

"Wow," exclaims Zelda, staring out the bus window. "The city is so empty."

"Yeah," the driver says, taking a left onto Cavendish street. "A detour 'round these parts'll do that."

"It's changed so much since the last time I was here," she says, seeing the bus driver nod in the rearview. "When I was a kid, I wanted to live here so bad." She studies the rundown buildings covered with graffiti. Their windows are boarded up or smashed out and piles of trash cover their sidewalks.

"Mario would always tell me..."

"Who's Mario?" the bus driver asks.

"My older brother," she answers. "I'm trying to find him. He's in the city."

Well, we're not in Kansas anymore, thinks Mario, as he examines the destruction. He imagines a house sitting on top of a Mighty wearing striped stockings and shiny silver shoes.

He scans left and right, surprised by the lack of carnage. Based on the size of the mobs of people, he expected a panoply of body parts all scattered about.

At least, not yet, he thinks, throttling the bike to trek further into what once was the Normals street market.

Watson screeches to a halt, no longer able to traverse the difficult terrain. Sheryl bolts from Watson in a burst of energy, flinging her arms to and fro. Tanalia and Jakandy crawl out of the passenger side, exchanging awkward grins before they separate to survey the destruction in their own manners. The two sky taxis descend behind them.

"I've never seen anything like this, sirs," the female taxi says in a belabored tone.

"No one has," Jakandy assures her. "What does it look like from up there?"

"It's a bloody mess," answers the dark-haired one. "There are body parts scattered all across this area." He points to an arm near them. The arm is still clothed in a yellow sleeve. "I can't be sure, but I think they belong to the Swiftglides. Isn't that one of their silly outfits?"

"Why were the Swiftglides here?" questions Tanalia.

"They likely believed the murderer was here, and so they came to confront said murderer," Sheryl explains. "It's very simple. They were a squad with superpowers and believed together they were invincible against any foe. Even if that foe has already killed one of their own. He was their president, right?"

"Right," answers Tanalia. "But now we have another murder. A mass murder of Mighty that we didn't foresee."

"The murderer must also be a blocker," Sheryl thinks aloud. "Hmmm. How interesting."

As the bus slows to a stop at 22nd Avenue and Cavendish Street, Zelda eyes the street signs, trying to orient her position.

"Be careful, kid," the driver says, as she exits. "You never know who's out there."

The bus departs, leaving Zelda stranded on the abandoned street. Many of the dilapidated buildings on the south side of Cavendish from 20th to 22nd Streets are overgrown with foliage, housing only those who want to be hidden.

Zelda jogs up 22nd toward Dalton Street, pretending not to notice the shadowy figures, standing in the alleyway she passes. She steadies herself, eyes straightforward, as she reaches for the key around her neck. She yanks it down and tucks it between her forefinger and middle finger, so it sticks out a bit and can be used as a weapon.

When I was a kid, Mario always protected me, she thinks, as she continues quickly down 22nd, crossing Dalton and the buzz of people on the opposite corner. In her peripheral vision, one of the shadowy figures follows her. She sprints down the street, thinking, *I was the princess and Mario was my knight in shining armor. Like in my Dad's bedtime stories.*

She makes a right onto Einstein and a left up 21st, and then another right onto Faraday. She bounds across 20th and makes a left up 19th, leaving the shadow lost behind. On the left side of the street are Normal buildings, mostly rundown, but they appear to be kept up as well as possible, unlike those dilapidated heaps south of Cavendish. She spies a couple of buildings that have odd-looking pipes and tubes jutting out and connecting them to one another.

Those remind me of PipeTown, she thinks. *Where I would be Ms. Shrum, always getting kidnapped by some villain, and Mario would be—*

Fucking insane! Mario thinks, as he stomps down the bike's kickstand and surveils the destruction all around him. He trudges southbound toward the center of the market, carrying the ledger at his side.

This is terrible. It's like a tornado ripped right through here.

He hunts around for survivors amid the scattered goods and toppled canopies and structures.

Where are all the bodies? This place would have been crowded. There should be blood and guts everywhere.

Mario continues to explore, working through his confusion about the situation. He shoves aside an upturned trinket stand blocking the pathway to uncover a bloody mess of strewn guts and severed limbs. For a second, he is excited to find what he has been searching for.

Wow. There's a lot of blood, he thinks, as his head begins to swim. He wobbles and his face turns green. He covers his mouth, turning away and swallowing hard to gulp down the disturbing putrescence building up inside of him.

"Uuuggghhh," a bloody body stump moans in the distance.

Mario staggers over to it, discovering nothing but a blood-drenched head and torso. Jagged bones flail around at its shoulders, dripping marrow and blood.

How is it still alive?

"Uuuuggghhh, mein... Gott!" the stump moans again. "It hurts."

"DerMööve?" Mario exclaims with surprise.

DerMööve bobbles his head. "Jah! Can you help?"

"Nope!"

"Nein?!? You can nicht leave me like dis," DerMööve begs, coughing up blood. "I vill die."

"Good riddance," Mario says without looking back, continuing his trek toward the south side of the market.

With each step, he accounts for every bloody stump, severed limb, decapitated head, and splayed entrails he encounters littered along his way. *I think they all belong to the Swiftglides*, thinks Mario. *How is that possible? Man, if the monks don't know, then something really is wrong!*

"You don't know?" asks Sheryl. "How can you not know?"

"I didn't feel a damn thing," shrieks Tanalia. "Did you feel anything?

"No," Jakandy replies. "I don't understand how this is happening."

"Unless we want it to happen to us," the female sky taxi blurts. "Maybe we could speed things up."

Zelda slows down upon approaching the market.

My God, she thinks, gaping at the aftermath of the massacre. She startles as unintelligible voices boom from the market. *Probably monks.*

As she seeks another route, she fiddles with the key in her hand. She spots an alleyway across the street, and as she hustles to it, the key slips back between her fingers. She flees through the alley unscathed and takes a right onto 20th on the other side. Without further hesitation, she dashes across A Street to take the bridge over Fellowship City Park.

"I would be kidnapped, and he would be my hero. Mario will always be my hero," Zelda says to herself through heavy breaths as she shoots across the bridge. "And that is all that—"

Mario stands in heroic form, one leg mounted on a fallen beam as he scours the area to the south. He catches sight of some shifting detritus in the distance and inches toward it. He zigzags through the wreckage, hiding behind various objects in the rubbish along his path.

As he draws closer, the echoes of distant voices become apparent. He follows the voices, growing louder and louder until he reaches a clearing. In the distance, a woman lifts a yellow-sleeved arm toward her face.

She's not going to eat that, is she?

"No," says Sheryl, inspecting the bloodied yellow-sleeved arm. "This is personal. The arm is severed here without any sheering. It's not a uniform cut. It's pulled apart. See the fleshy bits here. They're stretched. The skin lost its elasticity."

"How can you touch it?" Tanalia asks, averting her eyes and turning two shades of green.

"Someone must, deary," Sheryl says, dropping the arm to the ground as she squints at something covered by debris a few feet away. "Whatever is doing this killing is powerful enough to kill these—" She kneels, picks up the object, and finishing her spoken thought, "Mighties."

"It's the Mighty!" the dark-haired flyer corrects.

"Whatever," snips Sheryl, as she stands with the object in hand. "Doesn't matter. Because this thing seems to affect the Mighty—" she raises the undamaged TRIVIAL comic book for all to see. "—and nothing else."

"—matters," mumbles Zelda in a voice that fades away.

Stopping abruptly on the apex of the Fellowship City Park Bridge, she stands, shaking and shaken, gawking at the unlit neon sign for DerMööve's Arcade & Grill. Her brow furrows, nose wrinkles, and lip curls into a thin snarl.

Mom! she thinks, darting toward the restaurant. *It's been seven years! I haven't seen you in seven years!*

All this time, thinks Zelda, springing up the steps to the arcade door. *I'm so close now.*

A sign on the door reads CLOSED. She slams her fists on the door, beating it several times before giving up. *I need to find you!*

She glances around, snags a metal trash bin close by, and charges back toward the door. Then, she stops to assess her surroundings. *No monks?*

"Hey, I'm planning to do something bad!" she yells with her fist thrusting upward. Pleased with the lack of response, she locates a window she can reach and readies herself to slam the trashbin into it as hard as she can. *I WILL FIND YOU!*

Before she can bring the trashbin crashing into the window, something jerks at it from behind her.

A monk?!? she thinks, letting go and lunging toward the ground. She rolls to her back to get a good peek at the hooded figure, standing over her.

"Sorry to startle you," the figure says, returning the trashbin to its proper place.

Zelda appraises the figure from head to toe, realizing he wears a hoodie and jeans, not the traditional garments of a monk. He tugs the hoodie off his head, revealing his handsome, tanned face. Zelda loses herself in the dark pools of his eyes.

"If you want in, I have a key," he says with the whitest smile she has ever seen.

He retrieves a key hanging from a lanyard around his neck.

I have a key too, thinks Zelda, as she fiddles with the key still between her fingers, regaining herself once more. *And, I can stab you with it if you're not careful, Mr. Handsome-face.* But instead of saying that out loud, she asks, "So, why do you have the key?"

"Because I work here," he says, unlocking the door and holding it open for her.

"Makes sense," she says, tucking her key into her hand, not yet ready to return it to the shoestring around her neck.

He locks the door behind them and turns to her. She narrows her eyes, and he can read the suspicion on her face. He embellishes all his movements, making long, slow motions to unzip his hoodie. He removes it, revealing a name tag on his shirt.

"Tyler," she reads aloud. "Games manager."

"Yup," he replies. "And you are?"

She surveys the room, scrutinizing the details while trying to remember. She glimpses the stairs and rushes for them.

"You seem to know where you're going," he says, watching her zip away from him.

"No clue!" she shouts, as she races up the stairs. "I'm looking for an office!"

"Make a right," he says, following behind.

"Thanks!"

Zelda turns down a hallway, spying a door marked OFFICE at the other end.

"I've got a key for that—"

KKRRAASSHH

"—also," he says, face-palming himself and shaking his head.

He bolts the rest of the way, finding Zelda standing at the broken door of the office. She shrugs at him and steps inside.

14

AFTERMATH: PART II

She's not going to eat that, is she? Mario wonders, studying the woman with the severed yellow-sleeved arm.

She tosses it behind her and hobbles further into the rubble. Mario breathes a sigh of relief. The mystery woman shoves aside a wooden box and turns over a collapsed table. Mario inches out of his shadowed hollow, seeking a better view. She strokes her chin and kneels to pick something up.

A book, Mario thinks, spying the flutter of pages behind the debris. He tucks the ledger tight to his side and taps it.

Disembodied voices call to the woman. She stands and shows them the object.

Out of Mario's line of sight, he struggles to decipher their words. He crawls into the open, hoping for a glimpse. Then, the woman turns, and Mario recognizes the familiar comic book. He climbs over toppled crates to find the two monks with their sky taxis. *She must be the detective.*

Scrambling out of the clutter, Mario staggers toward them, shouting, "Hey!"

The motley crew assembled around the woman with the

comic book readies themselves for an attack. Acknowledging Mario as a nonthreat, they relax their stances and go
about their business.

"What happened here?"

"We don't know," answers Jakandy, turning his attention
back to the detective.

Dammit! Something really IS wrong!

"That's an understatement, Citizen," Tanalia interjects.

"C'mon," whines Mario. "I didn't even say it out loud."

Tanalia casts him a dagger-eyed side-glance that makes
him swallow hard. He shrugs, turning his attention to the
detective. He takes a few steps in her direction, but before he
can reach her, Tanalia lurches in front of him.

"What are you even doing here?"

"Same as you I imagine," he says, gliding past her.

She clasps his shoulder, turning him around to face her.

"I really do think your eyes are pretty," he blurts out with
an upturned grin.

Tanalia is unamused. She shakes her head, waving him
by. The dark-haired flyer grunts at him, as he passes. Mario
nods back stiffly, turning his attention to Sheryl.

Jakandy and the female flyer stand off to the side,
blocking Mario's way.

"I may have found something—" Mario says to Jakandy,
hoisting up the ledger.

"Take it to Tanalia, Citizen," Jakandy replies, giving
Mario no attention. "I'm busy."

Mario peeks back at Tanalia. She shows zero interest. He
returns his gaze to Sheryl, who notices the new addition to
their entourage. She winks at him. He blushes and turns
away.

"I need to commune with the Enclave," Jakandy says,
turning to the female flyer.

"What should I do?" inquires Tanalia.

"Find a reason for this," Jakandy says gesturing to the destruction, as he mounts the back of his sky taxi. "There's got to be something here. Something we can work with. When you find it, let me know."

"You heard him," Tanalia said, turning to the dark-haired flyer. "Go find something useful."

"You've got something you want to tell me, don't you?" Sheryl asks Mario.

Mario turns back to her and starts to speak, but she cuts him off.

"You've found something in that ledger."

Her eyes drift from the ledger to his shirt and then to his face, assessing every crease and blemish.

"You worked for the Realizer at QTs House of Jacks. Until recently, you just washed dishes, but now, well until this morning, you had a better job in the restaurant."

Mario cocks his head to the side, uncertain if he should speak or let her continue speaking for him.

"How'd you know that?"

"Oh, it's what I do," she says with a chuckle. Then, her face darkens, as she continues. "You were the last one to see the Realizer alive. They brought you in this morning expecting you to be the murderer, but of course, you weren't. And they still have no clue what's going on...you think you can help them."

Mario is speechless as Tanalia approaches from behind, overhearing the whole conversation.

"What did you find?" Tanalia asks, breaking the uncomfortable silence.

"There's a connection in the ledger with a comic book the Swiftglides found in—"

"It's trivial," Sheryl interrupts.

"No, I don't think so," Mario asserts. "I've been looking carefully at the ledger and there's—"

"TRIVIAL!" Sheryl says, lifting the comic book.

"Oh, yeah," Mario regains his composure. "They found that comic book in the Realizer's room."

"May I see the ledger?" Sheryl asks, but it is more like a command.

As Mario hands it over, she seizes it and turns away, flipping through the pages.

Meanwhile, Jakandy sits cross-legged, meditating at the top of the factory. The female flyer hovers in the sky about twenty feet away, guarding over her charge.

"*Members of the Enclave,*" his voice-thought reverberates from his meditative perch facing north toward the Monastery of Sol and Luna. "*I beseech your guidance in a dire matter.*"

A bright light erupts in the mind of the monk, taking over all other thoughts, becoming the one thought, the only thought. This was as close to omnivolence as Jakandy ever got, merging his mind with that of the Enclave.

Within the whiteness of the light, a dark form develops as a singular unshaped mass, slowly separating into various figures, until five white and gray-haired men and women in hooded, violet robes sit in meditative poses around Jakandy. They seem to float around him, and try as he might, he cannot envision them all at once.

"There have been criminal actions that I have had no foresight concerning," he began his debriefing. "Upon investigation, I lack hindsight and nearsight as well."

"Speak to the point," says a gruff-looking elder with a grayish-white beard covering light-brown, leathery skin.

"The Realizer was murdered," Jakandy replies. "We believe it occurred sometime after midnight."

"What??" shrieks a pale elder with long white hair draped on both sides of her hood. "That cannot be. It is impossible. You must be mistaken."

"I wish it were so, Madam Elder," Jakandy says reverently. "The Realizer is dead. I have seen it with my own eyes. His head and entrails were removed from his body."

"How did you discover the Realizer's death, if we felt nothing at all?" the Enclave collectively asks Jakandy.

"My protégé, Tanalia, was his monastery liaison," Jakandy answers. "She had a meeting with him and Ifton Upton III to go over their interests in the upcoming Sol and Luna Day celebrations. When the Realizer did not show, she attempted to focus on his location using nearsight, but could not find him. She took it upon herself to investigate his home and found his body. She called me in for support."

"Tanalia only recently advanced from communitor to monk," added an attractive elder with silvery locks, accentuating her olive complexion. "She is not yet able to commune directly with the Enclave. Her decisions are understandable."

"While this is an unfortunate matter," a younger-looking, dark-skinned, and gray-haired elder interjects. "We must discover why we were unable to sense anything. While some individuals are adept at blocking—"

"My apologies for interrupting, Madam Elder," Jakandy says with a bow. "But I have not gotten to the worst of it."

"How can this not be the worst of it?" she asks unnerved.

"The Realizer belonged to a social club called the Swiftglides," Jakandy begins.

"We are aware of his social club," interrupts an elder

with bushy white eyebrows and mustache, who resembles the stereotype of an ancient Kung Fu master.

"They are also dead."

At the epicenter, Sheryl raises the ledger in one hand and lowers the comic book in the other and vice versa, darting her eyes back and forth to each of them.

She's like a magician about to perform some kind of magic trick, Mario thinks, leaning forward, mesmerized by her ritual.

She closes her eyes, weighing the books against one another, lifting one and then the other back and forth, faster and faster, until she slams the two together.

"BOO!" she yells bug-eyed, thrusting her head toward him.

Startled, Mario jumps back, catching his foot on a box of fruit that sends him tumbling to the ground.

"Oh, I'm sorry," Sheryl says, offering a hand to help Mario up.

"What the hell?" Mario exclaims, knocking her hand away and trying to stand back up with dignity.

"It was supposed to be funny," Sheryl explains, spinning around with both objects pressed together.

"Be serious, please," begs Mario. "This is not a joking matter. Look around. Something bad is happening here, and these super-powered putzes have no earthly clue what's going on. We need you."

"Oh, the pressure." Sheryl stops spinning. "Fine. Give me a minute."

Mario nods, breathing out a long sigh.

Sheryl closes her eyes and opens them a few seconds later.

"Why are you so interested in this? You're not one of these Mighties. What's in it for you?"

"I—" Mario stumbles over his words. "I don't know."

"I'm sure you do," Sheryl coaxes.

"Can we just not worry about this right now?" pleads Mario.

Sheryl kicks the box of fruit, flipping it over and vomiting its contents all over the ground. Mario recovers from his surprise, tracking a red apple roll to a sewer grating along the curb.

Sheryl places the ledger and comic book on the box. She flips through both of them, pausing on the page where Trivial begins to write in the ledger and a page where Trivial answers a question in the game.

"The answer is unmistakably 42," she reads aloud.

Mario waits while she inspects the pages. When it appears that she might be done, he says, "You see. I think he's the same—"

"Quiet," she interrupts. "I'm thinking!"

How rude, thinks Mario, leaving Sheryl to do her thing.

Within the attic of her brain, images of Trivial, the ledger, pieces of the dead Swiftglides, the mushroom cloud of light, the monks, and Mario spin around in a vortex, making a central-focused brightness shine in the distance, like the answer to a question. *The answer is unmistakably 42*, she repeats over and over like a mantra. *There must be some connection.*

She considers everything she investigated in the market, as she climbs up to the highest height and examines each section with new focus.

What am I missing? She asks, scrutinizing each section. *Nothing.*

She scans another area. *What's here that shouldn't be here?*

She appraises another before opening her eyes and exclaiming, "There's no center point!"

Sheryl races toward the factory.

"Where are you going?" Mario asks, chasing after her.

"To see the big picture!" Sheryl howls, leaping toward a fire escape ladder dangling at the side of the building.

Wow, she's tall, thinks Mario as she grapples the ladder, scurries up, and bounds the stairwell. *And fast too!*

Sheryl reaches the top to survey the marketplace. Mario follows, much slower.

When he reaches her, she says, "Do you see it?"

"See what?"

She slips behind Mario and directs his head toward an unobstructed view. Waving her hand across the damaged area, she points out areas of amassed blood and guts and other body parts chaotically strewn about.

"You see," she says. "There's no blast radius! No point of origin! There's no damage to anything but—the Mighty—because it wasn't an explosion."

Mario jerks away, saying, "I saw an explosion!"

"Did you?" she questions.

"If not, what?"

"Now that's the question."

Pacing back and forth in the eye of his mind, Jakandy questions the Enclave, "How can I—"

"Use these Citizens at your disposal, as necessary," interrupts the Enclave, speaking in unison as if they knew his mind before he did. "But be aware that more undetected deaths of Mighty will result in a lockdown of the monastery. It would be best for you to be here before that happens."

"I understand," he says out loud, catching Sheryl's attention from the platform.

"Did you hear that?" Sheryl asks, turning toward the dilapidated tower atop the factory.

She searches for a way up. Finding none, she grasps the side of the building and peers over. The female flyer hovers in the sky not far away.

"The monk is here," she says to Mario.

"Jakandy?"

"Obviously," she says, pointing to Tanalia standing next to her flyer below.

Mario shrugs, as Sheryl yanks him over to the side of the building.

"Go ahead, give a look-see."

"You're right," he says, spotting the sky taxi. "Now what?"

Sheryl nudges him out of the way and cranes her neck around the side.

"Hey, you," she shouts to the female flyer.

"What do you want, Citizen?" she questions, flying closer to Sheryl.

"Tell the monk I have something to show him."

In the detritus below, something catches Tanalia's eye.

What's that? she thinks, stomping toward a flickering light within a pile of debris. Her sky taxi follows, hovering behind. "A little help," she orders, trying to clear away the wreckage.

He grumbles under his breath as he removes a massive chunk to reveal the sleek red paint of the Swiftglides van.

Tanalia ignores him, captivated by the light that continues to sparkle and fade. She reaches out to touch it, and a little static shock of lightning strikes her finger.

"Ouch," she says, licking her wound and sensing her flyer's judgment. "What? It hurt."

He shrugs, more worried about his tip than her pain.

"There's something here," Tanalia says with her hand on the van again, as she pushes her senses outward. "It's like frenzied chaos. It's all over the place." She opens the side door and calls inside. "Is someone in here?"

No one answers. Her sky taxi tilts his head and narrows his eyes.

"I'm getting something," she says, stepping into the van. "It's hard to describe. There's a mental warmth like someone's thoughts or dreams. It's a soft undercurrent."

The flyer shakes his head unable to follow.

"There's something here. I just—"

The van's dashboard lights up.

"That wasn't me."

The radio clicks on, sliding across channels and blaring with static. The clock on the dash blinks 00:00 three times before scrolling through the numbers and inputting the correct time of 10:12.

Tanalia hurdles forward into the driver's seat, placing her hand on the console.

"I'm sensing something familiar," she says to no one.

Her sky taxi stands outside the van, kicking his feet in boredom. Tanalia eyes him and punches the window button on the side panel.

"Retrieve Jakandy," she orders. "I need his help."

The flyer's eyes light up a bit as he launches upward toward the factory.

There's something here. Something I do not understand.

"*Understand what?*" a familiar voice penetrates her mind. She glances around uncertain of its origin.

"Who's there?"

The dashboard flickers again.

"*Ifton Upton the third! Who are you? Your voice is familiar.*"

"Tanalia."

"*Ahh, yes. The monk.*"

The radio flips through several channels of static before landing on 108.

"Reports are coming in about an explosion. Stay tuned to MYT Radio FM 108. We'll keep you informed!"

The radio clicks off.

"*What happened. I can't see anything.*"

I don't believe you can hear anything either, Tanalia thinks.

"*I heard that.*"

I didn't say anything. I believe you've developed your latent telepathy, Ifton.

"*What's happening?*" Ifton's panicked voice fills Tanalia's mind. "*I can't feel my body. I don't understand this. I can't feel anything. What are you saying?*"

"Your body is dead, and frankly, you've possessed your van."

"*What?*" Ifton says with a laugh. "*That can't be true. We are speaking, so I'm obviously—*"

"You're a technopath, right?" interrupts Tanalia.

"*Yes.*"

"Your consciousness survived death by merging with this vehicle," explains Tanalia. "Try to control the vehicle."

The engine turns over and revs up.

"*What was that? What just happened?*"

"You started the van."

"*Hmm, isn't that interesting. Let there be light,*" Ifton says, flipping the headlights on. "*Ah, there it is.*"

"There's what?"

"*I can see,*" Ifton says with a wicked laugh.

Ifton peels away from the curb, forcing Tanalia back into the driver's seat. She scrambles for the seatbelt.

"Take it slow," she pleads, catching the seatbelt and buckling in.

"*No way, Jose!*"

Tanalia braces herself as Ifton whips around a corner, tires squealing.

"Mind your control!"

Ifton slides to a stop leaving a burned rubber trail.

"*Smells good*," he says, turning back around and heading toward the market. "*I think I've got the hang of this!*"

In the distance, Tanalia spies Jakandy and the two flyers standing in the middle of the road, gawking at the van. Mario and Sheryl are a few meters behind, closing in on them fast. The van's back wheels start spinning, but it stays in place. Tanalia grips the steering wheel.

"What are you doing?"

"*I think they want to play chicken*," Ifton squeals with glee, launching toward them with violent velocity.

"Noooo!" Tanalia yells, trying to stomp on the brake, but it does not budge. "Ifton, stop!"

"*I think they'll move.*"

"Stop!" Tanalia yells again. "Please, stop!"

The flyers clamp onto Jakandy, heaving him back as the van screeches to a sudden halt right in front of them. Jakandy eyeballs Tanalia, betraying a sense of terror.

By Sol and Luna, Tanalia!

"I'm so sorry," Tanalia apologizes, exiting the vehicle. "It wasn't me."

She rushes over to Jakandy and the others.

"What was that?" Sheryl asks.

Mario stands motionless and speechless.

"What do you mean, it wasn't you?" Jakandy questions.

BEEEEEP BEEEEEP

The van's horn honks, and a voice-thought enters Jakandy's mind.

"*I'm sorry. It was me.*"

"What? Who?" Jakandy asks, shaking his head in confusion.

Sheryl and Mario shrug at one another as they witness a conversation where no words are spoken.

Sheryl taps the female flyer on the back. She turns, but her annoyance is palpable.

"Would you mind stepping aside?" Sheryl asks with a tight-lipped smile. "I'd like to speak to the boss. Thank you."

"I don't think so," the female flyer says, stiff-arming Sheryl with a palm in her face. "This is—"

Suddenly, the female flyer stops talking. She places a finger to her ear and locks eyes with the dark-haired flyer. Together, they launch into the air, leaving dark gray vapor trails in their wake.

As Mario stares up in shocked amazement, Sheryl hastens to the monks.

"Wait up," calls Mario, sprinting to catch her.

Sheryl observes the hands of the monks laid upon the red Swiftglides van and whispers to Mario, "The religious connotation of this is lost on you, isn't it?" Without waiting for a reply, Sheryl steps toward the monks, asking, "What is going on here?"

"We've found a survivor," answers Tanalia without looking at her.

"A survivor? Where?" Mario asks. "Inside the van?"

"Yes, I think so," Sheryl answers for the monks. "But not in the sense you're thinking. It's the van. It's talking to them."

"What do you mean it's talking? I don't hear anything."

"Only his consciousness survived," answers Jakandy. "It's

melded with the vehicle because he's a technopath. I can communicate with him through his thoughts."

"Technopath?" asks Mario. "You mean, the van is Ifton Upton"

"The third," Tanalia adds. "He wanted me to say it."

"Well, there's some excellent news," Sheryl says. "Can he describe how he was murdered?"

Tanalia blusters in offense, but she asks anyway.

BEEEEEEP BEEEEEEP

"He says he only saw a bright light and felt immense pain."

"Hmmm," Sheryl murmurs, pacing around the van.

"Whatever it was ripped them to pieces," Mario says, making a ripping motion and waving his arm across the marketplace. "There are body parts all over."

"Is this the product of some kind of power?" Sheryl asks herself, continuing to pace and think out loud. "Or some kind of individual? A violent genius?"

"Where are the flyers?" asks Tanalia, scanning the sky.

They all follow her gaze.

"Their vapor trails are gone," Mario says. "I swear they were just there a minute ago."

"Well, I don't sense them any longer," Jakandy says, pressing two fingers to the right side of his head. He thrusts out his left hand in various directions, trying to get a signal on them. "It's like they've vanished in thin air."

"That's what I was afraid of," says Tanalia, heading to the driver's seat. "Get in!"

Jakandy jumps into the passenger seat.

"Are you coming?" he asks Sheryl, who stands unmoving, other than her fingers fluttering on her wrist.

"No thanks, I've got my own ride," Sheryl waves, as Watson rolls toward them.

"Fine. Follow us," commands Tanalia. Ifton peels out, leaving Sheryl and Mario choking on dust.

"I guess I'm going with you," says Mario, as Watson arrives.

"Never assume, my dear Mario," Sheryl winks, stepping into the driver's seat. When Mario does not open the passenger door, she leans over and opens it for him. "Get in."

Even though she sits in the driver's seat, Tanalia is merely a passenger in Ifton's van. She sits back, trying not to interfere with the moving steering wheel and pedals. She turns sideways, directing a thought to Jakandy, "*Do you believe the Enclave will issue a lockdown?*"

"*If we cannot find the cause of this, it is a distinct possibility.*"

"*That will welcome riots.*"

"*I know*," Jakandy thinks.

CLACKETY CLACK CLACK

Zelda rips another drawer open from the filing cabinet and thumbs through the files. As Tyler stands at the doorway, he glimpses the clock ticking away above her with the small hand on the 10 and the long hand between the 3 and 4.

"There's gotta be something in here," says Zelda, as she tosses files on top of the files from the previous drawers piled on the ground.

"What exactly are you looking for?" Tyler asks. "Maybe I can help."

"How can I trust you? You work for that bastard!"

"DerMööve?" he asks, taking a step inside.

"Yes!" exclaims Zelda in a way to indicate his name should never be uttered again. "That son of a bitch!"

Zelda returns to shuffling through the paperwork in the file drawer. Tyler picks up a file from the floor and places it on the desk.

"I bet I hate him as much as you do," he confesses.

"I doubt it," she says without taking her eyes from the file drawer.

He steps toward her, places a hand on her shoulder, and asks, "What did he do to you?"

Zelda turns and loses herself in his warm eyes.

"You first," she says with eyes full of tears and without any of her usual spunk.

Tyler's dark pools quiver with tears.

"I don't even know how to say this," he says in a hush.

He turns away from Zelda and kicks the mass of files. Papers and manila folders go flying.

"Go ahead," Zelda says, this time placing her hand on his shoulder to turn him to face her.

"He's my father—"

"You're a Mighty?!?" Zelda interrupts, recoiling from Tyler. She slams the file drawer shut. "And, here I thought you were a good guy."

As he steps toward her, she prods a finger into his chest.

"You know, it's you guys who are fucking up this world! Not us anymore. There's not enough of us to do anything."

"You done?" Tyler asks, lingering on the finger in his chest. She pulls it away, appearing a bit calmer than before. "Listen, I'm not considered a Mighty."

"What? Why?"

"My mom's a Citizen," Tyler says, turning from Zelda. He takes a seat on the desk and continues, "I'm half Normal. They don't consider half-breeds like me real Mighty. We're forced to serve them just like you—and all the other Normals."

Zelda sits next to him on the desk. "I had no idea," she says, placing her hand on his shoulder. "I'm sorry."

He turns back to face her. She drops her hand from his shoulder, and it grazes his thigh. His eyes dilate and cheeks flush. She turns away and stands up again.

"He has my mother," she says, opening the next file drawer. "I'm trying to find her."

"He has your mother?" Tyler repeats, standing up, grabbing her by the shoulders, and turning her around to face him. "I think I can help," he says, clutching her by the hand. "Come on!"

As Tyler leads Zelda through the office door, she glances down at her hand and forgets that he is dragging her somewhere without having asked her permission first. Instead, she smiles at it and blushes. He guides her down the stairs into the arcade, not letting go until their feet are firmly planted in front of an enormous retro arcade cabinet game called SUPER MUNCHER BATTLE LORDS.

"Wait here," he says, placing both of his hands on her shoulders as he speaks. "I need to make sure it's safe. What's her name?"

"Lizbeth."

"Okay," Tyler says, heaving the video game cabinet away from the wall and revealing a secret doorway behind it. "I'll be right back," he says, stepping into the darkness.

As Zelda watches him disappear within, her arms begin to fold and foot begins to tap.

Inside the long and dark secret passageway, Tyler finds the darkness difficult to navigate. He turns toward the disappearing light, finding no sign of Zelda in sight. He turns back and snaps his fingers. A tiny electrical spark crackles at his fingertips as a light on the wall fizzles to life.

The hallway illuminates with a dull glow, revealing an old hospital corridor with doors stretched along it on either side. As Tyler sneaks down the hall, the lights flicker on as he approaches and fizzle into darkness as he leaves them behind.

15

ANSWERS IN THE DARK

"What the fuck?!?" screams the female sky taxi, as she plummets from hundreds of feet in the air. She crashes into the ground with a sick crackle of bone. Everything goes dark.

A loud thump and snap jerks her back into consciousness.

"I can't feel my legs," the dark-haired male wails in shock a few feet away. He is bent in half, and his legs splay out in unnatural ways. "I can't feel my legs."

As she whips her head around, searching for her partner, a wave of excruciating pain washes over her, radiating from her leg. She wills her arm to move, drawing her hand toward her hip. It creeps past her thigh to discover a bone protruding midway. She retracts her hand, tacky with blood.

"What the fuck?!?"

This doesn't make any sense, she thinks, as the adrenaline of shock wears away. *We're strongs. We are impervious to pain. We're invincible...unbreakable.*

"I can't feel my legs."

How are two strong-flyers lying on the ground bruised,

broken, bleeding? She bolsters herself, trying to focus all of her strength to roll over. She fights back against the pain, reaching for the other. "It's okay," she says, grasping his hand. "We'll be okay."

"No, you won't!" echoes an inhuman snarl from the dark shadow of a nearby alleyway.

"Who's there?" she whimpers, struggling to haul herself and her colleague away from the ominous threat.

His deadweight is too heavy for her. She tries in vain to tow him over, but her strength fades into oblivion.

Please, Sol and Luna, give me strength, she prays, as the footsteps grow louder and louder.

Mustering every little bit left inside of her, she turns away for greater leverage and yanks hard. Her arm flings over in front of her, still clenching the hand of the dark-haired flyer. She gawks at the black-checkered sleeve spewing blood from a gaping hole.

Am I strong again? Did I rip his arm off?

The insufferable throbbing of her broken body answers the question for her. She studies the detached arm, realizing that it is not pulled from the joint, but severed by some sort of blade. Terrified, she glimpses where her colleague lay, finding nothing now but a bloody red puddle.

SPLOOOSH SPLOOOSH

Entrails fall to the ground around her, blood splattering like heavy drops of rain. The dark-haired flyer's head plunges toward her, but she rolls away in the nick of time. It smacks the ground with a dull thud and crack of the skull. Nothing left but a mushy pile of bone and gore.

"Oh my god," she screams in horror, chills shuttering down her spine.

A shadow blocks the light from the sun above her, and she beholds the dark face of terror. A giant bloody blade glints red and sliver in the sunlight.

"Please don't," she begs as the blade comes slicing down. "I'm only a taxi. I have a wife! Kids!"

"So, did I."

SHHHFFFFTTTTT

Mario shuffles a deck of cards.

"Now, pick a card from anywhere in the deck," instructs Sheryl with her hands tight on the steering wheel. Mario follows her directions. "Don't let me see it. Memorize the card and put it back into the deck. Anywhere in the deck."

Mario etches the three of hearts into his eidetic memory before he shoves the card back into the deck.

"Now what?"

"Tell me why you care about these Mighties. Why do you continue this journey to help them?"

"Is this part of the trick?" questions Mario.

"No," Sheryl answers with a wink. "Inquiring minds want to know."

"I don't care about any of them. But the Realizer was good to me. I think I'm still here out of respect for him. I would like to know who or what did this to him."

Sheryl nods, as she turns to face the street. Her hands regrip the steering wheel, making a rubbing sound. Without looking at Mario, she whispers, "I was realized ten years ago."

Ten years ago.

The Realizer sat in his recliner, reading the Collected Works of Sir Arthur Conan Doyle. He pointed his finger at the page and pulled a figure from it, a tall 30-year-old, wearing late 19th-century apparel and smoking a long-stem briar cigar.

"That was exciting," said Sherlock Holmes, with a yawn.

"Welcome to Fellowship City," said the Realizer with a Cheshire cat grin. "There is much for us to discuss."

The Realizer placed his arm around Sherlock and ushered him to the door.

"Knock three times," the Realizer directed.

Confused and astounded, Sherlock accepted the direction.

"Am I being initiated?" Sherlock asked with a wink.

But when the door opened, his jaw dropped, and his eyes turned to saucers. Standing before him was a guard dressed in a 1930s style pin-stripe suit and bowler hat.

"That's a gorilla."

"Right you are, my boy," the Realizer said with a chuckle, patting Sherlock on the back. "This is Quell. He is my personal bodyguard."

"Hello," snorted Quell.

"He will take you to your new home."

'My new home?' he thought.

The Gorilla seized his wrist, dragging him through corridors covered in paintings the likes of which he had never seen before. Sherlock's head swam.

'Is this all a dream or reality? Maybe I'm suffering a fit of withdrawal or some kind of hysteria.'

He patted his pockets, seeking some calming narcotic, but found nothing.

"Where am I?"

"The Realizer's Mansion," Quell groaned, saying nothing more.

They traversed several massive chambers and long hallways before arriving at a colossal set of double doors on the other side of the house, which opened as they approached. Sherlock observed their apparent lack of handles on either side. Inside the room, automatic lights blinked into existence as the door closed behind them.

'What is this magic?' thought Sherlock. 'Some grand achievement of technology?'

He appraised the immense room, beginning with the extravagant damask drapes hung upon the walls.

'Of drab design and color,' he thought.

Between the drapes stood bookshelves filled with books of all shapes, colors, and sizes. In the middle of the room, he found a couch, armchair, coffee table, and side table with a lamp, all adorned in the same drab design and color as the drapes. Opposite the bookshelves, a lavish king-sized bed covered in a puffy comforter with a navy and maroon argyle design clashed with the other furniture in the room. Two doors framed the bed on either side.

'Water closet and wardrobe,' Sherlock deduced.

With his task completed, Quell about-faced and knuckle-walked toward the doors, which re-opened for him as he approached.

"If you need anything," Quell grunted, pointing to a contraption on the wall with several lights and buttons. "Push here and talk."

The doors closed, and Sherlock found himself all alone in the massive room.

'It's easily twice as big as my personal quarters on Baker Street,' he thought, circling around and taking it all in.

To confirm his deduction, he checked the doors behind the bed. They belonged to the largest bathroom he had ever seen and an even larger closet. He peeked behind the damask drapes, finding windows laid with brick. He inspected the brick for any inconsistencies and blemishes. Next, he surveyed the bookshelves, astonished to recognize only a few of the titles. He fetched one from the shelf and began to read.

"Call me Ishmael."

He flipped through the pages, scanning and recalling the story. He read the final line, "It was the devious-cruising Rachel, that in her retracing search after her missing children, only found another orphan. FINIS."

He tossed the book onto the ground beside the bookshelf.

BORBORYGMOS

His stomach echoed in the room, catching him off-guard. He tottered to the contraption with the buttons and light and punched one.

"Hello," he said into a speaker. "I'm famished. May I—"

"Hello," grumbled Quell.

"Yes, hello," Sherlock said before continuing again. "I'm famished. May I—"

"You need to hold the button when you talk," Quell spoke the words in a different voice, much clearer and less animal-like. "I can't hear you."

"Oh," spoke Sherlock, pushing the button down. "My apologies. May I inquire about sustenance? I'm famished."

"You want some food?"

"Yes, please."

"Yeah. I'll bring you something."

Sherlock soon learned he would never be at a shortage for necessities during his captivity. Even so, his head ached, and his stomach growled incessantly from the withdrawal. 'Even 3 and a half percent would do,' he thought, wondering if Quell might procure such a thing in this peculiar future.

He spent the next few weeks alone, other than the momentary visits by Quell to deliver something he desired. Otherwise, he read.

One day, he stumbled upon the Collected Works of Sir Arthur Conan Doyle. He opened the book to his amazement, reading all about himself and the adventures he would've had in his life had he not been realized. When he came upon the story, 'The Adventure of the Final Problem,' he was introduced to someone he had never met, but someone he found all too familiar.

Sherlock discovered that Professor Moriarty was a criminal genius who likely supported and protected many individuals he had already exposed. The vast organization directed by Professor Moriarty wanted Holmes eliminated, so they might be free to continue their criminal enterprise without his interference. The story ended with Moriarty chasing Holmes to Reichenbach Falls, where together they fell to their deaths. Sherlock slammed the book shut and threw it against the wall.

Unbeknownst to Sherlock, the Realizer also pulled Professor Moriarty into existence, holding him in captivity somewhere else in his enormous mansion. At that very moment, Moriarty sat in a very similar room to the one occupied by Sherlock, reading The Collected Works of Sir Arthur Conan Doyle. Unlike Sherlock, Moriarty read beyond 'The Adventure of the Final Problem,' flipping to the next series of short stories entitled, 'The Return of Sherlock Holmes.'

The Realizer had a grand design in play for these two arch-enemies.

"Welcome everyone!" The Realizer spoke into a microphone while gliding back and forth on a stage. "My dream has always been to entertain people, presenting them with something the likes of which they have never seen before. Now we are all aware of my mishaps in this endeavor."

The audience in the vast arena roared with laughter.

"Tonight, I am hoping to present you and all you viewers at

home," he pointed into a floating camera in front of him controlled by a telekin cameraperson near the side of the stage. "Something you will remember for the rest of your lives."

The Realizer waved his hand and two giant screens descended from above the stage, each screen pointed toward the audiences on either side of the stage in the arena. A giant array of screens near the middle of the arena blinked to life, casting the Realizer's face down in all directions. He wore a golden laurel wreath crowned upon his head, beaming over the audience like Caesar at the Coliseum. He flashed a broad toothy smile and said, "Welcome viewers—"

The camera zoomed out, revealing the Realizer dressed in a lavish toga, sitting upon a throne in the Royal viewing area of an ancient gladiatorial arena. On either side of him, fawning sycophants dressed in fancy togas of various colors and assortment cheered. He stood, raising both arms into the air, saying, "—to the Glory Battles!"

People all around Fellowship City, Mighty and Citizen alike, stopped and watched the new show. The media built up the show for months to culminate at this very moment. Everyone wondered if the Realizer's new experiment would be a success or a dismal failure like Gothmopolis. People watched in their homes, at bars, gathered in masses, or all alone. Some people even viewed it on their handheld devices while working or walking around. No one wanted to miss it and be left in the dark.

"For the inaugural event tonight, I have come up with something very special for you all. I hope you enjoy it as much as I enjoyed realizing it for you."

He waved his hand and the screens went black, as a loud bass rumble grew from the immense speakers hanging in the center of the arena. Horns blared and the screen filled with a close-up shot on a red and blue flag waving. As the camera zoomed out, the red and blue flag revealed itself to be a banner with GLORY

BATTLES emblazoned upon it. The horns blared in a kind of reveille, ending with a black screen once again.

"A long time ago, in a world not unlike our own," a deep voice spoke as the words appeared on the screens. An orchestration of music filled the room with such intense bravado that people applauded it.

"It is a period known as Victorian England," the announcer's voice continued as images of Victorian England appeared.

"Technology as we know it is but a dream of the inventors of this period. There are no Mighty yet, and so there is crime—sometimes brutal and violent."

Images associated with Jack the Ripper flashed.

"As in every age, such events prompted authors to create heroes and villains to reflect the world around them—"

The music reached its crescendo, accompanying the voice of the narrator and the images on the screens.

"—illustrating how they would change things if they could."

The screens dipped to black and an image of Sir Arthur Conan Doyle appeared. He was a dapper man with a broad pointed mustache and a pocket watch.

"For tonight's Glory Battle, two equal yet opposite reactions to the Victorian era face one another in mortal combat."

An image of Sherlock Holmes appeared on the left screen above the stage.

"The first is the world's greatest detective, Sherlock Holmes!"

An image of Professor Moriarty appeared on the right screen above the stage.

"The second is his arch-nemesis, the equally brilliant, yet evil in intent, Professor Moriarty!"

The Realizer's face returned to the center screens, "Both these men are great fictional archenemies, geniuses with dizzyingly brilliant intellects, who are certainly going to dumbfound us as we watch them battle!"

Spotlights shined down on the center of the arena. The floor separated, revealing a giant rock formation filled with trees and a waterfall, which lifted up from below until the scene filled the whole of the arena floor.

"Behold, Reichenbach Falls!" exclaimed the Realizer.

Both Sherlock and Moriarty rose from below trapdoors in the stage at different points around the falls. They scowled at one another, as the Realizer thundered, "Who will win? Hero or villain?"

The audience roared and the battle began.

The battle between these two would-be archenemies unfolded unlike any other gladiatorial battle ever conceived or experienced. Rather than a battle of strength or even a battle of minds, it was less of a battle and more of a game of hide-and-go-seek. Eventually, the men reached the point the Realizer had led them to, fighting fiercely with one another as they reached the falls.

"We don't have to do this!" exclaimed Sherlock, as he grasped Moriarty's neck, trying to shove him back.

"Yes, we do!" shouted Moriarty, as he walloped Sherlock's face.

Sherlock struggled to stop from falling back. Everyone in the audience sat on the edge of their seats. The Realizer leaned in from his throne, saying, "Here it comes!"

Moriarty ran toward him, trying to finish the job. At the last second, Sherlock dodged clear, allowing Moriarty's momentum to carry him over the falls. Sherlock breathed a sigh of relief. He stepped forward, peering down the falls and discovering Moriarty gripping a rock. Grappling a rock would be more apt, as Moriarty's arm had, in fact, become a grappling hook.

"You aren't Moriarty," he said, reaching down to help the false figure.

"BOOOOO!" yelled the audience.

As Sherlock tried to reach him, Moriarty turned into the form of a skinny young man.

The Realizer eyed the incident with contempt. He stood, and his face filled the screen, as he said, "I'm sorry dear audience. It seems we're having technical difficulties."

The screens all scattered in static and blinked off. Inside the arena, the falls stage descended back into the ground and the floor covered it once again. Under the ground, Sherlock continued to help the man back up from the edge.

"Who are you?" he asked. "Where is Moriarty?"

"You know me," the skinny young man said, shifting into the Gorilla and then back into the skinny man.

"My god, you're a—"

"Mimic," interrupted Quell. "I can shapeshift into anything. That's why Moriarty hired me. He said he knew he was going to die because the book said so."

"The book? Ah... the collected works of Doyle." Sherlock surmised. "Where is he now?"

"I... uh," Quell answered, shaking with uncertainty. "He's escaped—that's all I know."

Sherlock helped the mimic stand up, placing an arm around him to help him walk.

"I must ask; how did he hire you?"

"He didn't really hire me with money—it was different than that," Quell answered, lowering his gaze. "But I owe you a life-debt, and I know how to repay it."

The Realizer was not at all happy about the circumstances of his inaugural event. When he found Sherlock, he pointed his finger into his chest, yelling, "You failed! You cost me money!"

Then, Sherlock fell dead upon the floor.

"I watched from a window outside the mansion," Sheryl tells Mario, finishing her origin story. "He gave his life, so I could live. I ran from that place and hid myself as best as I could. I chose to wear women's clothes, because I figured that would be the last place Moriarty would look for me. And, I haven't been Sherlock since. I mean, I tried for weeks to find any sign of Moriarty to no avail. Undoubtedly, he is still out there."

"That sounds like a ghost story," Mario says with a shiver.

"It is my ghost story," she says. "I live it every day. I knew I had to be the one to kill him, and I had to do it before he killed me. I'm always looking over my shoulder, living in constant fear. Do you know what that's like?"

"I get the idea," Mario empathizes. "It's similar to our lives in the WPC, but we don't have it quite that bad."

Sheryl places a hand on Mario's shoulder. "My story is no greater or worse than yours, Mario. There's no need to compare."

Mario nods.

"You know it's weird though, your story," says Mario, trying not to sound rude. "I've seen the Realizer take a realization out, and they don't fall down dead like that. There's no body left over at all. They're here one second, and then poof—nothing but a puff of pastel smoke."

"Well, Quell was a Mighty," Sheryl responds. "So, I guess he didn't—"

"*STOP!*" Jakandy's voice-thought wrenches into the minds of Mario and Sheryl.

Sheryl slams the brakes of Watson, forcing a quick stop next to Ifton in the middle of the road. The air reeks of freshly burned rubber, as the parties exit their vehicles. In front of them is a giant bloody mess.

"Oh shit," says Mario, covering his mouth with his hand, choking back his nausea.

He tries, but he cannot take his eyes away from the bodies of the two sky taxis strewn about.

Sheryl kneels to examine the bloody concavity where the female flyer's face had once been.

"This is very fresh! Look around!" Sheryl orders, as she glares into the sky. "How did he get them to come down?"

"What?" asks Tanalia overhearing.

"They were strong-flyers, right?"

"Yes!"

"Whatever killed them is powerful enough to rip these flyers down from the sky and strong enough to tear them into pieces," Sheryl explains.

Jakandy stops his search and questions, "You're saying it's one of the Mighty?"

"Not necessarily," Sheryl answers, assessing the carnage. "Have you found anything?"

"Like what?" Mario asks, kneeling down and covering his mouth, trying not to vomit.

Sheryl steps toward Mario, studying the ground. She stops at a footprint in a puddle of blood.

"Footprints in blood, perhaps."

Jakandy and Tanalia halt what they are doing and tiptoe toward Sheryl, surveying the ground along the way.

Sheryl places her foot next to the footprint but off to the side of the blood puddle. "Men's size 13, I'd say."

"How can you tell?" asks Tanalia.

"They're slightly larger than my own," Sheryl says, showing off her oversized women's flats. "I can't do heels."

Sheryl starts to pace back and forth, as the other three stand by and stare. Her right-hand cups her chin and fingers her bottom lip while the other waves like a conductor to an invisible orchestra.

Tanalia leans toward Jakandy, thinking, *"Do you think she's sane?"*

"We need to see where this goes."

Mario leans against the van, gazing into the sky. He darts his eyes down at the carnage. Then, he cranes his head back up toward the sky, repeating it over and over, trying to process what is right in front of him.

"We're looking for a rather hefty man," Sheryl finally says, stopping her pacing and forcing each of them to pay attention to her. She steps in long lengths paralleling the footfalls in blood. "He made long strides, and his footsteps are deep."

"Well that narrows things," Mario responds without hiding his sarcastic tone.

"Will you inform the Enclave?" thinks Tanalia to Jakandy.

"Not yet," he responds. *"We need to help the community before we protect ourselves."*

Tanalia squints at Jakandy.

"Won't they already know?"

"This place is a void just like the others," Jakandy explains, wrinkling his forehead and motioning without sound. *"Until that dissipates, these areas are blocking long-range telepathic communication and other powers of the Mighty, I bet. That's why I had to seek high ground outside of its range in the marketplace. I imagine if we weren't right next to each other or completely focused on one another, we would not be able to communicate telepathically either."*

"But the flyers flew in the marketplace," Tanalia questions.

"Only when we were far enough outside the void," Jakandy answers. *"I think they flew into a void here and lost their powers. I've never seen a strong break like this, let alone ever bleed."*

Tanalia's eyes light up.

"Would you mind sharing?" Sheryl asks the two monks. "The silence is deafening."

"I was just thinking," Jakandy answers. "This place is a void where—"

"Yes, yes," Sheryl interrupts. "Where the powers of the Mighty are affected. I learned that in the marketplace, remember. I thought you had something new to share."

"The void dissipates, and powers return with time," Tanalia tries helping.

"Yes, makes sense since you can speak telepathically to one another right now and we're sitting in a goddamned bloodbath!" Sheryl emphasizes the end. "So, nothing, you have nothing."

Jakandy and Tanalia shrug.

"Maybe it's Trivial?" Mario chimes in.

"I don't think so," Sheryl answers. "But glad you're thinking. I read much of that comic and the ledger. There's nothing in them to indicate that he's such a sadist or even a killer at all."

"Oh," Mario says defeated. "But you do have an idea?"

"There is one person I can think of," Sheryl answers. "Professor Moriarty."

KA-HOFF KOFF-KAH

Tyler spins around, as the light in his vicinity flickers and fades.

"Is someone there?" he asks, scanning the darkening area around him.

"Only me," coughs a small childlike voice from down the hall.

Tyler snaps his fingers, illuminating the lights near the

origin of the voice. An emaciated, five-year-old child strains to cover his eyes with his arm. He wears dirty rags for clothes and sits motionless against the wall.

Tyler rushes to the child, helps him up, and asks, "Are you okay, kid? What's your name?"

"I'm Loo," the little boy says to Tyler with big brown puppy dog eyes.

"Where's your mom, Loo?" Tyler asks as he picks Loo up. "Is she in here too?"

"No," Loo says with deep melancholy in his eyes. "She died at childbirth."

"Oh. I'm sorry."

"It's okay."

Tyler stops to read the name placard on the door. TATIANA.

"What was your mother's name?"

"Mommy."

Tyler checks out another door. SARA.

"What are you doing down here all alone?"

"I don't know."

"I'm sorry, Loo," Tyler empathizes "I'm going to get you out of here."

"You will?" Loo's face alights with excitement.

"Yes, I will," Tyler assures with a caring smile. "But first, I have to find someone else. Do you know a mother named Lizbeth?"

Loo taps his little finger on his temple before answering, "I don't think so, but I met Mary Beth. Is that her?"

"I don't think so," answers Tyler, tapping on the next placard. GALATEA. "But, can you take me to her?"

"Yes!" Loo says, pointing down the hall. "She's just over there."

Tyler carries Loo to the door marked MARY BETH.

"Here!"

Tyler sets Loo down and pats his head. "Stay right here for me, okay? I'll be right back."

Meanwhile, Zelda paces back and forth in front of the Super Muncher Battle Lords game.

Why did I have to wait? she thinks. *What did Tyler not want me to see?*

She meanders around the room and stumbles upon the skeeball game. *I remember this game!*

Zelda pounds the button on the machine, sending a line of balls down the shoot. She remembers that day. The day she lost her parents. Suddenly, the room lights up and fills with sound, as it had on that fateful day.

Zelda twirls around and peers down, seeing the colorful floral dress she wore spinning around with her. She remembers the exact lane she played from, where her mother and father stood watching, and where Mario played, scrutinizing her every move. She remembers not caring what he thought and not listening to him about how to play. She was/is her own person and would/will do things her own way. So, she picks up the ball and throws it as hard as she can at the skeeball ramp.

KLANK KLANEKTY KLANK

She ducks as the ball bounces off the ramp back toward her.

"Sorry," she shrieks, recalling how she looked up at her father and said, "It's not working for me."

As she revisits her memory, she stands with her arms

crossed while stamping a foot, mimicking her childhood self.

She smiles from ear to ear as her father's voice speaks to her from within, "Come on princess. You can do it."

Mario said something snarky of course, but she cannot remember what. She only remembers how it felt when her mother embraced her, holding her arm out, pulling it back, and showing her how to throw underhand. She stands in front of the skeeball machine, feeling her mother around her, showing her what to do. Shivers crawl through her body as her mother's voice speaks inside her mind.

"See sweetie, you have to toss it underhand."

Everything felt warm and safe then, even Mario with his judging and teasing felt familiar. Basked in the warm glow of the memory, Zelda sits and smiles, watching her father and mother love one another and love her and her brother. She smiles, remembering her anger at her brother's gloating.

She shakes her head, thinking, *It was so important to him then. He never acted like that again with me. He only protected me after that.*

Suddenly, her memory darkens with panic as she recalls the chaos that ensued next. Something happened to her mother's dress. It rose on its own.

"Mommy," she cries, trying to warn her through the memory, but her mother turns as she did that day, thinking Mario had done something wrong.

Revisiting the surprise on her mother's face is torment to Zelda. She closes her eyes, trying to shake away the bad memory. Everything starts to go hazy around her as she spins around, trying to stop the vivid daydream.

"Noooo!" she screams, closing her eyes.

When she opens her eyes again, she is huddled in a

corner, clutching her knees with one arm and her other hand covering her mouth. She rocks back and forth, as tears stream down her cheeks and drip off her chin onto her knees.

"Zelda?" Tyler calls, stepping out of the dark hole in the wall, one hand still inside clasped to the hand of the hidden Loo.

"I'm here," Zelda says, standing up. She brushes herself off, wipes her face, and races toward him. "Did you find her?"

"I'm sorry, Zelda," Tyler says, stepping closer to her but still obscuring Loo behind him. "She's—she's dead."

Zelda stops in her tracks, cascading through surprise, sadness, anger, and grief.

"No, no, that's not right," she cries. Her hands cover her eyes as tears stream down the same paths they had come down just moments before. "She can't be dead. She was so strong. She was a fighter."

Zelda turns back to Tyler, questioning, "Are you sure?"

Tyler's face darkens in messenger's grief. She acknowledges the sympathy within him and drops her eyes, noticing the awkward positioning of his hand behind his back. She tilts her head sideways, peeking around him.

Behind his back, a small child cowers. He raises his eyes to meet hers and they fill to the brim with doe-eyed joy.

"Mommy!" yells the young boy as he leaps toward Zelda, hugging his little arms around her waist.

Zelda kneels down, peeling Loo off of her.

"I'm not your mom, kid."

Tyler steps forward, grasping Loo by the shoulders.

Loo's eyes are filled with joyous tears as he whispers, "You look like her."

"I thought you said she died at childbirth. How do you know what your mom looks like?"

"Not my childbirth," Loo explains, trying to reach for Zelda's. "My sister's. But you are here now—you're not dead! They lied to me."

"I'm sorry, kid," Zelda consoles Loo, allowing him into her arms. "I'm not your mom."

"Yeah," Tyler agrees.

Zelda's eyes meet Tyler's. Her face shows sadness, sympathy, and appreciation for Tyler's understanding.

"But I think you might be his sister."

For a moment, Zelda is struck dumb.

"What?" she asks, shaking away her bewilderment.

She stands up, picking Loo up with her and stepping toward Tyler. He backs up, motioning for her to calm down.

"How? What's behind the game, Tyler?" she asks, pushing Loo into Tyler's arms and barreling to the hole in the wall.

THRUUMP

Sheryl drops the trash bin she had been using as a prop for Quell in the retelling of her origin story. She eyes Mario to keep both his comments and thoughts quiet. They could share this little secret. Mario nods in agreement.

"I don't understand," asserts Tanalia.

Sheryl grimaces at Mario. He shrugs an apology.

"What part?" sulks Sheryl.

"How did you stay hidden so long?"

"Oh, that? I found Club Haberdashery, and I never left."

Sheryl sat in a third-row seat to the right of the stage in Club Haberdashery. On stage stood a magician wearing an old suit in front of a stool with an old, tarnished top hat.

"By the power of Magnifico, I will—" he said, trying to conjure something from the old hat.

Sheryl laughed hysterically. He squinted at her with contempt.

"You are interrupting a grand performance. I am trying to conjure this—"

"I can see the bloody wires!" Sheryl shouted. "You are no conjurer! You are a confidence man!"

People glance around at one another shocked and surprised.

"Oh yeah," Magnifico said, "Do you think you can do any better?"

"Yes, of course, I can," Sheryl assured him, jumping from her seat and climbing over people to get to the stage. When she reaches the platform, she shoves Magnifico to the side and steps toward the audience.

"Do you want to see a real trick?"

The audience loved Sheryl, so she got a regular gig.

She had a renewed confidence and a new life, but always in the back of her mind, she thought of Moriarty. 'I know he's out there somewhere plotting against me. I can feel him.'

Somewhere in Fellowship City, a dark figure reads a passage from the Collected Works of Arthur Conan Doyle. Then, he slams the book closed and yells, "Holmes!!! I know you're out there! I can feel you!"

16

HUSH LITTLE BABY

Ten years ago.

"I'm going to find you!" Moriarty shouted as he paced, flipping through the worn-out copy of *The Collected Works of Arthur Conan Doyle*. "And you will pay for what you did to me!"

He stopped behind the kitchen counter, fingering the knives in the butcher block. He shoved the book under his arm, yanked out the largest knife, and assessed its sharp point with the tips of his fingers.

"I will find you!" He exclaimed, marching toward the front door. "And when I do, I'm going to kill you!"

As he opened the door, a hand clamped on his throat and a second clasped his wrist, shaking the knife and book free. They fell with a clank and a thud. His eyes bulged in surprised panic as a strong-flyer lifted him inches from the ground.

"What? You can't do this to me. I'm a—"

"Citizen," the seer-path monk interrupted, stepping out from behind the flyer. He was in his early 20s and wore the traditional non-hooded brown robe of the communitors and adjudicators.

"By order of the Justice Assembly and the Enclave of the

Monastery of Sol and Luna, you are hereby reprimanded to the Fellowship City Solitary Internment Camp for hard labor for the rest of your days," the monk charged. "So says Adjudicator Muldivar, communitor Step 4."

"You can't—" Moriarty started to shout and flail his arms toward the monk, but the strong-flyer clenched his wrist and wrenched his arm back. The grotesque snapping of bone signaled a break.

"OWW!" he screamed, reeling back in pain. "You broke my arm!"

Adrenaline coursed through him, as he drew the fist of his unbroken arm back. He struck the strong-flyer, making a dull thud against him. The pain of the impact radiated through his hand and up his arm, but the flyer showed no such response. He was nothing more than an annoyance, a fly bothering a horse.

The flyer plucked him up and tossed him over one shoulder.

"Leave me alone!" Moriarty continued screeching, "I will not be imprisoned!"

The flyer leaped into the air.

"AAAAAAHHHHHH!!!" screamed Moriarty.

A second flyer picked up Muldivar and followed them into the air.

"Put me down! I'd rather die!" Moriarty shouted, flailing in the arms of the flyer.

"That can be arranged," taunted Muldivar, nodding to the flyer carrying Moriarty.

The flyer nodded back, letting Moriarty go.

"AAAAAAHHHHH!" Moriarty screamed, falling toward the ground with increasing velocity. "You bastard! Save me!"

Seconds before hitting the ground, the flyer swooped in to save him from impact.

Right now.

"He'll never stop until he kills me," Sheryl says, fighting back the tears. "And that is why I continue to disguise myself to this day."

"Sure it is," Mario says to himself.

"If Moriarty is as evil as you say he is," Tanalia says, "there is no way he's still in the city."

"I concur," Jakandy agrees. "If he so much as thought the wrong thing, our Justice Assembly would be on him in an instant. There's only one place a living man like that could be. SIC."

"Off to SIC, we go," Sheryl concludes.

"What?!?" Mario exclaims, bursting into laughter. "No one WANTS to go to SIC!"

"We must go," Sheryl says, narrowing her eyes at Mario. "If Moriarty is there, we can rule him out."

"It's not a question of if," Jakandy confronts. "He's there or he's dead. I'll commune with the warden to—"

"But he's more like me than I would like to admit," Sheryl interrupts.

"What do you mean?" asks Tanalia.

"Blocker," she says, tapping her forehead.

"Perhaps, but there's only so much blocking one can do," Jakandy assures. "He may be able to hide criminal thoughts, but he cannot hide actually crimes from the Enclave. As soon as his crimes involved someone else, we'd have him."

"Yeah," Mario says, flipping the ledger open. "The Realizer wrote about this. Hold on."

He flips to the end.

"Here. He says, *Blocking is easy enough for one person to keep these ideas from the Enclave, but as soon as you add a few more into the fold, which is necessary to actually—* it's smudged, so I'm not sure what that says, but then he writes, *somebody inevitably screws up, and the Enclave sooner or later discovers what is happening.*"

"You're assuming he follows the laws of this reality." Sheryl paces a few steps before adding, "As a realization, he may not. Something is causing a telepathic void. If it is Moriarty, he may be able to commit criminal activities right under the Enclave's collective noses."

"Does he possess such powers in your world?" Tanalia questions.

"No, but—"

"Then, we have no reason to believe he is the killer we seek," interrupts Jakandy, heading toward the van. "However, if he is not at SIC, you may be onto something, detective."

"Where are you going?" asks Mario.

"I'm going to commune with the warden. If this Moriarty is in the SIC, he will know."

"How?" asks Sheryl. "Moriarty can be anyone. I need to see him with my own eyes to confirm it."

Jakandy steps into the back of the van, sitting cross-legged and closing his eyes.

"You know the SIC is all the way across Summerland desert, right?" Mario asks Sheryl. "It'll take a while to get there."

"And the killer is still on the loose," Tanalia adds. "If it's Moriarty and he's—"

"Nothing," Jakandy calls from the backseat. "The void is too strong here. I can't reach out."

Mario races to the van and jumps into the driver's seat.

"What do you think you're doing, Citizen?" barks Tanalia.

"Getting ready to go to SIC," he says with a chuckle. "I

can sit here, right. It's not like I'm going to be driving anyway. Right, Ifton?"

"Fine," Tanalia says, taking a seat in the back next to Jakandy. "*This should be fine, right?*" she thinks.

Jakandy nods.

Sheryl slams the passenger door shut, saying, "Well, driver. Let's be on our way."

"OK, Ifton," Mario says to the van, massaging the steering wheel. "If you can hear me, let's go!"

VRRRRROOOOOOOOOM

The van's engine turns over. The gas pedal depresses under Mario's foot without his assistance.

Surprised, he jerks his feet from the pedals.

"I guess he can hear now," Mario says.

"Correctomundo! You've won two parade tickets for the Mayor's booth in front of Upton Tower number three," the radio blares before falling silent.

This is going to be interesting, he thinks, peering into the distance. *I hope my dad is still alive.*

Seven years ago.

High above the Summerland Desert, a strong-flyer carried Tommy Rickson. He screamed and flailed about, demanding to be set free, but the flyer paid him no mind.

'We're so far away from Fellowship City,' he thought as the skyline shrank smaller and smaller behind him and the vast desert spread out before him. In the distance, a dark blemish in the sand grew larger and larger. 'That's where I'll be spending the rest of my life.'

As they drew closer, the details of the fence-lined perimeter and buildings of the Solitary Internment Camp came into focus.

'There's nothing else around for miles,' he thought, glancing back toward Fellowship City, finding nothing but desert sand in every direction

"Let me go!" he croaked one last time, as they flew over the high fences topped with barbed wire. His throat was hoarse from yelling, and he was tired from the long flight.

The flyer lowered Tommy close to the ground and dropped him from about six feet up.

"What the hell?" Tommy yelled, losing his breath as he crashed on his back.

"This Cit's a little feisty," the flyer told the guard below. "You might need to keep him in the cage for a bit."

The fur-covered guard growled, "Easy to break!"

With sharp claw-like fingernails and pointed teeth, he gnashed at Tommy. Viscous spittle dripped from them and sprayed out as he spoke. Tommy had never seen a hybrid so animal-like. None of the guards at WPC remotely resembled this guy.

'Hybrids are a scary bunch,' thought Tommy, as he appraised the guards near him.

A snarling reptilian guard with a big green tail surprised Tommy. The furry guard hacked up a laugh and ushered Tommy toward the admin office.

A large barricade ran from the outer wall to the admin office, separating SIC into east and west wings. Slits in the concrete revealed female interns on the east side. After surveying the area, Tommy determined that there were far fewer females than males.

In front of the office towered a clear cylindrical tube filled with water like some piece of modern art. The amphibian guard swimming up and down within caught Tommy's surprise. He had scales, fins, and breathed underwater. Awestruck, Tommy followed the guard as he swam up, jumped into the air, tucked into a backward summersault flip, and landed on a platform at the top of the tube.

He yelled down to the furry guard, "Hey Foz, game on tonight?"

"Yeah," Foz snorted, smashing Tommy through the admin office doors.

Inside, a bird sentinel folded his feathered arms in front of him, tapping his talon-like fingers. A feathered tail protruding behind his back fluttered.

"Another one?" he squawked at the furry guard. "Take him to receiving."

Foz escorted Tommy through the office toward the back where another bird sentinel guarded a door marked RECEIVING. The bird nodded and opened the door. Foz shoved Tommy inside.

"Welcome, Intern!" sang an older woman with purple twinkling cat eyes and silver hair wrapped in a tidy bun on her head. "I'll take him from here, Fozzie."

She took Tommy by the arm and guided him to the back of the room.

"Please stand right here."

Along the long white wall, black lines marked metric heights at each major point. Tommy stood a little higher than the 1.85.

"Stand still," she sang.

GRRRRDDDDDKKKKKK

The wall shifted, opening in the middle. Mario attempted to jump away, but a mechanical arm reached out, seized his arm, and thrust him back against the wall. Another mechanical arm grappled his other arm, forcing him into position.

"What's happening? Leave me alone!"

"Don't worry," she sang again as two more arms snatched his

legs, and a strap braced his neck back against the wall. "Don't move, or it'll hurt."

The apparatus forced his left arm outward, revealing his ident-tag. The mechanical arm bifurcated, as a new device opened its articulating arm outward, revealing a series of needles. A thin tube filled with black ink sputtered, winding its way up one side, while a matching tube with milky white ink lined the other side. A tiny red laser dot emanated from the needle mechanism, scanning his ident-tag before digging into his flesh.

ZZIIIIZZZAAAAZZZZZIIIIINNNNG

The device zipped back and forth on the ident-tag, blacking out the numbers and leaving a perfect rectangular shape on Tommy's arm.

"Ouch!" he screamed in pain. "Son of a bitch! What the hell?"

"See," cat eyes said. "If you move, it'll hurt. Don't worry. It's almost done."

A second round of zipping back and forth left white numbers emblazoned upon the black background.

"Ahh, 11428. Very good," she said, poking a button.

The arms all withdrew from Tommy, forcing him to collapse onto the floor. He cradled his arm, still burning and pulsing from the pain of the forced tattoo.

"Geez, lady, that was uncalled for," Tommy said, trying to stand.

She punched another button, and two guards plowed through the doors.

Tommy sighed, struggling to raise his arms. The guards picked him up and carried him away.

"Bye now, 11428," the cat lady sang. "Have fun."

Outside of the Admin office, the bird waved goodbye as Foz led Tommy toward the barracks. They crossed a field with several

Normals wearing yellow jumpsuits with black stripes down the side and a giant C on the back.

"See that," Foz grunted, slapping Tommy across the back. "That's what your future holds."

A guard yelled a sonic boom at the field workers, forcing Tommy to cover his ears.

"Work harder!" echoed in the ringing.

At the barracks, a hulking, muscular guard in his mid-twenties stood watch.

'Isn't he a little too normal to be a guard here?' Tommy thought before the guard whipped around to reveal a flesh-colored prehensile tail waving behind him. 'That makes more sense.'

Foz tossed Tommy toward the guard, who caught him with his tail. Tommy shuttered in disgust. The tail fondled him like a boneless arm, grasping him in its tendril embrace.

"Enjoy," groaned Foz, as he turned away.

The prehensile guard grabbed Tommy's arm and scanned his fresh ident-tag.

"Welcome to Hell, 11428," said the prehensile guard with a southern twang to his voice. "I'll be your guard. You can call me Officer Julian."

The barracks address was 7734, but someone flipped the plaque upside down, so it read hELL. Tommy chuckled, as he entered.

Each barracks housed 8 interns who slept on 4 bunk beds. Below each bunk, two unlocked lockboxes affixed with the corresponding intern's ident-tag number stored two yellow jumpsuits, underwear, and spare shoes. Tommy found a folded yellow jumpsuit waiting for him on a bunk next to an oversized plastic zippable bag.

"Put your clothes in the bag, and then put on the jumpsuit."

Tommy startled and turned, discovering two interns cleaning the common bathroom. The tall, skinny one with glasses, dark *brown skin and wiry hair scrubbed a crevice on the floor with a toothbrush. The short, balding man with olive skin and a protruding paunch squinted at Tommy.*

"Whadda they git YOU fer?"

Tommy ignored him, getting dressed by his bunk.

"Heya," he said, standing up. "I'ma talkin' to you."

Tommy shoved his clothes into the bag and zipped.

"Where do I take this?" he asked.

"Leave it there," the tall intern said. "They'll pick it up later."

The short one darted his eyes at the tall one and then back at Tommy.

"Heya, I'ma no joke!" he hollered. "I killed somebody! That's why I'ma here!"

Tommy stepped forward, staring down the shorter man.

"You killed somebody?" he asked, taking another step forward.

"Yeah, yeah," the shorter man panted, his eyes widening and betraying his hard façade. "I'ma bad bad guy. Don't mess with me."

Tommy pressed forward, forcing the short man to step back or stand his ground. He stepped back.

"So, you're telling me that in this world where those godforsaken monks can see us do something or think something before we think it," Tommy said, jabbing his finger into the short man's chest. "You're saying, you got away with murder? I'll tell you this. If it weren't for those damned monks, I would have murdered someone. And that is why I'm here."

"Oh, okay," the short man said, trying to calm Tommy down. "I'm Meezer and this is Rahm," he says, reaching his hand out to shake Tommy's.

Tommy inspects it.

"He's harmless. He's all talk." Rahm said, sidling up to Meeezer and giving him a noogie. "And attention. He always needs attention. He's so damn needy."

"Nice to meet you, Meezer," Tommy said, gripping his hand. "Sorry about my attitude. I'm not real happy about being here."

"Yeah," Meezer said with a mile-wide grin. "None of us are."

Rahm nudged Meezer in the side.

"I mean, none of us are happy to be 'ere," Meezer corrected. "You'lla fit right in."

Tommy met his other five hELL bunkmates at dinner that evening. At every meal, the interns of each bunk sat together in the cafeteria during their assigned times. Bunkhouse hELL had third shift dinner, first shift lunch, and second shift breakfast.

Meezer and Rahm guided Tommy through the cafeteria line, suggesting what he should scoop up and what he should pass up.

"Git as mucha the meat-stuff as possible," Meezer said. "You never know when it'lla come around again, and you don't want it if it's turnt gray."

"There are two sorts of veggies available," Rahm chimed in. "Canned and stewed. It's hard to tell the difference, but you don't want the stewed veggies. They're the leftovers from the gardens. They stew them to hide the fact that they are not fit for human consumption."

Tommy examined the food options and chose the meat with the least amount of gray and the veggies least likely to be stewed. No fruits or bread existed, but he found vats of red, gray, and brown soupy mixtures. None of the tubs of mush seemed appetizing, so Tommy slid by without partaking.

Meezer nodded at him, saying, "Smart move. Avoid anything liquidy. It'lla run right through ya."

Tommy followed Meezer and Rahm to their assigned table where five other men sat. Meezer led the way, introducing Tommy to the "Hell Boys," as he affectionately called them.

"This here'sa Brubaker. He'sa here because he tried to git fresh with a Mighty. She didn't take too kindly to it, eh Bru?"

Brubaker, a squat man, a few inches taller and a few years

younger than Meezer, had a melancholy face even as he smiled and nodded at Tommy.

"Nice to meet you," Tommy said, nodding back.

Rahm stepped forward to introduce the older gentleman with white puffs of hair jutting out from under a plaid pageboy cap sitting next Brubaker. "This is Mr. Mendaeus. He's been here for a very long time, and he keeps quiet. None of us know much about him at all. He likes it that way."

"Rahm is the only guy he'sa talks to," Meezer spoke sideways to Tommy, as they took the empty seats at the table. "This guy sittin'cross from you is Kenji. He'sa a real badass. He used to train them Mighty in his-a dojo in downtown Fellowship City before they shut him-a down for—what was it again?"

"Treasonous literature," Kenji answered, bowing his head to Tommy. A yellow bandana covered his long, dark hair tied back into a ponytail. "I owned an old copy of an anti-Abnormal magazine from before Evol II called Lesser Than. The issue contained a reprint of a much older article written by one of my ancestors about his experiences in a Japanese Internment Camp. If anything, his perspective argued against such treatment, but the Mighty only cared that the magazine itself was contraband."

"Bad rap, man," Tommy said, taking a bite of his meat and veggies.

"What is three years on a rock?" Kenji murmurs with a shrug.

"Next to you is the Tailor," Meezer said, pointing his thumb toward the dark-haired, heavyset man to his right. "He can't talk."

"Tailor? Did he make contraband suits or something?"

"No," Rahm answered. "He was an assistant to an accountant. He made the unfortunate mistake of pointing out an error his boss had made. For that crime, he lost his tongue. The accoun-

tant was a Mighty. They can do whatever they damn well please with us, yet we're the ones labeled criminal."

"If ya need anything fixed, like socks or whateva, he's your man," Meezer plugged. "He does a real bang-up job."

Across from the Tailor sat a man with slick black hair and an air of prestige about him, like a proper gentleman. Yet, a darkness loomed around him, hiding some secret. His eyes sunk deep and flared with menace. He appeared more malicious and calculating than inviting.

"Ah, yes. A newcomer," he said with an accent Tommy did not recognize. "What is your name, sir?"

"Tommy Rickson."

"Welcome, Mr. Rickson," the man greeted him with a devious grin. "I'm certain we will become well acquainted over the years."

"What is your name?" Tommy asked.

"James," the man said. "Call me James."

"He'sa yer bunkmate," Meezer whispered, elbowing Tommy's side.

Tommy gave no air of apprehension, although uncertainty stewed within him. As he tried to sleep that first night, he tossed and turned. Below him, James slept completely still. He did not move one iota.

The others in the room snored and grunted, their bunks creaking with each minuscule shift of their weight. All except James. The silence of his bunk creeped Tommy out.

He stared at the window, admiring the dancing moonlight around its frame. The light too made sleeping difficult, shining in on him and growing closer and closer until the eclipse. The sudden dark alarmed Tommy. He lifted his head to find Julian glaring at him through the window.

He turned away, trying to feign sleep. Soon after, the false sleep became real sleep, sweeping Tommy away into a land of dreams.

Happiness overwhelmed him as he reunited with his family, clenching Lizbeth within his arms and bouncing Mario and Zelda upon his knees. He envisaged their faces clearly, recalling every aspect of their being, every essence of their personality. He remembered the way they spoke and the way they smelled.

He found fulfillment in his dreams. Even when they turned darker, casting recent memories into the fray, like those of DerMööve and Jakandy laughing at him, he faced them with courage. In his dreams, he fought back and beat them. They were not Mighty in his dreams. He was.

The same thing happened every day at SIC. Tommy woke up, showered, dressed, and headed to the cafeteria for second shift breakfast. Due to his youth and strength, he worked the mines. Between breakfast and first shift lunch, he would don his hard-hat, grab his pickaxe, and head into the dark caves west of the SIC.

The protective barrier the Enclave provided did not reach the caves, making his job one of the more dangerous among the interns. At any moment, a fleshie might break through the mine's blockades to pick off an intern, leaving the guards with a little extra paperwork to do.

So, Tommy hacked away at the rocks, trying to find pieces of whatever they wanted him to find, hoping the guards protected him from potential fleshie attacks. Usually, he had no complaints. The guards treated him decently or ignored him altogether. The pyrokin guard named Farrell would toss fireballs into the air, casting tremendous shadows in the cave, while the bird guard named DeLongue would practice flying a foot from the ground, trying to hover like the strong-flyers.

Tommy worked until the first shift lunch alarm, ate lunch, and, on most days, returned to the cave. One day a week, he did laundry or cleaned hELL house in the afternoon. Also, once per week, he earned four hours of rest and relaxation, wherein he did *whatever he wanted within reason. Most often, he played retro videogames in the common room.*

After third shift dinner, he showered, getting ready for his favorite time of the day.

Unlike the other interns whose constant plans of escape kept them going, Tommy's dreamworld kept him going. He didn't understand the others. Escape meant being surrounded by miles upon miles of sand with nowhere else to go. Without some means of swift travel through that desert expanse back to Fellowship City or being blessed with some peculiar means to repel flesheaters, the escaped intern would likely die.

'How would they elude the monk in charge in the first place?' thought Tommy.

Regardless, the thought of being on the other side of the wall motivated the majority of interns, appealing to their misguided sense of a free existence.

'Here or there, we have no freedom under the rule of the Mighty.'

Almost every day, Tommy witnessed a few interns mentally breakdown and end up doing something they immediately regretted. One of these moments happened during his first bunk duty. As he attacked the grime in the crevices of the bathroom tile with a wire toothbrush, he overheard the muffled sounds of would-be escapees. He craned his neck to peer out the open door of his barracks, catching a glimpse of two yellow-clad figures zooming past the door.

"Hurry! We're almost there!"

His curiosity got the better of him, so he scrambled up from his knees and sped to the front door. He recognized the runners from the first shift lunch. They sat only a few tables over from him and his bunkmates. The taller one worked in the mines with Tommy, but the other one, the slower one trying to keep up, worked elsewhere.

The tall one sprinted at the chain-link fence, jumped, and scurried up. He flung a bolt of cloth or something over the barbed wire to climb safely over.

'Clever,' thought Tommy.

The other one heaved heavily upon arrival, clinging the fence for support and losing all of his momentum.

"I... I'm... I can't," he stammered between labored breaths.

"C'mon! You can do it," the tall one encouraged from his perch at the top of the fence. He held the cloth down for the other man. "All you gotta do is climb up and over. And we'll be free!"

'Where are the guards—alarms?' thought Tommy dumbfounded. 'Where is the warden? He must sense what is happening. Is he toying with them?'

The smaller man climbed up and gripped the hand of the taller one. The taller one's face reddened and drenched with sweat, as he hauled his portly companion to the covered barbed wire.

ARRRRRRRGGGGGHHHH

The shorter man screamed, having plunged his hand onto a barb. He whelped, as blood cascaded down his arm. Trying to grasp it with his other hand, he lost balance and whipped him and the taller man back onto the prison side. They fell to the ground with a resounding thud.

At that moment, two strong-flyers landed in front of them, carrying the SIC warden between them. Tommy didn't find the warden familiar, except to the extent that all those monks looked the same in their traditional robes, whether they be hooded or unhooded. Tommy eyed the situation carefully but tried to focus his thoughts on cleaning, so as not to provoke the seer-path's attention.

"Interns, you are in violation of solitary internment regula-

tions. *Return to your bunk now or face punishment,"* The SIC
warden said, stepping toward the two men. *"So, says SIC Warden
Muldivar, monk Step 5."*

'We can't run without them knowing,' Tommy thought, still
keeping an eye in the situation.

Muldivar's head spun in Tommy's direction. Tommy shuttered and returned to his cleaning duty.

A few days after that incident, Tommy worked in the mine
and witnessed a scuffle. Three men on his shift, working in
another section of the mine, thought they could attack their
guards with pickaxes and start a riot.

"Kill them!" they shouted as they charged the guards. "Kill the
Mighty! Kill them all!"

Seconds before the first attacker brought his pickaxe crashing
down, four strong-flyers carrying additional guards and
Muldivar raided the mine, stopping the attack before anything
happened.

"Halt, Interns!" Muldivar commanded, as one of the telekin
guards fended off the three attackers. "We will not tolerate this
insolent behavior! Retreat now or be reprimanded."

'We can't fight them,' Tommy thought stupefied, as the
three men dropped their weapons and surrendered. Again,
Muldivar turned toward Tommy, who flinched and returned to
work.

One night after dinner, Tommy, James, Meezer, Rahm, and
Kenji sat at their table after all the other interns left. They
remained silent, waiting for the lights to turn out. When darkness
finally came, James pointed to Rahm.

"Countdown thirty seconds."

"Thirty-one-thousand," Rahm said aloud.

"Think about everything you know," James said, pointing to
Meezer. "Think loudly!"

Meezer nodded and squeezed his eyes in concentration.

James motioned for the others to lean toward him while Rahm chimed, "Twenty-five-one-thousand."

"They stop us at every move," James whispered. "We need a foolproof plan."

"Twenty-one-thousand."

"We cannot run. We cannot fight. But there must be something we can do."

"Fifteen-one-thousand."

"If we all meditate at once, perhaps we can confound the seer-paths," Kenji offered.

"Ten-one-thousand."

"If we were all meditating, we couldn't escape," Tommy countered.

"Five-one-thousand."

"We need more time," James said as the lights blinked on.

"One-one-thousand—" Rahm said, the words dying on his lips.

Muldivar and three strong-flyers poured into the room.

"Interns!" shouted Muldivar. "This congregation violates the—"

"Yeah, yeah," muttered Tommy as he stood up and pushed his chair in. "Regulations of the SIC. We know. We know."

The others followed suit, but Muldivar kept his eyes glued to Tommy. Perceiving the unwanted attention, Tommy flashed a smile and thought about everything he ever knew all at once.

'We—' he thought about Lizbeth, Mario, and Zelda. He tried to focus on their faces.

'Can't—' he thought of his favorite video games and played the 8bit synthesized theme songs in his head.

'Plan—' he thought about what life would be like if the Mighty did not exist.

Months later, the constant work and daily stress wore upon Tommy.

"I'm not well…lightheaded," he said in a strenuous whisper, as he scrubbed the barracks floor.

His head dripped with sweat and his skin glimmered pale and green.

"I need rest," he mumbled before crawling to his bunk, trying to escape the eye of Julian's patrol.

The Tailor nodded, continuing to work and trying to make up for his bunkmate's apparent inability.

Before long, Julian spotted the lump on Tommy's bunk.

"11428, stand up and work!" he ordered.

Tommy waved his arm limply, acknowledging Julian but doing nothing to change his position. Believing his order went ignored, Julian stormed into the barracks.

"Get your ass up, Citizen!" he yelled. "Before I break you in half!"

Tommy rolled his head toward Julian, lifted his hand inches from the bed, and moaned in a muffled whimper.

"You've asked for it!" Julian roared, reeling back his tail, ready to strike.

"Stop!" ordered a voice from behind, catching Julian's tail in his hand.

Enraged, Julian whipped around, but the sight of the warden urged him calm, as he straightened himself and humbled his posture.

Still clutching Julian's tail, Muldivar shouted, "Physically harming an intern is a violation of the work statute!"

He dropped the tail and clamped onto Julian's shoulder, conducting him out of the barracks.

"If they are harmed," he says, giving Tommy a quick once over. "They cannot continue laboring. Do you understand?"

Julian nodded, reddened by embarrassment.

'I guess it goes both ways,' thought Tommy.

This time, Muldivar did not turn to eye Tommy. His gait never faltered as he spoke with Julian.

Tommy listened to the noise of their conversation, trying to make out the words, but they were stifled by the drumming of his heart and pounding in his head. Every agonizing beat echoed in his temples. He counted the thumps, the rhythmic thumps, over and over and over until he finally passed out.

Even through fever-induced sleep, happiness filled him once more as he slipped away into his dreamworld. Bright colored weightless pillows of cloud bounced around his mind. Zelda jumped on them one by one, lighting up each as she landed. They dimmed as she jumped away. Mario followed her from the ground, jumping up and punching the clouds into nothingness. They burst bright with light and a chime.

BRRRDDDIIINGGG

Tommy tried to follow them as they bounded toward the castle in the distance. He shouted, "Zelda! Mario! Where's your mother?"

They did not respond, pulling further and further away from him. He tried to keep up, but a tollbooth arm fell in front of him, stopping him in his tracks. His momentum carried him into the bar, doubling him over.

"This way is blocked," shouted a guard from the small booth next to the bar. "You must take a detour."

Tommy shook his head in confusion, gaping as his children dashed across a drawbridge into the castle.

"But I need to get to that castle. I think Lizbeth is in there."

"I'm sorry, Tommy," the guard said. "Lizbeth is in another castle."

Tommy woke up, dripping with sweat. His mind tried to capture the dream, so he could remember their faces.

'The dreams,' he thought. 'I live for the dreams.'

The sun shone inside the barracks much brighter than usual. Tommy searched the room, finding all the bunks empty and beds made. Julian stood against the frame of the opened hELL house door, facing the camp. Tommy hugged his knees into his chest, drenched in pain and sweat as tears streaked down his face.

"Hey, you," he said in a soft muffled tone.

Julian turned.

"Yeah?"

"Come here. I think something's wrong."

Julian stepped toward him.

"Are you okay, 11428?"

"Oh God," Tommy squealed. "Please help me!"

Julian hurried over, asking, "What's wrong?"

He didn't finish the question, as Tommy's legs sprung forward, knocking him to the ground. Tommy staggered to his feet and stumbled toward the door in a haphazard run. Julian whipped his tail at Tommy but missed. Tommy exited the door, setting his eyes not on freedom but Muldivar and a strong-flyer landing before him.

"Took you long enough," Tommy mumbled, crashing down on all fours in front of Muldivar.

Anticipating the fall, Muldivar stepped back before Tommy hit the ground and far enough out of reach of the vomit spewing out of him. The strong-flyer jumped back, unable to evade the viscous chunks splashing onto his boots.

"Are you kidding?" he belted as he scraped them clean.

Muldivar stepped to the side and placed his hand on Tommy's forehead.

"I'm aware of your illness, so I'm willing to give you leave this time. However, let this be a fair warning,"

Muldivar said, raising Tommy's head to meet his eyes. "If you disobey the rules one more time, no matter how minor the offense, I WILL take away that which is most precious to you!"

Tommy stood up, resembling a belligerent drunken fool more than anything else.

"What can you take from me? Everything's been taken already?" he yelled at the warden, staggering a bit. "I have nothing, you son of a bitch! Nothing! You can do all you want, and you can't take away—"

"Your precious memories," Muldivar interrupted, tapping his forehead between his eyes.

Tommy stumbled back, speechless, trying to process this information. He fell to his knees and groped at his head. Muldivar placed a cold hand on his hot forehead once more.

"I can make you believe anything I want you to and strip you of your identity, removing every single memory of yours and implanting any memory I want."

Tommy's jaw dropped. Julian approached him from behind and yanked him up. Muldivar signaled his strong-flyer, who stepped behind him, wrapped his fingers around the warden's waist, and carried him into the sky.

"Can he really do that?" Tommy asked Julian with big sorrowful eyes.

"Come on," Julian said, ushering him back toward the barracks. "I've seen him do it before."

I only have my dreams now, thinks Tommy, as he examines his reflection in the windowpane. This face is old. I don't remember aging. I don't even recognize that face.

He waves his right hand to the reflection, half expecting the mirror image's left hand not to respond.

I guess it's me, he thinks. *How many times have I done this before?*

He glimpses the fresh, puffy scars on his arm and reads the names silently, "Mario. Lizbeth."

He struggles in vain to conjure the name of his daughter.

"What is her name?" he cries, wishing to carve those precious letters into his flesh next to the others. "If I could just remember. I'd never forget it again."

The memories of his family are gone, reduced to three hollow shapes devoid of any information. Every time he delves into the depths of his memoryscape, he finds nothing but Muldivar telling him to behave or suffer the fate of more lost memories. Now that is his only true memory. He has vague recollections about life in the SIC, but nothing from before—nothing but his dreams.

My dreams, he thinks. *I only have my dreams now.*

"You were sayin'," Meezer says, as he sits on the toilet. Tommy glances over with surprise. He forgot about Meezer.

"Yeah, where was I?"

"The dream you had last night," Meezer recalls. "You didn't wanna forget it, so you were tellin' me about it."

"What did I tell you so far?"

"You dreamed about your family. A wife. A son. A daughter."

"Oh, yes," Tommy says. "I dreamed I came home."

In his dream, Tommy opens the door to find his family welcoming him. Lizbeth greets him with a kiss and a *Welcome home, honey*, while Mario and Zelda scamper up and swing around his waist, saying things like, *We missed you, papa*, and *How was your day?* He dreamed of them sitting around a table, smiling and laughing at one another.

"We eat dinner together and discuss mundane things," he says to Meezer.

In his dream, Mario says, "Who was the host today, dad?"

"A puny guy with glasses and a guitar," Tommy answers. "I think they called him Holly."

"Isn't that a girl's name?" Zelda giggles.

He tells Meezer, "I dreamed that I tucked them into bed and told them a bedtime story."

"Yeah?" Meezer says with a grunt. "What's the story?"

"Tell us a bedtime story, please!" Mario asks in his dream.

"Please, papa!" pleads Zelda, as Tommy tucks her in.

Lizbeth peeks in from the doorway, and they share a loving smile.

"It's always the same bedtime story," he says to Meezer.

"Then, it'll be easy to tell," he replies.

"Once upon a time," Tommy says to his children. "In a world not much different from our own, lived a man named—"

"Mario!" shouts Mario.

In his dream, the story became a different reality unfolding before his eyes. A lush, colorful world of buildings with bulbous tops and skinny bottoms popped up all around him. Other buildings sprouted from the ground, bending in unnatural ways, like pipes and tubes. A sign popped out of nowhere: WELCOME TO PIPETOWN.

The buildings of PipeTown reflected its odd and unnatural population. Many half-animal or half-plant people buzzed here and there around the streets. But not Mario, a muscular construction worker wearing a hardhat and a cartoonishly big mustache. He worked at Cooper's Castle Construction site, jackhammering the ground.

A humongous COMING SOON banner floated above the construction site, held aloft at either end by chirping bluebirds. A frog person perched on a giant multi-colored mushroom nearby, keeping an eye on the construction.

"Hey baby, I like those ears," he croaked at an attractive young cat-eared woman walking by the site. "Maybe I can scratch them for ya!"

In this world, the Normals and Abnormals lived together in peace. Except, some of the Normals wanted powers like the Abnormals. Mario's little brother certainly did. He loved all the television programs featuring people flying in the sky, and he wished to be one of them.

"Mario!" he yelled excitedly, pointing to the television. "He can fly! I want to fly!"

As they grew older, Mario's little brother became discontent with not being an Abnormal. So, he packed his things and left one day. Mario watched out the window as his little brother waddled with heavy suitcases toward a rounded yellow taxicab, never returning home again. After that, Mario worked on the construction site for Cooper's Castle all alone, except for Mr. Toad, who monitored him daily, catcalling the cat women.

Years later, a pair of superpowered baddies called the WaWa Boyz descended upon Mario's city, making everything unpleasant for everyone. The day of their arrival, Mario jackhammered, as usual, stopping when he spotted two zigzagging lines streak across the sky. The trail pointed toward the giant building in the center of town where the Mayor's office was located.

"What's that?" croaked Mr. Toad.

"I'm not sure, but it looks like it's going to crash into Pipe Tower," answered Mario.

The streaks did in fact crash into Pipe Tower, right through the Mayor's window.

"Oh my?" shrieked Mayor Shrum, gripping his chest and stripping the color from his face. "I think I'm having a heart attack"

The feeble mayor quivered on the floor, his white-bearded mouth burbling. His beautiful blond daughter in a sensible business suit rushed to his aid, fanning his face with a file folder.

The WaWa Boyz wanted a payoff.

"Time to pay up, Mayor Shrum," the short, rounded one said, while the tall, muscular one adjusted his mask. They wore identical masks, save for one being gold and the other magenta, matching their vibrantly colored zoot suits.

"My father doesn't pay off terrorists!" shouted Ms. Shrum, trying to take care of her father. "You need to leave!"

"Honey, please," the Mayor said, trembling.

"Oh yeah, lady," the shorter WaWa said, approaching her with a twisted grin on his face. "If you don't pay us, we'll gladly take something else of value instead."

"Yeah?" Ms. Shrum challenged, "What's that?"

"You!"

He laughed, as the taller WaWa snatched her up and threw her over his shoulder. She hammered and kicked, trying to fight free, but he was too strong and too fast. He surged toward the window and flew away with a zoom.

"NOOOO!" cried the Mayor.

"HAR HA HUM," laughed the short WaWa, following his brother out the window and into the air.

"HEEEEEELLLLP!" cried Ms. Shrum. "PPPPLLL-LLEEEEEAAASSSE!"

Mario stared up at the new trails in the air, wishing he had the power to help. He raced to Mr. Toad.

"I must help her," he said. "What can I do?

Mr. Toad shrugged and jumped after a cat woman who strolled by, hollering at her all along the way. The mushroom he sat on twinkled, popping out the flat spot Mr. Toad made in its cap. Without thinking about any possible consequences, Mario ate the mushroom...

a magic mushroom. He started to glow. Then, he grew larger and stronger. The mushroom gave him temporary superpowers, making him almost like a superhero. He grabbed a sledgehammer and jumped into the air, catching flight and picking up the trail of the WaWa Boyz.

"I'll save you, Ms. Shrum!" he shouted.

He followed behind the colorful trails of the WaWa Boyz, trying to stay out of their peripheral vision.

"Do you hear something?" asked the taller WaWa.

"Other than AAAAAAHHHHHH! HEEEEEELLLLPPP?" quipped the shorter WaWa, mimicking Ms. Shrum.

"Yeah, it sounded like a sonic boom," said the taller WaWa. "The way it sounds when we take off from the ground."

"How ridiculous," the shorter WaWa said. "There's nobody who can fly like us in PipeTown. I did my research."

All the same, the shorter WaWa peered back.

"Did you see something?" the taller one asked.

"Pipe down will you," he squinted, trying to peep whatever might be flying through their colorful jet trails. "I'll take a gander."

The short WaWa hovered in place, searching for anything or anyone heading in their direction. Mario didn't notice in time. Both their eyes bugged out of their sockets as they locked onto one another.

The short WaWa flew as fast as possible at Mario, while Mario flew forward, swinging his sledgehammer backward. As they met, he swung the sledgehammer with all its momentum at the face of the short WaWa.

KARAAACK

Teeth flew from the shorter WaWa's face, as he went tumbling back into the sky and falling toward the ground. Mario pointed his arm straight ahead in a fist and flew toward the taller WaWa.

The taller WaWa glimpsed his brother plummeting to the ground in his periphery and reeled around. He landed hard with a boom, tossing Ms. Shrum behind him into a patch of mushrooms.

"Come at me, bro!" he yelled, placing his right hand behind his back. He flicked his hand and a spark of electricity pulsed from his fingertips.

Mario spied him on the ground and zoomed toward him, landing hard on one knee to face the tall WaWa.

"Are you okay, Ms. Shrum?" he asked, checking behind the tall WaWa and locking eyes with the beautiful daughter of the mayor.

"Oh, she's just peachy!" the tall WaWa answered for her.

Mario ran with breakneck speed toward him, readying the sledgehammer to strike, but the tall WaWa caught the sledge-hammer with his electric hand, frying Mario. Mario shrunk back down to his Normal self.

"You're only a Normal!" the tall WaWa laughs. "You can't hurt me!"

Mario scurried through the tall WaWa's legs and somer-saulted toward Ms. Shrum, fetching a glowing mushroom from the patch she lay upon. He bit into it, gulping several bites down.

When the tall WaWa turned around, Mario glowed with fire.

"No! This can't be," he cried as a ball of fire grew between Mario's hands.

He spun around and snapped his fingers, flickering electricity. As he turned to release his onslaught of lightning, the massive swirling fireball blasted into him, smashing him to the ground with a ring of fire dancing around him.

In the end, the tall WaWa lay suffering upon the ground with scorch marks all over his body.

Ms. Shrum found her feet and sprung into her hero's arms. She kissed him.

He turned red and yelled, "Wahooo!"

Behind him, the tall WaWa groaned and rolled over. With hands still ablaze and ready to strike, Mario approached his fallen foe.

"Mario?" the tall WaWa asked in a childlike voice.

Mario's eyes became saucers, as he realized his long-lost little brother had returned.

17

LOCKDOWN!

Zelda rocks under a flickering light with her back against the wall. Her arms wrap around her knees as she sobs into the space between her legs. Across from her, Tyler cradles Loo in the intermittent darkness.

"What is this place?" she asks, raising her red, puffy eyes to Tyler. "A harem? A brothel? Are they—for breeding?"

Tyler sets Loo down.

"Go to the arcade, buddy," he says. "Give us a minute."

Loo scampers away, as Tyler approaches Zelda. He bites his lip, unable to speak, trying to wear a sympathetic face.

"Are they sex slaves?" Zelda asks, lifting herself up and stepping toward Tyler.

"Yes. Yes, to all the above."

"Why?"

Tyler drops his head, and she pounds his chest with her fists and forearms. The impact isn't hard enough to knock him back, but he'll have some bruising.

"Why, Tyler? Why?"

Tyler clasps her hands, peers into her sad eyes, and answers, "Because they can, Zelda."

Zelda whips away from him and springs to a door, exclaiming, "We need to free them! Free them all!" She reaches for the door handle, and Tyler clamps onto her shoulder. She turns to him and says, "I'm surprised you knew about this place and haven't done anything about it."

She opens the door, yanking her shoulder free. As she steps inside the room, the mingled odors of disinfectant, bodily waste, and plastic tubing waft toward her. Her face sours, but she perseveres, tiptoeing inside to inspect the room.

A dark-haired woman with light brown skin and an emaciated frame lies on the bed, hovering somewhere between life and death. An IV tube feeds into her arm from a machine next to the bed. The monitor spurs and clicks as the IV pumps fluid into her veins. Next to the saline bag hangs another bag with a bright yellow liquid within. She examines the bag, but the only marking is a crude smiley face drawn in black ink. She follows the tube of yellow liquid down the woman's IV line to where her hand strangles a remote control wired to the monitor.

Zelda inches toward the woman and places her hand upon the woman's frail little hand. The woman's eyes roll open, groggy and red.

"You're free now!" Zelda implores. "You can go!"

The woman's eyes roll back into her head and close. She makes no additional movement, except to press the button on the remote. Her IV monitor buzzes and beeps, as liquid burbles in the yellow bag. Zelda observes the yellow fluid entering the other IV line in a controlled flow.

Zelda's huffs defeated, as Tyler steps closer to her and places his hand on her shoulder.

"I've been here before, Zelda," he says. "Maybe not with her, but I've tried so many times to free them. They're all hooked on Delirium. It's a free supply here, and they're unwilling or unable to leave."

"We need to disconnect them. Force them off," Zelda exclaims, shoving Tyler aside and surging to the other side of the bed to the IV monitor. "If we take it from them, they'll—"

"I tried that too," Tyler interrupts, placing a hand on hers as she reaches the monitor. He turns her to face him. "I got my mother out. I unhooked her from the feedlines and brought her to my apartment."

He leads her out of the room, holding her by the hand. He closes the door behind them and faces her again. She wears a face of sympathy, as he says, "My mother died. Believe me, they're too far gone at this point. They can't live without the Delirium. Anyone who's taken as much as they have for that long dies without it."

Zelda collapses into his arms.

"We have to get out of here. There's nothing we can do for them now. But there are some people we CAN help."

Outside of Fellowship City, Ifton races west on Summerland Highway toward the Summerland Desert wasteland.

"Well, that was the last city marker," Mario squeals from the driver's seat. Sheryl sleeps in the passenger seat, her head resting against her arm on the window. Jakandy and Tanalia sit next to each other in the back. The dashboard clock blinks 11:37.

"*If they find out, they will lockdown*," thinks Tanalia to Jakandy. "*They will block us, so we won't even know!*"

"*I imagine so*," he responds in thought.

Tanalia shifts in her seat. Jakandy reaches his arm around her and draws her toward him. She does not fight him, sensing his compassion, sensing his love. Her whole face smiles. He kisses her forehead.

"If it comes to that, I'll protect you."

Mario peeks at them through the rearview mirror, trying not to think about it, so they won't notice him being a creeper.

Sheryl wakes with a start, turns to Mario, and says, "We need provisions to ensure we arrive alive."

"Yeah," he agrees and taps on the dashboard. "I think we might need a fresh charge too. We don't want Ifton dying on us."

HRRRHAAA

The horn makes a deflated honk.

"He didn't like your comment," Tanalia speaks in Ifton's defense.

"I didn't mean it like that," Mario says. "What I meant was—"

"It doesn't matter," Jakandy interrupts. "Sheryl is right. We need food. We need water. We need to have a full charge if we are to make it through the wasteland."

"I said that," Mario whines under his breath.

"There's a supply store on Summerland Highway not too far from the city limits," notes Tanalia. "The owners are hoping their parade float will help with business."

Mario rubs the dashboard, asking, "Ifton, do you know the way?"

About ten minutes later, Ifton crawls into a parking lot next to an old building with a neon sign blinking CAMP.

"Don't forget to visit the little boy or little girl's room!" Mario shouts, hightailing it to the store. "Who knows how long it's gonna take to get there?"

"*I'm not going in,*" Tanalia thinks. "*I don't want them to ask me about better float positioning again. I'll stay and charge Ifton, okay?*"

Jakandy nods before following Sheryl and Mario out of the van. Tanalia exits last to find Ifton's charging port.

"*Are we really going to SIC?*" Ifton asks Tanalia.

"*It looks that way,*" Tanalia thinks, plugging into the port.

"*It's going to be a long, hot drive,*" Ifton says, cycling his dash on to view his electric charge. He flips to the nav screen and enters the SIC coordinates. "*It's 20 degrees hotter in Summerland. Do we have to go?*"

"The detective seems to think so," Tanalia says, stepping into the back. "Do you have any better ideas?"

"*Nope,*" Ifton answers. "*You?*"

"If I did, we wouldn't be here right now," Tanalia says with a yawn. Her eyelids droop, as the stress of the morning catches up to her. "I'm going to rest my eyes for a bit."

"*Fantastic idea,*" Ifton says, shutting his systems off, except the charge view.

As Ifton's electrical charge indicator switches from yellow to green, a red warning appears on the screen:

LOCKDOWN IMMINENT : ALL MONKS RECALLED

At the SIC, Tommy regales Meezer about his dream story.

"That's all I can remember," Tommy says to Meezer, who washes his hands in the sink.

"It's a good one."

Rahm darts into the barracks, wailing, "The monks are gone!"

"What?" Tommy asks confused.

"They're gone. They're flying away. Come see!"

Meezer is already out the door, running faster than Tommy has ever seen a short, round man run before. Outside the door of their barracks, interns and guards stand around, staring at a handful of dots in the sky.

"Those are the monks?" Tommy asks.

Rahm nods.

"So, there are no seer-paths?"

Rahm continues nodding.

"There are no seer-paths!" Tommy shouts.

Foz stands close enough to overhear Tommy. Horror flashes in his eyes, as he realizes he and other the guards are outnumbered by the Citizens.

"11428 back down now!" he commands.

Tommy pays no heed, plowing into the Furry guard at full speed. His shoulder spears into the guard's body, knocking him to the ground. Tommy punches his face into a bloody ruin. All around him the other interns acknowledge their chance to fight back, and they do.

Kenji jump kicks one of the birds as they try to fly away. The Tailor grabs a pair of scissors and jabs it into the eye of another bird guard. Three interns take turns cracking at the tank outside the administration office, trying to reach the amphibian guard within.

The pyrokin guard takes a cheap shot at Mr. Mendaeus, hitting him with a fist full of flame. The poor old man falls to the ground in a shambles. As Brubaker scrambles to his aid, the pyrokin opens flame on both of them. They scream in pain and the horror of being burned alive as they blacken with char under the scorching heat of the flame.

SAWWWWEEEESSSSHHHH

The water tank breaks and a flood gushes toward the

pyrokin. It is too late for the two charred interns, but his flame will no longer hurt any of them. The three who broke the tank pounce on the pyrokin as the amphibian guard flips around like a fish out of water on the wet ground.

A woman screams from inside the administration office, catching Tommy's attention. James exits the office, meets Tommy's eye, and nods. Tommy shakes his head and assesses the damage. The SIC is being torn apart piece by piece by these interns. He gazes out at the desert beyond the chained link fence and wonders, *what have I done?*

"To the gate, gentlemen!" yells James. "To freedom!"

Frantic interns pummel the gate, tearing it apart.

Tommy approaches James, still standing by the admin office.

"What's your game?"

James squints his right eye at Tommy as his nose slightly twitches.

"How do you mean?"

Tommy points at all the interns barreling through the gate and scuttling into the desert.

"You just told them to run—be free. Yet, here you are. What are you waiting for?"

"Me?" he says feigning innocence. He turns in the opposite direction of the gate and moseys back into the admin office. "There's always a bigger plan at work."

HONK HONK

"What did he say?" Sheryl asks the monks in the back.

Tanalia stretches and yawns.

"He's complaining about the heat," answers Jakandy.

"We know it's hot," Mario says, letting go of the steering wheel to wipe sweat from off his brow.

Ifton honks again, as the nav screen cycles up on the dashboard, showing green gridlines, a big red dot, and a white radar arm spinning clockwise.

"I didn't do it," Mario confesses, throwing his hands in the air. "I didn't do anything."

"Something's coming in on the radar," Jakandy says, leaning toward the screen for a clearer perspective. The big red dot blooms bigger on the screen with each sweeping pass of the radar's arm.

"You're telling me," Mario says. "That something's big, and it's coming this way!"

High above the desert, flying toward Fellowship City, two strong-flyers and two birds carry Muldivar and three other monks from the SIC. The heat is sweltering, and the birds are unable to keep up with the strong-flyers, who are almost immune to the heat. The bird carrying Muldivar on his back slips furthest behind the others and drops in altitude.

"Hey," yells Muldivar, kicking his sides.

"I'm sorry sir," the bird responds. "The heat."

"We must keep going," Muldivar urges, gesturing to the three others flying further away from them.

"I'm—trying—sir," the bird speaks breathless, falling another few feet.

Muldivar pivots around, searching for something to help. A red shimmer glints in the distance.

He points to it and orders, "Head that way. It might be a transport."

The bird spreads his arms out, allowing his feathers to catch the air. He glides toward the shiny object.

"It should be right on us!" Mario shrieks with his head craned out the driver's side window, trying to spot the unseen giant red blob. Sheryl's head is out the passenger side window, and Jakandy and Tanalia are leaning from the backseat, peering out the windshield.

"*I'm picking up a lot of panic,*" Tanalia thinks to Jakandy, "*but I can't pinpoint anything.*"

"*Yes,*" he replies in thought. "*It's all over the place.*"

"There it is!" Sheryl yells, pointing to the sky. "Ifton, stop!"

The van skids to a halt on the sand-covered highway. The passengers bolt outside. Mario raises his hand above his eyes as three dark objects fly past them. *Monks on flyers?*

Sheryl keeps her eye on the single dark object, growing larger with each second and heading in their direction. Jakandy and Tanalia stand, heads bowed and hands pressed together against their faces as if in prayer. Sheryl glimpses them in her periphery, trying not to take her eyes from the object.

"*It's a giant bird,*" she thinks as the feathered wings come into focus. "*No, wait. Something is on its back. It's not a singular object at all but two people.*"

Jakandy and Tanalia's heads shoot up at the same time. Their eyes meet those of the monk riding on the back of the giant bird.

"MULDIVAR?!?" they cry in unison.

Sheryl and Mario trade uncertain glances.

"I guess they're familiar," Sheryl says, winking at Mario.

The bird lands hard, falling to its knees and breathing heavy. Muldivar jumps from his back and hastens toward his fellow monks.

Sheryl motions for Mario to go to the bird. He shrugs. She rolls her eyes and trots to the back of the van. She opens the door, retrieves a cup from one of the supply bags, and pours some water into it. Then, she returns, bearing water for the bird.

"Oh," says Mario in sudden realization.

"Muldivar, what are you doing here?" Jakandy says, embracing his old friend. Tanalia stands back, nodding a greeting to her fellow monk.

"I'm on my way to the monastery. Why aren't you?"

"You're abandoning the SIC wardenship?" Jakandy asks, gripping Muldivar's left shoulder with his right hand.

"Abandoning?" Muldivar asks, recoiling as his face contorts with confusion. He studies his two colleagues. "Do you not know? How can you not know?"

"It's been a day for that," Jakandy answers. "What is happening?"

"There's a lot of confusion," Muldivar begins. "Much of what I sense is unfocused, but within the chaos is a clarity. The Enclave recalled me, and all the other monks outside of the monastery. Did you not receive the communication?"

"No," Jakandy says, shaking his head and turning away from his friend. "I have received no word from the Enclave since I communed with them this morning."

"Neither have I," Tanalia interjects. "Maybe you're confused—"

"No, the message is clear," interrupts Muldivar. He points toward the three dots becoming one and disappearing in the distance. "They all received it too and are on their way."

"We must be blocked," Tanalia says to Jakandy.

Jakandy nods. Then, he turns to Muldivar and explains, "We were on a mission for the Enclave—"

"A mission?" questions Muldivar.

"Yes," says Jakandy. "We are hunting a killer."

"A killer?" Muldivar asks, challenging his fellow monks. "I felt nothing."

"No one did," Tanalia says, shaking her head.

"Hey guys," Mario says, wiping his forehead with a fistful of napkins. "It's super freaking hot out here, and I feel like I'm cooking. I think Ifton might be—that rubber on the hot concrete is starting to smell. Maybe we can take this show on the road?"

Mario jumps into the driver's seat. Jakandy opens the back door and waves Muldivar and Tanalia in first. Sheryl helps the bird up and walks him back to the van. The bird slides over the passenger seat to find an uncomfortable seat on the console between Mario and Sheryl.

After shutting the door, Sheryl asks, "Did you say, all the monks are being called back to the monastery?"

"Yes," Muldivar's forehead wrinkles with uncertainty. "And who are you?"

"I'm the detective," Sheryl asserts.

"So, we're going to continue toward SIC, right?" Mario asks.

"No, the monastery is going on lockdown," Muldivar says agitated. "We need to get there before we are locked out."

"But...but," Mario stammers.

"How much time do we have?" asks Tanalia, spying the time on the dash clock." It's 12:24 now."

"Maybe an hour. Maybe less."

"We need to get to the monastery, Ifton!" Jakandy orders. Ifton burns rubber on the asphalt, peeling around in a U-turn back toward Fellowship City.

But my father.

Sheryl turns toward the monks in the backseat, nudging the bird forward and out of her way. "Excuse me, darling," she says, as she squeezes her shoulder behind him. He quietly squawks, intoning his discomfort. Sheryl addresses the three, "How well is the monastery fortified?"

"Very well," Muldivar asserts. "The five elders of the Enclave hold vigil, creating an impenetrable mental force-field over the whole complex, similar to the larger one surrounding Fellowship City keeping the flesheaters at bay, but much stronger. During a lockdown, all the monks within will meditate on the Enclave, strengthening the mental power, allowing it to last indefinitely."

"Yeah, I thought something like that might be the case," Sheryl says. "Now, I may not possess these powers you have, but I surmise with my keen intellect that a lockdown of the monastery before discovering who or what the killer is, might encourage nothing more than greater bloodshed."

"How do you mean?" Muldivar asks.

"Well, it's a one-stop-shop. A veritable smorgasbord," answers Sheryl. "All those Mighty gathered together in one place. They're sitting ducks."

Jakandy and Tanalia face each other at once with realization. "The mental shield won't work," Tanalia shares.

"What are you talking about?" confronts Muldivar. "The elders are the most powerful Mighty to exist—"

"The killer creates a void where the powers of the Mighty are temporarily...abolished," Jakandy says, placing a hand on Muldivar's shoulder.

"By Sol and Luna," Muldivar murmurs. "What can we do?"

"That's what we're trying to figure out," Sheryl answers. "You were the SIC warden, right?"

"Yes."

"Did you have a man named Moriarty among your inmates?"

"It's Interns," Muldivar corrects. "But I wouldn't know any by name. They're all encoded with a unique SIC ID number."

Sheryl turns back around. Staring out the windshield, she rubs her chin with her left hand as she tries to work out the next step.

Mario turns toward the monks. Muldivar lurches, seeing the driver turn away from the road. When the others pay it no mind, he eases back, still confused.

"I guess it's not worth asking if you knew my father then, eh?" asks Mario.

Muldivar narrows his eyes and tilts his head.

"Huh. I find you familiar," he says. "What is your name, Citizen?"

"It's Mario."

"Yes, yes," Muldivar says with a laugh. "You are Mario... and you have a sister, Zelda, right?"

"Yes."

"You are much more grown than the memories I have of you," says Muldivar.

"You know me?" Mario asks confused. "I don't think I—"

"I have your father's memories of you," he interrupted. "And your sister and mother."

"What?!?" Mario reaches toward Muldivar, his eyes reddening with rage as the bird wrests him back. "How?"

"Don't worry," Muldivar says, laughing again. "Your father, 11428, is very much alive. At least, he was when I left."

"Tommy."

"Excuse me."

"His name is Tommy," says Mario, glaring into Muldivar's eyes and pushing himself away from the bird. He turns back toward the windshield and mutters, "Tommy Rickson."

"How do you have his memories?" asks Sheryl, turning back around.

"We take them as punishment," Muldivar replies. "It's the only currency they still possess?"

"Are you the only one who does this?"

"Since I've been warden, yes," answers Muldivar, throwing a sidelong look at Jakandy.

Sheryl plunders a handful of napkins and snatches the bird's cup of water. She spins around and flips the mirrored visor down. She removes her wig and wipes her face free of make-up. When finished, she turns back around to show Muldivar her hidden face.

"Do you have any memory of this face?"

Fires burn all around the SIC, as Tommy follows James into the admin office. Inside, the bloodied corpse of a bird guard welcomes them. Tommy covers his mouth and pinches his nose. James rushes by without acknowledging the obstacle.

"Where are you going?" Tommy questions, easing past the carcass.

"The keys to the transport vehicles are in here somewhere," he says with a mischievous grin while ransacking a desk "Once we find them, we can be on our way."

Tommy begins a frantic search of his own at the next desk over. They find nothing in the first two desks and shuffle onto the next, and the next after that. Once all the desks in the room are emptied of their contents, they hurry toward the back.

James tries to open the door to Receiving but finds it jammed. He slams his shoulder into the door, making it budge enough to view the body blocking the way. Blood pools around the threshold.

"Little help here?" James calls.

Tommy dashes over.

"Three. Two. One."

They ram the door, plowing through and knocking the body out of the way. As the door swings out, they fall to the ground inside. Tommy's eyes linger on the cat woman's lifeless body tussled in a heap. Tears begin to well, but he shakes them away. *Why do I feel anything for her?*

"Got them!" James says, jingling a pair of keys in the air with one hand while grappling a book in the other.

They exit through the back of the admin building toward the warehouses. James surveys the area. About twenty feet ahead are three warehouses, separated by walkways between them and a guard tower in the center. Once it was a clock tower, but a makeshift balcony now extends around its core below the clock face: shorthand on the 12 and longhand on the 6. A guard still stands watchful and cocksure with the ladder drawn up. To the left and right of the tower, stragglers continue to fight the guards. James and Tommy crouch out of view.

"Keep an eye on the clock tower guard," James whispers to Tommy. "He'll run a routine, spending no more than thirty seconds on each facing. When he's on the opposite end, we run toward the walkway. Got it?"

They hunker down, watching the guard follow his routine even amidst the present chaos. James scurries toward the walkway as the guard crosses to the other side. Tommy follows right behind. They stop and wait for the guard to go back to the far side. Then, they creep down the walkway toward the front of the warehouses out of his sight.

The sounds of a scuffle echo against the warehouse walls along the walkway. James raises a finger, and Tommy hugs the wall. When the fighting ends with footsteps trampling off into the distance, James drops his finger and takes a step.

"Help...please, help me."

James halts, hearing the hollow cry for help.

"I know that voice," Tommy whispers to James, sliding by him and peeking out of the walkway. A bloodied body curls on the ground as a flesh-colored tail trembles.

"It's Julian," Tommy says, crouching over to him.

James follows him out the walkway, scanning around for any eyes on them.

"He needs our help," Tommy says, as he kneels next to Julian, putting his hand on his chest.

"Snap out of it, Tommy!" James orders, grabbing Tommy by the shoulder and whipping him up. "He kept you from your family! He's one of them! He doesn't deserve our help!"

"No... please," Julian begs.

"We'll get your memories back," James says, putting his arm around Tommy, ushering him toward the warehouse door.

A tear falls from Tommy's eye as they open the warehouse to reveal a transport truck.

"I'll help you find Muldivar," James says, sprinting to the driver's side.

Tommy takes his cue and zips to the passenger's side.

"And in return," James says, thumbing through the book, finding a page that reads: *The Return of Sherlock Holmes*. He caresses the print of the title with his right forefinger saying, "You're going to help me exact revenge!"

BEEEROOO BEEEROOO BEEEROOO

The siren at the monastery screams, followed by a voice booming from the speakers, "Twenty minutes until lockdown. All non-monastic personnel and visitors are to be evacuated."

Dozens of seer-paths, monks, communitors, and novitiates alike, file through the front gates of the monasterial complex. They head north toward the Main Cathedral. South of them, twice as many non-monasterial Mighty exit through a side gate.

A very tall, slender hybrid with blue and black striped fur stops to admire the giant spire emanating from the Main Cathedral. He wears the traditional non-hooded, white robes of the servants of the monastery with a lanyard and laminated ID hanging on his chest. Several other Mighty wearing the same robes scramble by him.

"Move it," yells a strong guard ushering the non-monastic personnel from the premises.

The hybrid turns and reaches for the hand of the nearest seer-path passing him. "I forgot to—" he tries to say, but the monk jerks her hand back in disgust.

"Don't touch me, filth!" she yells at the hybrid. "Guard! Take this creature from me and revoke his privileges."

"Wait... wait," says the hybrid as the strong guard prods him toward the exit.

"You need to leave now!" yells the strong guard, as he rips the lanyard from the chest of the hybrid. "And don't come back."

"But...but," the hybrid protests, taking a vicious right hook to the face. He flies out of the gate, knocking three other servants of the monastery to the ground.

"Anyone else?" The strong guard shouts, puffing out his chest and licking the blood from his fist. The last of the servants inside the complex spurt out. The guard exits behind them and locks the gate from the outside.

"Wait. Please. I need to tell them that I forgot to extinguish the candles in the library of the Main Cathedral," the blue and black hybrid tells anyone who will listen, as he tries to shake off his wounds and collect himself.

"They're fucking seer-paths!" the strong guard yells, overhearing the protests. "They know already." He tosses the laminate back to the hybrid. "Take this and go. They'll forgive and forget. It's what they do."

The blue and black striped hybrid bows before scampering away with the others. Behind them, the immense monastery grounds loom tall on the green, forested hill traveling northeast up a stone pathway from the Main Cathedral. The grounds are enclosed by massive walls, which easily repel Citizens.

They do not, however, repel the Mighty or flesheaters, which is why the elders of the Enclave maintain the mental forcefields around Fellowship City and the monasterial complex. The strength of the forcefields is determined by the number of elders and seer-paths connected and providing power. In general, the elders work one at a time in shifts, as the strength needed to maintain the forcefield depletes their energy. During their shift, multiple seer-paths meditate upon them, feeding them with supplemental energy to protect the barrier.

Until today, the elders never needed to work more than one at a time before. With all the non-monastic personnel and visitors relocated, and all the guards standing outside each of the four gates, the time for collective action was nigh.

Mighty spectators stand about outside the walls, speculating on what is happening at the monastery. Never before have they witnessed anything like this. The domain of the monks of Sol and Luna is supposed to be a quiet, solemn, reverent place. Because it lies north of downtown and east of Emerald Hills, the vast majority of the onlookers are Mighty, and rich ones at that.

An older woman wearing a fur coat and walking a hairless dog waves her right hand at a mound of earth not 50 feet from the high walls of the monastery. She moves her hands together in an arrhythmic gesticulation, fashioning an earthen bench from the ground. Taking a seat on the bench, she points to a spot near her pet. The earth opens up, creating a bowl, which begins to fill with water bubbling from below the earth for her dog to lap up.

A short, balding man wearing silk pajamas, a velour bathrobe, and leather, shearling-lined house shoes saunters up to the woman. He tilts his head in a greeting.

"I say. I've never seen them lock this thing up before. I'm not sure which side of this wall I'd rather be on."

"I'm not sure I'd want to be in there with them," says the older terrakin, petting her dog, as she sups from the earthen bowl. "They're all a bunch of mind readers. I hear some can even control people."

"You don't say," he responds, retrieving a cigar out from the pocket of his robe. He licks his lips and places it between them, snapping his fingers to create a flame to light it up.

18

THE EMERALD CATHEDRAL

HONK HONK HONK
Ifton races through a city street, whizzing by other vehicles and pedestrians.

Sorry. Out of my way! Coming through! he thinks, but it only comes out as another series of horn blasts.

Mario sits in the driver's seat, trying to keep his hands from gripping the wheel and feet from slamming on the brakes. Sheryl is still turned around, facing Muldivar with her right arm pressing down on the bird's back. He braces himself against the dashboard, desiring to be in the sky.

Ifton careens around a corner, forcing everyone to lean into someone or smash up against a window. In the distance, the sprawling green hill of the monasterial complex comes into view. Ifton follows the road until it becomes a single lane backed up with cars trying to either enter or exit.

Pedestrians stand along the side of the road, gawking at the happenings at the monastery. Some of them meander forward to get a better perspective on the situation while others shuffle away, returning to their homes in the magnificent Emerald Hills.

"If you want to get up there," Mario says, "You're probably going to have to walk—or fly."

The bird wrangles himself out of Sheryl's grasp and turns to Muldivar.

"I'd rather be flying than sitting in here, sir."

"I'll stay with Jakandy," says Muldivar without consulting the other two monks. "Take Tanalia."

Tanalia pleads with her eyes, but Jakandy only lowers his head, deflecting her gaze. Neither speaks outwardly nor inwardly.

The bird nudges Sheryl to open the door and jump out, so he can climb out behind her.

"But—" Tanalia starts to speak.

Jakandy stops her, placing his hand on her shoulder and giving her a light squeeze.

"You need to warn them. Make sure they take necessary precautions. If they stay isolated, they will—"

"Okay," Tanalia interrupts, placing her hand on Jakandy's and thinking, "*If I don't see you again, I want you to know that I love you.*"

"*I know,*" Jakandy thinks back to her, as she exits the van. "*I feel the same.*"

Tanalia climbs onto the back of the bird, giving everyone a reverent nod before the bird lifts up into the sky. They fly over the gridlocked road, which leads to the main gates of the monasterial complex.

"*It's the safest place for her right now,*" Muldivar's voice-thought tells Jakandy.

"*You better be right!*" Jakandy squints.

Sheryl turns back around toward Muldivar. "How much of his memory remains?"

"I can't be certain," answers Muldivar. "He's not a normal Citizen. He's one of the Realizer's imaginings. They're always temperamental."

"Yes, I know," says Sheryl. "I'm one of them."

Mario spies Muldivar's stunned face in the rearview and laughs.

"If the Enclave called for lockdown," Jakandy says. "There may be more murders than the ones I did not report."

Muldivar's expression is a mix of confusion, disgust, and intensity. Jakandy shrugs with indifference. Mario keeps an eye on them both in the rearview while Sheryl rubs her forehead between her eyes.

"I must commune with the Enclave and find out—" Jakandy blurts only to be interrupted by Muldivar.

"But you've been blocked, yes?"

"Yes."

"Then, it's on me," says Muldivar, as he climbs over the backseat into the storage area. He shoves the ice chest, bottles of water, and bags of supplies to the side to make room for him to sit in a proper meditative pose.

"Members of the Enclave," he thinks, sending his singular thought into the light of his mind to the beyond, where it would join the Enclave's vigilant meditation. "I require clarification," he continues, as the forms of the elders take shape within his mind's eye, floating around his line of sight, just out of reach.

The elders are more somber than usual, heads bowed in more than reverence.

"The unseen death is upon us, Muldivar," says the attractive elder with the silvery locks and beautiful olive skin. Her dark brown eyes with the yellowish tinge pierce his being. "The monks Avasent and Greeve have left this world before their eruption."

Muldivar's eyes open.

"Head northwest to the Emerald Cathedral!"

"What is it?" Jakandy asks with grave concern.

"Avasent and Greeve are dead."

Jakandy's face contorts with a combination of anger and despair, not believing that once again he did not feel or sense anything around these deaths. He knew those monks well. They were the caretakers of the Emerald Cathedral.

???
webnet.mightybase search results...
The Emerald Cathedral : MIGHTYpedia Entry
???

The Emerald Cathedral is lavish and strikingly beautiful, built in the style of French Gothic architecture. Though it was erected more recently than the ancient cathedrals of that style, the construction incorporated gargoyles and chimeras for support and waterspouts, as well as intricate stained-glass designs, carvings, and statues depicting events that followed WWIII, the rise of the Mighty, and the lives of Sol and Luna from birth to eruption.

???

Jakandy closes his eyes, delving into hindsight to retrieve a memory of his old friend Avasent. Each present thought advances outward from a central core of his mind's eye, where a small dark spot forms unmoving within the swirling colors escaping the void. The dark spot grows larger, driving away all else, as it forms into images from his first day of being a novitiate of the Monastery of Sol and Luna.

Jakandy opens his eyes to view his memory through the eyes of his younger self. He glimpses his youthful reflection in the mirror, admiring his new hoodless yellow robes.

"*Looking good*," a female voice reverberates within the heads of the current and past Jakandy. The younger Jakandy surveys the room, finding no one.

"Who said that?" shouts young Jakandy, searching the room for a culprit.

With no intruder in sight, he flees the room and scans the hallway. He slides his right hand along the wall, trying to discover the origin of the voice. He senses something draw him closer and closer. Turning the corner, he stumbles upon another novitiate in yellow robes.

Her long blond hair is braided with yellow ribbon hanging down the backside of her robe like a tail. She admires her reflection in the colossal window of the small sanctuary room, turning her head to and fro with an ever-widening smile.

"*Very good, if I do say so myself*," her voice reverberates once more in his head.

She wasn't trying to communicate telepathically with me, young Jakandy thinks. *Her thoughts came to me out of the ether. How interesting.*

Her eyes gleam with surprise as she catches sight of Jakandy approaching her from behind.

"Oh hi," she says shuttering. "I didn't realize anyone else was here yet."

The young Jakandy stands awestruck by her beauty, admiring her flawless early-pubescent skin completely different from his own face riddled with white-headed acne. After a long and awkward pause, he finally says, "I'm

Jakandy Tayo, but you can call me Jak if you want. All my friends do." He tries to regain his composure and sound cooler than he knows he is.

She smiles at him sweetly. "Hi, Jak," she says with a smirk. "How funny. You made me say hijack like you hijacked my conversation or something. If you were one of those comic book superheroes that would be your alias, Hijack."

Jakandy laughs, overdoing it a little. "And you are?"

"Oh yeah," she reaches out her hand to shake his. "I'm Avasentia Di Vienobo. But my comic book hero name is Avasent! You can call me that, Hijack."

"Just Jak is fine. I don't need to be a hero."

"You sure about that?" she asks, punching his shoulder and spinning around him. "I'd let you be my sidekick."

"Well, I'll think about it," he says, following her to the small sanctuary room door.

We were so close then, present-day Jakandy reminisces about his friendship and their lessons together as novitiates. *Even as we competed to be the best in class, we were inseparable and unstoppable. We were the first in our class elevated to the rank of communitor after completing Step 3: Practice. I'm not sure what happened to our bond after that.*

Swirling images and momentary interactions fill his mind's eye as he sifts through them in his hindsight. He observes his younger self become sharpened and focused, excelling in leaps and bound over everyone else. He achieves an early advancement to adjudicator and is promoted to warden of the SIC.

The youngest warden to ever serve the monastery.

"I bet you're going to be an elder of the Enclave before too long," Avasent jokes.

"I've got to achieve Step 8: Patience before I can even be

considered for that honor," his younger self replies in all seriousness.

"Oh, Hijack."

I didn't take it as a joke, Jakandy recalls. *I took it as a challenge. And so, I became the youngest monk in recent years to achieve patience. I wanted to be one of the first elders in ages that did not have silver or white hair on their heads. It was my dream —but I knew all my achievements were likely for naught, as I was not Omnipathic. The likelihood of being advanced an elder without being a Seer-Omnipath was close to nil.*

"Hey stranger," says Avasent. "While you've been cooped up in the monastery, doing Sol and Luna only know what, I've found my true calling."

While I excelled in my path toward monkhood, Jakandy thinks, envisioning the excited expression on Avasent's face as they stood in the doorway of the Emerald Cathedral. *Avasent stagnated. She never moved beyond Step 5: Emulate. She eventually transitioned from communitor to monk, but she never gave up her personal belongings or moved into the monastery. Instead, she found a passion somewhere unexpected.*

"Can you believe it?" says the ghost of her voice.

I couldn't believe it, he thinks. *I couldn't understand her choices. I thought she wanted more. Like I did. I thought she was more like me, a monk. Not a caretaker for the Emerald Cathedral.*

"It's so massive and beautiful. I absolutely love it."

Now she is gone and will never have the opportunity to reach parsimony let alone eruption, Jakandy thinks in silent meditation. *May Sol and Luna embrace her being into their omnivolence, regardless of her lapse in monastic progression.*

Muldivar grips his hand, sensing his fellow monk offering a similar prayer next to him.

And I love you, Jakandy wishes he had said to her. He wishes he had thought it, so she knew. *All those years together, I longed for her, but my ambitions would never allow me to get close to her. A relationship would've held me back from my dream. The impossible dream that I wanted so much to obtain and would not allow anything to get in the way of. That is why I strove to reach Step 7: Purge so soon in my monastic career.*

"I hope you visit me," her voice-thought enters his mind.

But I didn't visit her, Jakandy thinks. *I had to cast off my self and disregard any intimate relationships to allow me to focus solely on being a monk. I had to push my feelings for her out of my mind. Perhaps that is why Avasent did not progress.*

This realization causes his head to snap back as his eyes roll around under the lids. His myriad memories dance maniacally within his cortex, disrupting and erupting neuronal electrical impulses. Over all of the spinning images overlapping one another in a frenzied vortex, the face of Greeve looms.

Greeve, thinks Jakandy. *He was a few years younger than us, following us around like a puppy. We could never be alone together, which was altogether annoying. Even so, he was highly intelligent, very attractive, and extremely competitive. Avasent had a choice to make, and so did I.*

"You must put her out of your mind," his mentor's voice spoke, echoing in his mind. "Focus on your monastic progression rather than discussing the potentiality of inti-macy. True strength lies in the expulsion of the intimate. Intimacy is a plague consuming the weak, Jakandy. Are you weak?"

Her voice remains strident even now after so many years gone.

She taught me everything she knew about this world before she left it. Even so, she could not teach a teenage boy desiring a close relationship how to deal with his emotions. Those kinds of lessons were not in her wheelhouse.

"What do you want me to say?" asks his mentor. "Go get the girl? If you go get the girl, you can forget the monastery. It's your choice, Jakandy."

So, I made the choice to tell Avasent how I felt.

Jakandy recalls searching for Avasent, only to find her at play with Greeve.

They seemed happy, which made me feel debilitatingly insecure. Instead of pursuing her, I went full throttle into my monastic progression to become the pride of my mentor. I've forgotten this, Jakandy thinks. *I forgot that I blocked out these haunting memories. Now they stir around in my mind like festered wounds and clotted blood, disturbing my meditative peace.*

His memories surround him and penetrate his being, infesting him with those emotions of jealousy, envy, and doubt once again. He remembers how he withdrew from Avasent and left Greeve to pick up the pieces.

"If he can't see what's in front of him," Greeve says to her. "If his dreams are too great to include you, he doesn't deserve your time."

Those words resonate around him as what was once forgotten and repressed floods back in painful waves. At the time, his youth and impulsivity did not allow him to understand their meaning. Pondering on them now, he realizes he was the one who walked away from what he truly wanted. He now understands why Greeve also stagnated on his monastic progression, choosing to stay at Avasent's side.

Greeve loved her just as I had, thinks Jakandy. *But he made the right choice. He chose his desire over his dream.*

Jakandy bows his head and says a silent prayer for Greeve like the one he had for Avasent.

Mario peers through the windshield at the giant structure with the flying buttresses and tall spire. "I thought it was the Emerald Cathedral," he says, as they drive up the winding hill toward the back of the Cathedral. "Why isn't it green?"

"It's named after the suburb, not its color," Muldivar snaps.

"Oh."

HONK HONK

"What did he say?" asks Sheryl.

"He says he can see his house from here," Jakandy answers for Ifton.

When they reach the top of the hill, they park at the front of the Cathedral and exit Ifton.

"We'll be right back," Mario says, rubbing his right hand along the left front fender before catching up to the others.

He reaches the others as they ascend the steps toward the three pairs of giant doors at the front entrance of the massive Church. Above each pairing of doors are intricate carvings and statues.

"There is the Evangelist and her Beacon," Muldivar says, pointing to a statue standing between the two doors in the center and directly below an impressive carving, much larger than any others.

Mario's eyes linger on the statue of a young girl with one hand pointing outward and the other hand clasped to the hand of an elderly gentleman with a very long beard. Above it, two people with their heads connected like conjoined twins sit in a meditative pose upon a throne of fire.

"What's that?" he asks, pointing to the massive carving.

"They are Sol and Luna, first of their kind," answers Muldivar.

"That's Sol and Luna?"

"First of their kind," adds Sheryl, smirking at Mario.

Jakandy and Muldivar pay them no mind, as they both struggle to open one of the double doors.

"Sol and Luna have mercy!" exclaims Jakandy.

Candles lit in the massive grand entryway flicker their light upon a gigantic glinting puddle of blood. A crimson trail leads to the open doors of the main hall.

"They're too heavy to stay open like that," Jakandy says, scrutinizing the doorway. He tiptoes toward the doorway, trying to step around the puddle and not track any blood further into the room. "Be cautious."

Muldivar follows him, but he is mesmerized by the massive puddle. He stops in front of it and kneels for a better view. Blood splatters to his left in tiny droplets, capturing his attention. He tracks its trajectory toward a darkened corner of the room where the candles no longer glow.

Sheryl steps in behind Muldivar, surveying the room and studying the two monks' actions.

Mario remains by the doorway, dry heaving from the wretched scent of recent death and putrescence wafting toward him and sticking in his nostrils. As he turns away from the Church, he spots the top stories of the gigantic Upton Mansion popping out above giant trees lining a picturesque hill in the distance.

Jakandy investigates the doorway, discovering the mangled body of an unidentifiable Mighty split in two and wedged between the door and its jamb. Tacky blood crawls down the doors on either side.

Designer shoes, Jakandy thinks, exhaling in momentary relief. *This Mighty was not a monk.*

Lacking clarity in the darkness and unable to use his powers to increase his nearsight, Muldivar creeps toward the tiny splatters of red. He reaches out into the dark, narrowing his eyes to slits in hopes of better night vision.

Something is here that does not belong, he thinks, stepping closer and reaching farther. He touches something wet and sticky. *Blood*, he thinks before the horrendous odor catches him unguarded. He repulses back into the light, finding his fingers covered in a brownish-black viscous liquid that reeked of rank death and feces.

"Dammit," Muldivar mutters, wiping his fingers on a drape hanging from the wall. "I think I've found a pile of intestine and bowels."

"Probably," Sheryl quips, scanning around as she approaches Jakandy. "He seems to be missing some, yes?"

"Looks that way," agrees Jakandy, as he appraises the main hall leading to the outer sanctuary. Several tables and chairs are tossed to one side, and a small fire grows in a small trashcan. The room is lit with odd coloration as sunlight shines through the many-colored stained-glass designs decorating the otherwise unadorned high-ceiling walls of the main hall. "I think we are going to find a lot more death here than we anticipated."

Muldivar joins Sheryl and Jakandy inside the doorway of the main hall. Sheryl sniffs the putrid scent coming from Muldivar's hand and sighs with disgust. She is not so much disgusted by the smell but at his lack of investigative ability altogether.

"How does one exactly get a finger full of shit at a crime scene?" she asks, squinting sidelong at Muldivar.

He ignores her as he nudges by.

"There's a fire here," he says, scrambling toward the flames. "This can be a danger. We should extinguish it immediately!"

"Yes, yes, by all means, do," Sheryl says. "But, make sure you don't slip in that bloody mess."

"What bloody—" Muldivar says too late, unaware of the three bodies ripped to pieces and strewn about on this side of the room.

He recovers from his near fall, snatching onto the leg of an overturned table.

"There's a head here," he says, eyes glued to those of the dead Mighty gaping at him.

"Avasent or Greeve?" Jakandy asks.

"Neither of them," Muldivar responds, escaping the dead-eyed grasp of the severed head. "There are at least three bodies here, but none are monks."

Muldivar fetches a handful of cloth from the ground that once was a jacket. He shoves the dampened cloth into the receptacle to put out the flame. As soon as he does, something glints in the distance catching his eye before the dying light extinguishes. He slinks toward it, stumbling upon another severed head. Its eyes are agape staring back at him with a terrified expression.

Jakandy opens the door into the outer sanctuary, allowing an overwhelming odor of rot and sulfurous gas to escape from the captivity of the sealed room. Jakandy jumps back and covers his face. Sheryl follows suit.

"My God," she squeals. "I've never smelled anything this unholy before, and I've seen some bad things in my time."

"What the hell is that?" Mario screeches from the front doorway, as he doubles over. The sound of his vomit splashing to the ground on the marble floors of the grand entryway echoes through the chambers of the Cathedral. "Sorry," he singsongs. "I'll stay here and keep standing guard."

The room is alight with sun rays shining through broken

panes of stained glass. The body of a Mighty wearing a blood-drenched business suit hangs limply in a window on the left side of the room. A monstrous trail of blood drips down the wall below him, puddling on the ground in a heap of intestines and gore. On the far side to the right, another body hangs lifeless from a window. The upper half of her hangs down, arms reaching toward the ground, as her long hair drips blood onto the puddle forming below. Pews are tossed to the sides, possibly hiding corpses in the piles. In the center of the room are several size 13 bloody footprints leading toward the doors of the inner sanctuary.

"It looks as if people died here," Jakandy says, thinking aloud. "Then, they were drug to the next room."

"You don't say," Sheryl says, winking at Jakandy.

"If you're the detective," Muldivar says, pushing past Sheryl as he heads into the outer sanctuary. "Why are we doing all the work?"

"I don't want to break a nail," she quips. "Besides, I've been working this out. You gentlemen are doing your own thing."

"Yeah?" Muldivar questions. "You're working this out? In the meantime, my people are dying!" He turns toward her. "If you're so damned good, why haven't you figured this out yet?"

"I...I need more information," Sheryl says, stepping back and trying to fend him off with an answer. "There's simply not enough to go on. I can tell you what I know, what I suspect, what I can deduce, but at this point, it leads us nowhere. That doesn't mean I won't solve this case."

"This is not a fucking case!" Muldivar exclaims. "This is happening right fucking now, and we need to stop it!"

"Stop!" Jakandy shouts as he heaves open the door to the inner sanctuary. "Neither of you are helping anything right now with all this bickering. Leave the detective to her work, Muldivar. And you," he points to Sheryl. "Come here and find something!"

"Yessir," she salutes Jakandy, fashioning it into a middle finger that she flashes at Muldivar. She enters the inner sanctuary, and then seconds later she peeks her head back in and says, "Now you boys play nicely in here. I'll be back momentarily."

The smaller room of the inner sanctuary is lit up in the multi-colored glow of the stained glass and fluttering candlelight at the altar in the center. Sheryl follows the tracks toward the altar where they veer to the left and the right and culminate in gutted, headless bodies piled atop one another. The altar is covered in a crimson glow dancing in the candlelight.

"Do you see the monks?" Jakandy calls from the other room.

"Not yet," she calls back. "I cannot identify anyone here as a monk. There are a lot of people, but I don't see any brown robes."

As she draws closer to the altar, she discovers a pile of bodies lying against it as well. *Where are all your heads?*

"What was that?" Jakandy asks.

"Did you hear me?" she calls back. "I was thinking. The void must be lifting."

She inspects the altar, noticing the blood rippling outward and down the altar onto the bodies below.

Odd, she thinks, craning upwards.

High above the altar, the two monks hang upside down, blood dripping from their slashed necks onto the altar below.

"I think I've found your missing monks."

Minutes later, Sheryl sits on the edge of the backdoor of

the van, her head resting in her hands.

"Do you still think this is Moriarty's doing?" Mario asks.

"No."

AAAARRRRRRGGGGGHHHHHH

Pained screams bellow from within the Cathedral. Mario and Sheryl race inside the grand entryway to find Muldivar and Jakandy fallen to their knees, screaming in agony and gripping their heads with their hands.

"What is happening?" Mario asks in a panic. "Is the killer here? Are they dying?"

"I don't know what this is," spoke Sheryl in a slow cadence, trying to restrain her fright.

ERRRGHAAAMMMERRRG

Muldivar and Jakandy fall forward, drained of all their energy and wrenched in pain. After a few seconds, Muldivar rises back to his knees, shaking in shock. His face is white and his eyes red and full of tears. He wipes his knees, and then his arms as if he is wiping grime from his body.

Jakandy convulses on the ground, his eyes rolling back into his head and his mouth foaming.

"What's wrong?" shouts Sheryl, dropping to his side and trying to keep him still. "What is it? What is happening?"

Muldivar wobbles, clenching his head. Mario reaches for him to help him balance.

"Thank you," he says to Mario. "My equilibrium is gone —the ringing in my ears. It just won't stop."

"Here. Let me help you outside," Mario suggests, offering his arm for balance. Muldivar takes it, and Mario leads him outside.

Sheryl clamps Jakandy's shoulders to the ground.

"Break out of this, Jakandy!" she yells at him. "Get out of your head! Now!"

Jakandy's eyes snap open, as his face grimaces with overwhelming sadness. His eyes redden and well with tears.

Mario rushes back inside, asking, "Need help?"

"Yes," Sheryl says, hauling Jakandy to his feet.

Mario jumps to assist her, and together they carry Jakandy outside to the van.

"What happened?" asks Mario, as they maneuver Jakandy into the backseat next to Muldivar.

Muldivar only continues cradling his head as a small puddle of tears grows between his feet.

Jakandy raises his head, eyes red and full of tears.

"The Enclave is no more."

"What?" asks Mario. "What about Tanalia?"

"I don't know," Jakandy responds with increasing sadness.

"I can't sense anything," Muldivar says, lifting his head from his hands. "Is this what it feels like to be—to be a Citizen?"

Citizen is not a bad word! Mario shouts in his thoughts.

Neither Jakandy nor Muldivar pays him any attention. They are empty, like hollow shells of their former selves. Mario tries to think of something to say, something sympathetic. He turns from them and examines the Cathedral. After one glance at the giant red puddle within, he turns away, nauseous again.

Out of the corner of his eye, something moves near the back of the Cathedral. He double-takes and spies a skinny man wearing a pinstriped suit with a top hat and walking with a cane. Mario rubs his eyes, uncertain if what he sees is real or not. He takes another look, and the man is much closer and waving.

He seems familiar, thinks Mario. He jabs Sheryl's side and asks, "Who's that?"

She assesses the man and bolts upright.

"I think we found our missing comic book character."

Mario nods in agreement, upset that he had not figured that out first.

What is an eidetic memory worth if it does not work half the time, he thinks, reaching back into Ifton to retrieve the ledger and TRIVIAL #8.

"Can we help you?" Sheryl asks, stepping toward the man.

He motions his head to the right without taking his eyes off Sheryl and asks, "Is it a kill site?"

"I had a feeling we'd be running into you sooner or later," Sheryl says without answering the obvious. "You've been trailing us since the flyers, right?"

"Yes," Trivial answers. "How did you know?"

"That's where I left Watson," Sheryl says, pointing to the bottom of the hill where Watson is parked.

"That explains the programming," Trivial sneers. "I had to rewire him. Sorry about that, but I needed the transportation. Oh, by the way, she goes by Emma now."

Sheryl's eyes bug out in uncontrolled anger. She steps forward, but Mario jumps in front of her.

"You worked for the Realizer, right?" he says, blocking Sheryl's approach. "You were his assistant?"

"I guess you could call it that."

"This is you?" Mario asks, showing Trivial the comic and opening the ledger. "And this is your handwriting?"

"Yes, that is me," answers Trivial with a proud grin as he points to the comic. He takes the ledger from Mario and flips a few pages. "Yes, yes. Excellent work young sleuth. You've discovered the mystery behind the different handwriting in the Realizer's ledger. Congratulations."

Sheryl audibly smirks.

Trivial eyes Sheryl.

"I'm sure he learned it all from you. Right, Sherlock?"

Sheryl's right eye twitches as Trivial flashes a knowing smile.

I don't trust him, Sheryl thinks, hoping one of the monks might catch it.

"We must go," Jakandy breathes the words. "The killer—"

"Spit it out," Trivial interrupts, stepping forward and continuing to smile.

Muldivar adds, "The Enclave—dead."

"That's right!" Mario shrieks, running to the driver's side of Ifton. "We need to get to the monastery!"

Sheryl stares at the mechanism on her wrist, thinking, *Emma?*

"You coming, Sherlock?" Trivial asks, sliding into the passenger seat.

"My name is Sheryl, thank you," she says, prodding Trivial to the middle between the driver and passenger seats.

"My apologies."

"Alright, Ifton," Mario says, tapping the steering wheel. "Let's get rolling."

Trivial startles, as the van shifts gears and drives without any help from the driver. He shrugs it off and turns to Sheryl, flashing his wide-toothed grin once again at her.

"So, Sheryl, have you figured out who the killer is yet?"

"No. But I have a feeling you know who it is."

"As a matter of fact, I do."

19

HOW DO YOU HUNT A MIGHTY-KILLING MONSTER?

L oo clasps Zelda's hand as they both follow Tyler into a dark alley.

"Wait here," Tyler says, dashing ahead into the ever-darkening space.

He stops midway at a hidden alcove and waves before disappearing from their sight. Approaching a huge handle-less door with a panel box at one side, he rubs his fingertips and thumb together before placing his hand on the panel box. The box crackles as small electrical impulses course through the panel and all along the door.

KRRRK-KKCHK

The metallic clanking of multiple locks unlocking resounds through the alley. A line of light shines through the alcove, casting a giant Tyler shadow against the opposite brick wall. The shadow shrinks, as Tyler exits the alcove and waves for Zelda and Loo to join him.

He ushers them to the brightly lit room past the panel

on the wall still crackling with electricity and stinking of singed hair.

How'd he do that? Zelda wonders.

Zelda and Loo stand before the entrance, hands clamped together. Loo's doe-eyes peep up at her. She gives him a wink of assurance before spinning around to face Tyler. With a slight curtsy, she waves her arm in over-exaggerated gesticulations, indicating with all her esteemed majesty, her willingness to allow Tyler to enter first.

"So much for beauty before—" he jests.

"Nope," she interrupts, popping her finger into the air and following him inside the room. Loo keeps close behind her, still clenching her other hand.

Zelda examines the small room covered from floor to ceiling in riveted copper panels. On the ceiling, three lights shine down from copper enclosures. The floor is a single slab of marble or an amazing counterfeit.

As Tyler shuts the door, the room shifts under their feet.

"What the hell?" Zelda yelps, stabilizing herself against the wall.

Loo wraps both arms around her.

"Don't worry," Tyler says with a chuckle, pulling down a gate from inside the closed outer door. "This is one of those ancient elevators."

He reveals a control panel hidden behind him. Loo's eyes light up, and he loosens his grasp around Zelda.

"You want to do the honors, Loo?"

Loo shakes his head.

"I know new things can be scary, buddy," Tyler says, reaching for Loo's hand. "But don't you worry. I'll show you what to do, and I'll be here the whole time, okay."

Loo nods and takes Tyler's hand without letting go of

Zelda's. As he inches toward the control panel, he tows her with him. Before letting go of her hand, he glances over his shoulder at Zelda and whispers, "You're not going to leave me, right?"

"I'll be right here."

"Okay, Loo," Tyler instructs. "Flip these two switches."

A gear grinding sound emanates from the ceiling and the floor shifts under their feet. Loo stretches his hands out, clutching onto both Tyler and Zelda to keep his balance.

"I know it feels weird, huh?"

Loo stares up at Tyler with his puppy dog eyes and nods without letting go of his death grip

"Now, all you need to do is pull this lever to the right," explains Tyler. "Do you think you can do that, Loo?"

"I can do that," Loo says, letting go of Tyler and reaching for the handle. He tries to pull it with one hand, but it won't budge. He lets go of Zelda's hand and yanks the lever with all the effort he can muster.

As it cranks to the right, the room grumbles, and hauls them downward. Loo returns to the safe embrace of Zelda.

"So, where are you taking us?" questions Zelda.

"Before we get to that, there's something I need to tell you."

"I'm all ears."

"Okay. Here goes," he says, swallowing hard. "When Delirium hit the streets, like three or four years ago, it took a toll on the Normals, attacking like a plague. It's addicting from the very first dose, but if you can break it right away, then you can live without it—I know because I did."

Zelda tries to keep her jaw from dropping and eyes from widening. She bites her lip hard.

"I thought because I kicked the stuff, I could help her kick it too. But it doesn't work like that. Delirium becomes part of your physiology—something you need, like water or food. You understand?" Tyler folds his hands together and rubs them. "The Mighty use it to keep their slaves in check! It keeps us passive and numbs our brains."

The lever on the elevator snaps back, as they come to a stop. Tyler lifts the gate and opens the door, revealing a pitch-black hallway. The only light emanates from the elevator and casts three gigantic shadows into the long dark hall, each shadow larger than the next.

Tyler snaps his fingers with an electric spark, causing the dark room to illuminate in small bursts down the hall.

"Delirium did help some people though, like for headaches and other ailments," continues Tyler as he exits the elevator.

Both Zelda and Loo stand in shock, unmoving.

"I mean, it helped me," he says, turning to face her. "Without it, I may never have realized the extent of my power. I'm a technopath. I can communicate with electrical and mechanical objects. I can make them work for me."

"You ARE a Mighty!" Zelda exclaims as if she's uncovered a gigantic lie. She quickly maneuvers Loo behind her in the elevator before spinning around to face Tyler.

Tyler steps toward her, trying to explain, "No, I told you. I'm a half-breed—"

"Makes no difference to me," Zelda says, jumping up to grab a ledge on the elevator door while swinging her legs forward to kick Tyler with all her force.

Not expecting the attack, he is unable to brace himself. Her kick launches him several feet back, and he lands flat on his back out of breath. With amazing swiftness, Zelda spins around, rips down the gate, flips switches on the elevator's control panel, and jerks the lever.

Tyler reaches his hand out toward them. The elevator does not budge, only rumbling and grumbling in place.

"Son of a bitch!" Zelda cries out, glowering at Tyler through the gate. "Back the fuck off, right now! You sick son of a bitch!"

"Please Zelda, wait," he pleads while at the same time technopathically unflicking the switches and sliding the lever back in place. At the same time, he motions his other hand to the end of the hall and snaps. A door panel lights up. His fingers flutter, inputting the number keys on the pad, which depress as the corresponding number appears on the LED screen of the panel. The door opens.

"Zelda, I'm a half-breed. Just like Loo—"

Sounds of children playing fill the hallway, confusing Zelda. In her mind, she pictures the Orphan House. She drops her gaze to Loo. He is an innocent, her brother, and the son of a Mighty.

What powers do you have, little brother? she thinks before glaring back at Tyler.

In the distance, something by the door catches Zelda's eye.

"—and all these other kids."

Three small children peek their heads out the door and peer down the hallway. The first two squeal with glee and scurry to Tyler, still lying on the floor. The third raises his arms out and telekinetically grapples them, stopping them in place. They cry out in hushed whimpers.

"It's okay, Jorge," Tyler calls out as he rolls over and picks himself up.

Jorge lets the others free, and they barrel toward Tyler. He scoops them up in his arms.

"Where have you been?" one asks.

"Are we going to play Hide n' Spy?" asks the other.

He turns toward Zelda, carrying the two children not much bigger than Loo.

"This is Gwenyth and Gwendolyn. The twin Gwens."

Zelda stands awestruck, but Loo bounces with excitement.

"Games. I want to play. Please, Zelda."

Zelda smiles tight lips at Loo. Then, she turns to Tyler and shrugs an apology.

Tyler lowers the twin Gwens back to the floor. They scamper over to help Loo and Zelda with the elevator gate.

"Come on. Let's play!" One or the other or both say to Loo as they hurry down the hallway, zipping by Tyler.

"So, does Loo have powers?"

Tyler shrugs.

"Not all half-breeds have powers," he says, guiding Zelda down the hallway to his lair of lost children. "Some always have them. Some get them during puberty. Some never get them at all. It's a roll of the dice, I guess. Whether we have power or not doesn't matter to the Mighty though. If we're part Citizen, we're all Citizen—and that makes us slaves. Just like you."

Inside the enormous room are twenty cots with as many children playing together. Loo runs around with kids for the first time, laughing in gleeful excitement. Zelda surveys the room, assessing the number and ages of the children while taking note of those who exhibit power. Afterward, she steps toward Tyler.

"There's one thing that concerns me about all this, Tyler," she says, measuring him. "You knew where these breeders were, and you knew where these other kids were, but you didn't know who Loo was."

"I've been thinking about that," he says, scanning the room for Loo.

He finds Loo laughing and playing with the other kids. As if sensing the attention, Loo beams back at them and waves with excitement. Zelda smiles and waves back at him. Tyler gives him a thumbs up before turning back to Zelda.

"I knew the women were there, but I didn't know them. Some of them had children that went other places. I'm not sure why Loo was even in there."

"Maybe we should ask him," Zelda says, beelining toward Loo.

As she approaches Loo, she appraises his new demeanor. He is no longer the scared little boy. After mere minutes spent with other children, he is full of life with reddened cheeks and a playful bounce in each of his movements. She admires this new joy. Something he should have had his whole life. She did not want to take that from him now, but they must find the answers they seek.

She kneels in front of him, saying, "Loo, I must ask you some important questions. Do you think you can help me by answering them as best as you can?"

"Yes," he answers in his sweet quiet voice.

"You said your mother died when your sister was born, right?"

"Yes."

"How old is your sister now?"

"She's two."

"Why were you in the dark hallway, if your mother has been dead for two years?" Zelda questions.

Loo drops his head and whispers, "The mean man took me there. He said my sister was special. She would change things. He told me I would meet my mother again soon."

"How long were you in there, Loo?"

"I don't know," he cries with eyes swimming in tears.

Zelda cringes, not wanting to cause her little brother such pain amid his newly experienced joy. She cradles him to her chest.

"I'm here now, Loo," she says. "Everything will be okay."

"I'm tired," he replies, admiring the cots. "Can I take a nap?"

Zelda shrugs, glancing back at Tyler.

"Sure, buddy," he says, glimpsing the time on an LED clock hanging on the wall. "A little after 1:00, I guess that's a good naptime."

Tyler positions himself in the center of the room and hollers, "Alright, naptime everyone. Find your beds."

"Ahhh," a collective groan escapes from the kids, as they scramble for their beds.

Loo tugs Zelda to an untaken cot.

"Can you read me a bedtime story?"

"Yes, I can," Zelda says, mussing Loo's hair and taking a seat on the floor next to the cot.

Zelda loved the childhood bedtime stories her father regaled her with to lull her to sleep. Mario tried to tell them after the loss of their parents, but he never got them right. She appreciated the gesture though. In her head, she would always correct Mario's mistakes, not wanting to make him feel bad about forgetting some important detail. In truth, he never forgot any details, because of his perfect memory. He just didn't tell the story the way their father did.

The magical, colorful world her father created through his words blossomed into a lavish production in her mind. She would close her eyes and envision the lush landscape of vivid rainbows and oddly built structures with bulking, rotund tops and skinny bottoms, zigzagged buildings bending here and there, and others that seemed to defy the laws of physics altogether.

She imagined herself to be Ms. Shrum saved by the courageous mustachioed hero, Mario, once again. Her father never intended her to play such a role, as Ms. Shrum was the love interest of the hero and the damsel in distress. He told other stories about the adventures of the hero princess Zelda, but she wanted to live in Mario's world. In some ways, she identified with Ms. Shrum, especially after the Mighty took her parents.

"Brother!" exclaimed the mustachioed hero, trying to believe his eyes. "Are you okay?"

"It burns, Mario," the taller WaWa Boy agonized. "It hurts."

Ms. Shrum plucked one of the glowing mushrooms from the ground and hustled to Mario's side.

"Give him this," she said, handing him the mushroom. "It will heal him."

Mario took the mushroom from Ms. Shrum and studied it. The cap glowed green, except for several large white spots. His fingers and thumb did not meet as they wrapped around the bulbous stalk. He fed the mushroom to his bigger, little brother.

His brother turned a sick shade of green and started to convulse. Mario panicked, seeking help from Ms. Shrum.

"Don't worry," she said. "It takes a bit before the effect kicks in."

Within seconds, his brother's eyes bulged open as he leaped to a stance.

"I feel strong!" he shouted.

The short WaWa Boy recovered from the attack in time to witness the taller one's restoration. Filled to the brim with anger and betrayal, he soared into the air and screamed.

"Nooooo!"

Mario stood beside his brother, standing ready. Ms. Shrum found a sledgehammer and pickaxe lying against an old shed. She retrieved them and handed one to each brother.

"Godspeed, Mario," she said. "Brothers unite!"

Mario wielded the sledgehammer and his brother wielded the pickaxe. Behind both of them, Ms. Shrum stood punching her fist into her palm.

"You can't have him," screamed the short WaWa Boy, as he dove toward the three heroes. The heroes broke away from one another, but the WaWa Boy stayed headlong on Mario. "It's all your fault!" he yelled, pummeling toward him.

Mario brought the sledgehammer back and swung free, anticipating the short WaWa Boy's advance on him. The WaWa Boy flew backward where Mario's brother caught him with the pickaxe. He tried to shake himself free, but Ms. Shrum charged up and cold-cocked him.

Outside the battle area, hundreds of people of all shapes, sizes, and animal or plant natures came forward cheering, as the three heroes stood triumphantly over the unconscious body of their would-be attacker.

"Can I get a picture?" a photographer for the PipeTown Press said coming forward with her camera.

The heroes nod at one another. Mario and his brother signal for Ms. Shrum to join them front and center. She steps one foot onto the short WaWa Boy and pumps her fist into the air.

Suddenly, a light ray emanating from somewhere above them covered Ms. Shrum. Her eyes full of shock and surprise beckoned for Mario's help. Mario fell back into an attack stance, and his brother followed suit. The rest of the people gathered around gawked in confusion or scuttled away in terror.

As the light grew stronger, Ms. Shrum's form started to disappear. She tried to scream, but the light muffled her cries into a dull whimper. The light brightened until it blinded everyone before disappearing, leaving no trace of Ms. Shrum. Mario and his brother rubbed their eyes back into enough clarity to perceive a dragon-shaped spaceship zoom away.

Inside the spaceship, two Lizardmen guards, wearing their

techno-chrome armor and brandishing laser-pikes, tossed Ms. Shrum to the floor of the throne room/main deck. Without hesitation, she tried to jump from the floor and tear apart the iron manacles on her wrists, but the butt-end of the right guard's laser-pike smashed into her back, forcing her down to bow before the cyber-throne. She tried to lift her head, but each time, the guard thrust her head back down with the butt-end of his laser-pike. Before too long, she bowed before the cyber-throne, dropping her head in defeat.

"Welcome, Ms. Shrooom," a voice bellowed in a horrible animalistic, yet metallic growl from the throne.

She scowled at the Lizard King's giant Lizardman head leaning toward her, snarling and hungry. He turned his face, revealing one side to be mangled with robotics and tech weaving in and out of his scaled flesh. Revolted, she turned away.

Pleased with himself, he swiveled his throne around with his back to Ms. Shrum, laughing a mechanical roar. He waved one reptilian arm out to the left and one robotic arm out to the right, opening a giant viewscreen.

The stunned faces of the people of PipeTown appeared.

He wheeled back around to face Ms. Shrum and hissed, "I bettt your daddy will pay a handsssome penny for your sssafe return!"

ZZZZZZZZZZZ RON PSHI ZZZZZZZZZZZZ

Tommy smiled upon his sleeping children with their little snores. They loved his stories, but they rarely stayed awake for him to finish them. He patted Mario on his head and whispered, "Dream of being the hero you will become, my son."

He ran his hand through Zelda's golden hair, and whispered, "Dream of being the princess you are, my little Zelda."

"ZELDA!"

Tommy wakes up in a sweaty fit, drenched in fear. His

arms reach forward, grasping nothing. He examines the black mark on his arm with white raised numbers. 11428. The scarified names of Mario and Lizbeth protrude puffy and red from the flesh of his right arm. Ahead of him through the windshield is nothing but sand and sand-swept road for miles. As he stares into the vast emptiness, a glimmer of a memory alights in his eyes.

Zelda, he thinks, repeating the name over and over.

He retrieves a knife from his pocket and carves a Z into his forearm below the other two names. James notices the movement in the passenger seat.

"What are you doing?"

"Trying not to forget," Tommy says, scoring the letters E and L into his arm. The fresh marks redden with blood. James tosses Tommy a handful of napkins from the console. Tommy places them under his arm, sopping up some of the blood. "Thanks," he says, working on the D.

A small shiny object twinkles in the near distance.

"I think we're almost there," James says, pointing to a sign. "Look."

Tommy recognizes the highway sign.

"South Summerland Gateway exit half a mile ahead," he reads. "Take that! The gateway will take us right to the WPC."

James maneuvers to exit, while Tommy finishes carving into his arm.

"You sure there's an army waiting for us?" asks James.

"Absolutely," Tommy says, reaching into the back, prodding around for something. He recovers a white guard shirt, rips the sleeve off, and wraps it around his arm. A red rose blossoms through the bandage. "These people have every reason to hate their oppressors!"

"What if they don't feel oppressed?" questions James.

ERRRRRROOOOOOOMM

Ifton races down one of the many hills of the Emerald Hills suburb, heading east toward the monastery. Mario sits in the driver's seat, hands on the wheel, but only for show. Trivial squeezes himself together between Mario and Sheryl, pouting with discomfort. Sheryl sits in the passenger seat, legs crossed, gazing out the window in deep thought. The monks lie in pained heaps in the back.

Both these bastards are vulnerable, thinks Mario, glaring through the rearview mirror at Jakandy and Muldivar groaning in the back of the van. Mario keeps his eyes on them as he tests whether his thoughts register in their telepathic minds or not.

With no sign of reaction to his thoughts, he continues thinking, *Jakandy took my father from me and gave my mother to DerMööve! And, Muldivar took my father's memories from him as punishment, while he rots away at SIC for doing nothing more than trying to protect my mom from DerMööve! If there were any justice in the world, they'd be two of the dead Mighty right now. Hell, I should kill both of them myself while I can!*

"And who is the killer, then?" asks Sheryl, turning to face Trivial. "How do we find him? Stop him?"

Mario straightens up, anger flooding over him. He squeezes the wheel, as he squints at the agonizing monks through the rearview.

I don't want to find the killer! he thinks. *He's killing these fuckers who killed so many of us— made us their slaves—entertainment. He's doing us a fucking favor! I don't want to stop him until he's rooted out everyone with powers they shouldn't have!*

"I don't know if we even can," answers Trivial. "I mean, how do you hunt a Mighty-killing monster, let alone kill one?"

So, what's the bad news? thinks Mario as he feigns a surprise in Trivial's direction.

The Enclave is no more, Tanalia thinks as she opens her eyes, recovering from the intense pain of loss caused by the mass murder of her leadership.

She attempts nearsight but she cannot penetrate her mind's eye beyond the confines of the closet she hides within. She thinks with force, trying to find her mentor, latch onto him, and send him a message.

"Jakandy! Where are you?"

PATUMPATHUMP

A thunderous pounding hits the back of her wall, jolting her forward. She jumps up and plows through the closet door, finding the room splattered in blood and gore. Her eyes dart around, panicked. A heap of mangled body parts, guts, and feathers lies outside the doorway. She searches the room. Finding no other way out, she tiptoes through the crimson puddles and blood-soaked feathers lining the way from the closet to the dead bird guard.

She places her hand on what might have been a shoulder and whispers a quiet requiem before peeking out the doorway toward the origin of the noise. Several brown-robed bodies and limbs are strewn about the long white hallway now covered in splotches of red on the walls, ceiling, and floor leading to the dormitory. Someone screams in the distance. She flees in the opposite direction.

All around her is recent death, gruesome by sight and putrid by smell. She covers her nose and mouth as she hurtles by the bits and pieces of monks she once knew. They are now nothing more than red paint on a white canvas. Hoping against hope that not all is lost, she rushes toward the Enclave.

Someone might be alive, she thinks.

Without slowing her pace, Tanalia bursts through the immense, intricately etched double-doors of the Enclave's white meditation room. The blood within pools into a blackish-red lake in the center of the room, streaming from the maroon puddles blossoming around the five violet heaps on the ground. The white and gray heads of each elder are mounted on pole-sized candlesticks. All their eyes are open, gaping at Tanalia.

There is no hope here, she thinks, exiting the room. *I must seek another answer.*

She eyes the path to the Main Cathedral south of the Enclave. The path is straight but open. There is nowhere to hide. She spies the minaret high in the distance.

It's about halfway to the Main Cathedral, she thinks, calculating her odds. *There is more coverage if I hug the walls and hide within the bushes around the minaret, but it's out of the way and slower.*

Limp brown-robed bodies scatter all along the path to the Main Cathedral.

The killer has already been down this path. What is the likelihood he returns?

Someone screams from the minaret behind her. She swallows hard, turning her attention away from the path to safety.

They need my help, she thinks, appraising the high tower.

More screams follow as she sees monks flailing in the windows of the minaret high above the Monastery.

It's a fortress, they'll be safe, she reassures herself, turning back around. *If I go now, I just might have a chance.*

She decides to take the chance and barrels toward the Main Cathedral.

"Watch out!" a monk shrieks from the minaret.

She glances over her shoulder, confused by the several monks scrambling at the barred window near the top of the tower.

"Save them!" one yells to the other.

She keeps running toward safety, running toward freedom, toward life.

They'll be okay. It's—

KARAAAACK

More screams echo from the tower as something crashes into the minaret with a resounding boom all around Tanalia. She wheels around, surprised by the tottering tower. Panic overwhelms her as she stops in her tracks, unable to believe her eyes.

The tower is falling?

She stands in shock as the tower pulverizes the ground, scattering dust and granulated rock all around her.

There's no help for them now, she thinks, bowing her head in mourning and regret. *What could I have done but join them in death?*

As the cloud of dust settles, Tanalia stands motionless and dazed until she catches sight of rubble shifting in her periphery.

Did they survive?

Her momentary hope fizzles as a massive dark figure emerges. She turns, sprinting toward the Main Cathedral, but after a few steps, she topples over one of her fellow monk's bodies and crashes to the ground.

"Ugh, ouch!" she cries.

Panic wrenches her face as she tries to silence herself. She lies silent and still, staring at the ruin of the tower. Her heart pounds in her head against the sound of the rubble falling away, stone clashing against stone.

Her eyes widen in horror as the monster stomps free of the debris. She closes her eyes and thinks a silent prayer, hoping beyond hope the monster will miss her.

By Sol and Luna, she whispers as she opens her eyes, locking onto the eyes of the beast.

With utter terror coursing through her, she realizes she is now the target. She leaps up and tries to scurry toward the Main Cathedral's back doorway only 20 feet away.

FWWWUUUMMMPP

The sound is horrid, sending chills through her body. She cannot bear to peer back at their cause, keeping her eyes fixed on the Main Cathedral door. She hears the sound again, closer this time. Still, she stays fixed on the door and salvation. As she reaches out, a monk's brown-robed body slams into the doorway, blanketing it with dark red blood. Wide-eyed and slack-jawed, she halts in front of the flaccid carcass blocking her escape. Behind her, footsteps thunder toward her, pounding in her head louder and louder, deafening her ears.

She drops to her knees and screams, "JAKANDY!"

A monstrous fist grasps her, slams her to the left and the right, and bashes her head on the ground. She spits out blood and tears and teeth. She cannot breathe, as the grip tightens on her ribcage, crushing her lungs. Something snaps and a sudden warmth washes over her as she is consumed by darkness.

"Noooo!" Jakandy screams, bolting upright in the back of the van. He's sickly, gray, and covered in sweat.

Sheryl shoves Trivial into Mario and turns toward the monks. "What happened?"

"I dunno. I didn't do anything," Mario says, eyeing Jakandy through the rearview with tacit disappointment.

Jakandy tries to lift himself up. He grabs Muldivar's arm.

"Tanalia's dead!"

"You...saw...it?" Muldivar says through labored breaths, trying to sit up.

"No," Jakandy says, standing up and appearing healthier with every second. "She gave me her life-force. I feel her inside of me."

"They can do that?" Mario whispers to Sheryl.

Sheryl shrugs.

Jakandy yanks Mario from the driver's seat.

"Hey, what's the big—"

"Take care of Muldivar," Jakandy commands, climbing into the driver's seat.

You bastard, Mario thinks, burning dagger eyes into Jakandy. *I should fu—*

"I can hear your thoughts again, Mario!" interrupts Jakandy, squinting at Mario through the rearview.

Mario's eyes are the size of planets.

Jakandy turns toward Trivial and Sheryl.

"Tell me everything!"

"Everything?" chokes Trivial.

"Start at the beginning!" demands Jakandy. "Why were you realized?"

EPISODE III

SIGNING OFF

"Stay inside. Stay safe.
This is MYT Radio FM 108 signing off."

20

A REALIZED END, ERGO MURDER

S ometime last year.
    The Realizer sat at a booth in QTs House of Jacks, writing in his ledger.

There is nothing new I can do in the world. It is tiresome, and I am bored. I am out of ideas. I want some excitement... some adventure. Isn't that what this power is good for? Where can I find new ideas?

As he writes, a dark-haired man with five o'clock shadow, wearing a black suit, white shirt opened at the collar, and loosened black tie, saunters toward him, carrying a box overflowing with comics, books, and movies on discs and tapes. Around the room, several other realized characters from the films of one of his favorite pre-WWIII directors worked as waitstaff.

"Heya, Vic," greeted a tall, bare-footed woman with a short black bob and bangs, wearing a long white dress shirt and tight black trousers.

He nodded with a wink and a sidelong grin, checking her out as she swayed by.

"Ahem," coughed a longhaired blonde in a yellow and black-striped motorcycle suit with the same face, standing in his way.

"Excuse me, darling," he said, trying not to let anything fall from his box. He titled his head, glimpsed back at the other and asked, "You all sisters?"

She shook her head and scuttled away, zipping by the other woman without any acknowledgment.

Vic chortled and continued toward the Realizer's booth.

"Ey'yo, Vic," called a pale man with dreadlocks, a massive scar on the left side of his face, gold caps in his teeth, and a cloudy left eye. He wore a leopard print smoking jacket and a black leather hat. "Homie, we gonna play dat game tonight? I gotsta git my Benjamins back."

"Don't worry about it," interjected a salt and pepper haired man with a massive tattoo rising up his neck from under a black suit with a vest over a white ribbed tank top. "You'll get your chance to win back your treasure, little man. Just be cool."

"Whoa, whoa. It ain't white boy day already, is it?"

"See, I told you this place is amazing," said an excited man, recording everything with his datapad. He turns to the others sitting in his booth. "And you guys wanted to go the Moon Room."

Vic reaches the Realizer's booth and drops the box on the table.

"Here's your shipment, boss."

The first thing the Realizer extracted from the box was a comic book.

"Trivial number 8," he murmured, admiring the cover and flipping through the pages.

Something caught his attention within, so he flipped back to the beginning and started to read. The more he read, the more pleasure coursed through him until a sparkle glinted in his eye and a crooked smile formed on his lips.

Later, the Realizer sat on his recliner in his room, reading

Trivial #8. On the last page, the artist had drawn a full-size image of Trivial, wearing a pinstripe suit, top hat, and holding a cane, as he stands next to the Eiffel Tower.

"And how did he spend all his winnings from the game show?" the Realizer read the oversized red words on the page. "Why a shopping spree at the best shops Paris had to offer!"

The Realizer points his finger at the page and pulls Trivial from the comic book page into the real world.

"AAAAAHHHHH!" Trivial screams, as he erupts with life. "What in God's green earth was that?"

"I have a job for you, Mr. Trivial."

For the next year, the Realizer sequestered Trivial to a small room packed with boxes overflowing with an array of media. Trivial would sit on the couch-formed futon in the center of the room, writing notes in the ledger as countless television programs and movies flashed on the three giant viewscreens along the wall in front of him.

Each viewscreen was attached to various media players, allowing him to view any of the various, discs, tapes, films, and records he found within the hoard of boxes. When he was tired of the video media, he would read through an assortment of literature, including novels, magazines, comic books, and newspapers. The coffee table in front of him and the side-table to his left were covered in the print material.

"The Realizer was bored and wanted new ideas," Trivial says to Jakandy, recalling the many months spent exploring the myriad media. "He needed help to find the next big thing. Or so he led me to believe."

Trivial's eyes were hollow, and dark circles formed below. His cheeks were sunken, and he appeared to be much more than a year older. Any hope or desire he had for this interesting and new future left him months ago. He reached for a box on the coffee table, divesting it of any familiar material. Piles of junk heaped all around him.

"Ah hah," he said, uncovering a small leather case with a zipper. "This looks promising."

He opened the zipper to find a stash of videodiscs. He examined them one by one, eliminating duplicates already in the Realizer's vast collection.

"What he really wanted—what he was bored with—was this mundane existence."

Trivial found a disc with an image of a hillbilly firing electrical charges from his fingers toward a massive fist gripping a large, bloody knife. The scarred fist resembled the hand of Frankenstein's monster, sewn together from parts of different people.

In giant bloody typeface across the disc, he read, "ENDER'S REVENGE."

"You monks eliminated crime in this world. You eliminated anyone who committed crimes, including the Mighty. You killed or imprisoned any Mighty who might become —supervillains."

Intrigued by the possibility of something new, Trivial's eyes alighted with glee. He rushed to the player and popped in the disc. With wild-eyed wonder, he marveled as the electrically charged hillbilly fought a monstrous knife-wielding slasher. The electrical charge did not affect the monster, who slashed his knife into the hillbilly, releasing electricity like blood into the air.

"He wanted me to find his next big thing, but I learned his true intention too late. He was bored—he wanted excitement."

On the screen, the dark figure stood, knife down, dripping blood and electrical charge. Pieces of the Abnormal laid strewn about before him, electricity fizzling to death. Trivial punched the eject button, retrieved the disc from the player, and slid it back *into the black leather case. He opened the ledger and wrote Joey Ender. After he finished writing his report, he ripped out the page, folded it, and scribbled The Realizer. Then, he slid the letter inside the leather case and placed it on a tray by his door.*

"He wanted a supervillain. He wanted to be the supervillain. He needed a tool. Something that could survive here, elude the monks, and defeat the other Mighty."

The next day, Vic opened the door and escorted Trivial out.

"Thank you for your time," he said to Trivial, who stood in utter befuddlement. "The Realizer is no longer in need of your services. He says you are free to go."

Vic led Trivial to the front door of QTs House of Jacks and shoved him through.

"Have a wonderful rest of your realized existence," he said, mockingly saluting him before he turned back inside.

"He realized a Mighty killer?" Mario blurts out, trying to force a frown.

"Quiet, Citizen," Jakandy commands. "Continue, Trivial. Did you—"

Asshole, thinks Mario, digging daggers into Jakandy's back.

"I can still hear your thoughts!"

Dammit, Mario thinks again, helping Muldivar sit up.

"Did you witness him realize this Mighty killer from the movie?"

"Not exactly."

"What do you mean?" probes Jakandy.

"I was upset with the Realizer and I went to see him," Trivial answers with eyes glued to the ceiling before darting around like he's searching for a thought.

Last night, Mario was the last employee of QTs House of Jacks to exit. As he raced down the dark street toward the Normal slums, Trivial stepped out of the shadows from an alleyway across the street. He ambled to the door and pressed the COMM button on the panel.

BUZZZZZZZ

The door opened to Trivial's surprise. He hustled inside and up the stairs, making his way to the Realizer's apartment. As he drew closer to the door, he heard the Realizer say, "Come in, my sweet."

Thoroughly confused, he opened the door to find the Realizer lounging outstretched on the couch, wearing nothing but a maroon robe with black velvet trim.

"Heya, boss. I'm not sure it's me you're waiting for," Trivial quipped, entering the room.

The Realizer jerked upright and leaned forward, yelling, "What do you want, Trivial? I already set you free."

Trivial spotted the black leather case and the note on it, sitting next to the Realizer on his side table. The Realizer caught sight of his shifting gaze and covered the case with his hand.

"Did you come back for this?" he asked. "This is why I brought you into this world. You did exactly what I hoped for. It took you a lot longer than I had anticipated, but you finally did your job."

"You don't understand," said Trivial, taking a few steps toward the Realizer. "It's too dangerous. You won't be able to control him."

"If you get any closer," the Realizer's left eye twitched as he squinted at Trivial. "I will take you out of this world, just as I brought you in."

Trivial stopped and stepped back.

"This world will not survive him."

"I'll be the judge of that," growled the Realizer. "Leave now. I'm expecting company."

Trivial turned with his tail between his legs, scurrying down the stairwell and toward the front door.

BUZZZZZZZ

"That's funny, sugar," said an attractive 40-year-old woman, as she phased through the front door. She wore a flowing blue dress and glasses. Trivial stood awestruck. She giggled.

"You've never seen a phantom before, hun?" she cooed, stroking his cheek. Her hand dematerialized to pass through him as she glided by.

He shuttered, following her ascent up the stairwell. The little hairs on the back of his neck standing on end calmed a bit as she turned the corner. He exited QTs House of Jacks, returning to the alleyway across the street to keep an eye on the situation.

Her shadow entered the room, blocking the light in the window for a second or two before returning again. Their muffled laughter reverberated in the silence of the night like a hushed rumbling of thunder. The lights dimmed to a dull glow and Trivial relaxed, hearing their increasing laughter. He formed an almost comfortable seat from recycled Chronicles and waited, keeping an eye on the window until sleep overtook him.

A resounding bang roused him from sleep. He scrambled, collecting himself before returning to his surveillance. The light from the Realizer's apartment faded from blue to black to red, casting a multi-colored glow from the window. Another bang boomed in the empty street, this time followed by a banshee's wail and the familiar sound of over-produced synthesized music.

'He's watching the movie with her?' he thought confused.

He scooted to the edge of his makeshift seat and chomped his fingernails.

As the night wore on, he relaxed again, hypnotized by the pulsating light of the window. He tried to stay awake, pinching and slapping himself to no avail. Again and again, he faded in and out consciousness.

Blood-curdling screams woke him, and he wondered if they belonged to the phantom lady or the movie. The answer came with a splash of red hitting the window with a wet thud. Trivial bolted upright, as the woman screamed louder. He started for the street, but the screams ceased as another burst of blood splattered onto the window, casting an eerie red glow over the street below.

TUMPATHUMP

A couple blocks east, a blinding light shined and thundered with a sonic boom. Trivial covered his eyes, spying a massive dark figure materialize within. It bellowed a mechanical roar or so Trivial thought. The monstrous thing lurched toward an oncoming motorcycle, snatching the rider from the bike and tossing him like a ragdoll across the street.

The bike skidded to a stop in the distance, continuing to purr, as the rider's body smacked a wall with a crack and thud. The rider's bones breaking against brick echoed louder than the idling motorcycle. The dark giant stood, staring north for more than a few seconds. Trivial groped the wall, trying to keep out of sight. The monster turned, facing his direction. Trivial gulped and closed his eyes.

"He got more than he bargained for. He realized something he could not control."

"Who is this killer?" Jakandy asks, burning his eyes into Trivial.

"Joey Ender," surmises Sheryl. "He realized the killer from the slasher film. You've seen the film, yes?"

"Yes," Trivial says, "Your garden variety B-Movie slasher flick. Nothing extraordinary, except for the fact that the killer—"

"Is immune to superpowers," Sheryl interrupts. "We're aware. What is the film about? Tell us the story. We may discover something of use or a clue as to how to stop this—this slasher."

"It was produced around the first Evolutionary War—"

"The what?" Jakandy interrupts.

"I'm referring to the Evolutionary Wars where the Abnormals rose against the Normals to become the Mighty," he answers.

"You're mistaken, Trivial. That's not the true history. The Mighty rose following WWIII when the Normals as you call them wiped themselves out. Under the guidance of Sol and Luna—"

"That's a lie," Mario interjects. "That's the story the Mighty tell themselves and try to make all of us believe, but it's not fact. As my father said, 'The winners write the history books,' but it's not what really happened."

"And how would you know such things, Citizen?" Jakandy scoffs.

"I was taught by my mother and father," Mario asserts. "My family is one of many guardians of the histories. And because of my eidetic memory, I'm a perfect vessel to continue the tradition. We are taught the historical facts from a young age to be passed down orally generation after generation, so the truth may never be forgotten."

"And what truth is that?" questions Jakandy.

"The Mighty weren't always the top of the food chain," proclaims Mario. "Once upon a time, the Mighty were the ones in the cages and the camps. We aren't proud of what we did, but we must understand it to understand where we are today and to give us hope for a better tomorrow."

"And what would be a better tomorrow? To bring back the UCE and enslave the Mighty? We—" Jakandy stops as Mario's eyes go wild.

"What's the UCE?" questions Sheryl.

"The Unified Citizens of Earth," answers Mario. "They created the Citizens Army to protect the Normals from the flesheater and Abnormal threats."

"Abnormal threats? We just wanted to live in peace."

"And so do we!"

Trivial whips his head back and forth, watching the anger rise in his van companions.

"Do you want me to continue?"

"YES!" they shout in unison.

"As I was saying, the Normals feared the Abnormals extraordinary abilities," Trivial continues uninterrupted this time. "Ender's Revenge played upon those fears by playing up the classic tropes of a B-Movie slasher flick and turning them on their collective heads."

Like other films in the low-budget horror genre, Ender's Revenge began with an establishing shot of a lone car driving down an empty road. Ominous music played as the camera tracked the solitary Volvo wagon, focusing on the happy stick-figure family of five on the back window. With a slick transition through the window, the camera floated over luggage into the empty backseat toward the couple in the front, viewing the oncoming dusk through the windshield.

As the camera moved forward, the driver reached toward the radio, scanning through the stations. His wife tilted toward him as the camera maneuvered between them and panned around into a shot of them both. They were an average thirty-something couple, both caramel-skinned brunettes and somewhat attractive.

"Well Margot, I hope you're okay with the oldies," the driver said, settling on an old Motown tune. The camera went tight on him as he spoke. He wore a black and red bowling shirt with the name Ender stitched on the front. "It's either that, static, or some religious nut preaching about the end of the world."

As he leaned back, he draped an arm over his wife's shoulder.

"This is perfect, Joey," she said, batting playful big brown eyes and snuggling up to him. "I'm just so excited we were able to get away. We really needed a break—But are you sure your parents will be okay with the kids over the whole weekend?"

"Don't worry, babe," he said with a sly wink. "They raised me, didn't they?"

As the car journeyed down the long serpentine, forested highway, the gas-level light beeped on the dash. Joey grunted, tapped it with his finger, and peered out the windshield.

"It's getting dark and we're running low on gas. We might need to stop somewhere for the night."

As if on cue, they passed a sign that read GAS AHEAD ½ MILE.

At the gas station, Joey pumped the car with gas while the camera followed Margot. Three backwoods, hillbilly-types with similar faces and dull looks leered at her as she stepped inside. She flashed them an awkward thin-lipped smile while giving some obligatory greeting, but they didn't acknowledge her. So, she waited by the sunglasses stand, checking out new shades in the small mirror while Joey's reflection pumped gas.

When he finished, he entered the store, passed an empty

space where the hillbillies had been, and sidled behind Margot, covering her eyes.

"Guess who?" he started to ask, but she shuttered and escaped his grasp.

"Not funny," she interrupted.

"Sorry, sorry," he apologized, fetching his wallet and stepping to the cashier stand. "I'm on number two."

"That'll be $38.30."

Joey slapped down two twenties, and said, "If you can tell me how far we are from the closest hotel, you can keep the change."

"Well, the Golden Fleece Inn is just a ways up there in Argos," the cashier answered in a southern drawl. "But I might steer clear of that area, if possible. Next town after that with a hotel is about 2 hours."

"What's wrong with—" Margot started to ask.

"Well, it's getting dark," Joey interrupted, placing his arm around Margot and towing her to the exit. "We should head off. I'm sure we'll figure something out."

As they entered the car, the cashier exited the station, trying to wave to catch their attention. When the car departed, the camera stayed on the cashier.

"Avoid Argos! It's full of freaks!" he yelled before covering his mouth.

Something fluttered in the bushes, and he didn't wait to see what it was. He hurried back to the station, locking the door behind him.

"It seemed like he really wanted to tell us something," Margot said, keep her eyes on the cashier through her side mirror. "Maybe we should have listened."

"He probably has a deal with a hotel in that next city," dismissed Joey, sliding his arm back over her shoulder and

tugging her closer to him. "It'll be too late by the time we get there. I want to get some rest—"

He slid his hand behind her shoulder and under her arm to cup her right breast. "—and maybe some relaxation," he said, comically raising and lowering his eyebrows at her.

She smiled and sank into his chest, saying, "Oh you."

Seconds later, the Volvo wagon passed a sign that read WELCOME TO ARGOS: BEST LITTLE TOWN IN GEORGIA. The camera lingered on the sign, showing a bush blowing up against it. As the car passed, the bush fell, revealing Population 1881 with a red NORMAL spray-painted over that and an ABNORMALS 666 spray-painted next to it.

After entering the town proper, the camera followed as they cruised down an old street filled with a multitude of dilapidated houses.

"Well, this place could do with some gentrification," Joey joked.

"I'm not sure anyone would invest down here," Margot replied with her eyes glued to the various houses.

As they crept forward, her eyes locked with a greasy-haired, snaggle-toothed girl swinging on a tire swing in the front yard. Margot turned away for a second, but something swaying in her peripheral vision made her double-take. When she checked back, the kid stood outside of the fence and the empty swing still swung back and forth behind the girl in the yard.

"Did you see that?" she asked, still gaping confused through the side mirror.

"No, what happened?" Joey asked, his eyes drifting from side to side at each decrepit home.

"Nothing, never mind."

Up ahead a yellow neon sign blinked THE GOLDEN FLEECE INN and a smaller sign in red neon flickered VACANCY. The light for the NO was nonexistent.

"Looks like that's going to be home for the night," Joey said, parking the Volvo in the near-empty lot of the old motel.

The camera focused on Margot's concerned face as Joey parked. He jumped from the car, and the camera pulled back into a wide shot, showing him scamper to the back to retrieve their luggage. Margot exited, scrutinizing her surroundings.

"Are you sure you don't want to keep going?" she asked with a close-up on her worried eyes. "I can drive."

"No, babe," he said. "It's all good. I just want to get you into a bed, right now!"

As he skipped toward the front door of the inn, Margot continued her uncertain search. But she laughed as he opened the door with his back and spun around, saying, "We'd like your best room, garçon."

A white-haired lady in her eighties stood up from a seat behind the counter where a game show played on a small television.

"Oh sorry," Joey apologized, dropping the luggage to the ground. "I'm just a little delirious and need a good night's sleep."

"It's okay, youngin," she replied, winking at Joey and handing him a key connected to a bulky golden tag embroidered with a 13. "Lucky 13 is the best room in the place."

He opened up his wallet to hand her a credit card. She waved at him, saying, "You can settle up when you're ready to check out."

"Great, thanks!" he said, picking up the suitcases and heading back out the door. "Come on, my love! Destiny awaits us in lucky 13."

Inside the room, Joey tossed a suitcase onto the bed as dust flew into the air. Margot squinted, asking, "When was the last time they cleaned in here, you think?"

"Come on, baby," Joey said, reaching toward Margot and tickling her from behind. "It doesn't matter. So, we're in a *shithole in a shithole town in God only knows where. Let's make the most of it."*

He jerked his shirt off, unbuckled his belt, and let his pants fall to the ground. He stepped out of them, ripped off his socks, dropped his underwear, and streaked into the bathroom.

The camera stayed with Margot, who stood unmoving, still scrutinizing the room. From the bathroom echoed the sound of the faucets turning and water trickling into a shower.

"The rest of this place might leave something to be desired, but the shower is built for two!"

Margot smirked and shook her head. Then, she unfastened her dress as she sauntered toward the bathroom.

The camera panned right toward the golden curtain, as lightning flashed. Behind the curtain loomed several dark shadows. A cut to the outside of room 13 revealed several dark figures lurking.

"Blank out the innkeeper," commanded the figure in the middle to the taller one on his right.

The tall shadowy figure nodded in reply, as the camera followed him into the inn.

"What do you want?" The elderly innkeeper shouted as the dark figure placed his hand on her forehead. Her eyes shut, and she fell unconscious to her seat.

The tall dark figure returned to the others, as the light in Joey and Margot's room turned off. The figure in the center nodded to his compatriots, and they stepped out of the shadows into the light. Five separate figures emerged, all wearing blue jean overalls and trucker hats, and some had tattered plaid shirts on while others wore no shirt at all. The one on the far right flickered with electricity.

Inside the room, Joey and Margot made love under the dusty old comforter. The camera panned right as the five shadows approached the window. Then, the lock on the door started to turn.

Outside the room, a hillbilly raised his hand over the doorknob until the lock unlatched. Then, he spread his fingers apart and pushed the air forward.

As the door flew open, Margot screamed, wrapping the comforter around her. Joey rolled naked from the bed and snatched the lamp from off the side table next to him. He threw it at the disturbance, but the lamp stopped in mid-air. The hillbilly in the center of the five men had his hand up. A close-up of Joey's startled eyes filled the screen, then the lamp flew back at Joey, knocking him out with a black screen.

"Noooo! Stop! Please, stop!" Margot's voice cried in the darkness amid the moans and hollers of the hillbillies.

A point of view shot of Joey's eyes opening to slits indicated that he regained some consciousness. It tilted down, showing his hands strapped to a chair. He heard Margot choking, so it panned to the hillbilly with the telekinetic power holding his hand out, cutting to Margot clutching her throat like she was being choked. Then, it pulled back on the bare ass of the electrical hillbilly pumping on top of her, sparking electricity.

As Margot writhed in pain with each electrical shock, the other three hillbillies stood by, laughing.

One of them started removing his overalls, saying, "I'm next. I'm next."

"Nooo!" Joey cried, trying to lift himself up. "Leave her alone!"

"Don't worry," said the telekinetic hillbilly with a laugh, as he dropped his grip from Margot and raised his hand to Joey. "You'll get your turn!"

Hoisted up in a telekinetic chokehold, they forced Joey to watch each of them take turns with his wife. He tried to scream, but his neck clenched tighter and tighter until very little air *came through. After the last hillbilly finished and rolled off of Margot's bloodied body, she groaned in pain. Joey struggled again to free himself, but the pain was overwhelming.*

"Finish her," commanded the leader with an extreme close-up on his mouth.

Muffled screams came from Joey as the hillbilly standing over Margot re-affixed his overalls and raised his hands into the air.

Laughing, the leader let go of his telekinetic hold over Joey.

"What are you doing?" Joey coughed out in pain. "Leave us alone!"

Then, he heard the rattle of the chainsaw and darted his eyes at the hillbilly's hands. They had shifted into chainsaws and purred in the air above Margot.

"No! Please stop!" he cried through the pain.

Margot was too beaten and broken to even scream at the sight. Her half-closed left eye glared at the hillbilly with the chainsaw hands. He laughed at her, as his chainsaw hands dropped down, cutting into her flesh and spraying blood all over him and the room.

She loosed a soft and pathetic scream as the blood bubbled in her throat.

"Wasn't she a peach," said chainsaw hands, licking his lips, as he finished cutting her into pieces.

Joey's eyes streamed with tears, as he tried to break free.

Then, all five hillbillies turned to face Joey. The telekinetic leader flicked his fingers, severing Joey's ties. Joey lurched forward, but the leader raised his hand and lifted Joey into the air, splaying his naked body in unnatural ways.

"Now it's your turn," the leader said, signaling to chainsaw hands.

The hillbilly stepped forward and dropped the spinning saws onto Joey, cutting him into bloody pieces.

Blackout.

A phone rang as the darkness faded away, and an older, gray-haired, toffee-skinned woman with a Haitian accent answered.

"Allo. I am Ann-Marie Ender, Joey's mother," she told the caller.

The camera zoomed closer as the caller informed her that Joey and Margot did not arrive at their destination hotel in Orlando. Her face became almost monstrous in response. She sought help from the authorities, but when they were unable to find anything, she took matters into her own hands.

In a dark room, she lit a candle and killed a live chicken, letting the blood drip over the candle until the flame shifted from orange to green. Then, she used the green flame to light a fire inside of a charred human skull with the top cut off. A plume of black smoke billowed out and the voice of spirit spoke to her.

"No, no. It cannot be. They were—" She collapsed to the ground, her heart breaking.

The camera tracked in front of her, as she stumbled almost lifeless into the room where her grandchildren played.

"Hi, Grandmambo," the six-year-old girl said to her, but she did not pay her any attention.

The four-year-old boy scurried up to her, asking, "Grandmambo. Grandmambo. Can we go to the park?"

She placed a hand on his head and turned him around, saying nothing at all. Confused, he ambled back to his older sister. A two-year-old toddler sat between the other two children, playing with multicolored blocks and various plastic shapes. Their grandmother stood motionless in a corner, frowning out the window.

A balding, ebony-skinned man with a salt and pepper

power donut haircut poked his head into the doorway, "Allo, my little babies!"

"Pop, pop!" yelled the young boy, dashing into his grandfather's arms. "Can you take us to the park?"

"Why yes, my sweet little ones," he said smiling from ear to ear. "As long as your Grandmambo says it's okay."

She waved without looking at any of them, so he left with the children. After a few moments, she turned toward their play area. She lifted the rug from the floor, casting the toys off in all directions. From inside her blouse, she produced a small black leather bag hanging around her neck. She opened it and dropped out a piece of white chalk, using it to draw something on the floor where the rug had been. She returned the rug to its place and kicked the toys back onto it. Then, she went to her room and started a shower.

The steam filling the room dissolved into the steam whistling out of a teakettle on the stove the next morning. Ann-Marie came into the room and poured the hot water into three mugs on the counter. They swirled to the top with the chocolate within. She removed a leather pouch from her pocket and poured the contents into two of the mugs. Then, she topped those two with marshmallows and carried all three into the other room.

The camera followed the mugs still steaming a bit into the other room where the children played on the rug. She placed the mugs onto a coffee table and picked up the two-year-old. She smiled wickedly at the older children as she carried their younger sibling out of the room.

Eyeing the hot chocolate, the older children swooped upon the mugs with the marshmallows and began sipping. When their grandmother returned, she picked up her mug and said, "Let's go to the backyard and play."

As the children chased one another in the backyard, the

camera stayed inside and became a bird's eye view shot of the rug before cutting to the two-year-old crying in the crib. He stood in his crib, shaking the bars and staring out the window. The camera moved out of his room, through the hallway, and into the living room where his grandmother sat naked in the middle of a chalk pentagram with candles at each point.

"Écoutez-moi, dieux d'autrefois," she chanted, lifting up a golden bowl.

Subtitles on the screen read, "Hear me, gods of yore."

She poured the dark red oozing liquid onto her head, chanting, "Apportez-moi mon fils, MAMAN BRIGITTE! Le libérer de son linceul de mort, BARON SAMEDI!"

As the dark liquid covered her whole body, subtitles on the screen read, "Bring me my son, MAMAN BRIGITTE! Release him from his death shroud, BARON SAMEDI!"

The camera returned to the toddler in his crib, crying out the window of his room into the backyard. The shot transitioned through the window and into the backyard toward a shed. The door of the shed was cracked open with a small puddle of blood trickling out. The camera maneuvered to the shed where the bodies of Joey's two older children laid on the floor, drained of blood.

His mother's voice continued chanting, "GHEDE! Par DAMBALLA que je vous demande! Arrêtez-vous au GUINEE! Laissez mon fils revenir pour se venger!"

Subtitles on the screen read, "GHEDE! By DAMBALLA I ask you! Stop at GUINEE! Let my son return for revenge!"

The chanting continued over and over as day turned into night and transitioned to an establishing shot of an old rundown farmhouse with a huge shipping container in the back.

A shirtless, overall-wearing hillbilly walked the perimeter of the house and entered the backdoor. The camera followed him inside as he meandered through the kitchen and into the dining room. At a large table, other hillbillies gorged on plates of meat and gulped from massive metal mugs. They jabbered and laughed, spitting out chunks of food and liquid.

All the while, Ann-Marie's chants continued a layer behind their prattle.

The leader slammed his fist onto the table, saying, "I'm still famished. Don-John, git me another taste!"

One of the hillbillies stood up from the table and the camera followed him. He exited the kitchen's backdoor and headed to the large shipping container outside in the back. Inside, pieces of bodies hung from hooks, including the heads of Joey and Margot. He retrieved a large knife from the wall, cut a chunk of flesh from a slab on a hook, returned the knife to its home in the wall, and carried the chunk inside.

The camera lingered outside of the backdoor panning back toward the shipping container as the chants of Ann-Marie grew louder and louder, faster and faster. Through the cracks of the container, a light began to glow, and it shook with the low rumble of an oncoming earthquake. The chants continued as the camera tracked back toward the shipping container.

Inside, a bright light glowed in the center of the container as body parts flew all around, coming together to form a giant, dark figure. This new creature formed by the pieces of the body parts stood immensely tall in the center of the shipping container. From a pile of clothes on top of two suitcases, he snatched a black and red bowling shirt and a pair of ratty jeans.

He stretched the jeans over his legs, ripping them to fit around his massive thighs and calves with about a foot of high-water at the bottom. Then, he tugged the shirt over and busted through the sleeves as he buttoned three buttons around his hulking chest.

As he stumbled toward the exit, he passed a shiny panel on

the wall. Double-taking, he glowered at his reflection, not recognizing the creature he had become. It was his face, only massive and mangled, and his body was fused together by scar tissue in a patchwork of multicolored flesh. He touched his face as his monstrous mismatched fingers followed the lines of scarring. He looked more like a puzzle pieced-together than even Frankenstein's Monster. Then, he glimpsed the name on his shirt in his reflection.

"Ehn. Dehr," he grunted, trying to force words from his reanimated larynx.

He wobbled around, seemingly confused, as painful memories began to flash in a montage. He and his wife hugged their children and said goodbye as they left them with his parents. Then, he was forced to relive the rape and murder of his wife, as well as his own death.

An extreme close-up on his eyes revealed two different colors dilating and showing signs of intense anger.

"Rah. Venge," he uttered.

As he ambled toward the door, the camera revealed the hilt of a hefty carving knife in the wall. He wrenched it out, making a wretched metallic scratching sound. After he freed the knife, he checked its sharpness by slicing his left palm.

As black sludge oozed from the wound, the door opened, smash cutting to one of the hillbillies sinking his knife into some meat. Four of them still sat, eating their cannibalistic cuisine at the dining room table when something crashed into the house.

TUMPATHUMP

"What the hell?" the mind-wiping hillbilly shrieked, jumping out of his seat.

"Go! Go!" ordered the leader with the telekinetic powers.

The hillbilly with the electric spark was the first to reach the backdoor of the house. His hand sparked with electricity as he peeked outside at the door to the shipping container wedged into the side of the kitchen. One of his fellow hillbillies was split in half vertically by the massive door and half of the body lay next to it in a crumpled heap atop a giant puddle of blood. The electric hillbilly grimaced and stepped outside.

"Who's out here?" he yelled, sparking a fist of electrical light as he approached the shipping container. "We'll make you pay for this!"

Ender stepped from the shadow of the entrance of the shipping container, dragging the knife against the wall, making a shrill squeal. The electric hillbilly shuttered, squinting at Ender, unable to focus. Ender raised the knife, and the hillbilly's eyes filled with rage. Without pause, he rushed at Ender, surging the electricity through his body and into his fists. Ender jumped forward, hitting the ground with a loud thud.

As the hillbilly drew closer, his electrical power began to fizzle out.

"What the fuck?" he said, assessing his powerless fingertips.

Ender bolted forward, slicing the knife at the hillbilly. The hillbilly's eyes bulged in disbelief, as his fingertips flew into the air and spouted blood from the stumps left behind. He screamed but was abruptly halted when the knife came crashing down into the top of his cranium.

A fountain of blood spewed from his head as Ender yanked the knife free from the man's lifeless body. As the body fell backward, the blood spray covered the chainsaw-handed hillbilly as he exited the house.

"What is this?" he shrieked, trying to wipe the blood from his eyes without cutting himself with his sputtering saw hands.

Ender sprinted toward chainsaw hands and speared him back into the house. As the hillbilly flew backward in slow motion, his face distorted, showing great pain. Then, his hands morphed back to normal, but they were mangled and broken.

"What did you do?" he screamed in agony, cradling his hands to his chest.

Ender jumped forward, bringing his enormous bare foot down upon the hillbilly's face, crushing it into a red puddle.

"Who are you?" shouted the telekinetic leader of these cannibalistic Abnormal hillbillies, as he stood in the dining room doorway.

Ender stepped toward him, leaving huge bloody footprints in the wake. He pointed a patchwork finger to the nametag on his shirt and groaned, "Ehn. Dehr."

Suddenly, the mind wiping hillbilly reached out from a hidden spot behind the wall and grappled Ender's neck.

The leader smiled, shouting, "Blank him out!"

Ender's mismatched eyes filled the screen, narrowing with anger. He swatted his left hand at the hidden hillbilly before spinning around and snagging the hillbilly with both hands.

"No blank," the massive monster grunted, as he ripped the man in two, splattering blood all across the wall.

The leader's eyes were saucers on the screen.

"Stop!" he yelled, trying to force Ender back with his telekinetic powers.

He pushed harder and harder in vain, as the grotesque beast splashed bloody footprint puddles in his direction. Reduced to being a mere Normal, he could do nothing to stop the monster's approach. He stared through his useless hands, as Ender's monstrous mitts grasped him by the shoulders and lifted him from the ground.

"I have power! Why isn't it working on you?" he yelled right before Ender smashed his head into the ceiling. His body dangled there, twitching and convulsing, as a bloody puddle

formed below. A round light reflection in the puddle dissolved
into the moon above a forested skyline

Ender stood outside of the hillbilly hideout, screaming in a
brutish growl and thrusting his fists at the moon. As he howled,
he tore at his face like he was filled with pain. Then, he drew his
face down toward the lights of Argos in the distance. He
dropped his hands, revealing his eyes were closed. With a
dizzying effect, they filled the screen and opened before cutting
to his point of view.

The city of Argos became a field of red and blue lights
glowing with a few white lights shimmering here and there.
Panning around the hillbilly hideout, red and blue lights
dimmed where the bodies of the hillbillies lay slaughtered.
Overlooking Argos, the red and blue glows encroached upon the
white lights.

His slitted eyes filled the screen before cutting back to the
monster bounding down the forested hill toward Argos, knife in
hand and covered in blood and gore.

In the scenes that followed, Joey's mother brainwashed his
father, convincing him that their older grandchildren were
never at the house and had been with Joey and Margot the
whole time. From that moment, his eyes glazed over, and he
became a pseudo-zombie controlled by his wife. She forced him
to clean the shed and bury their grandchildren without his
awareness.

As her husband labored, she scoured the television for news
of her son, finding a report about a massacre of Abnormals in
Argos, Georgia. On the television screen, a neighbor of the
hillbillies wrested a microphone from a reporter and started to
rant.

"There I was mindin' my own gawdamn bidness, when
trespasses this big o' black boy lookin' all like Freddy fuckin'
Cougar or some shit, comin' through my property. I gits my

shotgun and flashlight and shine it at the sumbitch, tellin' him he better git his coon ass off my property before I blow him to bits. The dude don't move, even when I stick my shotgun in his chest. I shine my flashlight an' see he's all covered up in blood n' guts, wearin' a bowlin' shirt that says Ender on it."

She clicked off the TV set, packed the toddler, and instructed her husband to ready the car, so they can drive from Roanoke to Argos that instant.

As the News Reporters recorded their live broadcast from the cannibalistic hillbilly hideout, Ender stalked and slaughtered the red and blue glowing lights one by one in a montage of brutal death scenes of unsuspecting victims.

For example, one Abnormal man was walking his white fluffy dog down the street, when a long, dark shadow crossed behind him. The man did not see it. He just kept walking his dog; until Ender punched his fist through the man's chest, giving that poor white dog a red bath. He still had the knife in his fist through the man's chest when he yanked it back through, ripping the man apart. The dog whimpered, chewing away on the bloodied hand of his master.

Another scene was more massive in scale. Ender stomped up the steps to the Argos Church of the Mutated Christ, carrying his knife and an axe he had picked up from a previous kill. He kicked the door in, and the various Abnormals within started screaming. Men, women, and children met their bloody ends to the knife and axe as body parts flew all around and blood splattered the sanctuary walls. Apparently, the more Abnormals surrounding him, the stronger and deadlier he became, leaving decapitated heads, strung out guts, torn apart limbs, and dark pools of blood in his wake.

Shots from his perspective showed Ender no longer saw people, only the red, blue, and white lights. He also steered clear of red and blue lights that did not have a white light near them, indicating that he was not necessarily driven to kill all Abnormals, just those who he perceived as threats to the Normals.

When he was able, he would even find solace among the white lights, hiding in the shadows near them and acting like some kind of protector. After eliminating all the red and blue lights surrounding the Golden Fleece Inn, he returned to Lucky 13 to make his lair, basking in the glow of the white lights of the Normals around him.

Near the end of the film, his mother and father arrived at the Golden Fleece Inn, where they found Ender hibernating in his lair. As his mother approached his motionless body, she saw the knife lying on the bed and the axe propped up on the other side. She tiptoed to him and caressed his scarred, unrecognizable face, whispering, "What have they done to you, mon fils?"

His eyes opened and a gruesome grin formed on his lips.

"Muh. Thur," he groaned.

Then, his father entered the room, carrying his youngest child. He heaved himself up in an off-kilter wobble as his eyes shined with happiness. He peered around his father, seeking his other children. After a few seconds, he squinted at his mother.

"Chull. Drun," he grumbled.

His mother's panicked eyes filled the screen as she stood up and stepped back, raising her hands in innocence.

"They're no longer here," she tried to say calmly.

He jolted up, fire raging in his eyes.

"Why?" he growled.

"I did it for you, mon fils," his mother spoke in a calming whisper. "They are the blood of your blood. The only way to bring you back to me, mon cœur."

"No!" he howled, slamming his fist on the dresser. His face grew angrier and angrier with every passing second. He spun around and grabbed his knife from the bed.

His mother leaped away from him, reaching for her husband and her grandchild.

"There is still one," she offered, stepping behind her husband and motioning for him to go to Ender.

As his father presented him the toddler, Ender beamed at the face of his child and began to calm. But as he reached for his son, the two-year-old cried in terror. Ender's eyes enraged once more. He glowered at his mother, darting his eyes to the broken mirror. His deformed image reflected in the many shards.

Ender roared and jolted toward his mother, tossing his father out of the way. His father fell to the floor next to the bed, clutching his grandchild tight.

"You kill them!" Ender growled, raising his knife into the air. "I kill you!"

The knife came down fast with tremendous force, but his mother stepped back, clapped the knife between her hands, and stayed his blade. A close-up on Ender showed confusion in his eyes. The camera spun around to show his perspective of the white light shining, reaching toward him, and stroking his cheek.

A close-up on Ender's eyes revealed their search for an answer amid a world in slow motion. Then, they shot straight. His mismatched pupils fully dilated before rolling back as his head fell tumbling to the floor in front of his mother.

"I'm sorry, but you are no longer my son," his father cried, still clinging to the axe.

"Nooooo!" his mother screamed, as Ender's decapitated head came to a rest at her feet, his eyes rolling back and black blood oozing from his nose and mouth.

The film ended with red and blue lights shining around the Golden Fleece Inn, as police cars enter the parking lot.

"So, why did he have no power over his parents?" Jakandy questions. "How was his father able to kill him?"

"Maybe it was the baby," Mario quips from the backseat, still upset for having to be sequestered to serve Muldivar's needs.

Jakandy scowls at Mario before returning his gaze to Trivial.

"The problem is, I'm not sure which film this Ender comes from," answers Trivial. "That was just the first film. There are nine sequels."

"Nine sequels?" Mario says. "Shit."

"Did you view the others?" Sheryl asks.

"Yes," Trivial answers. "Briefly, the immediate sequel, Ender's Revenge II: Vengeance Reborn, begins with his mother sacrificing the baby to bring him back to life again. He goes on a killing spree, but his ultimate goal is to find and kill his parents. In the end, he kills them, but his mother traps his spirit in a Govi jar."

"So, we need one of those?" questions Jakandy.

"Yeah, no," answers Trivial. "The problem with that is at the beginning of the third film, Ender's Revenge III: Die Mutant Die, some children play stickball outside of Ender's mother's house, and they accidentally break that jar, releasing his spirit back into his body. So, that likely is not the best way to contain him, even if we were able to find one. The rest of the movie, he stalks and slaughters Abnormals in 'amazing' 3D. The film ends with him sitting quietly surrounded by white light and no red and blue light to be found."

"And the next film?" Sheryl asks, urging the conversation on.

"Ender's Revenge IV: Mother's Milk," Trivial snorts. "This one actually has nothing to do with him at all. In this one, his mother rises from the grave and stalks young Abnormals, sacrificing them to try and appease her Voodoo gods and bring all three of her grandchildren back to life. Ultimately, she is not successful, as the spirits of her grandchildren pull her into the spirit world at the end. The film does nothing more than showcase her power as a Voodoo priestess."

"Maybe we should find a Voodoo priestess?" asks Mario. "Do they still exist?"

"I don't think so," answers Jakandy in a way that made Mario uncertain as to which question he was answering. "What's next?"

"Well, the fifth installment is just ridiculous," says Trivial, shaking his head with his hand on his forehead. "From its awful subtitle pun, In the Habit of Dying, to its completely unbelievable plotline about Ender going on a rampage against Abnormal nuns running a sex ring in a monastery."

"What?" Jakandy eyes narrow with disgust. "A monastery. How sacrilegious!"

"I think that's the point," Mario quips.

"There's really nothing in that film worthy of mention," says Trivial. "Well, other than it ending with him befriending a young, blind Normal child named Sil, who was being groomed as a sex slave."

"That's sick," mutters Mario.

"Quite," Sheryl agrees.

"Sil returns in Ender's Revenge VI: Final Kill," Trivial continues. "This time she is played by a noticeably different, older actress, likely so she can do nudity. This film tries to recapture the vibe of the first by having Ender be in love with Sil, who is brutalized at the beginning of the movie by a gang of Abnormals on a subway. She survives, but the beating somehow brings her sight back. When she sees what Ender is, she kills herself by jumping in front of a subway train. Ender rampages against the gang and any and every Abnormal he can find. When it's all said and done, and he's covered in blood and guts; he finds himself back to the subway tracks where Sil took her life. He sits down on the tracks, mumbling her name and the name of his wife and children. Then, the light of a train barrels toward him, and he doesn't move. It honks its horn at him, and he doesn't move. It plows into him and his body parts fly all over."

"So, we can ram him with Ifton?" Mario asks.

Ifton looses two depressed honks.

"He said that's not funny," Jakandy answers for Ifton.

"Well, he doesn't really die. He goes into hell and fights demons and the Devil, winning his way out at the end in almost a fairy-tale ending, as he holds hands with his three children, spirits leading him out of Hell."

"It seems he cannot die," Sheryl surmises. "Is there anything else we can glean from the films, Trivial?"

"Well, the next two sequels are rubbish in that regard," Trivial says. "In the seventh film, subtitled Killing Time, he is sent through time to fight medieval mutants. And then in the eighth film, subtitled Ender in Space—well, he goes into space and kills aliens. However, the ninth film, Ender's Revenge IX: The End!, could have something interesting to note. This film acts like the previous two never happened, picking up with Ender's spirit returning to the world, but not having a body, so he possesses the body of an Abnormal Magician who wants great power. Instead, he winds up killing everyone he knows and loves."

"How does that help exactly?" asks Mario.

"To know how to fight him, we must understand him,"

Sheryl says, thinking aloud. "We must know which film version he is. I was realized from an earlier Doyle story, so I was not aware of my future he wrote. I read the stories and had no recollection. Likewise, this Ender will only have the memories and abilities granted to him based on which film he came from. You said there were nine sequels?"

"Yeah," Trivial nods. "Ender's Revenge 10: Born of Blood didn't use a Roman numeral, because they didn't want it called Ender's Revenge X. This was a prequel, telling the story of Ender's mother and how she turned her first son, Joseph, into a zombie killing-machine. In the end, she kidnaps another child who resembles her son and names him Joey. Then, she brainwashes the boy and her husband to believe he is their real son. This was supposed to explain the plot hole on why she killed her grandchildren and not herself or husband to bring Joey back in the first film. She needed his blood, and neither she nor her husband were blood relatives. I did not see this film, as it was released right as the second Evolutionary War began. I'm uncertain if the Realizer had a copy or not among his media treasure trove."

"Drawing this together, if this Ender character was realized from a later film, then he may possess some unkillable spirit," Sheryl reasons. "However, if he was realized from the first film, we may be able to kill him as they did."

"What? Get his parents to stop him," Mario says.

"Well, obviously that is not an option," Sheryl responds. "But we know he only kills Abnormals—"

"The Mighty," interrupts Jakandy. "They may have been derogatorily referred to as Abnormals in that film, but here and now, we will be called the Mighty and never Abnormals again. Am I clear?"

"My mistake," Sheryl clarifies. "He only kills the Mighty in those films."

"Aliens," Mario chimes in. "He also killed aliens."

"Fine, I grant you that," says Sheryl, hiding her annoyance. "Even so, as we have no aliens among us. His power is only over the Mighty here."

"I heard that flying guy with the red-cape was an alien," Mario quips.

"Shut up, Citizen!" Jakandy shouts at Mario. "Let the detective speak!"

Fuck you, you piece of shit, thinks Mario, expecting a reaction from Jakandy.

"He does have a point," Trivial interjects on Mario's behalf. "If he was realized from a later film, he killed more than just Ab—the Mighty. In the second film, he killed his parents and they were Norm—powerless humans."

Mario is surprised to find Jakandy unfazed with his focus kept on Trivial.

"His mother had powers," Jakandy responds.

Jakandy, can you hear me? thinks Mario.

"No, she used magic," Sheryl explains. "That's a different animal altogether."

Seeing a lack of response from Jakandy, Mario lunges forward, shoves Trivial to the side, and glares out the front window.

"Hey, watch it," Trivial grumbles.

"Where are we?" Mario asks, paying him no mind.

Jakandy peeks out the window.

"It looks like we've just pulled up outside the Main Cathedral. Why?"

"Because you're not responding to my thoughts—" Mario starts to say but is interrupted when the back of the van rips open, revealing the mammoth Mighty killer wearing the red and black bowling shirt with Ender stitched on it. He is covered in blood and grime, reeking of putrid death.

"Holy shit!" squeals Mario as he bolts toward Jakandy, struggling to reclaim his seat. "Punch the gas!"

Ender stabs his knife into Muldivar, who lets out a slight yelp, as he is plucked from the back of the van.

"Wait!" Jakandy yells, trying to slide behind Mario to peer into the back. "Muldivar!"

Ifton punches the gas, launching the supplies, water bottles, and ice chest out the open back doors. They crash down in front of Ender.

There goes lunch, thinks Mario, as the bottles of water burst open, spilling their contents in front of Ender.

As they drive away, Ender thrusts Muldivar in the air and rips him in two, spilling the contents of his body onto the pavement below. Muldivar screams a deathly wail, as blood sprays from his body onto Ender and the pavement below.

21

AND INTO THE FIRE!

"We're here," Tommy says, pointing out the window toward the WPC on the island across the river. "They stick us all on that island and force us to work for them. They give us some semblance of freedom, but we aren't free. They allow us to go places we might want to, maybe. Sometimes even if we make plans ahead of time and do all the right things, we still don't get what we should. We're not human to them."

Reaching Olum Bridge Way, Tommy leans forward and peers out the windshield.

"Is there some semblance of familiarity?" James asks.

"Yes," Tommy says, drumming his hands on the dash. "I could never have told you what any of this looks like, but as I see it again for the first time, it doesn't feel like the first time. Know what I mean?"

James nods not knowing what he means, appraising his surroundings and finding nothing familiar. He turns right toward the WPC.

"What's that aroma?" he asks as they cross the bridge over Olum River.

Tommy rolls down the window and sticks his head out, taking in a big sniff.

"Barbecue?"

"Is that usual?"

"No," Tommy says, as they round the corner to the entry gates.

The WPC is a war zone with fires scattered everywhere. A guard tower is toppled over, and hundreds of people scuttle about in disarray. A few Mighty guards fight off crowds of Normals near the bus stop. Some uniformed bodies lie in huddled heaps, and a charred body sizzles near the fallen tower.

"This is madness," James says sidelong through the window.

Tommy pays him no mind.

Mario und Zelda are out here somewhere, he thinks, taking in the chaos. *I only wish I knew what they look like.*

Mario's eyes are horrorstruck in the reflection of the rearview mirror as he falls backward in slow motion. He cannot peel his eyes away from the mirror and the realized monster splitting a Mighty in half with its bare hands.

Jakandy shoves Mario back into his seat as Ifton squeals away from Ender. Through the rearview, the monk grieves for another friend.

Trivial is turned to the back, amazed by the strength of Ender.

"We're going to need a big axe," Trivial says to Mario under his breath.

Sheryl rakes her fingers down her face, turning white with terror or withdrawal. Mario turns around just in time for Ender to rip Muldivar's head from his spine and lob it at

him. The head smacks the inside of the van just above
Mario with a disturbing thud. Blood splatters over everyone,
as the severed head lands on the seat next to Mario.

He sits silent and motionless in shock, waiting for the
head to roll to a stop. Mario tries not to stare into the whites
of Muldivar's rolled back eyes. Averting his gaze, he
discovers a freshly growing puddle of blood, which pools
around the place where the monk's neck once was. Mario
fights his nausea, turning away he locks eyes with Ender.

"He's coming this way," Mario warns as Ender bounds
toward them.

Ifton swerves in the road, making Muldivar's head
wobble and roll onto Mario's hand.

"Ahhhh!" Mario screams, kicking at the monk's lifeless
face and knocking it into the back.

The head totters a bit before a bump sends it careening
out the swinging backdoors. Mario shutters, taking his eyes
away from the bloody mess next to him, only to meet
Jakandy's eyes flashing anger at him in the rearview.

"What? You didn't need it for something did you?"

Trivial doubles over, wrenching in pain.

"What's wrong?" Sheryl probes.

SKKKREEEEL HONK HONK

The backdoors barely cling to their hinges as Ifton
whips around a corner. Mario reaches over his seat, struggling to snag the free-flying doors and shut them. Ifton hits
a bump in the road and Mario flies into the air, scrambling
to hang on. The back doors swing out and back, clanking
metal upon metal. He grasps one of the door handles,
clasping it tight as the other flies free and bounces down the
street.

The horn continues blaring, and Mario perceives Ifton's voice screaming in pain with every honk, "I feel pain! It hurts!"

He buckles himself into his seat, wondering if his sympathy for the vehicle is manifesting into a true ability to comprehend Ifton. He touches the armrest, closes his eyes, and listens. An agonizing whimper resonates around him. He opens his eyes, realizing they come from Trivial.

Sheryl tries to brace Trivial as they jolt around back and forth inside the van. Jakandy clutches the wheel, his right foot hovering over the brake pedal while his left foot presses firmly into the space to the left of the accelerator pedal. Mario peeks out the back, finding no sign of Ender.

Did we lose him? thinks Mario.

Jakandy searches in the rearview.

"I don't see him either," he says to Mario. "Keep a close eye though. We might want—"

"*You can hear my thoughts,*" Mario interrupts with his thoughts while staring into Jakandy's reflected eyes. "*We must be far enough away for you to regain telepathy.*"

"Ifton, find a safe place to park," Jakandy orders, peeling his hands from the steering wheel and turning toward the others. "We need to regroup and determine what to do from here, now that we know who the killer is. How's he doing?" Jakandy asks Sheryl while studying Trivial.

"I'm not sure. He's very unresponsive at this point."

Jakandy places his hand on Trivial's shoulder.

"Trivial, how are—"

He stops talking, and his eyes narrow as he scrutinizes Trivial.

"What are you?"

Something sparks confirmation in Sheryl's eyes.

Confused, Mario leans forward and asks, "What's wrong?"

"What did you sense when you touched him?" Sheryl probes.

"I don't know. It didn't make sense. It was all jumbled."

"He stopped moaning," Mario points out. "Maybe he's recovered."

Jakandy reaches his hand toward Trivial.

"Don't," Trivial says, turning toward Jakandy, wincing from the pain or something else.

Jakandy stays his hand, but Sheryl grabs Trivial's right shoulder and spins him toward her.

"Are you going to tell us what that was all about?"

"Probably not," Trivial responds, swallowing hard and regaining his composure. He sits up straight in the seat and shakes his head a bit. Then, he traces his fingers over his forehead and down his nose, turns to Sheryl, and asks, "Did I miss anything, love?"

Sheryl measures him with no response.

"Why can't I read you?" quizzes Jakandy.

"I have enormous brainpower," Trivial boasts, turning back to Jakandy with a wicked grin. "I'm a blocker. You can't read me unless I allow you to."

Sheryl eyes Trivial and then says to Jakandy, "Tanalia called me a blocker at Club Haberdashery. Could it be due to the Realizer?"

"No, no," answers Trivial, though he had not been the one asked. He taps his finger to his forehead. "It's because we are gifted, my friend. Albeit we are not gifted the way these schmucks are but in our brains."

"He is correct," Jakandy clarifies. "There are Cit...people with genius-level IQs, people of extraordinary brainpower, who have the ability to consciously block the monks."

"How does that work?" Sheryl questions. "How can you eliminate crime in a world where criminal geniuses may be able to block you from perceiving their criminal behavior? The monastery is a sham."

"Do NOT speak ill of the monastery," shouts Jakandy. "Without the elders, we would live in a world riddled with crime and violence. We stopped that. There is no evidence of any criminal behavior that is unknown to us!"

"Well, until today," Mario quips.

"Yes, none of you seer-paths were aware of this killer," Sheryl tacks on. "How many other criminal or violent acts might you have not been privy to?"

"I told you. Some geniuses can block us, but the blocking is generally momentary. It's not long-lasting."

"That Ender killer didn't really look much like a genius," Mario declares. "I mean, I guess he could have been before he became an undead killing machine."

"A revenant," interjects Trivial.

"A what?" remarks Mario.

"It's the term you mean to use," Trivial answers. "It's a collective term to refer to these creatures who return from the dead and are fueled by violence or vengeance. It differentiates them from other such similar creatures like zombies and vampires."

"Well, thanks for that," says Mario. "How does that help?"

"He's dead," Sheryl says, sitting straight up, thinking aloud, and trying to put the pieces together. "He doesn't have powers like the Mighty. He's no longer human, so they cannot read him. The void exists, not because he has the ability to block. He's not like us." Sheryl gestures to Trivial and then Mario. "The void exists because his ability is to turn off the powers of the Mighty." She turns to Jakandy, asking, "Can you search in your mind for areas that are blocked or areas where your sight is hindered?"

"I'm getting a lot of blocking right here," Jakandy says, nodding at Sheryl and Trivial.

"I told you, Holmes," Trivial says with his wicked grin. "We're a lot alike, you and I."

"I need somewhere quiet to meditate," says Jakandy, "I cannot focus on what is not present when the present is too much to process."

"I'm getting hungry anyway," Mario groans, rubbing his stomach.

Moments later, Ifton creeps down an empty street. The dashboard lights up and the clock blinks 2:24. "Thank you, Ifton," Jakandy responds, patting the dashboard. "Anywhere you can would be fantastic."

"That's really creepy," Mario says, sitting back into his seat. "If you weren't here, we wouldn't even realize this car was possessed at all."

The dashboard blinks.

"Ifton says you would figure it out in a hurry."

ARRRRRGGGGGHHHHH

Tommy bellows, cradling his head and screaming, "It hurts! It hurts!"

He falls to a clump on the corner of Dalit Way and Luxuria Street in the heart of the WPC. James stands over him confused, scanning around and hoping his companion does not draw any unwanted attention.

Memories of Tommy's past erupt within his head in painful flashes of color and images, bursts of sensations, thoughts, and feelings, and an overwhelming awareness of recognition. After a few moments, Tommy's torment starts to dissipate, and he lies motionless and silent.

"Are you okay?" asks James, placing a sympathetic hand on Tommy's shoulder.

"I'm perfect!" he says, jumping up wild-eyed and full of life. "Didn't you feel it? We have our memories back."

"I felt nothing," says James with grave concern in his voice.

"Don't worry about it, James," Tommy says, throwing an arm around his shoulder. "If all you remember is you want revenge, then let's go get some!"

As they walk toward the camphouse marked with a big 14 on the side, James glowers over his shoulder at the spot Tommy had just regained his memories.

I remember revenge, he thinks. *But on whom?*

Tommy barrels up to the door marked 1441.

"I remember this!" He exclaims, motioning for James to hurry toward him. When James arrives, he says, "This was our place." He grips the knob. "We never locked it during the day, so all the kids could come in and out of our place to play. Lizbeth loved that. She loved their smiles and laughter." He opens the door and leans in, hollering in singsong, "Hey kids, I'm home!"

"Get out of here, Cit!" says a naked bird woman, straddled on a strapping young prehensile. His tail wraps around her waist as his hands grope her feathered breasts.

"I'm sorry. I'm sorry," apologizes Tommy, raising his hands as he exits out the doorway. Closing the door, he takes one last peek at the two hybrid Mighty in mid-coitus, unsure if the sight is arousing or disgusting.

"Damn," he says to James. "Things have really changed around here."

In the secret lair of lost children, Zelda sits on a cot and observes the children play.

They laugh and play games just like Mario and I did when we were that age, she thinks.

She smiles as her eyes fall upon Tyler helping one of the children tie his shoes. Loo squeals with glee as he plays with the other children. Her heart melts.

A young girl seizes a young boy by the hand and says, "I'm the princess and you have to save me from the dragon."

"What dragon?" the boy says confused.

She points to an older boy with a small flame cupped in his hand.

"Put that out!" Zelda yells, hurtling in his direction. "Are you trying to kill us?"

The pyrokinetic boy startles as he closes his hand to extinguish the fire.

"I'm sorry. I was just—I was the dragon."

Zelda slows down as she approaches the three kids, saying, "It's okay. You just have to learn appropriate play. There are rules, you know."

"Yeah?" Tyler says with a huge smile and a sarcastic tone. "Who made you their mother?"

"Shut up!" she says, reciprocating. "No one was talking to you."

Loo runs up to Zelda, his big eyes filled with joyful tears.

"I've never played with kids before! It's fun."

Zelda picks him up and hugs him.

"I'm sorry the mean man did that to you, Loo. I promise I will never let him hurt you again. I'm not going to let him hurt anyone again." She waves to Tyler and says, "Come on.

We've got work to do. Let's get these kids to a safer place than this."

"A safer place than this?" Tyler asks, assessing the room. "We're three floors below the ground. I think your maternal instinct is running amok."

"Enough talk, electroboy," she says as she strides toward him, pointing a finger into his chest. "Are you going to help or wha—"

"Just shut up," he says, taking her by the waist and kissing her.

She shoves him back and slaps him.

"You presume too much, buddy!"

Ifton parks in front of a block of small businesses on 5th Avenue between U and T Streets. The cafe, barber, butcher shop, and bookstore are all closed. Signs adhered to the windows or blinking from viewscreens facing the street read CLOSED TODAY BY ORDER OF THE MONASTERY. The door to the bookstore is jimmied open.

Jakandy sits in a meditative posture in the back of the bookstore, as Mario paces back and forth by the front window with the backward stencil FELLOWSHIP CIRCLE FICTION & NONFICTION BOOKS. Every few steps, he glances with glaring intensity toward the back of the store where Jakandy meditates. Trivial stands aloft with his back to the rear of the store, fixating out the front window. About a meter away from him, Sheryl leans against a bookshelf, reading the various titles.

"You should probably close the door, Mario," Trivial advises. "Especially, if you're going to keep your back to it."

Mario pays him no attention. His mind is focused on Jakandy.

I'M— I can't think what I want to think because you can hear my thoughts.

Trivial meets Sheryl's eyes. She shrugs.

I can't think HAPPY what I want to think because you can hear my thoughts.

Trivial shakes his head and returns to the door to close it. He fetches a wooden chair nearby and wedges it under the handle.

"That'll do," he says, wiping his hands clean.

I can't think what I want HE'S to think because you can hear my thoughts.

"Sure, so long as he doesn't see that big window," Sheryl says with a smirk.

Her hand slips off the shelf, and she loses balance. She wobbles as she tries to regain her footing.

I can't think what I want to think DEAD because you can hear my thoughts.

Trivial squints at her, glimpsing some awkward movement in his periphery, but he is unable to register what happened.

"Right, so maybe we should move to the back?"

AND I— I can't think what I want to think because you can hear my thoughts.

"He'll inform us when he's finished meditating," Sheryl responds.

I can't think WISH what I want to think because you can hear my thoughts.

Trivial shifts his gaze between the front window and Mario heavy-footed pacing. Sheryl wipes her forehead with the back of her arm, trying to find a comfortable position to stand.

I can't think what I want YOU to think because you can hear my thoughts.

"Any good books on your shelves?" Trivial asks Sheryl.

She rolls her eyes.

I can't think what I want to think WERE because you can hear my thoughts.

Mario stops pacing and eyes Jakandy. Trivial takes heed, tilts his head toward Sheryl, and whispers, "You think he's all there?"

She flashes a pencil-thin smile at Trivial, blinks twice, and turns back to comb through her book titles again.

I can't think what I want to think because you TOO can hear my thoughts.

As Mario finishes his final thought, Jakandy jumps up from his folded leg position with exceptional ease and athleticism. The slight grunt he makes is soft, but it echoes in the quiet space, signaling to his companions that he has completed his meditation.

Mario shuffles toward the back of the bookstore. Trivial follows, gesturing for Sheryl to step between him and Mario.

"Ladies first," he jests.

She stops in her tracks and waves him by, following behind with a suspicious eye trained on Trivial.

"Were you able to track him?" Trivial questions. "Did you find the void?"

"No," Jakandy answers with his head bowed, still reflecting upon his most recent meditation.

Whereas before he always found a kind of serenity or at least a purpose within the confines of his mind's eye, he now finds nothing but chaos. A dark void swirls around him, like rich, dark chocolate marbled through vanilla ice cream. It does not originate from any single location, nor does it infiltrate like some kind of symbiotic organism adhering itself to a host's DNA through microscopic slimy tendrils. Rather, the void pulsates in a kind of arrhythmia, revealing no stability or pattern.

He senses the void all around him, yet not, depending on where he focuses. Not only is he unable to locate the origin of the void, but he is also unable to push into the beyond and see much through his mind's eye. The past, present, and future are all tainted by the dark void in some way, corrupting any means of sight. Instead, he uses his meditative space to focus on his own memories, reminiscing over his relationship with his recently deceased mentee. He also relives his most recent ones in the hope of discovering something unconsciously that he may have consciously missed.

"You said earlier that any Ender but the one from the first film would be virtually unstoppable, right?" he interrogates Sheryl.

"Yes," Sheryl answers. "If he was realized from the first film, we might have a chance."

"I've canvassed my mind's eye, seeking an answer to this question but I have found nothing," Jakandy says. "Do either of you recall any Citizens killed by Ender? If he is the Ender from the first film, then he should not kill any Citizens, right?"

"Right," says Trivial.

"I have—" Sheryl starts to say as she leans back into nothing, scrambles off-balanced, and hoists herself against a nearby bookcase before continuing. "I haven't seen any Normals singled out."

"Me neither," says Mario. "He only seems to have a hard-on for your kind."

Jakandy ignores Mario's facetiousness and Sheryl's off-kilter stammer while Trivial pays them greater attention.

"If he hasn't killed a Citizen," Jakandy states. "Then, can we assume he is from the first film?"

"It's harder than that, I'm afraid," says Trivial. "You see, he killed his parents who were Norm—Cit—people without powers. But that is not to say he would have killed any other person without powers. They were targets of his revenge. As his parents do not exist here, they were not killed."

"That doesn't matter," Sheryl says, wiping sweat from her brow. "Jakandy is right. We must assume he was realized from the first film. Because if he wasn't, we likely have no means to end this. That being said, it is very likely that only a Normal will be able to kill him."

Mario guffaws, crying, "Now they need us?!?"

"Citizen, you will never be needed," Jakandy exclaims, pointing to Mario and dripping with disdain. "I will rely on these two realized individuals to—"

Suddenly, Sheryl's knees buckle, and she collapses to the ground.

"Sherlock?" Trivial cries.

"No, no," says Sheryl as Jakandy and Mario try to help her up. "Call me Sheryl. I'm—I need—"

"Jesus, a fucking junkie?" Trivial exclaims, stepping toward them. "How did I not see this coming? Of course, Sherlock Holmes is a fucking junkie!"

"You're not helping," says Jakandy, narrowing his eyes at Trivial. "Take Mario and find weapons or something to fight Ender."

"Fine!" Trivial says, tugging Mario around. "Let's go, mon frère."

"You're lucky I have no idea what's going on!" Mario shouts to Jakandy as Trivial tows him out the front door.

Jakandy retrieves a small leather pouch from inside his robe. He holds it up for a second before handing it to

Sheryl. She eyes him and snags it, pulling the leather strings loose to open the pouch.

"My hero," she says, retrieving a small glass tube, clothespin, candle and matches, syringe, and baggie of crushed yellow powder from the pouch.

"I need you at your best."

She smiles with the nod of an excited toddler. Her fingers quaver as she prepares the Delirium.

"How long has he been like that?" Trivial asks Mario as they approach the familiar red and blue striped pole of the barbershop.

"Jakandy? He's always been a dick," answers Mario, peeping into the window of the barbershop.

"No, not him," retorts Trivial without stopping. "Sherlock."

"Well, SHE seems fine to me. Why?"

"You haven't noticed his fever fits?"

Trivial stops this time to gauge Mario's response.

"No," Mario answers, taking a moment to think back over the day. "Is that what that was? That's the first time I've seen it."

"Curious," Trivial murmurs, turning on his heels and heading toward the next storefront. "I thought you said you had an eidetic memory. Isn't that how you were entrusted with the family history?"

"Historical facts," corrects Mario.

"My apologies," Trivial says with a slight bow. "Regardless, what good is that, if you can't see what's right in front of you?"

"Excuse me."

Trivial stops to admire the sign on the storefront.

"Look at the details of this intricately carved and burned

sign," he says to Mario, pointing at the sign. "It gives it an endearing rustic look, wouldn't you say?"

"I guess," Mario answers with a shrug. "I bet we can find some pretty good weapons in a butcher shop though."

"That's a good boy," Trivial says with a wink, searching around the area and patting himself up and down. "Now you're seeing what's right in front of you."

"What are you looking for?" asks Mario with a fading, half-cocked smile.

"A way in," Trivial says, strolling over to a metal trashcan on the curb. He picks it up and throws it at the front window. It makes a dinging sound and falls to the ground.

"Well, that won't do at all," he says, scouring the area.

Mario dashes away.

"Was it something I said?"

A few moments later, Mario returns, carrying a hammer like it's a trophy he just won for being the MVP of some sporting event.

"This is how we opened the bookstore," he says, smashing the door handle with the trophy hammer. "Figured it'd be better than trying to climb through broken glass."

Back at the WPC, Tommy and James hustle through the immense spaces between the camphouses, slipping behind and in between the buildings as they try to avoid Mighty guards and Normal rioters alike. They reach building 17 and hide behind the bushes on the north side of the building.

"This is chaotic," James says, leering at Tommy. "It's just like the SIC. There is no army here. They're all a bunch of lunatics fighting their own battles."

"That's not everyone, James. There are people here ready to join a coordinated fight. We've just got to find where they're hiding. When I was here, the true historians met over there," Tommy says, pointing to building 22 around southwest down Invidia Street. "But who knows where they are now. You can bet they're all together, biding their time."

"True historians?"

"My people," Tommy says before hightailing it toward the camphouse across the way. "Now come on!"

James starts to follow Tommy when someone opens the back door of building 17 and waves at him.

"Come here! Quick!"

"Tommy," he howls with both hands cupping his mouth.

Tommy checks over his shoulder and puts on the brakes, making a quick 180 back toward the open door.

James slides over to the doorway where a teenage girl with auburn hair braided into a ponytail greets him. She waves for Tommy to hurry.

"It's safe in here," she says, closing the door behind them. "Go ahead and follow that hallway to the first door on the right. I'm going to keep an eye out for others who might need help."

"Thank you," Tommy says, nudging James in the ribs. "See, my people."

James rolls his eyes, whispering, "We will see."

The door leads to the common area of Camphouse 17, where they find twenty or so men and women huddled together. They all look frail, frightened, and suspicious of the newcomers. An older man with a long gray-brown beard and wearing a flat cap steps toward Tommy and James.

"Haven't seen you here before," he says to them.

"My name's Tommy. I used to live in 1441," he says,

reaching out his hand to shake the older man's hand. "But I've been in the SIC for the last seven years."

"The SIC?" a teenaged girl with tight black braids gasps.

"Yeah," Tommy says, pointing his thumb at James. "We were both there, but there was a riot today and no monks to stop it."

"It must be the same everywhere," says a beautiful thirty-something brunette woman, wearing a blue and white maid's uniform.

"We were in line for the buses when the explosion happened," the man with flat cap says. "Some people started to riot and attack guards, but we came in here to hide."

"This is your army?" James whispers to Tommy. "They're a bunch of cowards hiding from the fray."

Tommy shrugs him off, as the girl from the backdoor enters the room.

"I don't see anyone else," she says, wiping sweat from her forehead and heading toward a group of teenagers. As she passes Tommy, she says, "You know, you kinda look familiar. Do I know you from somewhere?"

"Have you been to the SIC lately?" asks her braided friend.

"You might know my kids. Mario and Zelda."

The two girls perk up and approach Tommy.

"We're friends with Zelda. I'm Keely," says the girl with auburn hair. "And this is Dorian."

Dorian waves, giggling, "Hi."

"That's great," Tommy says, scanning the room. "Where's Zelda?"

"She took a bus into the city after the explosion," Dorian answers.

Tommy's face contorts with terror and concern.

"Why would she do a damn fool thing like that?"

"She went looking for Mario," answers Keely.

Tommy slams his fist into the wall, startling all the people in the room.

"Son of a bitch," he says, shaking the pain out of his fist. "Both of my kids are out there in that mess."

James steps forward, taking the attention from Tommy.

"People," he says. "We need to organize. The monks have gone away, and who knows when they'll return. It is our time to rise up against the rule of the Mighty and fight for our freedom!"

The people murmur, glancing skeptically at one another.

"If not now, when?" Tommy says. "They're gone for a reason. Let's take advantage of it. Whaddaya say?"

Someone thrusts a fist into the air and shouts, "Fight!"

Tommy and James pump their fists up, shouting, "Fight!"

The rest of the people in the room follow their lead as fists fly into the air and cheers fill the room.

"Now, we just need some weapons," James yells.

The people chant, "Fight! Fight! Fight!"

James turns to Tommy and whispers again, "Now we have an army."

Jakandy eases Sheryl into a chair at the bookstore. He hands her a cup of water.

"Drink. You must."

Sheryl pushes it away, leans over, and vomits onto the floor.

"It's no good," she says, handing him her wig.

Jakandy cradles the wig in one arm and pushes the cup

to her mouth, forcing her to drink. Water and vomit drip off her chin.

"Don't worry," he says, handing her a strip of cloth. "You'll be back to yourself in no time."

"You don't understand," Sheryl says, wiping her mouth before she tries to stand up. "I'm not Sherlock Holmes—not anymore."

"I know," Jakandy says, offering her the wig back and an arm to brace herself with. "I know. You're Sheryl."

"No," Sheryl says, snatching the wig and slapping his other hand away. "That's not what I mean." She plops the wig back on her head and fixes it into position. "I haven't been Sherlock in ten years, but I've taken every drug this future has had to offer."

As she steps forward with a wobble, Jakandy reaches out again. She steadies herself between him and a bookcase, glimpsing the empty syringe of Delirium on the floor.

"At first, I used them to hide from Moriarty, and then they became my escape. Over time, the fear of Dr. James Moriarty waned, and so, I never thought I would need to be Sherlock again—the drugs have done me in. I can't think like Sherlock anymore."

She crushes the syringe under her foot.

"I keep trying to be of use, but I'm a fraud. I never even found James—"

"You may not have found this James," Jakandy interrupts, grabbing Sheryl by the collar and glaring into her eyes. "But you are our detective, Sheryl! You are the only one in Fellowship City. We need you now more than you've ever been needed."

"I doubt that."

"This is no time for games," he says, turning away from her. "The Enclave is gone! Tanalia is gone! Everything I have ever known about my world has changed! I am a monk by Sol and Luna! I have lived my life following the steps."

"*That's a good boy, Jak-Jak*," says his mother's voice from the memories swirling around in his mind's eye "*These are your first steps.*"

The voice echoes in his head, as images of his childhood race for prominence. They spin in nauseating wonder, pausing on milestone moments like his first steps. As they flitter by, he reminisces on a forgotten time. A time replaced by monastic service. Everything goes bright white, blurring his whole world out of existence. Then, two dark figures emerge through the dense white of the fog. As their faces become clear, he recognizes them.

They were his assessors, determining his acceptance to the monastery. The first was a graying monk with bushy eyebrows and mustache, wearing a hooded brown robe. The second was his mentee. She was beautiful, in her late teens or early twenties with golden-brown skin and dark brown locks hanging around her face. Jakandy was enthralled by the first and enchanted by the second.

For the first test, he sat with the older monk while the younger monk performed various tasks moving successively further and further away from him. Nearsight had always come easy for him, and this test revealed his exemplary skill. The younger monk was over five miles away before Jakandy found difficulty determining what she was doing exactly.

He also showed exceptional skill with hindsight, especially when he was able to touch the subjects and peer into their own memories. His empathic abilities were far more advanced than many of the other monks and potential monks. However, foresight was always tricky for him, as he seemed to connect to multiple possible future streams. Unfortunately, he had difficulty sensing which one would be the correct future, resulting in a failure on the foresight test. In reality, he possessed enormous potential, only requiring focus and training.

They also tested his latent path abilities, discovering that he was strictly a telepath. When he focused, the thoughts or voice-thoughts of others came to him like speech. They called that skill listening. They also tested him on communicating, but since he had never before tried to force his thoughts through his mind's eye, he did not succeed. He recalled being so disappointed to learn that his technopathic and zoopathic abilities were dormant if present at all. It destroyed his dream of one day being an elder, as one of the primary criteria was to be an omnipath—having all three path abilities at once.

Once discovered, he had to be initiated into the monkhood, which was in itself not an innocuous task. Presented to the Enclave, the elders evaluated his ability. He sat in a loose medita-tive pose as they probed his mind. They filled him with thoughts and sentiments, everything to direct him toward omnivolence— the all-choice, seeing all choices made by everyone all at once. After his successful completion of the initiation, he donned the hoodless yellow robe of a novitiate.

That memory faded away as memories of Avasent filled his mind for the second time that day. He remembered how they began their first steps toward omnivolence together, side-by-side.

Step 1: Enhance.

They would spend most of their days together reading from the collection of books in the library, studying for the sake of study. At dinnertime, they would eat their meals together, quizzing one another about everything they had just read that day. When they felt confident enough in their foundational knowledge, they both petitioned for advancement.

Step 2: Peace.

At first, they worked with one another, helping each other reach higher states of meditation and mindfulness. They would meditate for hours, turning their thoughts inward to create a massive mind's eye space, wherein they explored their sight abilities. Though their mind spaces were theoretically separate they created a dyad, allowing them to utilize their thought-spaces together, increasing their abilities faster than the other novitiates.

They were light years ahead of any others, but they could not yet be promoted to the next step, so they became bored and began challenging one another to make things fun again. At first, the challenges provided a little healthy competition, like who could meditate the longest. Eventually, their competitions became unhealthy, devolving into who could go without eating, sleeping, or taking care of themselves the longest. After that, they began to reek so foul that their instructors foresaw the only way to solve the problem would be to advance them both.

Step 3: Practice.

As so often before, they worked with one another daily to progress, practicing their seer-path abilities together to make them stronger and more acute. In turn, they progressed through each of the seven skills required of a seer-path to elevate from a novitiate to the rank of communitor: Focus, Push, Communion, Shield, Block, Absorb, and Control.

They learned to achieve greater Focus for exploring foresight and being able to sense which future would be the most likely while keeping their nearsight and hindsight finely tuned. Soon after, they learned to Push their voice-thoughts through their minds' eyes to communicate with each other and even share their sight. Communion required another seer-path, so they enlisted a new novitiate named Greeve to take part in their experimentation. After that, he accompanied them wherever they went.

For the most part, they easily mastered each of these skills. However, creating a mental Shield and Blocking other seer-paths proved much more difficult and strenuous skills to master. But the most difficult, the ones requiring the most amount of mental energy, were the ones requiring them to grasp onto an individual's mind to Absorb their memories or to Control them by physically or mentally manipulating them.

More than once, Jakandy and Avasent debated the ethics of the last two skills. Avasent believed no situation granted their legitimate use, whereas Jakandy, ever the practical one, reasoned for their use under the right circumstances. Regardless, they mastered each of these skills with the willing help of Greeve.

They were the youngest to achieve the rank of communitor in quite some time, but donning their new hoodless brown robes didn't seem to excite Avasent anymore. She seemed to want something else—something Jakandy had no idea how to give her. Something was happening between him and Avasent—something he clearly did not understand, even now.

After that, things were never the same. She began spending less time with him and more time with Greeve. Any desire to continue their healthy competition to mutually further their monastic progression had vanished.

He believed his relationship with Avasent had deteriorated beyond repair, so he focused solely on his monastic career.

Step 4: Preserve.

He was the first in his class to serve the community as an adjudicator and then later as the youngest warden of the SIC. In fact, he was the first communitor to ever achieve such a promotion. During this time, he had blinding pride in his position and avarice for his ambition, leading him to make choices he otherwise would not have made. These choices he believed led him toward the unachievable goal he so much desired.

Due to his singular focus on becoming an elder, he missed much and processed less during that time as warden. As memories lost and forgotten began to emerge, he only now remembered the time Muldivar arrived at the SIC with a man named James. Muldivar had been so excited to catch the would-be killer. It was *his first collar. Instead of congratulating him on the achievement, Jakandy told him to be neither prideful nor boastful, as real killers could not exist in a world without crime.*

Step 5: Emulate.

Not long after, Jakandy stepped down as warden and became a monk of Sol and Luna. Most people in Fellowship City referred to any robed Mighty as a monk. The true status of a monk, however, was not bestowed until the communitor reached Step 5, although the monk would not earn a hood for several more Steps and many more years. Jakandy was an exception. Upon achieving his new status, he returned to his old role as an adjudicator. Within the months that followed, he transitioned to a life in the monastery, selling off his personal belongings and small apartment in Upton Tower 7.

Step 6: Parsimony.

Without any belongings or home, save for that bestowed upon him by the monastery, he welcomed the next step with open arms. He had nothing else. He only lived for the monastic life. That is why it was so easy for him to become the youngest monk to achieve Step 7, as he removed all attachment to self and others. He had very little attachment to begin with.

Step 7: Purge.

During that time, he would often sit alone in meditation, waiting for something exciting to happen. He was an adjudicator in a world without crime. He believed he had no real purpose and longed for someone to do something that would trigger his foresight and send him on a mission.

He would settle for the elders sending him on a fool's errand when they sensed a Citizen would attack a Mighty. They couldn't have Citizens striking Mighty, so they ordered Jakandy to take care of it. And take care of it he did.

He took the sniveling male Citizen to the SIC and left his whimpering wife in the care of DerMööve. The task was beneath him. It was not a mission utilizing his skills and abilities. He realized the elders were no longer interested in him. He was now merely their garbage man.

With nothing left for him and resigning himself to the idea that he would never be an elder, he donned the hooded brown robe.

Step 8: Patience.

He would spend the rest of his life helping his fellow monks in the monastery and retiring from the outside world, as he waited to reach the final Step. It was during this time, however, that he became the mentor of Tanalia, and for the first time in his monastic life, he understood regret.

"I have waited patiently to achieve Step 9: Eruption," he says to Sheryl. "Leaving this earthly body to ascend into omnivolence, as Sol and Luna had before me."

"You might want to wait a bit longer," says Sheryl with a wink and a grin. "You're very likely the last monk in Fellowship City. We might need you."

"No, we need you, Sherlock," he explains. "We need a detective, not a monk. Not me, anyway. I must apologize, Sheryl. I only now remembered that your Dr. James Moriarty may have come through the SIC when I was warden. "

"What?" Sheryl questions with betrayal burning in her eyes. "You never mentioned that you were warden?"

"I'm sorry," Jakandy apologizes again, turning from her gaze. "I can only say that those years I spent as warden were not my finest, and I had chosen to suppress and forget many of those memories. In my defense, you always referred to him as Moriarty. It wasn't until just now that you called him by his full name. When I was warden, I had a James—a would-be killer that Muldivar had collected when he was an adjudicator. But if you're wondering if I remember your face, I don't."

Sheryl squints at Jakandy for a moment and then scurries toward the front of the bookstore, flicking her fingers on her wrist.

"Where are you going?" Jakandy protests. "We need you!"

"You do realize that the detective work is over," Sheryl says without looking back. "We know who the killer is. It's not Moriarty. It's not some Mighty supervillain gone wild. It's a realized revenant bent on vengeance against people with superpowers."

Sheryl opens the bookstore's front door and steps out.

"Please, don't go," pleads Jakandy. "I truly am sorry."

"I can see that, Jakandy. And, I do accept your apology, but I'm no longer needed," she says with a soft smile.

"WATSON!" she yells into her wrist mechanism as she steps to the curbside.

She surveys the area before dropping her head in recollection.

"Dammit! That's right. EMMA!"

Emma races down the street toward Sheryl.

"You can't leave us!" Jakandy begs. "We need your help!"

Emma pulls up to the curb next to Sheryl, opening the passenger door for her.

"You don't need me, Jakandy," says Sheryl, as she slides over to the driver's side. "You've never needed me on this. I've done nothing to help you whatsoever. I'm a shell of a man. I no longer resemble who I once was."

"Goodbye, Jakandy," she says, buckling her seatbelt. "Thank you for the one last hurrah."

Emma peels away with a squeal, slamming the passenger door closed with the momentum.

Jakandy watches her race into the distance. He waves, not knowing whether she can still view him through her rearview. He turns back to the bookstore, inspecting either direction for signs of Mario and Trivial. Faint voices echo from two stores down, so he makes his way to the door. The handle is smashed to bits. He opens the door and peeks inside.

"Trivial? Mario? Have you—" he calls but is interrupted by a horrendous sound.

BADOOOOOOM

Jakandy falls to the ground, covering his ears.

Sol and Luna, what was that? He thinks, regaining his composure.

He scans around, finding the telltale signs of an explosion in the distance. Flames reach toward the sky, as something moving toward him catches his eye. He braces himself for the worst.

A tire on fire rolls toward him in a wobble, spinning slower and slower until it topples over.

No, no, he thinks, searching for the source of the tire.

Below the towering flames, his eyes fall onto the destroyed carcass of Emma.

"What the hell was that?" Mario exclaims in a startle, trying to recover the knives he just dropped.

"An explosion of some sort, I'd say," Trivial says unfazed, filling a white canvas bag with sharp utensils. "There's a lot of that going around today."

Mario places the recovered knives into a similar white canvas bag on the countertop in front of him.

"It sounded pretty close," he says, picking up a large knife with a wide, curved blade and a Granton edge.

"Be careful not to poke yourself," jokes Trivial from across the room, as he ties a butcher's apron around his waist. "Those knives are sharp."

"Good idea," Mario says with a laugh, as he fetches a butcher's apron hanging from a hook behind him. He ties it on and raises the butcher's knife. "I think I'm ready to carve up a turkey."

"What do you know about carving turkey?" asks Trivial. "There aren't any around here anymore, are there?"

"I saw it in a movie," Mario says, sticking the butcher knife into the knife-holster at the side of the apron. "This guy sticks the knife into the bird, and it just kinda explodes in a grotesque dry puff. It was pretty cool."

"I'll say."

Mario snatches up his bag and exits the backroom toward the front door, while Trivial finishes scouring the backroom. Jakandy still stands horrorstruck, staring toward the remains of Emma and Sheryl. Mario steps out the door beside him.

"Wow. It WAS close," he says, peering around. "Where's Sheryl?"

"Dead," says Jakandy emotionless and mechanical. "Watson exploded."

"Oh my God!" exclaims Mario.

"How come I didn't foresee it?" Jakandy says, turning toward Mario. "I saw you two carrying bags full of knives and tying on butcher's aprons. I see a riot currently happening in the WPC. But I couldn't see Sheryl die!"

He ambles toward Mario, anger raging within.

"Why? She wasn't killed by Ender! That would explain it —but she wasn't."

Mario drops the bag and shows Jakandy his hands in surrender.

"Jakandy, you need to calm down. I think you're losing it."

"I'm losing it?" the monk bellows, shoving Mario back.

Trivial stands dumbstruck, uncertain how to intervene.

"Do you know how long I've been working on patience?!? I was the youngest monk ever to reach step 8! I could feel the omnivolence pulling me toward it. I was so gifted in the seer-path arts. I should have been made an elder."

"Careful, Jakandy," Mario says, keeping his hands up in front of him. "It's me, Mario! I've been helping—"

Jakandy interrupts him, grabbing his left arm and lifting it to reveal his ident-tag "You are 24VØR4VNØ, Citizen! Don't you speak up against me! I will punish you for such behavior."

Mario yanks the butcher's knife free from the knife-holster and thrusts it forward.

"Fuck you, Jak—"

SHPLISHCK

Blood splatters Mario's face.

The murderous rage in his eyes vanishes into horror as he wipes the blood away with his free hand. Jakandy wails in agonizing pain. Mario stares at his knife with stunned guilt.

His shiny bloodless blade gleams in the air in front of Jakandy. He drops his gaze to Jakandy's chest, where the tip of another knife pokes through from behind. Blood blossoms at the puncture, darkening the monk's brown robe.

22

A TRIVIAL PAST: PART I

What just happened, Mario thinks, standing slack-jawed and staring into Jakandy's eyes.

They squint in pain as blood drips from his mouth. The growing dark circle of blood on his chest seeps around the silver tip of the knife. Mario reaches out to touch it, but the point draws back with a squish, revealing a deep gash. Fresh blood begins flowing from Jakandy's wound as his eyes roll back into his head. He falls forward in a limp.

Mario shutters, shaking the butcher knife out of his hand in time to catch Jakandy.

CLANK CLANK

"It's okay. It'll be okay," Mario assures Jakandy as Trivial comes into view.

He stands behind Jakandy still wielding the bloodied knife.

"What did you do?" Mario murmurs with eyes the size of planets.

"I made a choice," he says, wiping the blood from the knife with his butcher's apron. "Him or you."

"What did you do?" Mario screams, helping Jakandy to the ground. He snags his white bag and flips it over, emptying the contents onto the ground. "Stay with me, Jakandy."

He cuts a strip of cloth from the bag to make a bandage and shoves it into Jakandy's chest, trying to somehow halt the flow of the gushing blood from within.

"Errrgh. Ugh," Jakandy grunts.

"It's not too bad," Mario reassures the monk.

"Muhtha fa—" Jakandy cries, as Mario bends Jakandy over and shoves another bandage into the wound at his back.

"I know it hurts," he sympathizes. "You're going to be okay. I promise."

He grasps the bandages on both ends of Jakandy, pressing together to stop the blood. Trivial hovers over them annoyed.

"Can't you do something? Find some help?"

"Not on my agenda today. Sorry," Trivial says, turning away. He snatches his white canvas bag and hastens toward the bookstore. "Let him bleed out. He's already dead anyway."

"Why—are you—help—" Jakandy tries to speak through bubbling bloody spittle.

"Shhhh," interrupts Mario, cutting off a hefty piece from the bag. "No matter how much I wish you were killed by that thing out there, I'm not letting you die at the hands of one of us."

Trivial bolts out of the bookstore, wailing, "Where's Sherlock?"

Mario ignores him, wrapping the makeshift bandage around Jakandy's chest. It immediately spots with blood.

"We may not survive Ender," Mario tells Jakandy. "But we are damn well going to survive each other!"

"Thank—" Jakandy starts to say, but Trivial interrupts.

"Where is Sherlock?"

Jakandy points a weak, trembling finger toward the burning wreckage of Emma/Watson.

"Try not to move too much," Mario says, propping Jakandy up.

"What happened?" Trivial shouts.

"Watson—" Jakandy groans. "—exploded."

"DAMMIT!" shouts Trivial, dropping his bag of knives and slumping to the ground. "That's not how this was supposed to end—"

At the WPC, Tommy and James lead a small army of twenty or so Normals armed with various appliances and utensils sharpened or broken into dangerous weapons. They march in line toward the bus stop.

"Stop Citizens!" a bird guard commands, as he lowers to the ground and levels a shock-cannon at the group.

Hurling a spear that was once a broom, one of the Normals lunges toward the bird guard, clipping his wing and grounding him. The bird shrieks, dropping the shock-cannon. While the guard lies helpless, several other Normals scurry up and pummel him with their makeshift weapons.

Not far away, Officer Lizardlips fights off a couple of rioting Normals. Tommy sprints at him, clamping onto his tail, whipping him around, and knocking him off balance.

"Send my regards to Julian," he yells as the rioters advance.

"Who?" the officer asks in a gruff whimper as he covers his face and body with his arms and tail, trying to block the onslaught of kicks and punches.

James rushes a giant fuzzy guard with an uppercut, saying, "Take this you beast!"

The fuzzy guard smacks the ground.

THWAP

"Ouch," cries James, rubbing his hand.

At the entrance of the WPC, Tommy scrambles up to an incoming bus, waving his hands.

"Help, help!" he yells as the bus stops in front of him. He hustles over to the side door and bangs. "Hurry, let me in. They're going—"

PSHOOO KALLUNK

Wow, that worked, thinks Tommy as he springs up the steps to the driver.

"Are you a Citizen?" he asks the driver.

"What? No."

"That's too bad," Tommy says, yanking him from his seat and throwing him down the steps of the bus.

The driver lands with a crackling thud and eyes gaping at Tommy. He tries to speak but only coughs up blood.

"Viva la Resistance!" shouts Tommy, calling his army of freedom fighters to the bus.

They charge forward, shouting, "Down with the Mighty!"

"He'll be fine," Zelda whispers to Loo as she peeks around the corner of an alleyway.

Loo stands behind her, clasping her hand. Behind him stand the twenty or so half-breed children in a silent, single-file line. She keeps guard, as Tyler sneaks across the street.

"Clear," he shouts, waving at her. "Come on."

"Okay, kids," Zelda says, turning around to address all the moon-eyed youngsters. "It's time."

One by one, the children slide by Zelda and scamper across the street to line up behind Tyler. Once the last child passes, Zelda urges Loo to take his turn, and she follows right behind him. On the other side, she performs a quick headcount with Loo always on her tail. When Zelda reaches Tyler, he sneaks across another street, surveys the area, deems it safe, and waves them over.

"Ugh," grunts Mario, helping Jakandy into Ifton's driver's seat.

Jakandy stretches back against the seat, groaning and clutching his chest.

"Careful," Mario says. "You need to move slowly."

Jakandy moves slower, catching sight of Trivial punching a brick wall.

"I don't think he is who he says he is."

"I'm beginning to have my suspicions as well," Mario agrees, bucking Jakandy into the seat. "I certainly don't trust him, and I definitely don't want him too close to my backside."

Jakandy looses a painful chortle. Mario meets his eyes and smiles an apology before closing the driver's side door.

"Thank you for saving my life."

Mario leans against the closed door, retrieving the butcher knife from his side-holster. "I just hope it was worth it," he says, sharpening the knife with a leather strap hanging from the apron.

"It was," affirms Jakandy, leaning toward Mario through the open window.

The last monk of the Monastery of Sol and Luna places a hand on the shoulder of the Citizen who just saved his life. He closes his eyes and whispers, "There were three. The Warrior. The Wanderer. And the Wise. That's the evangelical truth."

Mario's eyes roll back into his head in a flutter as he jerks back and forth seizure-like. His arms fall limp to his sides. His right hand still grips the knife. After a second or two, Mario's eyes open, and he resumes sharpening the knife like nothing happened.

"What did you say?" Mario asks, unsure if he missed something important in their conversation.

"I said, I promise if I survive this, I will work to change the system, Mario. We weren't meant to enslave one another. We are meant to work together. Like we are now."

"You called me Mario," he says with astonishment, stopping the knife-sharpening in mid-stroke.

"Yes," says Jakandy, shifting his discomfort. "You are not a number."

Trivial approaches them, overhearing the last part of their conversation.

"How sweet," he says. "The freak and the geek made up."

"We are armed now," Jakandy asserts. "We need to find and defeat Ender."

"Is that still on your agenda, Trivial?" Mario asks with

hate-filled eyes. "Or have you made other plans, while moping over there? Should I be scared for my life?"

"You should always be scared for your life," Trivial says, mirroring his expression. "As long as the Mighty are in it!"

Trivial glances at Jakandy, but their eyes do not meet.

"Did you not hear me?" asks Trivial, appraising the monk.

Confused by his nonreaction, Trivial leans forward to glimpse Jakandy's face. He finds the monk's eyes ever-widening in the rearview mirror as the color washes away from his face. Trivial cranes his neck around Jakandy and peers through the back of Ifton.

"WATCH OUT!" screams Jakandy. "Run!"

Mario leaps away from Ifton as Ender barrels toward them from a distance.

"Jakandy, come on," Mario shouts as the window rolls up and Ifton's engine revs. Mario clambers to his feet and reaches for the door handle. "We'll go with you. We can make it. We have time."

"No!" Jakandy shouts through the glass, slamming his fist on the door lock button.

KERRPOOK

"You need to go, Mario!"

His lips tighten as he grits his teeth and adjusts the rearview. Mario bangs on the window and yanks on the handles.

"Let me in, Jakandy," pleads Mario. "We can—"

"Go now!" Jakandy commands, pointing to Trivial fleeing down the street. "Follow him to safety!"

"No, we can—"

Jakandy turns to Mario with warmth in his eyes and

pushes a thought, *"Ender doesn't want you. He wants me. I'll distract him and you kill him, Mario. You kill him."*

"But," Mario begs. "You said you were going to make things right!"

"I will. I promise. Now—"

"What? Now what?" Mario asks in a panic as Ifton backs away from the curb and knocks him off balance. "I can't hear you in my head anymore, Jakandy," he says, stumbling onto the sidewalk and checking for the knife in his side-holster.

Bummer. I liked that one.

As Ifton drives away, Mario spots the white bag full of knives and other weapons. He retrieves a new blade and slides it into the holster, making a sawing sound against the leather.

"Good luck," he hollers before chasing after Trivial.

Jakandy eyes Mario through the rearview mirror and slams on the brakes.

What the hell are you doing, Jakandy? thinks Mario, hearing the screeching tires and smelling the burned rubber.

Jakandy spins the wheel around, whipping Ifton in the direction of Ender while pressing hard on the brakes. He pats the dashboard, saying, "I'm sorry, Ifton."

Ifton honks a reply as Jakandy releases the brakes and stomps the gas pedal. Ifton peels out and races toward the oncoming tank.

Mario's dumbfounded eyes are glued to Ifton's game of chicken with Ender. He breathes a sigh of relief when Jakandy's door swings open at the last possible second.

KAARRAAAAACK

The van slams like an unstoppable force into an immovable object, the back end flying upward a few feet and crashing hard to the ground. The sound of metal scraping and breaking echoes against the empty street buildings as tires roll away from the totaled van.

Did he make it? Mario thinks, seeking some sign of Jakandy amid the debris. Again, he breathes a sigh of relief as Jakandy rises from the rubble. *Okay, you did it. Now, get the hell out of there.*

Jakandy collects himself, taking little time to witness the aftermath of Ifton's forced sacrifice. He hobbles toward the back of Ifton, producing a substantial knife in his hand.

Ender jolts up, dislodging fragments of Ifton's glass and metal from his skin. He wipes thick black ooze away with a painful groan. The dashboard flickers and the radio blares with static, catching Ender's attention. He stalks into the van and roars with anger, smashing and trashing what is left as he approaches the front.

"Get out of the house!" blares the radio. "Come on down to the last—"

Ender jabs his fists into the dashboard and rips the guts out of the dash, making the radio fizzle into silence.

Jakandy winces as Ifton screams in pain, "*It hurts! It hurts! It—*"

Ender tosses the electrical guts out the side-door as a fire sparks behind on the dash. He steps out of the already busted up backend to find Jakandy standing in an attack pose, knife in hand.

"By the guidance of Sol and Luna, I beseech you to grant me the wisdom of the end, of the all, of the evermore—"

KAABOOOOOM

The inside of Ifton blows up, launching Ender toward Jakandy, who barely rolls out of the way. Adrenaline surging through him, he bolts up ready to strike but discovers the knife is missing. He searches around, spying it near Ender.

Dammit, he thinks, as Ender plucks the knife from the ground with an awful scratching sound against the asphalt.

His eyes meet Ender's mismatched eyes, and he accepts his fate. He sits into a cross-legged pose with his back as straight as possible. Fighting the overwhelming pain flooding him as the adrenaline begins to wear off, he begins to chant his final mantra.

"May I leave this world with an eruption and join you in the omnivolence!"

With the knife raised high, Ender hurdles toward Jakandy, crushing him in an explosion of body parts vaporizing into a red spray.

Mario screams, covering his mouth with his hands to stifle the sound.

The monster pays no attention, standing within the giant bloody puddle of Jakandy. He thrusts his arms into the air and roars.

AAAAARRRRRGGGGHH

James doubles over in the bus, screaming in pain. The Normal army surrounding him stares with confused faces, trying to keep their distance. His eyes burst open as he shrieks, "I remember!"

"WAIT!" yells Mario, trailing behind Trivial.

Trivial pays him no mind, ducking into an alleyway.

Mario follows, hollering, "I think you're going the wrong way!"

He rounds the corner of the alleyway and sees Trivial stop abruptly in the middle of the street ahead. Mario continues running toward him as Trivial turns to face him.

"We must make a stand," Mario says. "We're Normals. We can kill him, right?"

Trivial glowers down at the knife in his trembling hands.

"Here. Take it," he says, handing the knife to Mario. "Make a stand!"

"But you won't have a weapon," he says confused. "I can find something."

"No!" Trivial shouts. "Take it! I'll find something!"

Trivial turns back around and belts through the alleyway across the street. On the other side, he scans to the left and right before rushing headlong to the right.

"Stop!" yells Mario. "You're heading back to Ender!"

Mario darts to the end of the alley, stops, and throws his arms up.

"What the hell are you doing?"

TUMPATHUMP

Panic-stricken, Mario stands motionless, except for the shiver.

Oh, God. He's here.

Ten years ago.

Moriarty sat in the immense library of the Realizer's mansion, flipping the Collected Works of Sir Arthur Conan Doyle and marveling at each of the pages he read.

Quell in the form of a gorilla stood guard at the library door.

Moriarty slammed the book shut.

"Take me to the Realizer," he said, standing up and placing the book under his arm.

"I cannot defeat Sherlock in the Glory Battle," he said to the Realizer. "The stories all say he defeats me."

The Realizer reclined on his sofa, feeding himself with grapes. He picked one from the bunch, placed it between his teeth, and squeezed until it popped.

"So be it," he said, waving to Quell to remove Moriarty.

"My master," Moriarty beckoned in a soft respectful tone. "That would not make an entertaining experience. It's expected. Unsurprising. Dull. But do you know what will be unexpected? Surprising? Entertaining? Do you know what will make you a ton of money?"

The Realizer straightened in his seat.

"Go on," he said. "You have my attention."

"Do you think your ability would allow you to trade my body with his?" Moriarty asked, pointing to Quell.

"Hrrrmph," grumbled Quell.

"I don't understand," the Realizer said. "My ability allows me to pull something from a media source, like a video or text. But—"

"Oh, I need to write it down for it to work. All right," Moriarty interrupted, taking a pen from the side table and writing his idea upon a page.

The Realizer scrutinized his presumption as Moriarty handed him the paper. He snagged it from his hand ready to crumple it into a ball, but as he read, he became filled with wonder.

"Interesting," he marveled, studying the page. "I've never tried anything like that before, but I guess it might be worth a shot. The thing is, you have to be able to block it from the monastery. Do you think you can?"

"I'm always up for a challenge," Moriarty said, smiling his wicked grin at the Realizer.

"Quell," said the Realizer, gesturing to the page. "Are you up for it?"

"Whatever you wish, sir," grunted Quell.

"Well, it couldn't hurt to try, I guess," the Realizer singsonged like a giddy schoolboy. "Make sure, you're blocking too, Quell. We don't want any incidents."

"Always, sir."

"This will be fun," spoke the Realizer with glee as he waved his hands like a conductor and motioned to Quell. "Stand with your back to Dr. James Moriarty and change into something more his size."

Quell nodded, maneuvering into position while morphing into his true form. The Realizer stood between them, placing his right hand on the skinny young man's shoulder and his left hand on Moriarty's. He scoured over the hastily scrawled image and words on the page. They began to swirl in a vortex toward him, becoming a long thin translucent tendril beaming into the middle of his forehead until the page became blank once more.

His eyes burned with white light as he gazed upon Quell. The light pulsated from his eyes down his right arm with blinding vibrancy, reaching his right hand, and penetrating deep into Quell's conscious being. Like a fishhook catching a rare bite, the Realizer found what he sought within Quell and pulled it from him in an excruciating extraction of bright blue light. He withdrew his right hand from Quell's shoulder, cradling a tiny spiraling blue galaxy within the palm of his hand.

He performed the same ritual on Moriarty, pulling free a tiny violet galaxy into the palm of his left hand. After which, he crossed his arms and turned the palm-held galaxies toward the heads of Quell and Moriarty, thrusting them forward into each man's forehead.

Violet light rippled through Quell's body, as blue light rippled through Moriarty's. Both men shook in chaotic seizures as the light dazzled vibrantly within each. It coursed through their bodies, finding purchase in every vein and artery, blood cell and neuron until the light constricted into a tiny glowing circle in the center of their foreheads. Then, the light vanished, and both men opened their eyes.

They turned to face each other.

Moriarty viewed the world through Quell's eyes, tilting his head and saying, "I am devilishly handsome, aren't I?"

Then, Moriarty mimicked himself, so two versions of him stood in front of the Realizer.

"Now, we can beat Sherlock and really rake in the big bucks, boss!"

During the Glory Battle, it was Moriarty, not Quell, who fought Sherlock at Reichenbach falls. He fought with displeasure, not because he did not want to destroy Sherlock, but because he did not want to do it beholden to the Realizer. He did not want to be enslaved as he was to make the slob money while defeating the greatest foe he would ever have. He wanted to defeat Sherlock on his own terms.

He knew Sherlock would have read the Reichenbach story while he was a captive within the walls of the Realizer's mansion, so he played along. When it came time for the fall, he anticipated Sherlock's every move and counter. He allowed himself to fall, thus beginning the deception. He shifted his hands into grappling hooks and latched onto the edge.

As Sherlock peered down the falls, he caught sight of the grappling hooks and reasoned that the mimic was none other than Quell.

Moriarty believed Sherlock would save Quell to the dismay of the audience and the Realizer's pocketbook. Ingratiating himself with Sherlock, he helped him escape and took his place. He hoped Sherlock would stay long enough to witness him standing in front of the Realizer as Sherlock Holmes. When he spotted him in his periphery, he smiled a wicked grin.

"What are you smiling at?" the Realizer shrieked. "You failed! You cost me money!"

The Realizer pointed his finger into Sherlock's chest, and he fell to the ground in a lifeless heap.

Confused, the Realizer stood over the body of Sherlock, lying lifeless upon the ground. He examined the body, his finger, the body again, and his finger once more before kicking him.

"Ouch, Realizer," Sherlock said, balling his legs into his chest and turning over to stand. "That really hurt."

The Realizer jolted back. His startle morphed into anger, as Sherlock shifted into Moriarty.

"How dare you?!?" The Realizer yelled. "I brought you into this world! I can take you out!"

"Not this body," Moriarty said, flashing his wicked smile. "I'm a Mighty now! You can't keep my freedom from me! I will find and fight Sherlock on my own terms!"

Moriarty lunged toward the Realizer, shifting into a gorilla as he charged. The Realizer dove out of the way, rolling over as the gorilla crashed through the window and escaped the mansion. The Realizer recovered and rushed to the window. The Gorilla bounded down the street and into the shadows.

"I'm so sorry, my friend," the Realizer said as he stepped into the room where Quell remained hidden in Moriarty's true body. "You are going to be stuck in this filthy Normal body for now. But I promise I will find a way to return your body to you. Until that day, do what you can with this one's limited abilities."

He snapped his finger and a brown-hooded monk stepped into the room.

"This is only a precautionary measure, my friend," said the Realizer, nodding to the monk.

She lowered her hood to reveal a youthful beauty, if not for the gray hair braided around her dark skin, revealing her true age. Quell gazed into her eyes as she stepped toward him, raising her hand. He fell to his knees and she placed her hand on his forehead.

"This will only hurt if you fight it," she whispered as his eyes popped in anguish.

When all was done, he fell into a heap on the floor. She spun around and glided into the arms of the Realizer. She kissed him and stroked his cheek before clamping onto his manhood through his clothes.

He jerked back with a start, but her grip was tight, keeping him in place and submissive.

"Now, my dear Realizer, you understand," she purred. "This is the last time we will ever meet like this. My violet ceremony is less than a week away."

"I understand," he said with a nod.

"Good."

She dropped her brown robes from her body, revealing her stark-naked beauty.

When Quell awoke, he found himself sequestered to a wing of the mansion the Realizer never ventured. After that day, he never spoke to the Realizer again. Without his powers, he was of no use to the Realizer. He was a frail being stuck in a world he didn't belong to and a constant reminder of his employer's mistake.

He hated his new life. Anger swelled within him, and all he wanted was vengeance. But he had no clue how to even proceed, so he sought Moriarty's copy of the Collected Works of Arthur Conan Doyle and began to read.

Finding no resolve in its pages, he grew angrier and angrier, as his desire for vengeance never abated. One night, while flipping through the pages of the very worn copy of the book, he gave into the anger.

"I'm going to find you!" he shouted while standing at his

kitchen counter, clenching the book. "And you will pay for what you did to me!"

With the book tucked under his arm, he grabbed the largest knife the kitchen had to offer, and in a temporary fit of madness, he plowed through the front door of his home with murder on his mind.

"I will find you! And when I do, I'm going to kill you!"

They know what you think before you think it. He didn't even have a chance. In his frustrated anger, he had forgotten to keep his blocking vigilant. He had forgotten to keep himself calm. Surprise and panic rose within him, as the strong-flyer lifted him by the throat off the ground, shaking the knife and book free.

"What? You can't do this to me."

A second strong-flyer retrieved his treasured book. He wanted to say, "That's mine. Give it back to me," but the words could not penetrate his panic. He was weak, fragile, no longer a Mighty, and he had no way of saving himself.

"Citizen, by order of the Justice Assembly and the Enclave of the Monastery of Sol and Luna, you are hereby reprimanded to the Fellowship City Solitary Internment Camp for hard labor for the rest of your days," ordered the young monk, but to Quell, it sounded like he spoke from underwater. "So says Adjudicator Muldivar, communitor Step 4."

The face of his enemy, the face he wore every day, swirled around his head, laughing at him and provoking him. Anger raged within him once more, and he fought back, shouting, "You can't—" But that was it. Without warning, his arm snapped behind him.

"OWW!" he screamed, reeling back in pain. "You broke my arm!"

Without thinking, he swatted at the strong-flyer with his other fist, hurting himself more than anything. So, the strong-flyer hoisted him over his shoulder like he was nothing.

"Leave me alone!" he screeched. "I will not be imprisoned!"

But the strong-flyer did not leave him alone. Instead, he flew up into the air, causing Quell to scream, "AAAAAAHHHHHH!!!"

"Put me down!" he shouted, trying to free himself from the flyer's grip. "I'd rather die!"

The next thing Quell knew, he was falling to the ground and screaming again, "AAAAAAHHHHHH! You bastard! Save me!"

Then, everything went black.

He arrived at SIC, shaken and broken.

"What did you do to him?" asked the young warden in traditional nonhooded brown robes.

"He attacked us, Warden Jakandy," replied Muldivar. "We acted only in self-defense."

"Hmmmph," Quell, still in the body of Moriarty, groaned in disagreement.

Jakandy scrutinized him momentarily and placed a hand on his head.

'He's clouded,' Jakandy said through voice-thought to Muldivar.

'I know,' Muldivar responded in kind. 'Brain damage?'

'I don't know,' Jakandy thought. 'A portion of his memory is wiped. It's as if something is blocking me.'

"What does it mean?"

"I'm not sure, but I'm going to find out."

Jakandy placed him into regular rotation, but Quell was too consumed by hatred, anger, and vengeance.

"Moriarty! I will have revenge!" he shouted.

"Shut up!" yelled a guard.

"Fuck you!" he shouted, storming at the guard.

Inches from beating his face with his fists, a telekin guard pointed a finger at him, stopping him in his tracks.

"Trouble?" Jakandy asked the guard.

"This one needs a reprimand," the guard grunted.

Jakandy placed a finger on the forehead of Moriarty and pulled memories from him.

"It hurts!" screamed Quell. "Please stop! I can't remember!"

"Maybe now I can figure out who you are," said Jakandy as he finishes. "Hmm. All I'm getting is James."

23

A TRIVIAL PAST: PART II

"**M**y name is Dr. James Moriarty," said the tall, skinny man who did not resemble the Moriarty from the Glory Battles broadcast at all.

"You don't look like him," said the brutish Mighty bouncer at the door of the bar.

Moriarty examined his reflection in the window.

'I'm rubbish at this mimicry,' he thought and then said aloud, "Does it matter?"

"Only if you want in," the bouncer said followed by an overzealous guffaw.

"If you let me in, I won't need to hurt you."

"Now that's something I'd like to see."

"Oh, you would, would you?"

Moriarty spied an empty bottle sitting on the half-sized brick wall off to the side of the bar. He turned away from the bouncer, snatched the bottle, and bashed it into the brick, breaking glass in an echoing racket. He turned back to the bouncer, ready to strike.

Suddenly, a hand clasped his arm and wrenched the broken bottle free. He spun around to face this interloper.

"How dare y—"

"What is your name?" interrupted the unhooded monk in the brown robe with two strong-flyers hovering behind him.

"Quell," Moriarty, wearing Quell's body, blurted without pause.

"Well, Quell. I am Adjudicator Muldivar, communitor Step 4, and you are in violation," he said, letting go of Quell's arm. "Because you are a Mighty, I'll let you off with a warning. But, do not let me catch you ever again, Quell. Or it will be the last time. Do you understand?"

"Yes," he answered flabbergasted.

Muldivar brought his pointer finger down upon the forehead of the mimic and pulled from him all the memories he found of a baser nature.

"Ahhhh!" Moriarty screamed, his eyes pleading for help from the bouncer.

"See. I knew you weren't that Moriarty dude," he said. "Will he remember tonight?"

"No, I can pull that too," answered Muldivar.

"Good," the bouncer said, spitting a cruddy wad of phlegm into Moriarty's face.

Over the next year, he followed his natural inclination toward villainy, attempting to enlist would-be supervillains out of susceptible Mighty. He believed an organization rife with super-powered criminals with him at the helm would make a killing. However, at every turn, every possible recruitment opportunity, the monastery halted him, and each time, the adjudicators' punished him by removing memories.

In time, the monks extinguished all of his memories of life before Fellowship City with Sherlock and after with the Realizer. His inherent nefarious tendencies drove him toward activities that society deemed anti-social, although he learned to work within the law rather than try to circumvent it.

After making some wise investments, he purchased a former

hospital in southwest downtown Fellowship City on the north-west corner of 20th Avenue and B Street. He planned to turn the first floor into a restaurant, keeping the higher floors as luxury apartments.

'Real estate is all about location,' he thought, exploring the building. He found a south-facing panel window and surveyed the southside ghetto. 'A lucrative investment with plenty of potential, and an opportunity to serve Mighty and Citizens alike.'

He signed the deal only after viewing the basement levels. He left them alone, refitting and refurbishing them for some possible future need.

Not long after the purchase and remodel, he interviewed potential tenants for his restaurant space. One suave, young German-speaking telekin named DerMööve made the grade. He took a liking to the young man, sensing in him some suppressed criminal tendencies. However, he did not like the budding restaurateur's ideas for the establishment.

"The location is ideal for pulling from both sides of the tracks," conveyed Moriarty. "If you make this something too upscale, you are only gearing up for one clientele."

"But I vant only to serve Mighty in mein restaurant," DerMööve said with conviction.

"My dear fellow, you're not seeing the bigger picture," Moriarty said, placing an arm around DerMööve and waving his arm across the empty room awaiting construction. "This is not to serve Citizens, but to serve us."

Moriarty spun DerMööve around, revealing the secret room in the restaurant wall leading to the basement.

"Was ist das?" asked DerMööve as he stepped toward the open space in the wall.

"That, mein freund, is where the magic begins," Moriarty said with a laugh. "The monastery does not want any affliction to come to the Mighty. But they turn a blind eye when the same *thing happens to Citizens. I think we can come to some kind of arrangement here."*

DerMööve stares into the dark hallway fluorescent light flutters throughout, revealing door after door down the long corridor.

"Ich halte es für sehr wahrscheinlich," he said grinning sideways.

"Sehr gut," Moriarty says, reaching to shake DerMööve's hand. "We're in business."

A few years later.

Moriarty returned to DerMööve's bustling arcade to revisit their previous arrangement.

"Here's an interesting proposition for you, Herr DerMööve," he said, standing in the restaurateur's office. "I understand you've curated a harem of Normal women in the basement level."

DerMööve squinted at Moriarty.

"How did dis information come by you?"

"Oh," Moriarty said, waving a hand. "Let's say, a little birdy told me. Now show me what you've done with the place."

DerMööve led Moriarty through the dark corridor behind the SUPER MUNCHER BATTLE LORDS game to a door with a nameplate that read Guinevere. He motioned to a drawn shade and retracted it to reveal a two-way mirror. Behind the mirror, a woman sat in a rocking chair breastfeeding a baby. A 13-year-old boy sat cross-legged entertaining his 5-year-old sister by touching an unplugged radio, sparking it to life and making it play music.

Moriarty eyed the boy's sparking fingertips.

"A Mighty?" he asked.

"Not according to law," DerMööve said, winking with his sidelong grin. "Sie are half-breeds."

"But they have powers."

"Ist nothing. Ist residue. Tiny gifts by virtue of ihres Vater's DNA. Sie ver born from a Citizen. Das ist all dat matters."

"Do all half-breeds have powers?" asks Moriarty.

"Sometimes sie have powers, but sie are not Mighty," assures DerMööve. "Sie are still slaves."

"Fascinating," Moriarty said, stroking his chin. "You know, a harem is just one man's brothel. If you shared, you might make a hefty little profit from this venture."

"Cash ist king!"

Before long, DerMööve's harem transformed into a Mighty brothel. He anticipated pushback from the monks, but Moriarty assured him the monastery had more important things to do than concern themselves with the plight of a few Citizens. With the brothel up and running, Moriarty went to work, interviewing the occupants of the basement level.

"And do you experience these headaches when the child isn't around you?"

He punched notes into a handheld touchpad as he sat at a table in a small white padded room across from a mother cradling a small child.

"Yes," the mother said, frowning at her child. "I get them all the time."

On the touchpad, Moriarty swiped his finger across the woman's info in an X.

"Thank you for your time," he said, standing from the table and moseying toward the exit.

"Do I get the extra meal now?"

"I'll notify someone to bring your meal forthwith," he said, exiting the room and locking the door behind him.

After the interviews, Moriarty sought to purchase more property. He liked the old hospitals and found another for purchase in East F.C., northeast of downtown between O and Summerland Highway and 7th Ave and 8th Ave where Puissant Way ends. This area of town was quaint and less populated than the rest.

"It's perfect," Moriarty said, assessing the dilapidated building.

"Oh no, hun," said the attractive, brunette real estate agent. She appeared to be in her 30s and wore a periwinkle blue pantsuit and glasses. "I forgot the keys. Give me a second will ya, sugar," she said, phasing through the door.

Moriarty stood awestruck, as the door click—clicked and opened. The phantom held the door, inviting Moriarty in with a wink and a grin.

"I believe you'll find all the amenities you require," she said, leading him toward a stairwell.

On the second floor, she guided him to a door marked with a bio-chemical hazard sticker. Inside, a small observation room sealed with glass hung above a much larger room.

"Here's the scenic view, sugar."

Moriarty stepped forward and peered over the massive laboratory below.

"I'll take it."

"Excellent," the real estate agent said, shaking his hand. "I'll be right back with the paperwork."

Moriarty startled as she disappeared from in front of him, leaving only a puff of smoke where she had been previously standing.

Less than a year later.

Moriarty gazed through the overhang window at his refurbished lab, sparkling clean and gleaming white. Several workers in white lab coats scurried around below. He palmed an intercom button and said, "Thank you all for making my dream of Delirium a reality!"

He gripped a book in his hand, something he found among his possessions but had long since forgotten, the Collected Works of Arthur Conan Doyle.

At home that evening, he read about Sherlock Holmes and

found the words too engrossing, too captivating to put down. Some four hundred pages later he discovered Moriarty, and his mind went adrift with recollection.

He began to think of himself as Moriarty, although he did not understand how he could come to exist in this world.

'I know you're out there, Holmes!' he thought with his hands pressed against his head. "I cannot believe that I would exist in a world where you were not. Where are you hiding? Does this strange future scare you to death? While you're out there somewhere in the shadows, I am thriving."

Within weeks, Moriarty returned to DerMööve's brothel bearing a gift. They stood outside the doorway of a room with a nameplate that read Virginie. Moriarty appraised a vial of yellow liquid in his hand.

"We've discovered among Normals—"

"Citizens," DerMööve corrected, opening the door.

"Whatever," Moriarty said with a shrug, stepping in behind. "Delirium causes acute pacification."

"Was ist pass-if—"

"Pacification. It makes them easier to control."

Virginie lied strapped to the bed. She fought against the constraints, as one of Moriarty's lab workers fit her with a catheter for the IV. Another set up the IV and pushed buttons on the monitor. In a series of beeps and whirls, the IV started its saline drip into the tubing and into Virginie's arm.

"Stop!" she cried. "Don't touch me!"

"Now watch," Moriarty said, pointing to the small bag of yellow liquid a lab worker affixed to the IV. "The response is almost instantaneous."

The yellow fluid dripped into the clear, trickling toward Virginie's convulsing body.

"Leave me alone!" she yelled, as her eyes followed the yellow fluid creeping toward her vein.

She tugged and pleaded with DerMööve, tightening her muscles and trying to resist up until the moment the Delirium entered her vein. After that, a wave of pleasantness radiated from her face, as she loosened her muscles and relaxed.

Moriarty signaled for his lab workers to leave and closed the door behind them.

"She is completely pacified. You can do whatever you want to her and she will not fight."

DerMööve approached Virginie, ripping the blanket from her and revealing her naked flesh beneath. He placed a hand on the inside of her ankle, slid it up her calf and to her thigh. Then, he stopped and turned to Moriarty.

"I see," he said with wonder. "Und how does it affect das kinder—children?"

"Similarly. Small doses will pacify them and make them controllable."

"Perfekte. Start now!" DerMööve demands, and Moriarty is more than willing to comply.

The first child given Delirium was the 17-year-old son of DerMööve and Guinevere. Moriarty remembered his face from years ago.

With a syringe filled with a bubbling yellow liquid, Moriarty said, "It's an inoculation."

"What will it do to me?"

"We've found that it will ensure you stay healthy," Moriarty half-lied, handing the syringe to the boy "It will enable you to be the best you that you can be."

"What if I don't want to be the best me I can be?" Tyler asked, studying the needle.

"Then, I'll be forced to call in support," Moriarty said, gesturing over his shoulder to the two Mighty in lab coats behind him. One was a fuzzy, hairy and massive. The other was a strong or strong-flyer. "It's your choice, Tyler."

Tyler gulped.

"Believe me, you don't want that. It's better if you learn how to do this yourself," Moriarty said, nodding at him and narrowing his eyes.

Tyler found a vein popping from his skin and slid the needle into it, emptying the strange yellow fluid within. His head whipped back, and his eyes gaped open, dilating into dark spheres. His body convulsed, knocking the needle from his arm, as a strange energy flowed through him.

He shuttered and raised his hands into the air. Electricity sparked from his fingertips. He gulped and teepeed his fingers, shooting a bolt of lightning from his hands and burning a black hole in the ceiling tile.

"What did you do to me?" Tyler belted, as he fell backward.

'We also found it enhances the abilities of half-breeds,' thought Moriarty, smiling a wicked grin at Tyler. 'Superpowered children that I can control.'

"How ist everything coming along, mein freund?" asked DerMööve, as Moriarty exited the dark hallway into the arcade.

'Everything is falling into place,' Moriarty thought, but said, "It's going very well. We have almost completed all of the inoculations."

"Sehr gut," DerMööve said, placing an arm around Moriarty. "I vant you to meet someone."

DerMööve ushered Moriarty toward the booths in the dining area of his Arcade and Grill. A bulky figure sat at one of the booths.

"Das ist der mensch I have been telling you about," DerMööve said as they approached.

The man in the booth turned to face them. Moriarty did not recognize him, but the man recognized Moriarty.

"Quell," the man said with a breath. "Or is it Moriarty."

"You know him?" DerMööve asked, his eyes narrowing.

"I'm not sure that I do," Moriarty said.

"Oh, you definitely do. We're old friends, you and me. I'm sad you've forgotten."

"Well, interactions with a monk tend to do that to you," Moriarty said tapping on his temple as he sat at the table. "How do we know each other?"

"I'm the Realizer," he said, seeking a glimmer of recognition.

"Oh yes," Moriarty said. "You have that interesting restaurant on 17th. I haven't been yet. I should come by."

"Yes, you should," the Realizer responded, taken aback by the complete lack of recognition. "It is always an interesting experience. I would especially like to know your thoughts."

Moriarty wished he could remember this man. He scanned what memories he had, trying to find something about the Realizer, but nothing came to him. His mind was wiped clean of any impression this man may have made, and the way the Realizer glared at him was worrisome.

Acknowledging the threat was one thing but acting upon it was impossible. Both men knew nothing could be done. Though they both were blockers, neither of them knew how successful they could be at killing or thinking about killing a Mighty without a monk showing up and eliminating one or both of them. So, they faked their smiles, enjoyed their meals, and congratulated each other on their achievements.

"I think you vould be fine addition to der Sviftglides," said DerMööve, revealing his motive for the meeting.

"Oh, thank you," Moriarty said, standing up from his seat, and before the Realizer could negate the request. "But, I'm not sure that is something I would like to do. I'm more of a loner, you see. I'm not really a—team-player. However, I do thank you with all sincerity for this opportunity to meet with the two of you."

DerMööve appeared to be as disappointed as the Realizer appeared to be relieved.

"Well, it's certainly something you might want to consider," the Realizer said, exerting tremendous effort on his part.

"Again, thank you," Moriarty said, bowing his head. "I'll keep that in mind."

After that meeting, Moriarty could not let go of his worry. He wanted—No, he needed to know exactly who the Realizer was and why he felt threatened by him. So, he changed his form into something he hoped was unfamiliar to the Realizer and visited his restaurant.

The host was a man with a black pompadour, wearing a golden jacket and a pair of gold aviator sunglasses.

"You here for a big hunk o' love or are you takin' care of business?" the man asked with a southern drawl.

"Which one means I'm here to dine?" responded Moriarty in his disguise.

"Hunk it is," the man said, raising his lip and pointing at Moriarty.

He waved over a dark-haired man with five o'clock shadow, wearing a black suit, white shirt opened at the collar with a loosened black tie.

The man sauntered over, saying, "Come on, kid-o, let's get you some grub."

As Moriarty followed the man to a table, he spotted the Realizer sitting in a booth on the other side of the room.

"May I sit over there?" he said, pointing to a seat near the Realizer's booth.

The man in the suit shrugged and guided Moriarty to the new table.

At the table, Moriarty did not sit right away. He stood for a second, but it must have been longer than the man in the suit thought appropriate.

"You gonna bark all day, little doggy, or are you gonna bite?"

As Moriarty slid into his seat, the man handed him a menu

and sauntered away. Moriarty surveyed the room. He saw a thin man with shaggy dark hair wearing glasses and a white tuxedo taking an order from a couple at a table near him. When the waiter left, the couple squealed with glee.

"I can't believe it's actually him," the woman said.

"Of course, it's him," the man said. "That's what the Realizer does. He creates these experiences for our enjoyment. This is just like being in the movie!"

Moriarty teepeed his fingers as he began to put the pieces together. He scrutinized all the workers in the restaurant, identifying how anachronistic and alien they were to this world. They did not belong and neither did he. The Realizer had brought them all into existence, and that meant, he had brought Moriarty into this world as well.

He thought back to the book that triggered the memory of his true being.

'He is able to materialize beings out of ideas,' Moriarty thought. 'How did I miss that? His name is literally the Realizer. It's painfully obvious. Sherlock would never have missed that.'

"Why can't I think of anything?" Moriarty overheard the Realizer say. "I'm so bored. I need something new—something big —different."

'I'll give you something different,' Moriarty thought.

Later, Moriarty perched in a shadow near the dumpster in the alley behind QTs House of Jacks, holding a syringe of Delirium. He waited hours before the door cracked open and a man in a black suit carried a trashcan out the back.

The man whistled as he sauntered to the dumpster.

'He's of a decent physique,' Moriarty thought, inspecting the man who sat him at his booth earlier that day.

As the man dumped the rubbish into the dumpster, Moriarty sprung from his spot and injected the needle into the man's neck, causing him to fall almost lifeless to the ground. He shifted, becoming the man in the black suit. He picked up his doppel-ganger and tossed him into the dumpster. As Moriarty expected, the monastery did not respond. No monks showed up to haul him off to SIC. The man had no powers, so he meant nothing in this future.

Moriarty as the man in the black suit returned to the restau-rant to complete his shift. He found no difficulty learning how to be this new character. No one detected the change. Their jobs required too much fast-paced movement, too much labor, and too much independence for anyone to pay attention to anyone else at all. As demanding as it was, he enjoyed the work. He considered it a respite from his previous life.

Over time, he ingratiated himself into the Realizer's company, making himself a much-needed confidante.

"I need something more, but I can't think," the Realizer confessed to him. "I can no longer bring myself to read through the same drivel over and over, trying to find something new I can use. I sit on my couch and watch show after show of nothing. I've become a drone and I hate it. I hate this world and what it has made me."

'I can use this,' thought Moriarty.

As the confidante, he would go out into the streets on a quest to find media for the Realizer to consume. He would scour book-stores and thrift shops, libraries and museums, and other remains from the years before the reign of the Mighty. He found a virtual treasure trove of resources when he discovered the remains of a comic shop deep in the Normal slums among the derelict build-ings south of Cavendish Street. Within the ruins of the Arcana If You Cana Comics shop, Moriarty scanned comic after comic, trying to find the perfect character for the Realizer to bring into existence. One day, he found a comic full of promise and retrieved it for the Realizer to read.

Moriarty carried a box overflowing with various forms of

media into the back of QTs House of Jacks, through the kitchen, and into the dining area, acknowledging several members of the waitstaff along the way. He nodded with a wink and a smile to the tall, bare-footed woman with the black bob with fringe who was always pleasant. He nearly crashed into her bitchy blonde twin with the tight yellow motorcycle suit. He escaped talking to the freak in the leopard print smoking jacket thanks to the brooding, salt and pepper haired man with the massive tattoo on his neck.

"Here's your shipment, boss," Moriarty said, dropping the box onto the table.

At the top of the box lay the comic book Moriarty salvaged for the Realizer—the perfect one to help him find what he thought he needed to find—something to shake up his mundane world and bring chaos into this utopian future.

The Realizer picked it up and examined it. "Trivial number 8," he read.

The first part of Moriarty's plan for the Realizer had come to fruition when he saw Trivial sitting at the Realizer's booth the very next day.

'Now he just has to find that present I've left for him in one of the boxes upstairs,' Moriarty thought, steepling his fingers.

He had no idea it would take a year for the second part of his plan to come to fruition. The lack of success left him so frustrated when the day finally arrived, he felt less joy than annoyance. His only pleasure that day came as he escorted Trivial out of the restaurant, never expecting to lay eyes upon him again.

The explosion in the Normal slums changed everything.

'So soon?' thought Moriarty, as he stared at the billowing cloud of light in the sky. 'No reason to go to QTs now. As Sherlock would say, the game is afoot.'

Tucking his book under his arm, he raced toward the explosion. His plan was now set in motion and time would tell if the chaos would bring forth Sherlock from the shadows. When he arrived at ground zero for the explosion at the Normals market, he found only scavengers and Delirious D-heads scrounging for anything salvageable. He sought any sign Sherlock might have been there, but nothing jumped out at him.

He opened the book, read a passage, and slammed it shut, yelling, "Holmes!!! I know you're out there! I can feel you!"

From a distance, he heard the faint sound of a muffled scream and a squealing of tires. He sprang toward the noise.

As he approached, a small, skinny man in a pinstriped suit and top hat stood at a corner, peering around it.

"What are you doing here?" Moriarty said, approaching Trivial.

Trivial startled, calming only after recognizing the familiar face.

"Oh, it's you," he said. "Take a peep."

With cautious curiosity, Moriarty stepped forward and peeked, spying a van and a sports car parked to one side of the street. To the right, he glimpsed a group of people huddled around a mass of redness in the center of the street. He scrutinized each member of the group, hunting for Sherlock. Disappointed, he turned back to Trivial.

"Did you see what happened here?"

"No, I only just arrived," Trivial said, averting his gaze and cracking the knuckles of his folded hands. "I do know what this killer is though," he continued. "I was about to approach them and offer my help. Only, I'm not entirely sure what to say."

"Maybe I can help," Moriarty said, trying to show a sympathetic smile. "Tell me what happened. What do you know? I'll go with you...for support."

So, Trivial recounted his last 24 hours.

Moriarty placed an arm around his shoulder in an effort to comfort him as he spoke. When he finished his story, Moriarty *smiled at Trivial as he brought his arm from behind his shoulder to below his neck.*

Trivial tried to squirm away, flailing his arms about and trying to stop the pressure on his throat. He choked, trying to scream for help, as Moriarty placed his other forearm behind Trivial's head. Trivial's eyes filled with fear as Moriarty's hands gripped his face on either side.

SNAP

His eyes went blank as his body fell to the ground. Moriarty reached down next to Trivial's corpse to pick up his cane and top hat. As he placed the top hat upon his head, he shifted into Trivial, pinstripe suit and all.

By the time Moriarty dispatched Trivial and hid his body, the group in the street had already left in the van, but the sportscar remained. Trivial headed toward it, stepping over any entrails, body parts, and puddles of blood along the way. When he reached the car, he touched the handle and the door swung up.

"Welcome," a male computerized voice said from within. "My name is Watson. How may I serve you?"

Moriarty stepped into the driver's seat.

"Oh, my dear Watson," he said with a wicked sidelong grin. "You already have."

At the Emerald Cathedral, Moriarty finally caught up with them. He parked Watson at the bottom of the hill, ascending the pedestrian trail toward the cathedral. As he crested the hill, a wave of pain rushed into his head, as memories from all over flurried back into him. Memories pulled from him as punishment by various adjudicators long ago now returned in a painful reintegration. He doubled over, wanting to scream but forcing the pain down, trying not to reveal himself to anyone above. And then, he heard tormented screams echoing from the cathedral, and he wailed too.

KRUNKAKRUNK

Ender snatches a trash can and crushes the metal into a ball. Mario feels the weight of the knife in his hand and turns to Trivial.

"Kill him!" Trivial yells, scurrying away. "Kill him now!"

"Coward!" Mario yells. "Help me!"

24

SHOULD EVIL BE LEFT UNPUNISHED?

The grotesque beast's scarred and blood-covered face scowls as he lurches toward Mario, still wielding the metal ball.

Mario stands his ground, knife in hand, readying himself to strike. As Ender closes in, he hurdles over Mario, clearing him by several feet. Mario whips around, trying not to let Ender behind his back, but the monster charges away without attacking him. Confused, Mario glances at the knife and back to Ender. Without further hesitation, he follows the rampaging beast.

Over his shoulder, Trivial glimpses Ender exiting the alleyway, storming toward him, and picking up speed.

"Kill him!" he yells back. "Please!"

"He's after you!" Mario yells, chasing after Ender "Why is he after you? Are you a Mighty?"

Unable to move fast enough with the small legs of Trivial's body, Moriarty shifts into the familiar shape of the gorilla guard from the Realizer's mansion. He quickens his pace, bounding down the street with his massive arms as well as his legs, lunging him further away from Ender.

Mario screeches to a halt, stunned by the sight of the gorilla taking shape.

He's a shifter? Mario thinks. *That's not in the comic.*

With monstrous power, Ender hurls the metal ball at the escaping gorilla.

BADDDONK

The force of the ball knocks the gorilla to the ground. Ender leaps forward, landing a few steps away. The gorilla rolls over, trying to stand up and defend himself. Ender gives the gorilla a once over, retrieving a gigantic knife from somewhere, although it appeared to come from nowhere. The gorilla stands straight, pounds his chest, and roars before lunging at Ender with his raised fists ready to plummet into his chest and knock the knife free from his hands.

As his fists pummel Ender's chest, they turn into the smaller hands of a young man, bouncing off and doing nothing against the rampaging monster. Moriarty's face freezes in horror, as he realizes his powers are gone and he is nothing more than a fragile bag of blood and bones ready to be ripped apart. He tries in vain to turn and run, but Ender jabs the knife between his legs and yanks upward, slicing Moriarty from crotch to cranium.

KERPLOP-PLOP

The guts of the body Moriarty possesses spill onto the ground. Each half of his body stands a second or two before Ender brings the knife back around to lob off Moriarty's head.

The head rolls to a split in front of Mario, like an upside-down, unzipped bowling bag oozing brain matter and blood. Mario stares at the mutilated head as a shiver starts to surge, but he fights back, clenching his teeth and resetting his fingers tight around the hilt of the blade. He glares at Ender with narrowing eyes, raises the knife, and bolts toward the beast with all the strength he can muster.

Before he can attack, someone or something drops down from a building between him and the monster. Mario stumbles to a stop, assessing the new development. The figure stands and dashes toward him. He braces himself, trying to make the best defensive stance possible.

"Mario!" the familiar voice calls.

"Sheryl?" he yells, relaxing a bit. "I thought you were dead."

Sheryl strides up to Mario with unshaken confidence.

"Who me?" she says, fetching a playing card from her pocket and flicking it to Mario. "I've got two more hearts in me yet."

Mario claps the fluttering card between his hands, opening them slowly to find a three of hearts. He lifts his head in astonishment as Sheryl faces down Ender.

"Allow me," she says, sliding forward into a defensive stance as Ender approaches them. "Years ago, I trained in the martial arts at a downtown dojo. After hours of course, when they would let Citizens in. I needed to ready myself for any future confrontation with Moriarty."

Ender lunges at her. She jumps, kicking his face and knocking him backward. Astounded, Mario cheers.

"Thank you," she says a little breathless. "I've always had my suspicions about Trivial." She kicks Ender's hand, knocking the knife to the ground. "Obviously, Moriarty's ego didn't allow him to kill me from afar. He wanted to get close to me first. Toy with me."

"Moriarty?" Mario asks confused, peeking over Sheryl's shoulder.

"Oh yes, Moriarty was Trivial the whole time," Sheryl clarifies, nodding in the direction of the split head. She kicks the knife away. "Well, the whole time we knew him."

"Wow," exclaimed Mario. "How'd you know?"

She strikes Ender in the chest and uppercuts him, knocking him back again.

"When Muldivar died, he became debilitated by pain. I suspected the restoration of all his memories was the cause." She kicks Ender's knees, crumpling him downward. "I had to play up the drag queen junkie role, so he'd drop his guard. I needed to free myself to observe him unnoticed."

She roundhouse kicks him in the face, knocking him to the ground.

"I faked the Delirium fit and set Watson to self-destruct," she says, trotting back toward Mario. Ender rolls over and begins to stand up. She turns and kicks him back to the ground.

"I rolled free before he—oh, I guess, she—exploded. Knife?" she requests, turning back to Mario with her hand out.

He obliges.

"You see, Mario," she says. "Ender is the balance, between power and control." She raises the knife, ready to strike down upon Ender. "He vanquished the gods from the heavens and set a new stand—"

With breakneck speed, Ender jutted his knife up and sliced open Sheryl's abdomen. She swallowed hard, as the pain washed over her, trying in vain to keep her guts in place while blood sprayed from her body.

"Nooo!" cried Mario.

"But, I'm a Normal," she says, staggering with her entrails spilling out in front of her and making a wet smack.

She falls in a slump, splashing in a puddle of her own making.

Ender stands up and picks her up by her head. He plunges his sausage fingers into her eye sockets with a sick popping sound. Blood oozes around them, as he jerks upward, ripping the top of her skull off.

"Brain not normal," he says, as her body plops back to the ground.

Ender steps toward Mario. Mario closes his eyes and stands motionless. Ender sniffs Mario for a second before taking his arm. Mario stiffens as Ender places something into his hand. Mario stays still until the clomping sound of the monster's footsteps fade away in the distance.

He opens his eyes to find the cap of Sheryl's skull in his hand. He drops it, shuttering in disgust and falling to his knees in relief.

AAAAARRRRRGGGGHH

James screams, gripping his head in pain, freaking out the people around him for the second time in a matter of minutes. Little sparks of lightning crackle across his body, lighting him up in bright blue light.

"What's happening?" he cries.

Tommy rushes to his aid.

"What happened?" he asks the person closest to James's seat. "Did you see anything?"

"He just started freaking out again," the person answered. "Then, electricity."

Tommy places his hand on James's head.

SSZZZLLLKK

Violet light and electricity strike his fingertips and fizzle out.

"Ouch," cries Tommy, snapping his hand back from the electrical shock. "Are you okay?"

"I think I'm fine," James says, shaking his head as the sizzling electrical crackle ceases at his fingertips and a pale blue light fades into the veins of his hands.

"James?"

"I'm not sure what this was, but earlier I got my memories back like you—" he says, turning to the others, who gasp in terror. "What? What's wrong? Why are you looking at me like that?"

He turns to the window and faces his reflection. He no longer has the face of Dr. James Moriarty.

"Who are you?" Tommy asks the tall, skinny stranger. "What did you do with—"

"It's me," Quell says in a panic. "It's still me!"

The Normal Army surrounds Quell, brandishing their weapons and stomping toward him. Anxious and scared, he shifts into the gorilla and beats his chest with a roar. They back away frightened both by his ability and the Mighty ape raging before them.

"Back off!" he growls, clasping the ceiling rail and swinging to the front of the bus. "Careful," he grunts, flying by a few scared passengers. "Out of the way," he snarls as he reaches the door.

He shoves the guards aside, bursts through the door with a voracious roar, and bounds down the street. The bus riders ram their faces into their windows, watching him fade into the distance.

"Should we go after it?" asks one of them.

"If you want to, go ahead," replies the other. "I'm staying right here."

Mario sits on his knees, staring at the cap of Sheryl's skull resting before him. Her lifeless, gutted body lies mere steps away, pooling in a thick red puddle. Not much further, the corpse of Moriarty lies in its own massive pool of maroon.

I am WPC Intern, Mario Rickson, identity tag 24VØR4VNØ.

Mario's hand shakes as it clings to the knife in front of him. His eyes rise from the skullcap to the knife.

I live in a world where the HAVES are super-powered, and the HAVE-NOTS are their slaves.

He grips the knife harder, willing the tremors to cease and raising it up for his eyes to follow.

I've always wanted to have superpowers, but I'm alive now because I don't have any.

He stands up, focusing on the knife before lowering it to his side.

If I let this thing run its course, it'll kill all of them. Then, we'll be the majority. We'll have all the POWER.

He brings up the knife again. As it glints in the sunlight, he closes his eyes.

If I let them die—

His eyes shoot open. He turns around and launches toward the impending danger.

Just give me a reason to let them live!

He rounds the corner of the street to find the dismembered body of Jakandy.

Jakandy said he would change the system!

He sprints by the remains of Ifton.

He said we weren't meant to enslave one another but to work together.

He races down a street littered with the remains of bloody corpses of the Mighty.

If he can change, maybe they all can.

To the left, an array of body parts, blood, and entrails spreads out along the side of the street.

He didn't survive this. They didn't survive this.

To the right, he finds the same thing.

Together, we may all survive this.

In the distance, Mario hears the dulled cry of someone screaming for help. Without thinking, he charges toward it, knife in hand.

As the bus heads downtown, the familiar skyline with the two tallest buildings looms over the rest in the distance. From Tommy's perspective, the one with the giant U and superscripted 3 is larger than the other. As he stares out the window of the front seat of the bus, his face darkens.

A beautiful brunette a couple of years younger than him leans forward from the seat behind him, saying, "He was your friend? The mimic?"

"Didn't really know him," Tommy says, peeping over his shoulder and getting a full view of her ample bosom kept in place by the blue and white maid's outfit she wore. He quickly meets her eyes, trying not to redden with embarrassment. "We were both interns at SIC."

"Oh," she says, sliding around the seat to sit next to him. He scoots over to make room. "But you used to live in the WPC. I remember you and your wife, and how you didn't come back. Your kids were put in the Orphan House. I volunteered there."

"Poor kids," Tommy says, trying to hide tears welling in

his eyes. "I didn't mean for them to grow up without us. Have you seen them? Are they good kids?"

"Oh yes," she says with a calming smile, placing a tender hand on his arm. "Mario works at a restaurant in the city. I think he's a dishwasher."

"A chip off the old block, eh?"

"Zelda's always leading the other kids her age around, and she volunteers at the Orphan House," she says, squeezing his shoulder. "She's a born leader. Like you are."

"Me?" asks Tommy, taken aback. "I just fell into this. It all happened so fast. James was more of a leader. All I want to do is find my kids."

"I'll help you find them," she says, beaming at him. "I'm Madrigal, by the way."

"Hi Madrigal," he says, reaching out to shake her hand. "I'm Tommy."

"I know," she says, shaking his hand.

"So, you think Zelda is a leader?" he asks after a few awkward seconds. "That's good and all, but who is she going to lead. There's no place for us in Fellowship City, except to be followers."

"Aren't you trying to change that?" she says, tilting her head. "Isn't that why we're here right now?"

Tommy eyes the empty sidewalks of downtown Fellowship City, thinking for a few belabored seconds before turning back to Madrigal.

"You're right! We are going to fight back!"

Tommy stands up and commands the attention of the people on the bus.

"We are all here because we are tired of being treated like we have no place in this world but to serve the will and whims of the Mighty!"

Madrigal slides behind him, edging him to the center of

the bus. The people on the bus stop talking to others around them and pay attention to Tommy.

"We will not be relegated to the camps and the ghetto any longer! We are worthy of much more than what they allow us to have! We are people and we deserve respect!"

The bus riders cheer and pump up their fists.

"We will not back down! We will not waver! We will fight the Mighty to ensure our rights to justice, fairness, and equality!"

"FIGHT, FIGHT, FIGHT!"

EHHHHIIRRRRRRRKKKK

The bus driver slams on the brakes jolting everyone forward.

"What the hell?" Tommy yells at the driver, marching to the front console of the bus.

The driver gapes dumbfounded ahead of him. Tommy follows the driver's gaze.

"What is it?" Madrigal calls, leading the others to the front of the bus for a better view.

"It looks like—" Tommy starts to say before drifting off, his face contorting in confusion and terror.

"Casualties of war," Madrigal whispers at his side.

"Yes," Tommy says with subdued excitement. "Like in the old movies."

As the bus idles on Fellowship Way and 15th Avenue, the streets ahead of them are covered in bodies and blood. Tommy taps the driver's shoulder.

"Take it slow," he orders, motioning for him to take them forward.

The driver obliges, depressing the gas with slight pressure. Aside from the crawling bus, nothing else creeps in the usually busy street. The passengers press their faces to the windows, surveying the carnage. They pass blood-splattered walls and walkways marred with severed limbs. Further on, they drive through bloody puddles full of intestines and organs that pop and squish under their tires. Everywhere broken pieces of bodies are strewn about.

What could have done this? Tommy thinks, unable to peel his eyes away from a pile of heads tossed into an overturned dumpster.

"These are Mighty," Madrigal whispers to Tommy.

"I know," he replies, considering all the telltale signs of the Mighty, like scattered feathers, scaled flesh, and expensive clothes. The expensive clothes and jewelry indicated just how Mighty some of them were.

They drove until the piles of bodies blocked the bus from continuing further.

Tommy stands again, speaking with an air of command, "Alright people. This is our moment of truth! Let's get out there and show them we mean to be free!"

MEEEEP MEEEEP MEEEEP

A few minutes later, the bus reverses to the other side of the street, crushing a severed head under the tire as it maneuvers back and to the side. The driver spins the steering wheel around and turns the bus across to the other side of the street. The tires slide through several slippery blood puddles, making braking difficult, as the bus careens toward a dumpster.

MEEEEP MEEEEP MEEEEP

The reverse lights flash onto Tommy and Madrigal

standing amid the bloodied war-torn street, casting them in a white and reddish glow. They cover their eyes with their hands as the bus reverses back toward them before rolling forward and away.

"Thanks for coming with me," Tommy says, as his eyes linger on the bus's blinking turn signal as it approaches 15th. He rests the sledgehammer against his right shoulder and scratches the back of his neck with his left hand. "I have no idea what I'm doing leading this little army."

"We're not an army," she says, tapping a baseball bat against her foot and gesturing to the others who were brave enough to stay and fight. "We're people—citizens trying to do what we think is right. We're finally able to stand up to tyranny and oppression. So, here we are."

Tommy appraises the eight people, already paired and standing with their weapons at the ready.

"We need to head to the monastery!" he exclaims. "Because they're on lockdown, they won't be able to stop us! But be careful! No telling what else or who else is out here!"

Tommy and Madrigal pair up. They deftly maneuver through the obstacles in the center of the street, while the other pairs follow behind, fanning out across both sides of the street.

"You don't remember me at all, do you?" asks Madrigal, as they trudge shoulder to shoulder through the bloody puddles full of Mighty guts. She laughs as his face twists with embarrassed confusion, and he kicks a head of a Mighty off to the side. "You used to play with my older brother, Paolo."

"I remember Paolo," Tommy says with a sidelong glance. "I don't recall him having a sister."

"You sure?" She asks, stopping in place. "You don't

remember me? You both called me bratty Maddie. You don't remember?"

Tommy stops and steps to her with an apologetic, sad face.

"I'm sorry," he says, shaking his head. "I've only recently got my memories back…in a very painful way. They're still coming together, like puzzle pieces finding the right connection. I'm sure, I'll remember you soon."

AAAAAAAHHHHHHH

A scream echoes through the street, forcing the 10-person army to take stock and listen.

"Help!" someone cries from an alleyway up ahead in the distance.

Tommy and Madrigal hurry down the street, following the sounds of the cry. Tommy is faster and rounds the corner of the alley, stopping suddenly in disbelief. Madrigal rounds the corner and nearly slams into him.

"What the h—" she starts to say, but the words hang in her throat as she spies what stopped Tommy in his tracks.

Before them, a middle-aged aquakin woman, wearing a designer pantsuit screams. She stands with her back against the wall, shooting water out of her fingertips toward something massive and hidden by shadow.

At the other end of the alley, Mario rounds the corner with his knife at his side.

"What's wrong?" he calls to the woman spraying a doorway with water.

Through the water spray, he gleans the blurred outlines of two people standing on the other side of the alley. He presses forward, waving his hand when a dark figure lunges from the shadows. Mario falls backward, trying to keep an eye on the aquakin's attacker.

Ender's knife cuts the water in two as he lurches forward with unrelenting ferocity toward the frightened wet woman. The knife pierces her neck, pinning her to the wall.

"Guuurrrgggggglllee," she groans, as bloody bubbles fill her mouth and blood sprays from her neck onto her killer.

Her hands grasp her neck, trying to stop her blood from flowing out of her like water. As Ender yanks the knife out with brutal force, her head falls forward, hanging by a small piece of flesh. Her hands drop to her side, dripping water from her fingertips into a reddish puddle. It streams toward the center of the alley and gathers into a murky pool.

As the aquakin's body falls lifeless into the puddle below, Ender jumps up the wall behind her, grapples onto the fire escape, and leaps toward the roof of the building.

Mario follows Ender, trying to keep tabs on his trajectory. Tommy and Madrigal stand motionless, unsure of what they witnessed, as the other eight members of their army gather behind them.

"What the hell was that thing?" Tommy says to Madrigal.

"No clue," she says, eyes fixed on the heap of a dead aquakin. "But I hope it's gone."

Unable to follow Ender further, Mario advances toward the people on the other side of the alleyway.

"Are you Mighty?" he yells, as he approaches them.

They all stand ready, weapons in hand.

"Hell no!" Tommy yells, brandishing his sledgehammer. "We're Normals! You?"

Mario slows down, narrowing his eyes at the man.

"Dad?"

Tyler hugs the wall, trying to stay out of sight of the bus racing past him. He makes no movement until the bus is gone. When all is clear, he waves at Zelda, who is hiding across the street in an alleyway and peeking around the corner. She gathers her twenty-something followers and marches them across the street toward Tyler.

"That's the first movement we've seen," she says out of breath.

"Yeah," he says, puzzling over the blood and guts on the ground.

"Stay here. I'm going to scout ahead."

"No, we should—"

"Zelda," he interrupts, pointing to a severed arm in a puddle of blood. "I think this is going to get a whole lot worse before it gets better. I don't want these kids getting traumatized any more than they already are. I need you to wait with them, please."

Zelda turns away from him.

"Please, Zelda," he says, turning her around and clasping her by the shoulders. "I don't know what's out here today. But it looks bad. We need to get these kids away from it."

She kisses him.

He stumbles back, unable to speak.

"Be safe! I'm counting on you!"

He waves awkwardly before turning on his heels and hustling across the street. Peering around the corner, he spots a bus parked in the distance. He turns back and nods at Zelda before scrambling toward the bus.

As he approaches, he notices the OUT OF COMMIS-SION sign on the bus.

It looks completely abandoned, he thinks, surveying the perimeter.

He checks the door, giving it a tug. Nothing. He closes his eyes and places a hand on the door. The engine turns over and the door opens. He steps inside and is greeted by the barrel of a shock-cannon.

"Who the fuck are you?" says the bus driver hiding behind the front seat.

"I'm not armed," Tyler says with hands up in surrender. "I'm just trying to help some kids."

The bus driver grabs Tyler by the collar and shoves the shock-cannon in his face.

"That's too bad," he says, hauling him up the steps and tossing him into the front seat. "You could've stood a fighting chance."

"What's this about?" Tyler presses, still holding his hands up. "What's wrong?"

"Something's out here killing everyone," the driver says, flashing his long, sharp canine teeth and stroking his short-cropped beard. He growls at Tyler, nuzzles the cold metal of the shock-cannon's barrel against his temple, and says, "Convince me it isn't you."

"You're a hybrid?" Tyler asks, squinting into the eyes of the bus driver and seeing his cat-like pupils glaring back at him.

"Yeah. So?"

"Not too smart, eh?"

Tyler rolls his eyes back into his head and raises his hand to the weapon. Little pulses of lightning strike the shock-cannon, shorting it out and shocking the bus driver.

The bus driver grimaces in disbelief as he steps back, trying to brace himself.

"I'm going to fuckin' kill you!" he purrs.

Tyler jumps into a protective stance.

KARRAAACK

The bus driver's eyes roll back into his head as he falls down cold. Zelda steps up from behind him, wielding a lead pipe.

"Are we taking this show on the road or what?"

Tyler steps over the bus driver toward Zelda.

"I told you to stay with the kids. What if you'd been hurt?"

"That's cute," Zelda says with a laugh. "I'm not letting anything happen to you while I'm around, electroboy. You better get over that real quick. Now toss this asshole in that dumpster over there and let's take these kids somewhere safe."

"Yes, your highness," Tyler says, dragging the bus driver out of the bus.

Tommy drops his sledgehammer and hugs Mario.

"You're so big!" he says, fighting back tears of joy. "I can't believe I missed it."

"It's okay. You're here now," Mario says with one arm around his father and the other trying to keep the knife from stabbing anyone.

"What was that thing?" Madrigal asks, eyes still glued to the aquakin lying in the puddle of water and blood.

"That was Ender," answers Mario. "He's a Mighty killer. We need to stop him."

"Whoa," Tommy says, taking a step back. "If this guy kills the Mighty, why do we need to stop him?"

Mario steps toward his father and meets his eyes.

"As much as I hate them for what they have done to us, I can't be responsible for allowing them to be eradicated. Not if I can do something about it. If we do not stand against evil, are we not just as evil?"

"Wow," he says, awestruck. "Kid, you've certainly grown up."

"Thanks!" Mario says, rushing past them and hollering back over his shoulder. "But it's all in the historical facts you taught me. I'm sure you would've come to the same conclusion."

"I'm not sure I would," Tommy mutters, glancing innocently at Madrigal.

"I think he went that way," Mario shouts, pointing at a tall building with a panel of windows along the third floor busted out with an Ender-sized opening through them. "Let's go!"

Tommy nudges Madrigal and says, "Born leaders. Both of them."

Zelda ushers the children onto the bus one by one while Tyler sits in the driver's seat. When all the kids are on the bus, she sits next to Loo behind Tyler.

"We have to find Ahah, Zelda," Loo says with his puppy dog eyes.

"Who's Ahah, Loo?"

"My baby sister."

Zelda's eyes pop wide.

"Do you know where to find her, Loo?"

"The bad man said he took her to the lab," Loo says ashamed.

"What's the lab?" Zelda asks Tyler. "A hospital?"

"I think I have an idea where she might be," Tyler says, stepping on the gas.

"I think he went in there," Mario says over his shoulder to the ten members of the Normal Army now following him. He points to a tall building just ahead. "Let's go!"

As they approach the building, Madrigal whispers to Tommy, "What is this place?"

"It looks like an old hospital."

Mario charges up to the door at the side of the building and kicks it open.

That was easy, he thinks, trying to stay cool in front of his dad. He collects himself and turns to face his father.

"This is an electrical closet. We can't get in this way."

As Mario searches for another possible entrance, Tommy puts his arm around his son's shoulder and whispers, "That looked super cool though."

Swelling with confidence, Mario darts to the dumpster area near a fire escape. He climbs up the dumpster closest to the railing, jumps up, grasps the dangling ladder, and pulls it down.

"This way," he yells, waving for the others to follow him.

He climbs the ladder and springs up the stairs, checking the door at the second-story level. When it does not budge, he dashes up to the third level and checks. When that door also does not open, he leans out to assess how far away the broken windows are and the width of the ledge leading to them.

"That's doable," he thinks, climbing onto the ledge and shimmying over to the broken windowpane.

Mario climbs through and finds himself in a grimy old office that reeks of at least a century of disuse. Dust still lingers in the air from Ender plowing through and kicking it up. Mario sneezes into his elbow as he scrambles to an open door. He scans the hallway, finding the safety door to the fire escape and forces it open.

"Excellent work, son," Tommy says, clapping his son's shoulder.

"No big deal," Mario says smiling from ear to ear. "Now let's find Ender!"

Because the third floor is a dust-covered memento of a time once forgotten, they can follow Ender's path like footprints in the snow. The small army marches headlong toward the stairwell, descending the stairs as fast as possible to the second floor.

"I can't tell, but I think he may have gone through here," Mario says panicked.

"He may have continued downstairs," says one of the soldiers, brandishing a tire iron.

"You're right," Mario says. "And there are several more possibilities. He may have even gone up. Split up and take each floor. Dad, come with me."

"Sounds good," Tommy says, nodding to Madrigal. "You come with us."

Mario, Tommy, and Madrigal head to the second floor to investigate. After a few fruitless rooms, they find a promising door marked with a bio-chemical hazard sticker. Inside, they discover an overhang room observing a massive laboratory below.

"Ay, Dios mío," cries Madrigal, as she appraises the dozens of people in white lab coats ripped apart in the lab below.

The once white room is covered in red splotches throughout, and the usual bright yellow of the Delirium is now a dark orange, almost a sick shade of brown.

"We need to get down to that room," Mario says.

"Why? There's nothing we can do now?" asks Tommy.

"Not that room. That room," says Mario, pointing to a doorway where one of the lab techs' severed legs is jammed and keeping the door from closing.

They bolt out of the room, through the hall, and down the stairwell, finding the door to the laboratory. Mario turns the knob and pushes, but it doesn't move.

"I think it's blocked by a body," Madrigal says.

"Push harder," Mario urges, plowing against the door. Tommy and Madrigal help, but the door barely budges. Dark red blood seeps out from under the door. "It's no use. We need to find another way in."

"I didn't see one," Tommy says. "Did you?"

"No," says Madrigal.

"Son of a bitch!" Mario yells. "Give me your sledgehammer."

Mario sprints back upstairs with the sledgehammer. Tommy and Madrigal throw questioning glances at one another and then follow. As they reach the stairwell, they hear a strange thud and glass shattering. When they reach the door with the hazard symbol, they find Mario jumping through broken glass into the laboratory below.

"Do you hear that?" Mario asks, creeping toward the door being propped open with a severed leg.

"No," Tommy responds. "What does it sound like?"

The muffled sound grows louder and clearer as he approaches the door.

"My God, it sounds like children crying!" he says, scurrying to the door and swinging it open.

25

SHOWDOWN AT DR. DELIRIUM'S LABORATORY

"We're here," Tyler says, pointing out the window of the bus toward the top of a five-story building coming into view.

Zelda leans over from behind him and points to a faint H faded away with time.

"What's the H for?"

"Once upon a time, this hospital helped people, but now it's the lab of Dr. Delirium. I've only been in once, but I remember everything about that place."

Zelda placed a sympathetic hand on Tyler's shoulder.

"Tell me about the security," she says, trying to steer his thoughts toward strategy instead of tragedy.

"A couple of guards, I think," he says, shrugging at her through the rearview mirror. "10 or more working in the lab. Not sure, but they're all Mighty. Most of them have pretty sophisticated powers necessary for the lab, but I encountered at least one strong and a fuzzie."

He stares up at the building as he drives closer.

"They would strong-arm us if we fought the inoculation, so none of us did."

"Where do they keep the kids?" asks Zelda.

"In the basement below the lab—the kids are kept in small side rooms around a massive common area," answers Tyler, recalling his time spent in one. "They're small and padded, blindingly white. They put two or three kids in each."

"Can we access the basement without going through the lab?"

"Yeah. Yeah, I think we can," he says, gripping the steering wheel and stepping on the accelerator. "I'm pretty sure, an underground parking lot leads to a hallway. I think they took us through there. If not, it'll be close anyway."

"Sounds like we've got a plan," she says, beaming at his reflection.

As the bus approaches the old hospital, Tyler turns to the right down an alleyway to its side. He drives up to a closed gate and glances back at Zelda and the kids all sitting with their hands clamped on the seat bars in front of them. Zelda nods. With a squeal of the tires, Tyler punches the gas and rams the gate.

KRRRRRRRRREEEEEEEEEEEEEE

The sound of the metal gate tearing apart is like nails on a chalkboard. Zelda tenses and grits her teeth, remembering how much she hated hearing that sound at the Orphan House when volunteers used it to induce silence. Loo tugs her arm around him and tucks his head into her side, covering his ears.

Finally, the gate breaks free, allowing the bus to veer down a ramp toward the basement level parking lot. Tyler parks the bus in a long space next to a brick wall with a yellow and black trefoil radiation sign.

"What's the sign mean?" Zelda says, standing up as the bus comes to a halt.

"Radiation waste, I think," he answers. "I'm pretty sure the room is lined with lead or something. Maybe it'll stop a Mighty with X-ray vision from discovering the bus and the kids."

"Good idea," Zelda says, but after a moment she wrinkles her nose and forehead. "Wait. Some Mighty have X-ray vision?"

"Maybe?" shrugs Tyler, as he opens the bus door and steps out.

Zelda follows him down the stairs, and Loo follows right behind her.

"Okay, everyone!" Tyler shouts to the kids inside. "We're going to find some more kids. So, make room for them. Put your smile faces on and welcome them when they get here."

The kids on the bus start shifting seats.

"I'm impressed," Zelda says, grinning at Tyler.

He winks and clicks his tongue.

She punches his arm, saying, "Come on, you big softy. Let's put our smile faces on and find some kids."

The sound of children screaming and crying for help fills the overhang above the blood-splattered laboratory. Tommy and Madrigal search for a way down, as Mario slips through the doorway and disappears. Tommy peers through the broken glass window.

"I can see a table just below this window. If we jump down here, we'll cut the distance. It won't be too bad."

Madrigal nods, whispering, "Okay. But you go first, handsome."

"Beauty before brains, eh?" Tommy quips.

"Por supuesto," she says with a wink.

Tommy scales through the glass and drops to the table.

"Come on," he says, helping Madrigal down. "That is a beautiful brain you've got. I wouldn't want anything too bad to happen to it."

They race to the door and the sound of crying children.

At the bottom of the long stairwell, Mario reaches a doorway. He hears Tommy and Madrigal behind him but cannot wait for them. He plows through the door, finding Ender on the other side of the room stalking a young half-breed magnokin boy.

The boy magnokinetically forces Ender's knife away with one hand and beckons a loose rod hanging on a window with his other.

The pathway to Ender is littered with several small bodies of children, broken, bloodied, and dead. Mario spies others hiding in various places around the room and surmises more are likely behind the dozen or so locked doors.

"Noooo! You monster!" he screams from the doorway. "They're just kids!"

Ender glowers over his shoulder, scowling at Mario with a breathy groan. The distraction is long enough for the magnokin boy to yank the rod free from the window and send it hurtling missile-like toward Ender. As if sensing the threat, Ender turns back toward the boy and lunges forward, plunging his knife into the boy's shoulder and pinning him to the wall.

"Uuunnggh!" cries the boy in pain, as the rod falls to the floor, not finding its mark.

PDING DING DING

Mario charges toward Ender with his knife ready to attack. Ender snatches his knife from the magnokin's shoulder and whirls around. The boy falls to the ground with a thud as Mario dodges Ender, jumping right and juking left, causing Ender to jab his knife in the wrong direction.

Mario slices across Ender's abdomen. Black sludge oozes out of the gash, smelling of putrid flesh.

"ERR!" Ender groans, turning back to face Mario.

"Come at me!" Mario yells in his face.

Ender steps toward Mario with his bloody knife in the air.

The magnokin boy crawls to the fallen rod and thrusts it upward into the left side of Ender's back, right under his ribs. Ender rails backward, reaching his arm around to retrieve the rod. He bellows in pain as he grapples the rod from the front and pulls it through his chest. Without warning, he spins around and plunges the rod into the magnokin boy, impaling him onto the wall.

"Nooo!" Mario screams as Tommy and Madrigal enter the room.

He leaps at Ender. They follow his lead, scurrying toward the monster ready to strike. As Mario comes down hard upon the beast, Ender reaches his right arm back without looking and catches Mario by the neck. He struggles to break free, but the massive fist shakes him, forcing the knife from his hand.

Ender faces Mario, draws him close, and sniffs.

KAAARRACK

Tommy's sledgehammer slams into Ender's knee, driving the monster to the ground. Mario rolls free from Ender's grasp and reaches for the knife. Ender stands and reclaims the rod from the magnokin boy now passed out from the pain. The boy slumps into a bloodied heap.

Ender turns to face Tommy and Madrigal. Mario gasps, clenching his throat with one hand and hoisting the knife up with the other.

"We need to get these kids out of here," Mario chokes out. "I think they're Mighty. He gets stronger when they're around."

"How do you know this?" asks Madrigal.

"It's in the movie!" exclaims Mario as he swipes at Ender.

Ender steps back, his face contorting with confusion. He perceives Mario as a white light in front of him, but the white light attacks him. He shakes his head and two other white lights come into view, standing with weapons ready to strike. The red and blue lights of the magnokin and the other children around the room fade away in his periphery. He scans the room, finding a new source of blue and red lights pulsating from behind doors in the room.

"They must pay!"

"No!" Mario yells. "They're not like the Abnormals who killed you. They're children. They're innocent."

Madrigal dashes to the closest door and opens it, finding two scared children inside, embracing each other with closed eyes.

"It's okay," she whispers. "We're going to save you...somehow."

Tyler opens the door to the common room, surprised by the massive figure of Ender looming between the two men.

"What the hell?" he says under his breath.

Zelda pushes the door further open and peeks inside.

"Oh my god," she says, seeing all the bodies of the dead children strewn about the room. "What happened?"

Loo cranes his neck around her and points at Ender, saying, "He's a bad man!"

Zelda hides Loo behind her.

"You need to go back to the bus and hide with the other kids, right now!"

"But Ahah," Loo protests.

"Now, Loo!" Zelda commands. "It's not safe!"

Loo scampers back alone, crying, "Save Ahah!"

"We will!" Zelda promises. She turns to Tyler. "Right?"

Tyler shrugs while trying to give an optimistic nod before returning his gaze to the massive figure in the room.

"What the hell is that?"

Ender growls and stomps toward Madrigal. Tommy swings the sledgehammer wildly in front of him, trying to keep the monster back. Mario rushes from behind and jumps at Ender again, bringing his knife down into his massive shoulder blade.

Ender whips backward with such force, he launches Mario into a post in the center of the room. Mario slumps. His eyes slowly open and close.

As the monster tries to reach the blade in his back, Tommy smashes the sledgehammer into Ender's cranium. Ender stumbles back, howling with rage.

Tommy yells to Madrigal, "Get them out of here!"

"Over here," Tyler waves to Madrigal.

She ushers the two children over to the stranger at the open door.

"Who are you?" she asks as she surrenders the children to him.

"He's okay," Zelda says, stepping from behind the door. "He's with me."

"Zelda!" Madrigal exclaims. "It's so good to see you. We—"

"We need to get these kids to safety," interrupts Zelda. "Can you free more and send them this way? Tyler will free the others. We have a bus waiting."

"Yes," Madrigal says. "I can do that."

"Great!" Zelda says, squeezing Madrigal's shoulder. "Be careful."

Madrigal hustles to the door closest to her and opens it. Tyler hurries past her to the next door. Zelda waits to retrieve the children and send them to the bus.

KLANKETY KLANK

Tommy smashes the sledgehammer into Ender's monstrous fist. His knife flies free, sliding across the floor toward Mario, recovering by the post in the center of the room.

Ender stops again confused, surveying the room. The white lights and red and blue lights dance all around him. He closes his eyes and rakes his face. A white light slams a sledgehammer into his side, knocking him off balance. He fumbles to the side, catching himself on the wall.

"You okay, Mario?" Tommy hollers.

"I think so," he answers, shaking the cobwebs out and lifting himself against the post.

"You see that knife? Grab it!"

As Mario reaches for the knife, he spots Zelda at the doorway, retrieving children from Madrigal. He squints sideways, uncertain if his eyes deceive him. He shakes his head and yells, "Zelda?"

"Zelda's here?" questions Tommy, not taking his eyes off Ender.

Tyler zigzags toward the magnokin boy hunkered on the wall.

"It's okay, buddy," he says, helping the child up.

"Ugh," the kid groans as blood trickles from his shoulder and gut.

Tyler yanks his shirt off, makes it into a bandage, and puts pressure on the wounds.

"Don't worry. I got you," he says, picking the boy up and carrying him toward Zelda.

"Hurry!" she yells.

Tyler glances over his shoulder as Ender turns in his direction. Their eyes meet. Then, Tommy's sledgehammer slams Ender in the stomach, causing him to double over. Ender grabs onto the sledgehammer and wrestles it from Tommy.

"For fucksakes!" Tommy shouts. "Watch out!"

Ender whips the sledgehammer up and trudges toward Tyler, knocking Tommy hard against the wall. As Tommy falls back, Madrigal erupts with righteous fury. She darts toward Ender, leaving the children behind with Zelda. Just out of Ender's periphery, she swings her baseball bat back, and with all her might, she cracks him square in the face, knocking him to the ground.

"Take that! You sick fuck!"

Mario stammers over to Madrigal's side while keeping an eye on Zelda at the door. She opens it, letting Tyler through with the injured magnokin boy.

"Zelda!" he yells with certainty.

"Mario?" she calls back. "Is that you?"

A clock in the common room chimes three times in an

electrical jarring noise, causing Ender to stop and cover his ears.

Madrigal takes advantage of the moment, pummeling Ender with blow after blow. Tommy retrieves his fallen sledgehammer and swings away. Mario plunges the knife into Ender's side. Ender swings his arm back, knocking Mario on his ass. He blushes at Zelda.

"Yeah, it's me!" he yells, picking himself off the ground. "I found dad! What are—"

Mario falls forward, smacking his face to the ground. Over his shoulder, he glimpses Ender clutching his ankle. He tries to break free, kicking and scrambling, but Ender tugs him closer.

"Nooooo," Zelda cries as something snaps inside.

All she can see is Mario and Ender, and Mario is losing. She barrels toward them, hell-bent on saving her helpless brother. As Ender hauls him up by the foot, Mario dangles upside down, trying to shake free.

"Drop him!" Tommy yells, slamming his sledgehammer into Ender's back.

Ender tosses Mario like a ragdoll at a pillar.

"Uuuunnnghh!" Mario cries as his back cracks against the pillar with a sick thud.

Zelda scurries to her brother's side. Tommy and Madrigal take turns hammering and swinging at Ender, keeping him on the ground and buying her time. Mario's body is twisted around the pillar unnaturally.

"Stop!" Ender groans, clasping the sledgehammer in one hand and the bat in the other, stopping the melee.

"My back," Mario says, pained, as Zelda clears the foam around his mouth. "I think it's broken."

Zelda's eyes glisten, swimming with tears.

I am more than the Story-Keeper, she thinks, shaking that weakness away. *I am not some helpless princess waiting for a prince to save me.* She glowers at Ender, her eyes narrowing as she fills with rage. *I'm a SOFA King monster slayer! And it's time to take this motherfucker out!*

"Zelda?" Tyler cries from the doorway as she bursts toward Ender. "No! Zelda, no!"

Tommy struggles, trying to free the sledgehammer. Madrigal does the same with the bat. Tyler's voice echoes in the room, beckoning Zelda to stop, but she cannot hear him. Her focus is solely on her target as she races toward the monster.

She eyes the knives in the monster's shoulder and side, calculating her attack in seconds and readying herself to pounce. As he turns his back toward her, she leaps at him, ripping the knife from his shoulder. He wrenches back, stripping the sledgehammer and bat away. Zelda spins around and jerks the knife from his side.

Ender howls in pain, dropping the weapons. He lunges forward, clamping onto Tommy and Madrigal's necks and lifting them into the air. They flail and fight to free themselves, clawing at his massive patchwork arm and kicking with their dangling feet. Their eyes go bloodshot and faces turn violet as they lose oxygen and strength.

Zelda drops back a few feet, grips both knives downward in her fists, and sprints full speed at Ender. She launches into the air, bringing both knives down into the back of his neck. His hands shoot open, dropping Tommy and Madrigal to the floor. Zelda rips the knives out, leaving two gaping holes, gushing thick black ooze. Ender compresses his neck, trying to stop the flow.

Tyler marches toward Ender, waving an arm at an array

of lights. They spark bright at first and then dim, burping out electrical current. With his other hand, he draws the electricity from other electronics around the room. The devices fizzle, filling the room with a burnt plastic odor. He rolls his hands, forming the freed electricity into a tiny lightning storm, crackling near Ender.

"No! Stay back!" Mario tries to yell. "He gets stronger when Abnormals are around."

Tyler stops, placing his palm on his forehead and closing his eyes. Mario breathes a painful sigh of relief. Then, Tyler opens his eyes and a barrage of blue electricity blasts the monster.

Zelda jolts back away from Ender, crossing the knives in front of her. Little electrical pulses sizzle through Ender as he falls to his knees. Tommy and Madrigal roll out of the way and into each other.

"You okay?" he whispers.

"Yes," she answers with eyes magnetized to the blue voltage rippling across the beast.

Tyler waves his hand again and the storm surges, striking the monster with an onslaught of electrical lightning bolts.

"STOP!" Mario cries through the thundering noise. "Stop. The power of the Mighty will make him stronger!"

"I'm not a Mighty!" Tyler yells over his shoulder.

Ender turns to Tyler, lightning flickering in his eyes as his scarred mouth curls into a wicked smile. He slams his fist into the ground, blazing with blue electricity.

"I don't think HE knows that!" Tommy yells, reaching for the sledgehammer.

Ender starts to rise.

"Get out of here!" Madrigal yells to Tyler as she retrieves her bat. "Get everyone with powers out of here, now!"

Tyler apologizes with his eyes.

"You didn't know," she says. "Now you do. Go!"

He scuttles through the door, locking the deadbolt behind him. Zelda, Tommy, and Madrigal brandish their weapons and take defensive stances.

Ender rises. His muscles ripple with electricity through the patchwork of scars on his flesh.

"He can't be that strong," Tommy quips.

Ender spins around, knocking Tommy and Madrigal onto their backs before turning to face Zelda. He takes a step toward her. She steps back and raises her knives.

"Come at me, Lizard King!" she beckons. "I dare you!"

He lunges toward her, but she is ready and quick on her feet. She deftly dodges him, jumping to the side and bringing the right knife down against him with quick fast jabs, as she spins around behind him. He tries to swing his arm out behind to hit her, but she anticipates the attack and ducks. He spins around hitting nothing.

He stumbles back with bulging mismatched eyes as she springs upward, thrusting one of the knives under his jaw and into his mouth. He staggers backward with his mouth forced open, revealing the knife tip through his tongue.

He reaches for his mouth, trying to free the knife. She slices at his hands, sending several severed fingers flying. He stands back flabbergasted. She smiles and curtsies. He tilts his head sideways and tries to find a defense. She readies the knife in a fighting stance. His eyes narrow, as he bolts forward. She somersaults through his grasp, thrusting the knife into his belly and yanking upwards. He reels back, bellowing in pain.

She throws the knife at his leg. It sticks deep, black ooze seeping around the hilt. He drops to his knee. She jumps at him, grabbing the knife in his jaw with both hands. Then, she pushes her feet off his chest, ripping the knife out of his face and splitting it in half.

She flips backward, landing on her feet with knife in hand. He reaches toward her, but she steps back out of range.

Out of breath, Tyler reaches the bus. He takes a second before he opens the door and steps in. Loo greets him from the front seat, sitting next to the wounded magnokin boy. His hand glows white on the boy's shoulder. Tyler stands dumbfounded, as the boy's injuries heal right before his eyes. The white glow emanating from Loo's hand grows around him until the wounds are completely healed.

"You're a healer, Loo!" Tyler exclaims.

"His glow was getting dark. I gave him more light."

"We need to get away from here, Loo! That monster draws power from people like us. We need to go as far away as possible."

"Yes," Loo says. "The bad man glows less bright when we're not around."

"Let's hope so."

With his jaw split in two up to his nose, the gruesome beast continues swiping at Zelda, Tommy, and Madrigal.

"I think he's tiring down," Tommy says as he bludgeons him with the sledgehammer.

"Don't stop, Dad," Zelda says, attacking from the rear. "Keep hitting!"

"I will, princess! I will!"

AAAAAAAARRRRRGGGGGHHHHH

Ender rages, throwing his arms into the air.

"No end," he growls, burbling through the black tar dripping from his split mandible.

He spins around, trying to attack. Zelda jumps back hitting the wall, barely escaping his mangled hands. Madrigal whacks him in the side. Tommy cracks the sledgehammer into the knife sticking out of his leg. It flays him open as the knife tears out of him, spraying thick black blood at Tommy and Madrigal. Ender falls to his knees, and Zelda rams her knife into the side of his neck, hanging on tight.

GGGUUUUUURRRRGGGGLLLLE

He tries to yell but only blackness oozes from the wounds in his face and neck. Zelda dangles from the knife in his neck and he tries to knock her away. He misses as she swings out of his reach.

Her feet hit the wall behind her, and he is almost amazed as she runs along it like gravity does not exist for her. Everything goes into slow motion as the white light of her feet stamp against the wall. Step after step, she lures him toward her, offsetting his weight and dragging the blade through his neck in a warm gushing wave.

An orchestra strikes somewhere in the ether, playing its heavenly music. Resounding in his head, the beautiful song is in a harmony he can only understand in a dream. Lights of white, red, and blue flutter all around him, merging into shapes and abstract forms. Images of his wife and children flash before his eyes. He begins to remember their lives together, memories that were never captured on screen.

They are the real memories of a man who once had a family.

Pain cascades over him as he relives the anguish of losing his wife, his family, himself. The loss streaks through him, feeding his anger and hate, prompting only wrathful vengeance. The darkness of death encompasses him, sending him into a deep oblivion. But it does not last. A bright white light with the voice of his mother beckons him.

Bathed in this light, he feels warm and calm, but this too does not last. The chaotic swirling glow of red and blue encroaches its frigid darkness upon his peace. His mother's voice speaks of fury, rending him from his final slumber and setting him on a path of righteous revenge. He is filled with a desire to extinguish those lights.

In a killing frenzy, he stalks and slaughters the ominous red and blue lights beset before him, as if they were patiently waiting for their impending deaths. He brings down doom upon one of them, forever snuffing out its light. Then, some new strange sensation overwhelms him and enshrouds him in a new light, tearing him from the fabric of his reality.

As the strangeness subsides, he is able to differentiate colors from the bright light. Colors of red and blue emanate before him, focusing into forms. He still grips the hilt of the knife in his fist and swipes at one of the solid lights. The top of the red light flies up into the air, spinning and spraying essence all around. He brings the blade back across the dimming light, opening it up and spilling darkness from its center.

The top of the light lands upon the floor, rolling around before coming to a rest in front of him. The light dims, fading into a reddish-purple. He picks it up like a bowling ball, swings his arm back, and launches it at the pale blue light with the high-pitched banshee wail. Somehow the projectile flies through the light that blinks off and then on again. Behind it, glass shatters and the dimmed ball bounces into a box on the floor.

Taunted by this vacillating light, he lunges toward it, trying to destroy it before it flickers out once more. He misses and tumbles against the wall of boxes, latching onto something massive mounted upon the wall. He jerks it down and hurls it at the pale blue light as he lunges toward it again. This time, he captures the light within his embrace, squeezing harder and harder until it dims into nothingness.

But before the light is blotted out of existence, it grows brighter and brighter until it blinds him and explodes in a flash, spraying its essence all over the room. The light subsumes him, filling him with a sudden surge of energy. As the light fades, he stands outside in the middle of a street, facing another bright white light coming his way.

Just beyond the oncoming light, a red light glimmers. He readies himself to attack. Once the small white light passes him, he grabs the light that follows behind. Spinning with momentum, he flings the light against a wall in an alleyway across the street. It smacks with a wet thud and dims.

Confused in this new world, he takes stock of his surroundings. In the north, he finds a massive red and blue aura emanating around him in the vast city. To the south, he discovers the bright, welcoming radiance of white light. He seeks solace in the white light, however short-lived it may be.

In the morning, the sun begins to shine upon this new world, and the blue and red glow in the north begins to encroach upon the bright white light of the south. He waits until the last moment, but when the blue and red lights penetrate the sanctity of his new home and attack the innocence of the pure white lights, he can take no more. He rushes headlong toward the oncoming enemy.

Grappling the first red glow he finds startles him. As he applies pressure, it begins to cast bright white light from its appendages. He stops the crushing to scrutinize the figure and ensure the light was not more than mere deception. Finding the red glow to shine within the bright white light, he viciously rips the top from the light and flings it toward other red and blue lights glowing in the distance. The bright light grows larger and larger as it hurtles toward them.

KAAAAAATOOOOOOUUUUM

A thundering boom shakes him from his feet as a massive stream of light bursts into the sky above him. Moments later, glowing red and blue forms charge toward him, attacking him with their infernal abilities. As they draw closer, his strength increases.

The first one flies into him with great strength, but it diminishes upon impact. As he squeezes the life from its violet glow, he finds a white light shining brightly within. He grasps onto it, tugs it free from its prison of red and blue light, and positions it behind him, protecting it from the oncoming red and blue lights. Then, he makes an easy end to the aggressors, slicing them into pieces and extinguishing their light.

Finding no more threats to the white lights in the vicinity, he stalks away toward the red and blue glow of the city.

Now the memories of his efforts to protect the white lights—the sacrifice he makes for their benefit, spin around him in a hazy glow. In the center of those swirling images, a small pinprick of black appears and begins to grow into a spiral, spinning around him until he is enveloped by the darkness. As the last little twinkle of light disappears, a sense of peace and happiness and warmth overwhelms him.

In that warm darkness, the last thing he hears is his wife's voice saying, "Welcome home, Joey."

26

TO HAVE OR HAVE NOT

Zelda stands back as Ender falls to his knees. His body slumps forward, and his head topples off, rolling toward Tommy and Madrigal.

"What do I do with this?" Tommy says, placing his foot on the head.

"Destroy it!" Zelda yells, returning to Mario's side.

Tommy finds a knife lying on the ground, moseys over to Ender's head, stabs it through the cranium, and picks it up.

"Shit. This is pretty heavy."

He carries the head to the stairwell leading to the lab. Madrigal follows behind.

"That was insane," she says, covering her nose while trying not to slip in the foul-smelling black sludge dripping from the monster's severed head.

"Yeah, it was," Tommy says, keeping his eyes on his feet.

"What are you going to do with it?"

"I've got an idea."

Tommy heads to a lab table and plops the head down while Madrigal stands by the doorway still covering her nose. Tommy fetches a burner and a stand, setting them next to the mutilated head.

"Watch this," he says, finding a pot big enough to put the massive head into and placing it on the stand. Then, he snatches a vat of untarnished yellow liquid from another table and dumps it into the pot.

"You sure that's a good idea?" asks Madrigal, as Tommy lights the burner.

"What's the worst that can happen?"

She casts a questioning glance.

When the yellow liquid starts to bubble, Tommy drops Ender's head into the boiling yellow liquid.

"Do you feel that?" Tommy asks Madrigal, tottering a little off balance. "Is there an earthquake?"

"No," Madrigal replies from the doorway. "I think it's the fumes. They're making me feel a little loopy too. Maybe you should watch from a distance, cowboy."

Tommy saunters back to Madrigal's side, trying not to fall over. She places an arm around him to keep him steady. Together they stand at the doorway, observing the yellow liquid bubble over. It turns darker and darker as Ender's head boils away into the fluid, turning into an explosion of pitch-black oozing goo.

"How you doing, bro?" Zelda asks Mario, wiping her eyes free of the tears.

"I could be better," he says through pained breaths and a weak smile.

A tear drops from her, landing on his forehead. His eyes close in a flinch, but his body is motionless. He opens them again.

"Did we win?" he asks, laboring between the syllables.

"Yeah," says Zelda with a huge toothy grin and eyes full of sorrow. "We won. What was that thing?"

"A revenant."

"What's that?"

"Long story. Remind me to tell you someday," Mario says, closing his eyes.

"Mario, keep your eyes open," she pleads.

He doesn't respond.

"Mario! Please, Mario! Open your eyes!"

Nothing. She scans the room for help, finding no one.

"Dad!" she yells. "Dad!"

Tommy barrels down the stairs, answering the call of his long-lost daughter. He finds Zelda sitting next to Mario, crying and cradling him in her arms. He falls to her side.

"Is he—" Tommy starts to say but lets the words die in his mouth.

"I don't think so," Zelda answers. "But, I'm not sure how much longer he has."

"I just got to see him again," Tommy blares, tears streaming down his face. "This is so fucking unfair. After all these years they took from me...from us. He pays with his life for them. What the fuck?"

"I saw a stretcher in one of the rooms," Madrigal says as she approaches. "I'll get it and we can take him with us."

Tommy nods, caressing his son's cheek.

"He grew up to be a really good kid, eh?" he says, trying to smile. "You both did. I can't believe how amazing you are. You're both gawdamn superheroes to me."

Madrigal returns with the stretcher, and they work together to lift Mario. Tears fall from Tommy's chin onto Mario's forehead without response as they roll him away.

Outside, Tyler taps on the steering wheel, staring down the hospital ramp at the broken gate. Movement in the rearview catches his attention. He glimpses Loo and the magnokin boy playing a game with their hands. Behind them, the children he saved from DerMööve played with children he helped save from Dr. Delirium's lab. The scene brings joy to his heart. He returns his gaze to the darkness of the basement parking lot and thinks of Zelda.

Is she still alive? She has to be.

He opens the door, steps out, and surveys the area.

"Loo, I'll be right back. Shut the door, okay?"

Loo scurries to the front of the bus and shuts the door. He sits in the driver's seat and peeps through the windshield.

"You think he'll be okay?" the magnokin boy asks over Loo's shoulder.

"I think so," Loo says as Tyler jogs through the broken gate and down into a black hole.

When Tyler reaches the bottom of the ramp, a strange metal clanging catches his attention.

"Is someone there?" he calls, blinded in the darkness.

"Tyler!" Zelda's voice calls back to him.

"Zelda," he says, darting to her voice.

He hears her footsteps racing toward him before he discerns her shadowy outline. When she reaches him, she jumps into his arms, wrapping hers around him and kissing him with passionate relief.

"Ahem," Tommy clears his throat, wheeling the gurney with Madrigal.

"Oh yeah. Dad," she says. "This is Tyler. He's my boyfriend now—and he's a half-Mighty."

"Well, I guess you can't be half bad then, eh?" he says after some deliberation, reaching to shake his hand.

"Is he okay?" Tyler asks, motioning to Mario.

"I think it's fatal," Zelda says with teary eyes. "He's my brother, Mario."

"Oh god, Zelda. I am so sorry."

"Did we find Ahah?" Zelda asks.

"She's not among the living kids. I'm not sure if she—" Tyler says, bowing his head and rubbing his eyes. He stops and tries to be optimistic. "There's no way to know if she was even down there. I'm not sure if I'd want to ask Loo to see if any of the bodies in there are her."

"No, we can't do that," Zelda agrees.

It takes all of them to heave the stretcher up the ramp. When they reach the broken gate, Loo spots them and honks the horn. He opens the door and bounces down the bus steps.

"Did you find Ahah?" he shouts, scampering toward them.

Zelda frowns at Tyler and shakes her head, starting to cry.

"I'll get him," Tyler says, squeezing her shoulder. He hurries to Loo, scoops him up, and says, "She's not here, buddy. We'll find her though, okay?"

"Okay," Loo says, but his attention is drawn down the ramp. "That makes me sad."

"I know. But we will find her," Tyler assures him as they walk toward Zelda and the others.

"No, his glow," Loo says, pointing to Mario as they meet halfway up the ramp. "It's almost gone."

"What?" asks Zelda.

"His glow is almost gone," Loo says. "It makes me sad."

Tyler's eyes light up.

"Zelda, Loo is a healer! I totally forgot. Maybe he can help, Mario."

Zelda snags her little brother out of Tyler's arms.

"Loo, do you think you can help our brother?"

"Our brother?" asks Tommy.

"I can try," Loo says, reaching toward Mario.

Zelda sets him down, and Loo touches Mario's forehead.

"What do you mean our brother?" asks Tommy.

"He's our half-brother. We have a half-sister too."

"He is? You do?"

"That DerMööve fucker bred mom—"

"Watch your mouth, young lady!"

"Sorry, daddy," she apologizes. "He used her and other Normals to breed half-Mighty kids to be slaves. Slaves with powers."

"Your mom's a—" Tommy stops as Loo begins to glow white. "What the fuck?"

"DAD!"

"Sorry, sorry," Tommy says. "I just wasn't expecting that."

MMMMMMMRRRRRRRGGGGGGG

Loo's face twists painfully as the white light radiates out of his body. Zelda places her hands on Loo's shoulders.

"Hang tight, Loo!" she encourages. "You can do it!"

He glows brighter. Tyler places his hands over Zelda's. Loo glows even brighter. Tommy and Madrigal each place a hand on Loo. They all glow even brighter. The kids in the bus turn their heads, hiding their eyes from the blinding brightness of Loo's glow. The alleyway becomes consumed by the brightness until all turns into a bright white light.

Mario's eyes move rapidly under his eyelids, coursing images and memories through his cranium in bursts of colors and shapes. The recesses of his mind fill with light, focusing the abstractions into darker unfamiliar forms. He focuses on each, trying to bring them into view, but the more he tries, the more they blur and fade into his periphery. He perceives warmth and love, as he floats alone, trying to scream without a mouth and grasp something without any hands.

Something floats in the back behind everything else, something small and shiny. He urges himself forward, trying to identify the object. It grows larger as he looms nearer, becoming a blinding light drawing him in. The struggle makes him frantic, as he tries to halt his forward momentum, but the light seizes him, pulling him closer and beckoning him to enter.

He surrenders, purging himself of his fears and merging into the new dimensional space, as he sacrifices his essence for a physical form. Before him stands an enormous mural of colors and shapes painted upon a gigantic brick wall. He finds neither an end to the height of the wall nor an end to the mural itself, as the wall extends into infinity in all directions.

A sudden movement in his periphery catches his attention. He turns away as a giant pink hand clamps onto him and drags him into the mural. He reaches outward with his left hand, envisioning it now for the first time. He grips it with his other hand, willing himself forward. He touches the soft skin, sinewy muscle, and hard bone of his own arm. On his pink flesh, dark shapes emerge, etched into his skin, and everything becomes clear as he relives an old memory.

"So, my ident-tag is 1CUR4QTTØ, which can also be read as something called a numeronym," Tommy said, pointing to the characters one by one. "I See You Are A Cutie Too. I would just need to change my 4 into an A somehow."

"You could cut it," said nine-year-old Mario. "The scar might make the letter."

Tommy tilted his head, measuring his son. Mario raised his left pointer finger. Tommy recognized the lightning bolt-shaped scar crossing the knuckle of his little index finger. He flashed him a sidelong grin and said, "You're lucky we didn't have to remove your whole finger after that." Then, he grabbed the finger and pretended to bite it off.

As Mario recoiled and laughed, Tommy glimpsed Mario's ident-tag and started to make a numeronym from it.

"To Have," he said, reading the alphanumeric code. "If you change the 4 in yours to an H, yours would say To Have." He tugged Mario's sleeve up all the way and read the remainder of his ident-tag. "To Have Or Have No."

"Have no what?" asked Mario. "Maybe I can draw a picture of vegetables next to it."

Tommy laughed.

"You're always going to need to eat your veggies, buddy," he said, fingering the empty spot after the second Ø. "You know, you could cut or tattoo a T there and it would say TO HAVE OR HAVE NOT. That's cool, Mario. I'm kind of jealous."

Mario laughed, yanking his arm away, but sneaking a peek and reading it as his dad did.

'To have or have not,' he thought.

He read the ident-tag on his father's arm once more.

"I see you are a cutie, too."

"Who's a cutie?" Zelda asks as Mario opens his eyes.

"What?" he says, squinting at her confused.

"You just said before you opened your eyes, I see you are a cutie, too."

"I did?"

Mario shakes his head and rubs his face. After a few seconds, he realizes he is surrounded by a lot of people who are beaming down at him. He sits up in a hurry.

"What's going on here?"

"Mario, you're okay!" Zelda says, hugging him.

"Of course, I'm okay," he says, hiding anxiety as he hugs her back. He stands up and brushes himself off. "Why wouldn't I be?"

"Well, you were practically dead, son," Tommy says, stepping into Mario's view.

"Dad?" questions Mario. "It IS you!"

The two men hug.

"I think you're having some memory issues, kid," Tommy says, tapping his temple. "We've already done this. But I'll take as many hugs as I can get. There's a lot to make up for."

Mario spies a small boy hiding behind Zelda. He tilts his head toward him before surveying the room, finding many more children, as well as some adults. He scans the area around him, trying to recognize the place. Recent memories begin to pop into his mind as he recalls the faces of the people around him.

"I should be dead," he whispers, forcing the words out of his confusion. "My back was broken. I had to have been internally damaged."

He touches his body, sliding his hand from his chest to his stomach.

"How am I not dead?"

"This little guy saved you," says Zelda, ushering Loo out from behind her. "He's a healer. And, he's our little brother."

Mario is taken aback. His face contorts in greater confusion.

"Brother?" he asks, shaking the cobwebs loose. "I don't understand."

Tyler reaches for Loo's hand and picks him up, as Zelda steps toward Mario.

"His name is Loo. He's half-Mighty," she says, placing a

hand on his shoulder. "That sick fu—ool, DerMööve, made mom a sex slave. Had her locked up in the basement of his restaurant. All this time and she was right there."

"Mom's alive?" Mario asks, starting to smile.

"No," Zelda says, shaking her head and wiping a tear from her eye. "They had her and the other women hooked on Delirium. She died in childbirth."

"Oh," Mario says, studying Loo. "So, he never knew her, huh?"

"He did," Zelda says, smiling while glancing over her shoulder at Loo. "She died giving birth to our sister, Ahah."

Mario's eyes well with tears as he searches for a girl younger than Loo. When he does not find one, he turns and asks, "Where is she?"

Zelda signals Tyler to carry Loo away.

When her little brother is out of earshot, she says, "We thought she was here. We didn't find her, and we're not sure if she—is among the other children."

"They were just kids," Mario cries, tears streaming down his face. "How many did we save?"

He peers around, trying to count the kids.

"We got about eight or nine out of there," answers Madrigal.

"Plus, the twenty or so Tyler saved before," interjects Zelda.

"Tyler?"

Zelda gestures to Tyler and Loo off in the distance. Mario sits down and wraps his arms around his knees.

"So, all these years, she was stuck in a prison under the arcade? I avoided going by that place like a plague. What if I had just gone by there? I might have been able to do something."

"There's nothing you could have done, son," says

Tommy, kneeling next to Mario and placing a hand on his bowed head. "The monks were always watching, even before we did anything. Hell, if you even thought of doing something, they would've taken you to the SIC."

"The monks," says Mario in a bitter bite. "She was stuck in some prison and repeatedly raped for the enjoyment of some Mighty, just to die there. How does that happen? How did the monks not see this happening? Why didn't they stop it?"

"Because we weren't anything to them," answers Tommy. "We were their fleas—pests. But that's all changed now. Because of us, the Mighty are going to live."

"How do you know that?" asks Mario, wiping tears from his red cheeks.

Tommy stands and reaches for his hand. Mario grasps it, and Tommy helps him to his feet.

"The monks are all dead," says Tommy, putting his arm around Mario and walking him out toward the alleyway behind Zelda and Madrigal. "Hell, a lot of the Mighty died today. It's a new day out there now."

"Jakandy told me that he would help change the system if he survived. He said we weren't meant to enslave one another. We were meant to work together. He's dead now—and that dream died with him."

"No, it didn't," Zelda says. "Look."

Mario notices for the first time the chaotic sound of people coming from the street beyond the alleyway. He cranes his neck around Zelda to find hundreds of people cleaning up the streets. Both Mighty and Citizen do their part to clean the mess left by Ender.

"What is happening?" Mario asks dumbfounded.

"It's the future, Mario," Zelda says with a huge smile.

In the distance, a tall, skinny man sprints toward them.

Tommy catches sight of him and squints, trying to recognize the man.

"Does he seem familiar to you?" Tommy asks his kids and Madrigal.

They all check out the man rushing in their direction.

"No," Mario and Zelda respond in unison.

"Oh," says Madrigal. "I'm not sure, because I only saw him for a second, but isn't that the mimic who turned into a gorilla on the bus?"

"Yes, you're right," Tommy says with glee, taking Madrigal by the waist and kissing her lips. Surprised by his impulsivity, he jolts back, apologizing, "I'm so sorry. I'm not sure what—"

"Cállate," she interrupts, placing a finger on his lips before dropping it to kiss him back.

The tall, skinny man approaches, saying, "I hope I'm not interrupting."

"Com'ere, James," Tommy says, giving him a welcoming hug. "I'm so sorry for what we did earlier."

"It's okay," he said with a nod. "By the way, my name is Quell, not James." He taps his forehead. "Memories. Go figure."

"You're the shapeshifter who worked with the Realizer," interjects Mario.

"I prefer mimic."

"You helped Moriarty!" Mario accuses.

"You're right," Quell admits. "But I didn't do so willingly. He manipulated and used me. I served my time for that with another friend of yours."

Mario narrows his eyes at Quell.

With a devious half-smile, Quell says, "Jakandy."

AAAAARRRRGGGGHH

Quell as James doubled over in the bus, screaming in pain and wrenching his face as the influx of old memories flooded into his mind. He opened his eyes, finding himself standing in a white room across from a hooded monk in a brown robe.

"Do you remember me?" the monk said, lowering his hood and revealing himself to be Jakandy.

"Yes," answered Quell. "You were the warden when I arrived at SIC."

"Good," Jakandy said. "The memories I took from you have been fully restored since my untimely death."

"You're dead?"

"I was slain by a creature, not of our world, who preys on those who are Mighty," Jakandy explained. "He will kill us all until we are all gone. Unless those we oppressed and considered lower than ourselves take on our fight as their own. We should not expect that. We should expect them to let us die given the way we have treated them. How we repeat the violent cycle over and over and learn nothing from our past, I will never know."

"Why have you come to me?"

"You worked for the Realizer. You knew both Sherlock and Moriarty. And, you spent time at the SIC. Your story is inter-twined with everything happening today," clarified Jakandy. "I need you to find a Citizen named Mario Rickson. If we are lucky, he will help the Citizens to accept us for our wrongs and encourage them to help us based on our shared and collective humanity. For we are truly one species, one people, human beings all. I need you to remember to do this. Do you remember?"

"I remember!" Quell said, as his eyes burst open.

Not too long thereafter, Quell regained his true physical form and abilities as a Mighty in a bus full of Citizens ready to fight against the Mighty. He shifted into his gorilla form and escaped the wrath of the Normal Army and returned to QTs House of Jacks only to find the Realizer had been murdered. Uncertain and confused, he trudged through bloody streets toward the monastery, the only other authority he knew.

When he arrived at the monastery, the gates had been broken and the grounds were covered by the blood, guts, and body parts of several hundred monks. There were also a few small fleshies already scavenging the corpses.

'There is no Enclave to hold them back,' Quell thought. 'What will we do?'

He raced to the dormitory building, searching all the rooms for a sign of life and finding nothing. He checked the Enclave's white meditation room, where the stench of death ensured nothing lived within. He called in anyway.

"Is there anyone in here?" he said, pinching his nose and covering his mouth.

With no answer, he rounded to the back, where the immense grounds led southward to the Main Cathedral. He found a dozen or so flesheaters of varying size gathering around the fallen minaret and thought, 'There must be a lot of death that way.'

Quell as the gorilla crept to the side of the fallen tower, keeping an eye on the amassed fleshies with grave concern.

'They might get spooked by a gorilla,' he thought.

As he drew closer, he realized that none of the animals paid him any attention, and none of them paid much attention to one another at all. In fact, one resembling a giant wolf and one resembling a massive deer both dug at the ground below the tower next to each other. Quell approached the area where most of the fleshies were digging, discovering a hole had been dug out under a window. He shifted into his tall skinny form to crawl into the hole and up through the window.

He climbed through the ruins and over the bodies of dead monks, sensing some unearthly force drawing him forward. When he reached the locked door at what would have been the top of the tower, he placed his hand on the lock. His index finger shifted into a key, which he used to open the door.

Inside, he found five children between the age of two and four years old.

'This is the Enclave,' he thought, appraising the vastly diverse children.

The oldest of the bunch was a four-year-old with light brown skin, jet-black hair, and very large brown eyes with an epicanthic fold.

"I thought you would be taller," she said, scrutinizing Quell.

"What's your name?" he asked her.

"Meiwen," she answered.

"I'm Gruber," a three-year-old brunette boy said, pointing to himself with his thumbs.

Two dark-skinned twins around two-years-old played with one another, tossing a ball back and forth.

"They're Aja and Frou," Meiwen answered without being questioned. "And that's Anna."

A blond-haired, green-eyed two-year-old girl sat cross-legged with her hands outstretched, touching the walls of the fallen ruin. Quell tilted his head, studying her.

She tapped to the spot next to her and said, "Seet."

When he sat down next to her, all the children came to him. Each of them placed their hands upon his head. He sensed a warmth stemming from within him, coming outward and into each of them. He closed his eyes and found himself in the white room again, standing before Jakandy.

"I will be leaving you now," he said to Quell. "These children will be a new Enclave and will start a new monastery, one based on justice, fairness, and equity for all of humanity, not just the Mighty. I need you to take care of them and ensure their survival. And, Quell—"

"Yes?"

"Remind, Mario to study his historical facts. He might find some new ones to add to his oral tradition."

Quell opened his eyes to a blinding light. The children drew the light of Jakandy out from within Quell, and each of them received a small portion of his life-force. Each of the children glowed brighter and brighter until they absorbed all the light offered to them.

When they returned to normal, Quell helped them escape the fallen minaret. As he escorted the children out one by one, he knew they would not be harmed by the flesheaters. Something inside of him purged any thought of them as harmful. When he witnessed Anna touch each of the fleshies digging around the fallen minaret, he realized the scope of her power. They nodded at her and scampered away, and others followed them back into the woods beyond the monastery.

Quell guided the children on a long circuitous route to avoid the scenes of death all around the monastery. He found the Arborium to be clear, but the door was electrically dead-bolted.

'I can't get in,' he thought, hearing a click of the door opening.

Anna smiled at him with her hand firmly planted on the wall.

"Are you a seer-omnipath?" he asked her.

"Ahah," she answered.

"I think this world is going to be a much better place," Quell says, shaking Mario's hand. "And you're the hero who made it happen."

"I didn't kill Ender," Mario says, shaking his head. "My sister did."

"A hero doesn't kill the monster, Mario," Zelda interjects. "A hero brings the people together."

Zelda waves her hand at all the people in the streets like she's the princess of the land. She glances back at Mario with a huge grin.

"You are the reason all these people are out here right

now, working together, trying to make a difference," Tommy says. "Without you, I would still be hating the Mighty, trying to figure out how to oust them now that they're vulnerable. You have made me, and all these other Normals who have felt all this injustice for so long, want to try to live in harmony with the Mighty."

Tyler and Loo approach Zelda. She kisses Tyler while holding Loo's little hand.

In the future, people will live together in peace and harmony, thinks Mario.

Tommy and Madrigal kiss.

In the future, monks will no longer prescribe the morality of society. Instead, the monastery will be a beacon of light for justice and equality.

Zelda picks up Loo and kisses him on the cheek. He blushes.

In the future, people will not be scared of one another. They will respect others for their differences and treat those differences as the strengths they are.

Mario stares at his ident-tag.

In the future, there will be no Normals or Abnormals. There will be no Mighty or Citizens. There will be no Haves or Have-Nots. There will be only human beings.

27

ON TOP OF OL' MACGUFFREY

onstrous golden eyes bulge from the cover of darkness within the woods, beaming down their yellowish glow upon the cabin in the distance. No smoke plumes from its fireplace. No lights flicker from within. There is no movement at all.

Unusual, thinks the giant beast, stepping toward a cleared pathway, expecting at any moment to feel the usual pain of the invisible barrier.

Closing its eyes tight, it pushes its giant clawed paw through the air to find no painful electrical mental shock forcing it to draw back. It stumbles forward.

"Hyack, hyack," echoes behind it in a thunder of animalistic laughter from not one, but many similar such beasts as itself.

Hundreds exit in a mercurial march out of the woods, continuing their uproar. Then, all at once, they halt. Several hundred gold eyes glimmer for a second before turning into golden threads, as they sprint to the cabin.

Within moments, the beasts scatter away, leaving

nothing but a dust cloud of pulverized mulch, splintered beams, and broken antiques in their wake.

CUCKOO CUCKOO CUCKOO CUCKOO CUCKOO
CUCKOO CUCKOO CUCKOO

A small bird cuckoos from an antique clock lying in a heap of shattered timbers. Its call echoes into the open sky full of stars, shining bright in the moonless night. The starlight above is only outshined by the bright lights of Fellowship City in the distance, which beckon the beasts to come and play.

THE END

THANK YOU

Thank you for reading my book!

I sincerely hope that you enjoyed the first book in my TO HAVE OR HAVE NOT Universe, as much as I enjoyed writing it. I've been a story-teller for as long as I can remember, always writing stories that I want to read and creating worlds that I want to see. My hope is that you will like them as much as I do.

I truly appreciate getting feedback on my work. Please consider leaving me an honest review on Amazon, as word-of-mouth is the best way people can learn about new and wonderful books to read.

If you see any issues (typographical, grammatical, or otherwise) or have questions, concerns, criticisms, please feel free to email me:
author@jaredkchapman.com

COMING SOON

FOUNDATIONS OF FELLOWSHIP CITY

Book I: The Warrior
Book II: The Wanderer
Book III: The Wise

Before the Mighty were the majority, they were merely ABNORMALS struggling to survive.

Without three women, separated by time and linked by blood, the Mighty would never exist. Evie lives in a hunter-gatherer tribe, trying to survive in the desolating heat of the deep desert. She discovers a dark truth that changes everything she has ever been taught. Evangelical is an Abnormal born in a brutal concentration camp. Following a riot that leads to war, she escapes into the desert wasteland, finding 'safety' in the hands of a nomadic cult led by a charismatic prophet. Esther is haunted by a mysterious call beckoning her from her desert home to somewhere unknown. As darkness and death loom all around her, she accepts the quest, seeking light and wisdom.

Where the *X-Men* and *Mad Max* meet, the true history of the conflict between the Normals and Abnormals will be revealed.

To read the first chapter on the webnet.mightybase, sign up for my email list at jaredkchapman.com

ABOUT THE AUTHOR

Jared K. Chapman is an author, filmmaker, and educator. He is a native Californian who spent his formative years at school in frigid Alberta, Canada with his father and summer vacation in arid central California with his mother. He holds degrees in psychology & religious studies and is currently a doctoral candidate studying the social psychology of extreme groups. He lives in a little oasis just east of Los Angeles with his wife and three sons. You can find him at...

jaredkchapman.com
2hvorhvnot.com
Facebook: @jaredkchapmanauthor
Twitter: @redchapCREATIVE
Instagram: @jaredkchapman

CPSIA information can be obtained
at www.ICGtesting.com
Printed in the USA
FSHW010955230920
74047FS